The Everlasting

LEONARD BISHOP

The Everlasting

POSEIDON PRESS
NEW YORK

Copyright © 1982 by Leonard Bishop
All rights reserved
including the right of reproduction
in whole or in part in any form
A Poseidon Press Book
Published by Pocket Books, a Simon & Schuster
Division of Gulf & Western Corporation
Simon & Schuster Building
Rockefeller Center
1230 Avenue of the Americas
New York, New York 10020
Poseidon Press is a trademark of Simon & Schuster
Designed by Ed Carenza
Manufactured in the United States of America

1 2 3 4 5 6 7 8 9 10

Library of Congress Cataloging in Publication Data

Bishop, Leonard, 1922-
The everlasting.

I. Title.
PS3552.I7717E8   813'.54   81-17808
ISBN 0-671-44154-X   AACR2

Acknowledgments:
Michael Kaye: a splendid attorney who has allowed me to draw from his expertise and knowledge—which I have used at my own discretion.

Dr. Ron Linder: a thorough and conscientious doctor who has offered me invaluable advice—which I have used at my own discretion.

For—Celia

"And it shall be, if thou do at all forget
the Lord thy God, and walk after other gods,
and serve them, and worship them, I testify
against you this day that ye shall surely perish."

Deuteronomy 8:19

The
Everlasting

Chapter 1

I became a Catholic priest, not because of my zealous devotion to God, but to avoid meeting the woman who was destined to destroy my life, and my soul. I believed my eternal salvation was not only in God, but in celibacy.

I decided to become a priest when I was twelve years old. It was then that I became tormented, and fascinated to learn there were two other lives—lives I had lived but had already died, long ago—still living within me, in my present life.

The woman I was terrified of meeting in this lifetime was the same woman who had destroyed me in those other lifetimes. I had loved her in the fifteenth century, in Italy, and in an ancient century before that, when we belonged to a pagan and savage society. I had loved her with a passion and lust so overwhelming that my love became transformed into madness.

Now I am forty-one years old and no longer a priest.

In a little while I will be placed on trial for murdering the same woman who had caused my death in those two other lives I believe I lived long ago.

I heard a heavy metal door slide open and two men spoke to each other as they walked toward my cell. I leaned forward on the metal bed frame and muttered a prayer to God, for it is written in Romans, *"I will have mercy on whom I will have mercy, and I will have compassion on whom I will have compassion."*

I stood up, ready to be taken to the courtroom.

I was led through long corridors, past underground cell blocks. Prisoners pressed their faces to the bars and snickered to each other, "That's the priest—Father Jerod—the one who killed that young chick he was balling." I stared ahead. They forget I am no longer a priest. I stepped through the final door, pretending I was sleepwalking in a grim dream, and was led into the courtroom, where my attorney and the public were waiting for me.

I did not let myself see the hundreds of faces staring at me. They had come to witness a carnival of legal procedure. Will that infamous, craven ex-priest, Stephen Jerod, get his justly deserved punishment? I glanced at the jury. Seven men, five women. Ordinary people whose hearts are now heavy with the weight of judgment. I felt compassion for their burden. The prosecutor would harass them with one undeniable fact. "Stephen Jerod did, without a shadow of a doubt, strangle Shara Medford to death." He would poke his finger at each jury face and remind them of what I said when they found me—my hands still gripped around her throat. "I had to destroy her. It was the only way I could save my soul!"

I was afraid to die. Not for the natural, human reasons. After I died, would all of me be ended? Or would I become again, in another man? And would Shara, as another woman, appear in that life?

I sat beside my attorney, Martin Lormer. We did not speak. He began arranging his long yellow pads and sharply pointed pencils. On the floor, beside his right leg, was an old-fashioned leather briefcase. Among his documents was the journal I had written about the two men who lived in me. I had begun the journal on the day that I was ordained as a priest.

Shara, Shara, my beloved Shara. I have loved you for ages and my love was so absolute it transcended natural Time, and natural Life. The world will misunderstand why I killed you. Even I cannot understand really. Did I kill you for the ordinary reasons any man would kill a woman who was causing his insanity—or was it because I did not want you to destroy me throughout eternity?

I will know—I swear: as God is my creator—when this trial is over.

The bailiff stood and requested that the entire courtroom do the same. The judge, a middle-aged woman with a beaked face, wearing rimless eyeglasses, walked to the bench. She did not look at me. She arranged her black robe and sat down. We did the same. The court stenographer began putting a new roll of paper into his machine.

My attorney opened a manila folder and studied his notes. We did not like each other.

Perhaps my trial would have been conducted in the average anonymity of other trials if Martin Lormer was not a man who demanded constant public attention—who told a newspaper reporter, "I cannot tell you what Father Jerod thinks—I can't tell you how he feels about anything because he refuses to talk to me. All I can say is that he has granted me, as his defense attorney, the right to conduct his defense any way I believe appropriate to his welfare. He will not talk to me because he has taken a vow of silence."

The Church, disturbed that the public would believe they had abandoned a former priest, had retained the noted Martin Lormer. He was a brusk, impatient man of about thirty-eight. He stated that my tale of having two other lives alive in me was either the irrational invention of a man who was insane, or the desperate lie of a man who could not justify his act of murder. He said that he had accepted my defense only as a favor to Bishop Francis Alerton. I accepted this as a half-truth. My life was now a public scandal. He was using me for another gain in his reputation.

During our first interview there was a uniformed guard stationed outside the room. Martin Lormer paced from wall to wall. Energy and intelligence dominated him. He was tall and lean, his gestures dramatic. Even while standing still he appeared to crackle with motion. He said, "My first inclination, after reviewing this situation, was to plead Diminished Capacity. But I'm not satisfied. Something else is trying to get through to me."

I sat, my hands relaxed on my knees, and watched him pace the room.

Diminished Capacity, as a defense, is usually defined as the result of an overwhelming shock, or intoxication, or any disease that can be proven to have altered the condition of someone's mental state—thus causing the crime to occur. It eliminates the factors of malice aforethought, premeditation, or deliberation. The prosecution has to prove that the defendant was sane, while the defense merely has to establish "reasonable doubt" that his mental capacity was in a "diminished state" at the time of the crime.

I had told Martin Lormer that I had choked Shara Medford to death and that we knew what I was doing. This statement annoyed him. He was a man in the profession of specifics. He distrusted the abstract. He had defended many murderers and believed he knew their souls. They were rotten with psychological diseases, and all liars. I was just another killer to him, and he did not like me.

"When you say we knew what you were doing, what, exactly, do you mean? No, wait. Let me put this question to you. Do you mean those other lives you claim to be in you can view what you are doing in this life?"

"No. They do not know of me. But by some supernatural phenomenon I believed that once they were avenged we would all have peace."

"Then what do you mean by we knew what you were doing?"

"I'm not sure I know what I mean."

"I find that unacceptable. Most unacceptable."

He began pacing. I could feel his mind cluttering with ideas. He kept muttering, "None of this makes sense." He jammed his hands into his pockets. "I mean," he muttered, "none of this makes a damn bit of sense." He pulled his hands from his pockets and snapped his fingers.

"Father Jerod, will you please stand up."

"It would please me if you stopped calling me Father Jerod. Mister Jerod will do. I am no longer a priest."

"You can forget that little bit of honesty, right now. There is no way the jury will think of you as plain old Stephen Jerod. To some you'll be a priest out of his habit. To others you'll be a defrocked priest. Juries and the mass media need hooks to hang identities on. Yours will be 'The Priest.' And the prosecutor will use that as a heavy character weapon. He will brand you as a sexual deviant who spit in the face of God and left the church just to have himself some young hot pussy. Now, will you please stand up."

I eased the chair back and stood up. He put his hands on his hips and stared at me. "Six foot one?" he asked. I nodded. He scanned my physique. "Still trim, still in good physical condition?" I nodded again. He pinched his lips thoughtfully.

"How much did Shara Medford weigh?"

"About one hundred and fifteen pounds."

"I have studied her photographs. She was slender, small-boned. Petite is an obsolete word, but would you say she was petite?"

"Yes, I would say so."

"It doesn't seem likely that she could hurt you if she attacked you, does it?"

I smirked. "Hardly." There was no violence in Shara.

He drew a cigarette from his shirt pocket and tapped it onto his thumbnail. "Did Shara Medford ever attack you with the intent of committing bodily harm?"

"If you knew Shara, you would never ask that kind of a question."

"Did she ever behave in a way that could be construed as a threat to your person, and were there witnesses present at the time?"

"No, no, the question is ridiculous. A more gentle person never lived."

He returned the cigarette to his shirt pocket and grinned. "Good. I have just recognized your defense. It will be weird, but if I succeed, it will establish a legal precedent that will be studied for all time." I shrugged. I did not care. *Shara was dead. I was alone in this lifetime. I was only a substance.*

Shara and I met, almost two years ago, when I was listening to confessions. I heard a woman step into the box and say, "Father, I confess that I have sinned. I carry a hatred in my heart for a man who is intimidating me. His intentions are of a sexual nature." Suddenly, the horrible fear ever present in my life—that I would meet in this lifetime the women I believe I loved in other lifetimes—burst into my sensibilities.

How could I know it was she? There was no logic to my belief. If you could explain the fantastic, it would become ordinary. I am like anyone. I know more than I realize and cannot trace back to where I learned it. There are mysteries that will never be understood.

My recognition of her was a painful scream in my mind. I could not breathe. "Father, are you there?" she asked. I could only moan, "Yes." I had known of her since I was twelve years old. This was the woman once named *Letitia*. This was the woman once taken captive by an ancient tribe who used me as their god of the Dark Above.

Sitting in my part of the confession booth, I was suddenly raw and savage with rage toward the man who was trying to molest her. I sat clenched in the narrow confines, trying not to tremble.

She asked, "Father, what am I to do?"

I could not answer. Confession is a secret sacrament. The priest, although a sanctified instrument of God, is anonymous. The penitent feels unembarrassed and free before God because no man is viewing her sin. I could not answer because currents of excitement were swelling through my senses. I sat, my arms hugged about my body, feeling dizzy with passions I knew to be lust. She sobbed softly. It was Wednesday, early afternoon. We were alone in the church.

I breathed deeply and said, "My child, hatred is understandable. It is quite human. Although that does not excuse it from being sinful. God forgives you and tells you to avoid this man as best you can. God will protect you, and deal with him."

I stood up and left the dark, humid booth. I waited. She stepped from her portion and frowned at me. She was lovely. Her auburn hair spilled across her shoulders. Her eyes were wide apart above high cheekbones. The shadows in the sanctuary made them seem black. Almost Oriental. The loveliness was not in her look, but in her essence. She did not resemble the other women she had once been.

I said, "I'm sorry. I should have waited for you to leave first." Her eyelids fluttered and she smiled.

"This is the first time I have ever been to a confession."

"I'm very sorry if my seeing you makes you uncomfortable."

"I understand, Father, and I'm fine. You look familiar to me, Father. Do I know you?"

I felt a spurt of panic. Did she know of the other lives she had been? Would she say, "You are Barthelamo Vecchio, and before that you were an albino shaman." I stared at her and shook my head.

"We have never met before, I'm sure."

"How strange. You look so familiar to me."

"Perhaps you have seen my photographs in the newspapers where I was . . ."

"Oh, yes, now I know. You are *that* Father Stephen Jerod, the reincarnationist who led a committee to that fabulous art treasure, in Italy."

"I am not a reincarnationist."

She reached out and touched my forearm. "I'm sorry, Father Jerod. It's only a foolish term." I wanted to bring her hand to my lips and tell her, "I have always loved you."

I said, "No harm done, really." She glanced at the small circular watch on her wrist. "My supervisor at the university is a tyrant. I had better leave before I'm late." I stepped back and nodded, thinking, yes, leave, go from me. Vanish. Meeting you now does not mean we have finally been united in Time.

She said, "Thank you, Father," and walked to the aisle. She glanced at a statue of our beloved Savior. Beneath her white blouse her breasts were handful large and firm. I quickly confessed to the sin of lust and closed my eyes. I did not want to watch her leave.

I listened to her steps along the varnished wooden floor. I was praying that because I could allow her to leave that my recognition of her was a mistake.

Yes, it was a mistake. This was not the woman I had avoided while waiting for her to appear.

I heard her step onto the tiled floor outside the sanctuary. I stood and prayed that she was a lie, or, if she was the truth, that because I could allow her to leave, we were done with each other. She would inhabit her parts of the city and I would remain in the confinements of my parish and perhaps God would protect us by preventing us from ever meeting again.

Yes, God would do that. For God is good. It is written, "*Because you put your faith in God, you are under the protection of his power until salvation comes.*"

But it is also written, "*O the depth of the riches both of the wisdom and knowledge of God! How unsearchable are his judgments, and his ways past finding out!*"

The attorney spoke sharply to me. "Father Jerod, you are

drifting again. Please pay attention." He lifted his briefcase from the floor and opened it on the table. He withdrew a thick binder. I closed my eyes, ashamed, and afraid. It was my journal. The detailed record of the other lifetimes within me. Shara had read the journal before I killed her.

He placed the journal onto the table. He flattened his right palm on it. He leaned to me. I could sense his agitation, his hostility.

"I want to tell you something, Father Jerod, and I want you to understand that I mean it for all time. I don't believe one damn word of what you have written in this journal. It is nonsense and, quite frankly, a crock of fantastic bullshit."

There was no anger in me. I moved my hand forward to touch the binding. He shifted it from my reach. Some months before Shara found my journal I had decided to burn it. It contained parts of the devil. I had a can of paint thinner and a book of matches. But I was stopped from pouring the fluid. An invisible power gripped my wrist. The can suddenly became too heavy to lift. Then the metal gave me an electrical shock. The journal, I knew, was part of some satanic power and I had been away from God too long to break its hold on me. I remember crying aloud, "Jesus, my beloved Jesus, help me." But I had abandoned Him.

The attorney chuckled.

"Don't be disturbed, Father Jerod. I don't have to believe you in order to defend you. Nine-tenths of the people defended for major crimes are guilty as hell, and the attorneys know it. There are only two immutable ethics in criminal law. Win your case any way you can, and collect your fee. Any other attitude is stupid, and betrays incompetence. I don't believe in people. I believe in myself. Now, I'm going to smoke a cigarette and relax. Then I'm going to ask you some questions. I want honest, straightforward answers. And by the way, if you're at all interested, I intend pleading self-defense."

"That's ridiculous. Shara never once did anything to harm me. Not once. And I will not lie."

He drew a cigarette from his shirt pocket and tapped the tip on the journal binding. He grinned. "I am going to do what no other lawyer in recorded history has done. Prove that reincarnation is not only real, but, when a crime is committed because of reincarnation, it is defensible in this day and age. Now, sit back and allow me to enjoy my cigarette."

I was not in a direct, intimate relationship with the remote male living within me. I knew of him only because Barthelamo Vecchio was bedeviled by him. Although Barthelamo did not believe in the lunatic superstitions of his times—incubi, succubi, witches and goblins, magic amulets and religious indulgences, relics like the whiskers of St. Peter or a flask of the Virgin Mary's milk—what he could not explain, what he could not comprehend, he accredited to a supernatural unknown that was demonic. He was a Physician and a Surgeon—in advance of his times, but still limited by his times.

I was fascinated by Barthelamo's life in me, and anxious for the remote male to appear, because I could not always observe that remoter life until it was brought into Barthelamo's awareness.

I was a large window which, when uncurtained, revealed a smaller window which, when uncurtained, revealed a still smaller window. I could see into the first window, but not through it. Only when the curtain of that small window was drawn aside by Barthelamo's consciousness could I see the still smaller window. Only when Barthelamo was forced to look through the still smaller window could I know some of that other man's life.

But there were times in which an urgency, a feeling of desperation happened within me, allowing me to bypass Barthelamo—to directly see through the smaller window—and experience the Albino I had once been. I did not know why this sometimes happened.

The remote male could not look ahead to see Barthelamo who could not look ahead to see me. It was a relationship of the past.

Barthelamo Vecchio was a hawkish looking man whose brooding character was known through his deep-set, cindery brown eyes. His black hair was worn long, after the fashion of his times. His look was sinister, capable of evil, but that was not his heart. He favored the color black in his clothes. His only adornment was a slender silver chain from which dangled a medallion symbolizing his profession. He would have been tall had he kept his bearing erect. But he carried a deformity. There was an ugly hump straddling his right shoulder like an overweight cat. Its hind legs and stubby tail clutched his back. This deformity estranged him from the society he lived in. He believed himself to be continually mocked, or pitied.

He began his life in me when he was thirty-four years old. All I could know of him was from his present. He was a man who dismissed the sentiment of memories. He would not dwell on recalling his youth. I could only determine that his parents had been weavers, who sent him for hire to a wealthy trader who believed the boy's deformity to be a talisman of good fortune. Before he was thirteen years old Barthelamo had traveled throughout Europe. Once, he had sailed to England with a cargo of costly silks.

From a scattering of infrequent reminiscences I had glimpsed Barthelamo as an intense, continually fatigued student attending courses at the School of Medicine in Bologna.

In France, he gained medical experience at the Hôtel-Dieu, which was used as a charity hospital. I felt his disgust, his horror, at the unlighted and sealed rooms. Men and women on splashes of straw, lying like the corpses they would soon become. While he performed his treatments, the nuns stood at his side fanning away the clusters of flies, stamping on the hordes of vermin. In one room there were eight beds, each holding six people. Men and women and children. Three women were giving birth, five children shook with feverish convulsions. Barthelamo would not hold that memory for too long. Once, I felt him vomit.

I had sights of him stooped over soldiers slain and wounded on battlefields. He became engrossed in his profession of Physician and Surgeon. It was a rare duality of careers. Surgery was the avocation of hog-gelders and barbers—medicine was conducted by apothecaries and corrupt monks. He did not wear the long robe of the Surgeon to distinguish him from the barber-surgeon, who was allowed to wear only the short robe. He would become known through his skills, not by his attire. The only possession he guarded was a box of papers he called "medical indulgences." They were his own invention. The paper was signed by the patient, declaring before God and King that no member of his family would seek revenge upon the Physician-Surgeon if, in the course of treatment, he passed from this life. As his reputation spread throughout the provinces of Italy, he became more isolated. Medical practitioners, like priests and court-emissaries, were often used by the nobility for intrigue and assassination.

He became a secretive man. He conducted his practice in the city of Romagna. When he was not repairing a shattered leg or concocting a poultice for the easing of a rash or festering sore, he left his rooms and walked about the township streets. His pleasure, his amusement, was staring at people. They thought him odd. They could not know he was searching for someone. He did the same when he was summoned to heal a noble in Fabriano, in Perugia, in Viferbo—in all the cities that required his enlightened services. The populace could not know he was waiting to be found by the woman he was destined to love. He did not know if she was to be his blessing, or his doom.

He believed himself to be a man bewitched by the devil and this woman he would meet was part of his secret madness.

He had visions of another man residing within his existence. A man so white in complexion and hair, he seemed to be an ivory statue given life before the demonic powers had colored him. He could not stop the visions of this man from appearing in his mind. He could not reveal his visions to anyone. The nobility and church were offering rewards for information directing them to the witches and warlocks who were intruding upon their rule of the people. Anyone with visions was damned as a "spawn of the devil" and was put to the rack before being burned at the stake.

Barthelamo began to experience the feelings and thoughts of this strange white creature, as I was able to experience Barthelamo's feelings and thoughts.

The vision always appeared to Barthelamo as this white man struggled among a column of dark-skinned, squat, and thick-limbed people who were being marched across a long and arid stretch of land. They were bound at the wrists and attached to each other by heavy, fibrous ropes. Their village had been raided and they were taken captives by a warrior tribe. While Barthelamo's vision included the captors who strode beside the prisoners and beat them with carved staffs, Barthelamo's vision was concentrated on this male with his bizarre complexion, his white-gold hair, his watery pink eyes. He was not being beaten or prodded.

Because of his greater height and rare pigmentation, the warriors believed he possessed great and magic powers.

They believed they had captured the son of a god. A god whose white eye could be seen when the Great Above became black.

They did not yet know that sunlight was his enemy. Too long an exposure in the heat of the day would cause his body to swell. When he had been marched from his village to where his captors lived, he had been naked. His body began to bloat; spittle bubbled from his mouth. He began jerking at the ropes binding him. His eyes rolled in their red-rimmed sockets. He wailed and screamed and contorted. The warriors, all black-haired and darkly burnished from the sun, became troubled. Was this child of their god calling to his great father to release a curse upon them?

To stop the spell from reaching his great father, the warrior-chief ordered that he be covered. A blanket with the symbols of their tribal power was draped over his heated body. He was now protected from their greatest god, the Great Burning Eye. He was given water. Soon, he quieted and walked as though one of their people. He knew that when he reached the village he would be treated as the son of a god. They would give him peace and honor. He would live in their village and not run away. The son of a god belonged to everyone.

My attorney finished smoking his cigarette. He pressed it into the octagonal glass ashtray and stood up. He flattened his hand on my journal. I breathed deeply, resigned to being questioned.

"Now, Father Jerod, I want to go over some of your background in reincarnation."

"I have no background in reincarnation. It's a myth of pagan religions."

"Can we avoid these denominational polemics and get on with some information? You were first brought to public attention when you directed a committee of art historians to a secret cache of paintings hidden in the summer home of Cesare Borgia, in Fabriano, in Italy. You claimed you were able to do this because you were alive in the fifteenth century, as Barthelamo Vecchio."

"No. I made no such claim. That was the news media's misunderstanding. I said that Barthelamo Vecchio was alive at that time. But I was not him, reincarnated. To me, reincarnation is false and satanic."

He muttered, "Lord, give me patience," and paced around the table. I glanced to the small window set into the door. I could see the back of the guard's head. Martin Lormer began shaking his head.

"I find that unacceptable. So will the jury. My defense in your behalf will be the validity, the reality of reincarnation in your relationship with Shara Medford."

"Then I will be forced to deny the validity of your defense, as pertaining to me."

"Father Jerod, wouldn't you agree that it is stupid to fight the attorney who is trying to save your life?"

I shrugged. The life he was trying to save was no longer real to me. Before meeting Shara my reason for living was to avoid her. After knowing Shara my reason for living was to preserve my soul. When I killed Shara my reason for living had become forfeit. I suddenly wanted to slam my fist onto the table and shout, "Give me a reason for living and I won't fight your schemes to keep me alive!" I made myself breathe deeply, several times, to regain my control. My attorney pinched his lips thoughtfully, and stared at me.

"Father Jerod, I am not too clear about why you left the church."

"It was by mutual consent. That's all I intend saying about it."

"Father Jerod, I am becoming impatient."

"I'm sorry."

"Sorry won't cut it. I would rather be dealing with an illiterate than with some self-deprecating ex-priest who hasn't the balls to try and save his own life."

"I'm sorry. Really. I can only tell you what I feel is the . . ."

"Stop it, damn it, stop this charade of remorse. I am not interested in your personal feelings. I am interested in convincing a jury that you were justified in what you did. To do that, I will need not only facts, but concepts. Ideas. You have committed the act of murder in a most compatible era. Our society has become freaky with exotic religions. People believe in the occult, in Ouija-board revelations, in karma and hypnotism. The District Attorney will talk fact, and I'll talk impression. He'll establish law and I'll establish justice. If you're concerned about your integrity, then consider your present status and how it all came about. You have taken the life of another human being. You are a criminal, a murderer. You are no longer entitled to integrity. Your only remaining rights are legal. So stop being a damn fool and let me use them intelligently."

"I appreciate your . . ."

"No, Father Jerod, I won't accept your mealy-mouthed bullshit. I want information. Now answer my question. Why did you leave the church?"

I looked down at the scuffed linoleum floor. I was angry. Not at his dislike of me, or his sleazy approach to the law. There was a greater meaning in what he intended to do, and I could not grasp that meaning. He was a cunning man, with vision. If I were Barthelamo Vecchio, I would have quickly understood. Barthelamo was a man who lived through his perceptions. He not only interpreted facts, he absorbed personalities.

"Father Jerod, I want that question answered."

"I was asked to resign by Bishop Carmondy."

"Did he have grounds for that proposal?"

"No, not really. But the church is an authority unto itself, and I had become disenchanted as a priest. My reasons for becoming a priest were less than spiritual, and the priesthood did not offer me what I believed it would."

"That's interesting, but too abstract. I want more."

"I had also broken my vows."

He grinned. He would not inquire into why I had broken my vows. He returned to the table and sat down to begin writing on one of his yellow legal pads. "Tell me about your conflict with Bishop Carmondy, and your disenchantment with the church."

I leaned forward and intertwined my hands. I said, "The public has no idea about the power plays and politics that go on in the Catholic church." I looked at the journal positioned at his left arm.

He had read it. There was no reason to be secretive. I squeezed my hands together and began talking about my attitudes.

I told him that I was not shattered in soul or spirit when I left the church. My devotion to God, at its most intense intimacy, had been distracted. God could not hold me because I had never given myself to Him. I could not love the church because it was a lie. It was grudging about the wealth it collected from its parishes. More was spent on public relations than on charitable programs. The naive priests were overworked and always in want—the politically astute priests lived in tax-free affluence. Religion was their profession. The church was their civil service. They were devout in appearance and ritual, but corrupt in their flesh. I was able to restrict my observation and knowledge of their blatant sexualizing by convincing myself that I must follow in the steps of Christ, and not impose judgment on His servants. I did not let myself see. What I could not avoid seeing, I ignored. I was engaged in my own maddening survival.

If I was at all unique it was because I was thirty-seven years old and still a celibate. Sustaining that celibacy in the church was an anguishing difficulty. Either the homosexual priests were always after you, or the nuns were trying to entice you into their beds. Young priests let their bodies be used to solicit favors and position from the older priests. I became an oddity because I would not establish sexual relationships. I was not a passive homosexual, not a guilt-burdened bisexual, not any manner of contemporary sexual deviant. By learning how to insulate myself against my normal sexual nature, I had become asexual.

I was treated as though a leper; suspected of trying to spread the disease of celibacy. After leading the art historians to the cache of hidden art Cesare Borgia had once shown to Barthelamo Vecchio, I was summoned to the Bishop's office and warned, "You have not only brought embarrassment to your Order, you have stigmatized the church with your dabblings in the occult."

"I have never dabbled in the occult. I have only . . ."

"You will be silent until I indicate that you are to speak. I am telling you, Father Jerod, that such an event must not happen again. Not ever again."

We stared at each other. His round face was mottled with controlled anger. His jowls quivered. I had to silently pray for forgiveness for disrespecting him. His hypocrisy was well known. While he had a lavish parsonage, he owned another residence in San Francisco where he had been living with the same woman for twenty years. In three weeks his oldest illegitimate son would be graduating from high school. He placed his chubby fist onto the desk and struck the top, snarling, "Not ever again. Is that understood?"

I leaned over the ornately carved oak desk. "And if it does happen again, what will be done about it?"

"I will arrange for your voluntary resignation."

"Just like that?"

"Father Jerod, I have always known you to be an indifferent priest, but I did not know you were an idiot. The church can absorb all sorts of men and women, but what it cannot absorb is a fool who becomes outstanding, or notorious."

"Bishop Carmondy—your excellency—let me tell you something. I have only . . ."

"You have nothing to tell me, Father Jerod. I find your presence in my church most distasteful."

He picked a sheaf of papers from the desk and began reading. Our interview was concluded. I would not be able to explain that I had used the art historians in an attempt to prove that the life of Barthelamo Vecchio was nothing more than a recurring dream that had fallen from the dimension of Time. It was a dream happening to me while I was awake. There are mysteries of natural life that contain deeper mysteries which, when realized, open upon more baffling mysteries. And on, *ad infinitum*. Proving there was an art treasure served only to make me believe in the possibility of weird coincidences.

I still would not accept that another man lived within me.

Three months after meeting with Shara Medford, I was transferred to a small church in Pinole where I assisted an elderly priest who was hovering near senility. But I was no longer anonymous. Catholics from all over Contra Costa County sought my counsel, not to be comforted in sorrow, not to become more intimate with God. They wanted me to describe my reincarnation. They believed I was a psychic and could tell what the future was planning for their investments, their children. Some brought Ouija boards and asked me to conduct séances. Women began making sexual overtures.

I began to recognize the frightening puzzle I was living.

I would not believe that I had once been Barthelamo Vecchio or the tribal Albino who had become what we call a shaman—a witch doctor. Yet I had already met the woman I was destined to love, as I know I had loved her twice before, in other centuries. If I was not Barthelamo Vecchio, or the Albino, reincarnated, then why was I compelled to love the woman they had loved? Was I the average boy of twelve years old until, by a caprice or warp of some supernatural power, I was suddenly victimized by another man's reincarnation? How was that possible when I knew reincarnation to be a lie—a public hoax?

I began having erotic dreams. All the sexual experimentation that others had told me of in their confessions became my nocturnal pastime with Shara. Where the penitents believed these unconventional positions of fulfillment were sin, I felt only the joy of innocence in what we did. Soon, the nighttime erotics became part of my day. I had to wear my cassock to conceal my imaginings. Wherever I walked or stood, Shara was there, naked and awaiting my attention. It was when I was forced into continual masturbation—which all priests believe to be sin—that I decided to learn, conclusively, if my life and my sanity was being destroyed by a power which I had to accept because it was above my comprehension—or if in the hidden depths of my reason, I believed reincarnation was possible.

I contacted the archaeology department of the University of Mexico and told them about the city to which the Albino had been taken. Its location, by my study of Mexico, was approximately three hundred miles southeast of the present city of Uaxactun. The university responded with a detailed map and letter informing me that an ancient ruin had already been discovered at that site. "It is now in the process of being restored."

I thanked God, I blessed Jesus Christ, for revealing the truth to me.

I was not insane. I was merely being driven insane by unexplainable supernatural forces. Now that I knew the truth these demons would tire of harassing me and seek out some other poor soul.

Martin Lormer interrupted me. "You said that you had proven reincarnation to be a lie." I looked to him, suddenly alert.

"Yes. I had proven, to myself, that reincarnation was a lie."

"Let's back up a little, Father. What you actually did was to try and prove it a lie because you believed—I will now quote you—'In the hidden depths of my reason, I believed reincarnation was possible.' Did you actually prove it to be a lie, or did you merely accept some half-baked coincidence as irrefutable proof?"

It was then that I decided to take the vow of silence until the trial was over.

I felt as though a wire veil had been torn from the surface of my mind, allowing me to think. To know.

When he had said, earlier, that he would prove ". . . reincarnation is defensible in this day and age," I should have understood the terrible impact of his intention.

He was leaning toward me. His narrow face a wedge trying to split my character into pieces for the game he was playing. His eyes were stark with intensity. I could smell his deodorant, see the dry film of anxiety on his lips. He wanted me to submit to him so he could use my life and Shara's death to give reincarnation a legitimacy that science had not been able to establish.

Legality establishes reality.

No, I thought. No. God will damn me for being used in this satanic scheme. "It is a fearful thing to fall into the hands of the living God." No. Reincarnation was a corrupt and lunatic lie.

I shifted back and put my hand to my forehead, shielding my eyes to avoid looking at him.

I did not understand what was happening in my mind. There was no natural intelligence to define what I had realized. I knew only this—that I am to die. That I must force my death to occur through the dictates of the law.

Martin Lormer made his mouth shift into a pleasant smile. He spoke softly. "Father Jerod, if you didn't believe that you were reincarnated from Barthelamo Vecchio, and the Albino, why would you have caused yourself such misfortunes and made such sacrifices to prove your beliefs to be a lie?"

I flattened my hand across my eyes and looked into the darkness of my own mind. I could only whisper to him, "My reasons for entering the priesthood may have been false, and my conduct as a priest may have been despicable—but there is forgiveness even for someone like me. What cannot be forgiven is an open and knowledgeable rebellion against the truth of God. Reincarnation is a corrupt and vicious lie. Not even the stupefying power of the devil has been able to make it otherwise. You will not be able to do it either."

I could not see his face but I knew he was frowning at me. I heard him shift on the chair, I felt his presence move closer to me. His voice was an angry slap of sound.

"Father Jerod, will you please stop your theological crapola and talk sense. All I'm trying to do is save your damn life!"

I would speak with him only a little while longer and then I would be done with speaking.

He reached to me and grasped my wrist. "How can I help you if you refuse to help me? How can I do what . . ." He stopped talking suddenly and snapped his fingers, cursing, "Shit—I know your game." He started to laugh. His voice was a derisive cackle. "How many times have you tried to commit suicide, Father Jerod? How many times did you try, but stop, because you didn't have the guts to do it?" I tensed. "That's what's in your mind, isn't it? You haven't the guts to do yourself in so you want the people of this state to do it for you. You want to be taken to the gas chamber and have your death done for you. In that way your creepy little soul will escape being sent to Limbo or Purgatory or wherever the hell creepy little souls are sent after committing suicide. That's it, isn't it?"

Shara, Shara, my beloved, listen to me. He lies. The times I tried to kill myself I tried only because I could not endure what I was doing to you. But you are dead, my beloved. We are no longer a torment to each other. I have reason to live now. So I may die properly. Not as a suicide, but as a sacrifice.

Martin Lormer stood up and lit a cigarette and blew the smoke at my face. It was his way of displaying contempt.

"I ought to plead you insane. Because that's what you are. Reincarnation, suicide, defrocked priest, murder—it's all like a Hollywood horror movie. Well, it won't work, Father Jerod. I'll save your life. Do you hear me, ex-priest? I'll save your silly life!"

Shara, Shara, my darling. If this clever devil can establish to the world that reincarnation is actual, it will be written into the law of the land. People will believe as I have believed, that we live and die and are reborn to die again to again be reborn, over and over and endlessly over—and the agony and sacrifice of our Jesus Christ will be reduced to a psychotic gesture. You are dead, my darling, not because you deserved to die, but because I believed what this devil will try to make the world believe. Beloved, beloved, listen to me. It is assigned to some people, by divine selection, to use their life for a purposeful death. I will use myself to stop this devil the church has retained. I must, beloved, you know I must.

I lowered my hand from my eyes and looked at him.

"I will tell you one thing, Mr. Lormer, and then I will take a vow of silence for the duration of the trial. It is written in Hebrews . . ."

"When you say a vow of silence, what do you mean?"

"I won't speak to you, or anyone."

"But I intend putting you on the stand. Your testimony is important."

"I will not speak once I have taken my vow."

"The gesture is ridiculous. Your testimony is important, but not crucial. I can manage without it."

Shara, beloved, you see, even the devil is a fool. The jury will stare at me, study me. They will see small smiles when absolute seriousness is vital. They will see sly winks. They will see the disturbed fidgeting of a man made ashamed by his own deceptions. They will be fascinated by the devilish persuasion of Martin Lormer, but it will be my silence that convinces them that reincarnation is a lie, and I must die for living a falsehood.

I stood up. I was four inches taller than he. My shoulders were broader, my physique more muscular. He edged back, not liking the differences in our size. I looked at the journal on the table. He would use what I had written about Barthelamo Vecchio and the Albino. I shrugged. They were dead. Irrefutably. Not even he could revive them. They had never lived in me. They were the fancies of a lonely boy toying with excess—who had made them real.

I walked to the door and turned to him. "It is written in Hebrews, nine, twenty-seven, '*And as it is appointed unto men once to die, but after this the judgment.*' That is the word of God telling you that reincarnation is a lie. I believe in God. I now take my vow of silence."

I tapped on the door and waited for the guard to lead me back to my cell.

Chapter 2

The judge drew off her eyeglasses and asked the court clerk to read the indictment. The clerk stood up, blinked and nibbled his mouth.

"The people of the state of California, represented by the District Attorney, accuse the defendant, Stephen Jerod, of the felony, to wit, murder. In that, on the day of March 29th, 1978, the above named defendant did unlawfully and feloniously take the life of another human being, to wit, Shara Medford, and with malice aforethought. Signed, the District Attorney, Charles R. Solenzi."

He sat down. The judge muttered, "Thank you," then turned to the jury. She twitched a smile at them. "Ladies and Gentlemen." Her voice was a cranky sound. "This is the information which has been filed by the District Attorney. I will remind you that these charges have not yet been proven and that it is for you to decide the guilt or innocence of the accused."

She looked to the District Attorney. "Do you wish to make an opening statement?" He nodded. "Yes, your honor." He winked at the two men seated at his table. I could sense the courtroom become tense as he walked toward the jury box. He was about forty years old. He kept touching the wispy strands of black hair he had combed over his frontal baldness. He was a short man with rounded shoulders, neatly dressed in a dark brown suit. He stood and tapped his black-rimmed glasses against his chin. The twelve people watched his contemplative pose. I wondered if he was as superb a performer as Martin Lormer would be. He brushed his hair again and began his opening.

"Ladies and gentlemen of the jury, I have been with the District Attorney's office for twelve years. I want you to believe that I have been in on every type of capital crime you can imagine. Murder, kidnapping, poison, sabotage, causing death by the use of a deadly reptile, malicious destruction of an aircraft, bombing, arson, machine-gunning, even train wrecking—but in none of these crimes have I ever come across a defense for murder comparable to the defense you are about to hear."

He paused and tapped his glasses against his teeth. He turned to me. His mouth looked chubby and curved down into his fleshy chin. Shara would have enjoyed this, I thought. She loved to see great institutions ridiculed by the way people exploited them.

"I will not allow the people of California or the integrity of our legal system to be hoodwinked, conned, or made fools of. There is always a determinable reason when one human kills another. I will bring into evidence the defendant's confession. Yes, he has already confessed to the crime. Yes. But in that confession there is only one fact. That is correct, only one fact. And, except for this one fact, the confession is a concoction of lies, fabrications, deceptions—it is a confession so cunning that it staggers human reason—but still, it does contain one fact. On the night of March 29th, the defendant, Stephen Jerod did, in fact, kill Shara Medford. Yes. He choked her to death. Yes. Now, let me tell you some of the circumstances surrounding this . . ."

Gradually, I drifted from listening and began looking at the faces of the people seated in the north area of the courtroom. I recognized some who would be called as witnesses. Ordinarily, witnesses were kept outside the courtroom, waiting their turn to testify. But Martin Lormer had not objected to their presence. It was his way of bullying the District Attorney.

I saw Franklin Jimson seated on the aisle. He kept twitching his thin mustache and sniffling. What would he say in behalf of Shara's character? Would he admit that he had continually tried to molest her? Could I blame him for driving Shara into the church, to confess, so we could meet?

". . . and when the defendant, Stephen Jerod, was taken into custody and transported to the Alameda police department, he was confined to a cell. He was not badgered, hounded, or even mildly harassed. He was left alone, to remain in his cell. Time passed. What was he doing in that long interval? He was thinking. Yes. Thinking. This former priest who, through a careful study of the

Renaissance era was able to direct art commissions to hidden treasures—to direct archeological expeditions to discover hidden cities, was thinking. It was in that time that his confession came
about and . . ."

Seated beside Franklin Jimson was Mrs. Lefkowitz, the elderly woman who lived in the next apartment. Her husband was a
real estate salesman forced into retirement by Parkinson's disease.
She had entered the apartment while my hands were still gripped
around Shara's throat. Would she sit in the witness box and state,
"Shara Medford was an awful bitch, and a drunk. When she
moved in with that man, we never had a moment's peace. The
drinking and sex and wild things going on were—were disgusting."
Or would her statement be, "Shara Medford was the dearest,
sweetest person I've ever known. She was always so good to my
husband. Why, she even baby-sat—I mean, kept him company
while I went shopping." I closed my eyes, wondering, even now,
what was the truth about Shara—what was the lie?

". . . but we have more than a confession. Yes. You, ladies
and gentlemen, are going to realize, as this evidence is presented,
that this is a man who knew exactly what he was doing. When he
killed, and after he killed. You might ask, how can I know that?
Wasn't it enough that he was found with his hands still on Shara
Medford's throat? No. His confession, by its very nature, proves
that Stephen Jerod is a devious, scheming, premeditated murderer.
His confession is a carefully planned cover-up. He was no man
caught in the grip of passion, who was having diminished capacity.
He was not insane or under the influence of intoxicants or depres-
sants. If you believe the defendant's confession, then you must also
believe that this murder was planned hundreds of years ago. No.
Thousands of years ago."

I could hear some gasps, and some people laughed derisively.
The District Attorney nodded repeatedly, as though trying to believe what he had just said. "Yes, yes—we are supposed to believe
that this murder was the result of events that happened thousands
of years ago—because of reincarnation." I could see the people
shifting and looking at each other, then at me. The judge squinted
and tapped her gavel to achieve quiet. Martin Lormer patted my
arm, whispering, "Relax, relax. He has to prove you *aren't* reincar-

nated." The men and women in the front rows were writing notes onto their pads. I carefully looked at the jury and grinned. I wanted them to know that even I thought such a defense was foolish.

"This man, this former priest, this teacher of theology at one of our great universities, told the officers that he had murdered Shara Medford to prevent her from killing him, as she had in several other lifetimes. That Shara Medford was here, in this life, in a state of reincarnation. Ladies and gentlemen, did you ever hear of such . . ."

I knew that somewhere in the courtroom Bishop Carmondy, in his street clothes, was watching me. He was leaned forward, squinting at me, his poorly fitting bifocal glasses not allowing him a clear sight of my face. Beneath his squint was a scowl. He was a man who enjoyed the grudge, the rancor he held for other men. Could I blame him for forcing Destiny—for hurrying it?

I was preparing to administer Communion in the church he had transferred me to. Only twenty or thirty people would attend. While I was placing the bronze wine chalice onto the linen corporal and covering it with the white chalice veil, the church door opened.

I turned to welcome the person who had entered. I suddenly constricted with fear. She was standing in the opened doorway. I wanted to lift my cassock and race from the sanctuary. I wanted to scream to God to stop letting the devil harass me.

Because within the depths of knowing I would love her—that I already loved her—I felt a shocking hatred for her. If she was these other women, come alive again, then she was ambitious, treacherous. She brought into this new life a compulsion for depravity.

She walked toward me. "Father Jerod," she said. Her voice was a whispered melody. I placed my hands at my sides. I must look on her as nothing more than a lovely young woman come to Sunday Mass to partake in the blood and body of our beloved Jesus Christ. . . . *"Do this in remembrance of Me."* She was carrying a small leather purse held against her stomach.

"Father Jerod, may I speak with you about a personal matter?"

"Yes, of course. But why have you come to this church? Surely there are other priests, in San Francisco, in Berkeley, who can advise you."

"This also concerns you, Father. Ever since our first meeting I have been unable to sleep. I have had . . ."

I could not stop myself from saying, "You have had dreams of an unusual type. And I am the male in your dreams."

She shook her head, bewildered. "How could you know that?"

I eased my hands behind my back and looked at the dusty ceiling. The wings of two semi-relief plaster cherubim were broken. Three feet behind the balcony rail was an enormous gap in the wall. The organ had been removed for repairs and not returned. My superior, now in his dotage, had forgotten about it. She shifted closer to me, her eyes staring at the chipped tile floor. "Then you have been dreaming about me."

I shrugged. "An oddity of circumstance, nothing more."

"No, Father Jerod, it must be more than that. Night after night you are with me. I have no way of understanding why this has happened. I've even consulted a psychiatrist."

"What did he advise you to do?"

"To find you and tell you about it. And if the same thing was happening to you, then he would have to research the problem. He was not too experienced in psychic phenomena."

"Psychic phenomena is just the grab bag for all things that scientific minds can't explain. Most of it is demonic."

"Whatever it is, doesn't the kind of dream we're having disturb you—a priest, sworn to celibacy?" Her tone was troubled, sad.

She glanced down, her long lashes lay a fragile design on her cheek. A pulse throbbed in her slender neck. Her mouth trembled. I would rather taste her mouth than sip the Communion wine.

I began puttering with the Communion arrangements. I placed the stiffened linen pall over the chalice. I felt flushed and tingled. My chasuble, newly laundered, concealed my sexual response. While putting this vestment on I had prayed, "*O Lord, who has said: My yoke is easy, and My burden light; make me so able to bear it, that I may obtain Thy favor. Amen.*" My hands trembled to reach out and touch her. My head throbbed. We were so irreversibly connected that we even reach into each other's dreams to embrace.

Then, suddenly, I became irritated. This was all a farce of God and Time and satan. We were being jiggled and bandied about by supernatural whim. I made myself frown at her.

"I am a man of God and I cannot dare propose a reasonable solution, Miss . . ."

"Medford. Shara Medford."

I could not tell her that once her name had been Letitia and at another time her name had been the sound, Onadyh. I could not tell her that in both other times she had been a gloriously sensual woman, so charged with sexuality that she interested Cesare Borgia and, before that, the sons of the Great Burning Eye and the Great Cold Eye. I could only stand and stare at her.

"Father Jerod, let me be frank. I have never been with a man. I'm old-fashioned enough to still believe that that belongs in marriage. I want you to be as honest with me. Are you responsible for my dreams?"

I was swept into a mood of exhilaration. She was a virgin! No man had used her. There we were, both unspoiled in our flesh, standing in God's sanctuary, like Adam and Eve.

"You can be assured," I said, "that I am not responsible for causing you those dreams—as I am not responsible for the dreams I am having. I do not have psychic powers, as people believe. My reputation is based on coincidence."

"Then what is it, Father, what is it?"

"We have been caught up in some peculiar dimension of Time. But whatever it is, it will pass. It must."

She reached out to touch my hand. I drew back. Was there any part of her I did not know, that my hands and mouth had not explored in my dream life? Were her dreams as lavishly erotic with me? Was she looking at me now and thinking, is there any part of his body my hands and mouth have not explored? God, God, why are you letting this happen to me? Your Word promises that you will not let us be tempted beyond our capacities to endure. I am beyond that endurance now. Remove her from me.

I placed my hands behind my back and intertwined my fingers. I deliberately sighed.

"We must not let it affect our lives to any harmful degree."

"Then what am I to do?"

She was so slender, so small standing before me. Her fingers wiggled nervously on the purse she held. I could smell her subtle perfume. Her mouth, tinted with a cosmetic, seemed to throb. The worried lines in her brow accented the steady intensity of her eyes. I smiled at her.

"Now that we have talked about it so openly, perhaps the dreams will disappear. For both of us. Why don't we wait and see. If the dreams persist, in both of us, after a few weeks, perhaps we can talk again."

"All right, Father Jerod. But will you pray for me?"

"Let us both pray, for each other."

Two weeks later the church was crowded with newspaper and television reporters wanting to interview me. The University of Mexico had reconsidered my letter and had conducted an exploratory excavation beneath an ancient ruin. They had uncovered the presence of another, more ancient civilization. They had found artifacts with the surfaces covered with picture writing and language. To the archeological community it was an astonishing find.

Voluntarily, I mailed my resignation to Bishop Carmondy. My dreams of Shara intensified. What we did with each other, sexually, became more imaginative, more elaborate.

" . . . and after this ridiculous confession was taped, what did the defendant demand? You will hear him sobbing, moaning all through the confession—in which he admitted to the crime of murder—what did he demand? Absolution, from a priest? Sleep, because of the weighty burden just lifted from him? Solitude—to be alone with his remorse, to grieve the love he himself destroyed? No, no, no. The defendant demanded that he be fed. Yes. He devoured a hearty breakfast that three lumberjacks would find hard to . . ."

My attorney muttered, "That really was stupid, Father Jerod," and reached for the leather briefcase beside his chair. He drew out my journal of Barthelamo Vecchio and the Albino. The jury shifted their gaze to him. I wanted to lean to him and plead, "Please don't use it. The past is dead now. It ended when they buried Shara." He placed the black binder beside his legal pad and sat back, listening.

" . . . there is no defense of insanity in this case. You will not be asked to believe this man is insane. The evidence will show that the defendant sincerely wanted the officers to believe that he was a reincarnated being who murdered another reincarnated being—that they were not real people at all. Just one spook doing in another spook, so what does it matter. But police officers are not naive bumpkins who . . ."

I could only stare at the journal.

I began each entry with the year and month and time of day— then a quotation from the Bible, in Latin. Then, on a whim, I interpreted it. I opened the journal with Barthelamo Vecchio the night he was dissecting the corpse of a woman. He was demonstrating to four students the miraculous order and provisions God had devised for woman in the process of pregnancy.

There was danger for him in conducting this clandestine autopsy.

The church, relentlessly diligent in seeking out offenders of its canons, had spies throughout the city of Romagna. Were a Physician or Surgeon even to be suspected of dissecting a cadaver, the Papal guards apprehended him and news of his sacrilege was quickly spread about the city and provinces. He was then tortured in the church dungeons until he confessed to his pagan practices, thus providing cause for his execution. The less agonizing death was by garroting, if he avowed his blasphemy—or the witch's stake and fire if he upheld his innocence.

While Barthelamo was worried about what the church might do to him, he was not terrorized. He was waiting for circumstance to alter the design of his life. When this happened, it would cause him to live in a manner similar to the utterly white creature who was existing within him. But while the other man had failed to gain absolute power and happiness, he, Barthelamo Vecchio, knew he would succeed.

Before the Fates guided him into this experience he wanted to pass on the knowledge he had acquired. While he was teaching other men, perfect in physique, he ignored the deformity on his shoulder and back. While he was teaching he was greater than other men.

I had written the journal as though I was Barthelamo Vecchio.

Date: 1498   Month: April   Time: Evening
"Ecce quantus ignis quam magnam silvam incendit."
Behold, how great a matter a little fire kindleth.
James 3:5

My anatomy theater was the rear of a tavern an innkeeper allowed me to use. He believed I had preserved his life when I removed a scabrous growth from his forehead. A canker of peculiar but harmless origin, which I had become familiar with when performing surgery after the battle of Fornovo. Needing a secret place for these dissections, I did not reveal that his growth would have eventually reached its limit and dropped from his skin. His gratitude served my convenience.

The cadaver was a grotesquely fat scullery maid whose death was wrongly diagnosed by a district barber-surgeon. When the body was purchased from him, he told my agent that the devil had implanted a demonic growth into her, then caused it to burst. It was clear, from the once-festering bruises and breakage of bones in her face, that she was beaten to death.

My four students did not breathe whilst I drew a scalpel across the fleshy abdomen. They feared a putrid gas, brewed in the bowels of hell, would issue from the bloated innards to poison their lungs. I leaned over the body and began separating the flesh I had incised, when we were startled by a loud pounding on the bolted door.

"Open! In the name of the Duke de Valentino. Open!"

Hurriedly, we stepped back from the table. A soiled blanket was flung over the cadaver. The pounding continued. The *bravo* shouted, "Master Barthelamo Vecchio, you are summoned for service by his excellence, Cesare Borgia." My students hastened to the narrow side door, a secret exit used for just such dangers.

As I watched them scurry in departure, I too was in fear.

Not for the violence that would be done upon my person. I was not yet destined for death. I feared the demented agents of the Papal hierarchy, quick to reach for amusement and *divertimento*, would render me naked and march me through the streets, chained to a dray cart drawn by an ass, where all could see the veiny, mottle-scarred hump grown on my shoulders and back. I would be jeered and mocked, pelted with dung and spat upon. They would believe my deformity was a sign of Cain, a leprous tumor cast onto me by the curse of the devil.

"Open, I say! The Duke de Valentino will not be kept waiting."

The *bravo* kicked at the door, rattling it. "Open, *figiol d'un can*." I shrugged, thinking, *finito*. I am finished. But even as I resigned myself to certain disgrace and outrage, I was overtaken with calm.

I called out, "*Pazienza*," then quickly donned my teacher's robe and hat while snuffing out the torches and all but one candle, leaving the small room in near darkness. I unlatched the door and opened it to see a tall, muscular youth in velvet *farsetti*, and bright green stockings, the color *calzoni* favored by Cesare Borgia. His velvet *berreto* was worn at a rakish angle, the edge of it emphasizing the scimitar scar slashed onto his right cheek. He was of low birth, like myself, but clearly a ruffian used in the service of Borgia because of his pleasure in violence and killing. Unexpectedly, he smiled. "*Buona notte*, Signor Vecchio," he said, and held out a sealed parchment with the royal stamp upon it.

"This is for you, from the Duke."

"*Grazie*," I said, ignoring his attempt to see beyond me into the room where the bulge of the cadaver lay. I tore open the parchment and read that I was summoned to Borgia's *palazzo*, where I would perform an examination for him. I would be escorted into the palace by the *bravo*, and brought before the great Cesare Borgia. I wanted to laugh then: to laugh at myself and brand myself as *idiota* for having been so frightened.

Rumor had been spreading throughout Romagna that Borgia had tired of his current mistress and, though about to marry the daughter of King John of Navarre, he betrayed her in favor of another comely wench. But unlike other sovereigns of great or petty republics, Borgia was in dread of contracting the diseases contained in the female and passed during the ecstatic intervals held in the bed chamber. Marius Vitto, his court physician, was now aged, his vision affected by the natural dimmings of time and from the constant use of infant urine to cleanse his eyes. He could no longer see the minute blemishes and fractive lesions of that monstrous malady of Venus.

I stepped into the kitchen, forcing the *bravo* to step backward. The aromas of *scaloppine* and *cacciucco* and *stufato* caused me strictures of hunger. I closed the door behind me. "I will be there, presently," I told him.

"I am obliged to escort you, Signore."

"I must cleanse myself, and change my attire."

"My obligation is to bring you to his Excellence, when I find you, and as you are, Signore."

"You will address me in the proper manner. I am not some *campanilista* you can trifle with. I am a Physician, and Surgeon."

"Forgive me, Master Vecchio."

"I will be with you shortly. Wait for me at the carriage."

"*Grazie*, Signor Vecchio," he said, his voice derisive. "*Grazie mille.*" He left the kitchen and I instructed the troubled innkeeper on how to rid himself of the cadaver.

In the carriage ride to Borgia's palace, the *bravo* sat opposite me, and slept. From his erratic snoring I suspected he carried a cloggage within his lungs. The vehicle jounced along the poorly paved road but I ignored my bodily discomfort and the offensive stench of garbage and excrement that littered the narrow streets of Romagna. I was held in my concern for this remarkable opportunity presented to my by Borgia's lusts.

Physician-Surgeons from as many leagues distant as Venetia and Campania were scheming to replace the aged Marius Vitto. A court physician was lavishly rewarded, in monies and lands, if he served his noble well. Eventually, if he was cunning, he could achieve political position and perhaps be raised to a Prince.

Although, as in all grand enterprises, there was the risk of falling into disfavor during any of the tempestuous and unreasonable rages of Cesare Borgia—or if the Duke's own fortune began to decline through military defeats and political treachery—the greater the jeopardies the more glorious the gains, if you endured.

I desired that coveted station. Truly. Physician-Surgeon to the House of Borgia. I was fatigued with the unvarying days in which I treated the low-born and mercantile ill. I needed not only the power and influence I could gain—I needed the danger, the steady sharpening of the senses caused by ever-present fear. Only in this mode of life would I be able to free myself from a satanic curse.

The ghastly white creature given refuge within my life was myself, as I had been, centuries bygone. The devil, being what he is, had gained cause for tormenting me. The burden of a deformity was not satisfaction enough for Crooked-Foot. I could not freely fulfill my present life while my former life was incomplete. A satanic curse is cast from the human soul only when the devil chooses to remove it, or when the bewitchment reaches the end of its cycle. I perceived this alabaster creature that I had been, only in part. By altering the pace of my life—by shrilling its intensity—the veils about my depths would be torn away, thereby allowing me to view more and more of him. Until I knew his conclusion. At his conclusion my freedom would begin.

The carriage clattered across the immense courtyard. The *bravo* awoke and wordlessly I was escorted through winding corridors lined with the lewd sculpture Borgia enjoyed gazing upon. I was hurried upward along a dank passageway. My deformity did not hamper my pace. It was an encumbrance I had learned to balance with a stooping motion. The *bravo* rapped the hilt of his sword onto a thick door and it was opened. I was told, in a guarded whisper, "This is his excellency's private chamber." The door closed behind me.

Standing, idly awaiting my approach, was Cesare Borgia.

He exuded a brawny roughness that betrayed a disposition for power and violence. Although he was hardly past twenty years, the impression of his size was greater than his actual substance. His shoulders seemed granite cliffs jutting from the sides of his sturdy neck. Beneath his gold embroidered doublet his chest was muscular and his torso tapered to a slender waist. There was a jeweled dagger fixed in the band of his *brache* and pressed against his flat abdomen. I wondered how many throats he had, himself, slit—how many hearts he had punctured with that very blade.

His legs were long and contoured with athletic grace. Legs which, it had been said, could propel him onto a horse without needing to touch the saddle. His black hair was an imperial mane framing the muted almond complexion, making the stark cast of his features appear burnished. The illusion of his boldness and strength seemed suitable to the legends of his deeds. The myths about him declared that he could mangle a silver *scudo* in his fingers, bend a thick prison bar between his hands. But the physical force contained within him as though it were a furious beast still untamed by civilization was second in its impact to his startling blue eyes—a color rare in this part of Italy.

His eyes gripped me, pierced me until the essence of my character was diagnosed for ambition, assessed for cunning, and analyzed for threat. Though he gazed silently upon me, I saw evidence of inner speech in those remarkable blue eyes. He was resolving intangibles and speculations into conclusions, even as his mind was moving to newer thoughts, grander alternatives.

I knew that I was already fixed in his estimation, but that his estimations could be altered either by his whim, or by my conduct—by his need of me, or his disregard for my function. Though I did not know what he estimated me to be, in truth, I did not care. My life, to him, could be nothing more than a single grape among acres of vines. I could be crushed, or cultivated. I was but a Physician-Surgeon to him. And he was a noble by birth, a former Cardinal by special dispensation of his father, Pope Alexander.

I stopped three feet before him and bowed low. "Your Excellence," I said, then stood erect, slowly shifting to the side to keep my deformity from his sight—though I knew he had seen it. A nerve below his left eye twitched but he seemed unaware of it. I recalled a gypsy poultice of the fruit of the Tamarindus indica, crushed rose roots, and bees' honey, applied three times daily, for one week, would alleviate the tic. I did not offer it. He was a conqueror of cities and republics—Perugia, Piombino, the duchy of Urbino—he was a regent of Destiny. A mere tic would not inconvenience him.

"You are aware of why you have been summoned?" he asked. I nodded. He glowered and his lips were taut across his teeth. "Have you no power of speech, Physician? Or are you so steeped in the sacrilegious dissection of human cadavers that the presence of the living mortifies you?"

I concealed a sudden spurt of fear, but though I felt the agonizing scrape of the devil's tail across my soul, I stared back at him with the reverence of court protocol, but no more. He is dangerous, I cautioned myself. But he is still only a man. He waited, perhaps expecting me to cringe and plead for my life.

I sighed. "I am a Physician, and a Surgeon, my Lord. I do what I must do to uphold the integrity of my profession. Danger always trails after dedication. As my Lord well knows."

"Yes, yes, that is why *you* have been summoned. Your reputation for skill and honor has been growing. That is why I have allowed you to continue your dissections. I first learned of your mastery from the Duke de Gaspari. You succeeded in saving both his legs. Then a *bravo* I used in Mantua lay on the field bleeding to death, and you stanched the flow from his neck. A remarkable feat, worthy of Galen himself."

"Impressive, my Lord, but hardly remarkable. There are vital arteries in the human anatomy which, when pressed, can . . ."

"Yes, yes, I will attend your discourse at another date. Preparations for the examination are already made. The wench awaits you."

"Forgive my impertinence, your Sublimity, but I am aware of how the honorable Marius Vitto conducts his examinations and I cannot lend my services in those primitive methods."

He suddenly grasped the hilt of his jeweled dagger and roared, "What—you deny me!" His dark complexion turned florid with rage. His blue eyes bulged. I did not breathe lest my fear tremble my frame, while deep within me, I was not truly afraid. He had allegiances and allies, but no companions. No trusted consorts. His court, as in other courts throughout the land, was crowded with lackies niggling at him for favors and high stations. Their service offered him no pleasure. And though his conceit was vast, I sensed it had not warped his appreciation for pride, nor the refreshment gained from witnessing honor.

If I served as he commanded, I would be merely another tool. If I served him as he should be served, I risked his displeasure in the chance of achieving his respect. And I knew that his brilliance as an administrator of principalities depended upon his instinct for recognizing the authentic.

The deformity clutched to my body stung as blood rushed into the tendril veins spread throughout the ugly flesh. My hump always pained me when I suddenly decided to engage in a great endeavor which, before it could gain life, risked being suffocated. I bowed low again, offering my courtesy, my homage.

"I do not deny you, my Serenity. I would not declare to you '*Io servo chi mi paga*' as your da Vinci once did. 'I serve out of loyalty, not payment.' But as I would not counsel you on procedures for conquest, I would not accept, blindly, your counsel on how to conduct an examination for the French malady, and virginity."

His look softened and his hand gradually eased from the hilt of his dagger. He sighed.

"I will forgive your insolence and speak no more of it. It will be as I have decreed."

"Forgive me, my Lord, it cannot be that way. You will have four ladies of the court in attendance and their gabble will distract me. Your presence, though a veritable endowment to any lowly Physician, would also hamper my examination. You must either allow me to serve you to the ultimate of my skills, or find another Physician. I will name several who will serve you as you wish."

He cursed. "Fool! Will you destroy yourself for one idiot moment of glory in resisting your sovereign?"

I remained silent. He strode to the wall and pulled a drawstring, summoning his personal guards. Two appeared instantly. They were burly youths, Spanish in origin, who grinned in anticipation of my abuse. I bowed low again, sweeping my arm before me, and muttered, "Does your Magnificence believe he can examine the wench himself and bed with her in perfect safety?"

I turned full around and walked to the massive oak doors. The guards followed me. My hump bristled painfully. It was at these times the white creature within me chose to reveal his existence. Whilst I saw Borgia in his fury, I could also see the companion of my horror. He was kneeling before the altar of a great stone temple. Light was beginning to dawn, soaking the shadows on the immense rise of stone steps. He wore a cluster of bright feathers upon his white hair. His milky arms were upraised in prayer. Below him were many square stone dwellings, with thatched roofs. He shook a container of bones and green ornaments to awaken the sun. *Great Burning Eye our warriors are doing their weapons. They will bring many captives to your hungers. I will cast the teeth of the dog that howls and the bird that sleeps. I will tear out many hearts to fill your bowls.*

Suddenly, Borgia shouted a command. "Hold fast, fool!" The vision of this chalky creature at prayer in me dispersed. Borgia strode to me. I did not turn. He stepped around me and stared at my face. The tic below his eye twittered furiously. He gestured to the *bravi.* "Await outside. Be alerted." He continued staring at me as they left the chamber, their sword scabbards thunking against the metal of their leg shields. Borgia smiled slyly, then bowed to me in mocking obeisance.

"What, oh grand and glorious Physician, will you require?"

"To have the maiden completely disrobed and to examine her alone."

He bolted upright and stamped his foot on the carpeted floor and bellowed, "Physician, you go too far!" I waited for his anger to soften even as he waited for his anger to terrify me. But I have lived with other terrors more monstrous than he could incite in me—to view yourself as you were, as another man, in another time, with feelings so real that your current feelings pale to them, inures you to fright from higher authority—and I remained before Borgia, silent, seemingly fearless, and his anger calmed to curiosity.

"Physician, you puzzle me. Other men wilt before my lesser frowns. I have caused barons and prelates to wet themselves when I harshen my tone. Yet you are unperturbed. Is it outrageous courage, Physician—or are you an *idiot savant*—brilliant in your profession yet *idiota* in all else?"

"Neither. Rather than cause my Lord, the greatest Prince of our day, one uncomely blemish upon his illustrious flesh, I would suffer the rack—nay, more than that, I would suffer his disdain of me."

He clapped his hand to his forehead and rolled his eyes upward. "Ye Gods, Physician, the dung that comes from your lips could fertilize a nation. Let us have no more of this. You will do as I require."

"Will my Lord place himself and his republic in jeopardy because of ancient proprieties? To learn if she is free of the malady of Venus, will he trust that to an untutored inspection, or chance? Is it a malady that reveals itself not only in the most precious of womanly parts, my beloved Sublimity? No, Sire. Its presence is often a mere speck indiscernible to the untrained eye. Can I know if she is contaminated without viewing her for this contamination? Do you require the services of a physician, or a quacksalver?"

"You are also a male. Her nudity would distract you. Her nudity is for my eyes only."

"Has my Lord looked upon me closely? Am I like other men? And were I perfectly formed and divine of countenance, what is that to the incomparable Cesare Borgia? Is it not known that the moon fades when brought to bear on the radiance of my Lord?"

I could sense his smile though his lips did not move. He was amused at the game that had suddenly sprung between us. "You are a snake, Physician. A clever reptile not to be held fast, for too long," and he laughed and his merriment was a melodic rumble throughout the expansive chamber, and I suddenly loathed him: loathed his good fortune, his physique and his birthright, bastard though he was. And I could not forget, as the white creature brought himself into my memory, that once I too possessed the latitudes of power.

I tried to force the vision from my mind. I did not want to be distracted from the instincts I would need to deal with Borgia. But this creature, whom I call Bianco, would not leave me. I saw him being escorted across the sun-baked stones leading to the chief's residence. The structure was an immense rectangle of precisely carved stone blocks. Three massive dogs with upright ears barked fiercely at the entranceway. Bianco was in his regalia. His body was covered with the skins of animals. His head was protected from the sun with a golden encasement. The people knew he lived only during the time of his father—the Moon.

I go into the great house. Our leader waits for my power. My

enemy, the son of the Great Burning Eye, looks his hatred at me. He
wants to be the son of both fathers. I fear him. I stop before my leader
and kneel. At his feet are the sticks and green stones cast by my
enemy. They tell my leader not to war when the Above has no shadows.

He wants to war with a far city. Our God will need many hearts
for his hunger. The women have opened the earth and put in the
little gifts of God. Soon, waters will fall from the Above. Slaves will
be needed to pick the gifts of God. My leader wants my signs. Should
he war when my father's eye is full? Will there be many round blankets to cover my father's eye? Are his warriors to march or to sit upon
the beasts that run?

I shake my bag of signs. When I cast, I will look at the eye of the
long beast who swims. I will dance. I will look at the teeth of the bird
who howls. I will sing. I will touch the black feet of the beast that
shouts. I will fall to the earth and claw my fingers. I will say to march
in the day and war in the dark. This will make my enemy needed.
They will bring him to the war. Many warriors will be left in stillness.
A weapon that sings in the air could find the heart of my enemy.

I do my casting.

Whilst I watched Bianco toss the peculiar objects before the
feet of the chief, Cesare Borgia reached to me, as though to a com-
rade, and gently patted my arm and chuckled.

"No, no, Physician, you will not see this maiden without attire. You cannot persuade me to allow you that offense. Come, let
us think upon it. How may it be done?"

He pinched his lower lip thoughtfully. His blue eyes became
slightly glazed, as though he had withdrawn his vision and fixed it
into his inner mind. I did not offer to think of what he desired. He
was Cesare Borgia, custodian of great cities. Brilliant general.
Courageous leader. A master at timely assassinations. A Duke
whose ambitions had gained favor with the monarchs of France
and Spain—who was, at this very moment, acquiring an army of
mercenaries to invade the Republic of Florence. He would conceive of a method for this examination and it would be clever—
cunning. He made a bridge of his long, thick fingers, and touched
the thumb tips to his nose. Then he smiled.

"She will be examined in this manner. She will lie upon the

examining table. Each part of her will be cloaked. You will examine only one of her portions at a time. As each is done and found acceptable, it shall be concealed again. In that way you will see only parts of her, never the whole."

"I am not astounded at my Lord's brilliance. The intelligence of Cesare Borgia is not legend, it is truth."

"Yes, yes, Physician. Enough calculated subserviance. I do not believe your reverence. But it is a quality that appeals to me. I am fatigued with the fawners who court my favor and affection."

"There is only one difficulty, Magnificence. I do not mean to offend, but I must speak of it. It has to . . ."

"Yes, yes, Physician, the core of her womanhood. That oasis of delight in which every parched traveler seeks everlasting succor. You may examine that without my surveillance. You cannot conjure the entire female from the mere sight of it, nor can you derive delight from the touch of it. Without the soul of her, it is a *thing*. Come, we are done with this talk. While the arrangements are being made you will take some wine with me. We will talk of your blasphemous dissections. That will humble you, Physician."

There was a sudden noise in the courtroom, then a scuffle. My attorney grabbed my hand, saying, "Sit still. This all works for us."

I watched the heavyset bailiff pull a miniature camera from a youthful reporter's hand. He held it up to the judge. "I spotted him snapping the defendant, your honor." The judge tapped her gavel onto a wooden plaque. "I'll have order in this courtroom." The people quieted. She pointed to the reporter. "You know the consequences of such an action." She motioned to the bailiff. "Remove him from the courtroom." While the people watched the reporter being escorted away I glanced at the District Attorney. He was sweating. The judge spoke to him. "You may continue with your opening statement." He studied the jury. This interruption had broken his rhythm.

"Ladies and gentlemen, this will be a long trial. The state will show, through expert testimony, that this confession, this carefully arranged and systematic story of reincarnation, is a malicious deception. We know from pre-trial discovery that the defense will attempt to persuade you to believe that this man acted reasonably in committing murder in fear that a reincarnated person was going to kill him. In that defense . . ."

My attorney raised his arm, saying loudly, "Objection, your honor. He's prejudicing the defense's case."

The District Attorney glowered at him. "Your honor, we have a statement here and we are entitled to comment on the evidence we intend to put before this court. And it's very clear that this man, from his statement, argued to the officers that he had killed in self-defense."

The judge nodded. "I overrule the objection. You may proceed with your opening statement."

The District Attorney's voice became emphatic as he pointed at me. "This confession took two and a half hours in which this man rambled and repeated and . . ."

"Your honor," my attorney said, his arm raised. "He just said the defendant was making a carefully arranged and systematic confession, and now he's saying he was rambling and repetitious. I object to that."

"Counsel, will you please save your argument for your closing argument and let the prosecution complete his opening statement."

He lowered his arm and made a show of an exasperated sigh, even as he muttered to me, "We have to show the clowns in the jury box that we're still in the ball game." The District Attorney held his arms out as though offering a tray of food.

"If the defendant is a reincarnation of someone, who was a reincarnation of someone else, and on and on, backward to the origin of our species, or the Garden of Eden, then why haven't we, as well, been accorded that mode of transit through the centuries? If a defense of this kind is given credibility, it becomes dangerous. People can kill, willy-nilly, and claim they were avenging a relative in the tenth century. To what age does our present law and order then apply? And if the defendant is really in the mainstream of reincarnation, then perhaps in the sixteenth century he was a cockroach."

Some people laughed. I grinned. The District Attorney continued with his argument but I stopped listening. He was ridiculing reincarnation and he was convincing. There was little I could do to assist him. I sat, a smile fixed on my face, but there was no joy in me.

We cannot know what forces are affecting our lives—their origin or the purpose—when those forces are from a supernatural source. We can only try to explain them after they have happened.

The only personal gain I experienced from the notoriety of having led to the discovery of the ancient city was to receive an offer to teach Theology at Calvin Coolidge University, in Alameda, California. I accepted quickly. It would be a personal gratification to me to stop teaching children that the blessed Mary was a virgin all her life—though everyone knew Jesus Christ had younger brothers. I realized the adjustment would be difficult. After seventeen years with the church, how does one stop being a priest?

While I waited for official approval of my resignation I remained to assist my doddering superior. But I was anxious to leave. I wanted to rent an apartment in Alameda and then seek out a prostitute. I believed the only way to stop the recurrent sexual dreams of Shara was to experience the physical reality of sex.

Two days after I submitted my resignation, Shara Medford telephoned me. Her voice was strained.

"You must help me, Father Jerod. Unless these dreams stop, I know I'll go insane. Are you still having the dreams?"

"Yes."

"Oh, God, Father, what is happening to us? Have your dreams become more—more . . ."

"Unconventional?"

"Yes. I can't believe the things that happen. I've never read books or magazines of that sort, so it can't be a projection of fantasies. I don't know where they come from."

"I'm really sorry, Shara. I don't know what to do either. I'm leaving the church, by the way. In another week or so I'll no longer be a priest."

"Has something happened to you? Are you ill?"

"No, nothing like that. I've been considering it for a long time now. This new wave of notoriety merely forced it a little sooner."

"Can I come visit you today? About five o'clock? For just a little while, Father. I can't go on like this. I hardly sleep at all. I don't want to live like this."

"All right, Shara. I'll be here, in the sanctuary, waiting for you."

She looked haggard and grim. Her eyes were sunken, the flesh of her cheeks drawn. Her fingers twitched when she touched her hair. Even her clothes seemed unpressed. I wanted to hold her against me and comfort her as a father does to a distraught daughter. I was afraid to touch her. I did not know what I looked like to her.

She stood before me and we looked at each other. There was no language to explain what we were realizing, to convey what we were feeling. The horror that happened in our sleep moved us beyond the bounds of propriety. While I knew our connection in Time, she knew only that her sanity was being destroyed. We were strangers sharing a mutual shock. Our recognition now was equal. We were gripped by unexplainable forces and we could not, by our own moral struggle, extricate ourselves.

While we could not know if our lives should be one, we knew that separation was doom.

There was no need to speak.

I extended my hand. She placed her fingers on my palm. Silently, we walked from the sanctuary to the room in which I lived. This was the dream we shared. Devoid of fury. Impassionate. We were to conduct each other into a sexual procedure. Our eyes were held in a locked stare as we undressed. I did not think.

We moved as though in a placenta of warm liquid. Slowly. Effortlessly. Flesh to flesh—the entry to each other. Entwined in Time and unraveled in Space and embraced in the instant of Now. "What must I do?" she whispered, and I said, "It has all been done for us, in our dream," and we became instincts groping to desire— stroking, we eased upon each other and were branded into an impeccable unity—torn apart only to breathe until we could join again, and she moaned, "Oh, God, it hurts," and I sighed into her mouth, "Long before I knew you, I loved you," and her pain dimmed and she was youth and I was ageless, and though I heard her muted weeping there was another voice of laughter in me, saying, *"Sie sente meglio?"* and I wept while I listened to the laughter ask again, *"Sie sente meglio?"* and I shouted, "Yes, damn you, I feel better!" She stiffened, afraid, and I soothed her as we moved, "It is nothing, darling," and beyond that foreign voice there was an ivory laughter, brittle and polished, and the laughter rattled with bones and trinkets and animal symbols, and then I knew that while I was loving her, we were sharing her, and I was in an orgy of women, and while my flesh smoothed in sweat upon her flesh I understood that I was mad but my madness had not yet reached my sanity. . . .

. . . and then she screamed and I screamed and suddenly I wanted to beg her, "Don't kill me, my beloved, let me live, let this be my final lifetime," and she screamed again and in that scream I believed her lunatic with lust and the wish that I could die burst through me, and then it was done, we had spilled ourselves into each other and she was no longer as she had been and I could never be the same.

"Shara, Shara," I muttered, kissing her forehead, her cheeks. She murmured, "What will happen to us now?" and I inhaled her voice in the dark light as she began to sob. I stroked her hair and laughed softly, "I don't know, darling. Except that we have begun."

When the District Attorney completed his long opening statement, the judge asked my attorney, "Does the defense wish to make an opening statement at this time, or to reserve it?" Martin Lormer leaned to me and winked. "If the DA knew the investigation I've put into this case, he would swallow his dentures." He stood up and shook his head at the judge.

"Your honor, we were going to make an opening statement— but from what I have heard—which I consider to be misleading and totally argumentative, I don't believe we will make an opening statement. The issue before us is not only of self-defense and possibly reincarnation, but also of God and the . . ."

The District Attorney quickly rose and shook his hand like a schoolboy in class. "Your honor, he just said he would not make an opening statement and now he's making an opening statement."

The judge frowned at my attorney. "Is it your intention to reserve your opening statement?"

He nodded. "Yes, your honor. We want to see what evidence is actually brought forth to establish the facts which the prosecution now claims they can put forward. Therefore, I will not make an opening statement at this time, but will reserve our statement for our own case."

The judge turned to the jury. "Ladies and gentlemen, you are now instructed that the defense is not required to make an opening statement following the prosecution's case, and are entitled to reserve their statement." She patted a fluff of gray hair and nodded to the District Attorney. "Now proceed with your case, Mr. Prosecutor. Call your first witness."

While the district deputy coroner was being sworn in, my attorney drew several manila folders from his briefcase and stacked them neatly at his right elbow. The courtroom listened to the coroner's qualifications and the District Attorney asked him about the autopsy he had conducted. The man put his report before him and squinted at the pages.

"The body was of an adult female, approximately twenty-two years old. The body was identified to me as that of Shara Medford."

"Would you describe the body on which you performed the autopsy?"

"There were hand prints and bruises on her throat. Also a pattern of small scars at the base of her spine. They were obviously the result of being burned when she was a child. Other than that the body had no unusual markings."

"Do you have any opinion concerning the cause of her death?"

"Yes, I do. She died as the result of suffocation."

"In other words, she was choked to death."

"Yes."

"Thank you. No more questions."

The judge looked to my attorney. "May this man be excused?" Martin Lormer stood up and spoke to the judge. "I have no questions at the present time. But I ask that the witness remain subject to recall."

I was puzzled. I did not know why he wanted to question the coroner. There was only one possible cause for Shara's death. I had choked her. The District Attorney frowned at him. He too was puzzled. Martin Lormer sat down and began doodling the word S C A R S on his yellow pad.

While the arresting officer, Detective Sergeant Essex, was sworn in, I kept staring at the word S C A R S. I did not want to think about Shara but I knew the importance of the scars on her back.

After making love in the church I insisted that we separate. She argued, "We can't, Stephen, I've just found you." She touched my face, my shoulders, her eyes were damp from her pleading. I made myself adamant, I spoke with pretended anger. I lied because I was afraid. "It won't work, Shara, I tell you it's all wrong!" Dear God, how I lied.

If we remained together I could not deny her existence. Separated, I could convince myself she did not exist. If we became lovers I would never find my own life, in this time. The exhilarations, the passions I had felt with her could not dispel my knowledge that she would someday destroy me. I wanted to love a woman—not have an affair with my death.

Then I softened. Tears warmed my eyes. I caressed her cheek with my mouth. I whispered, "Shara, darling, listen to me. I can't see you again until I understand what is happening to me." I was telling her adolescent nonsense but she closed her eyes and nodded. "All right, darling, I'll wait." You will wait in the eternity where you belong, I thought—and we kissed, and separated.

But while a man and woman can force themselves apart, they cannot disrupt the intentions of a supernatural power.

My dreams of Shara were sustained.

They became more frightening.

Throughout our sexual unity, in the dream—wherever we conducted our lovemaking—the air was cluttered with small, luminescent eyes. The eyes floated about us like buoyant confetti. The eyes never touched us. They only stared. Their presence soured my sensations. I became ashamed. At my time of climax the eyes twirled and churned and I could not always release myself into Shara. I would push her from me and begin cursing the eyes. I would stand naked and scream damnations at the eyes. But they never left us. Shara did not seem troubled by their invasion of our lovemaking. "They are only eyes," she would say.

And while I stood and cursed the glowing orbs I was cramped with jealousy and hatred. The eyes belonged to the spirits of the men who desired her. They were the eyes of the men who already had used her flesh. The eyes were laughing at my ineptitude, my crudeness. I became less and less absorbed with lovemaking and more interested in the eyes. My body performed mechanically while I studied the eyes. There was pain in them. And grave sorrow. I knew they were the eyes of the men she had betrayed. The eyes were sent to warn me.

She would lie on her stomach in sleep. I would lie on my back, staring at the eyes staring at me—my hand idly stroking her skin until I touched the scars across the base of her spine. My fingertip would trace each rippled contour, and I would silently cry because I knew that some male lover had branded his name onto her body and only when I loved her exactly as she wanted would the scars disappear. I cried because my love was imperfect. The scars were there and they would never vanish.

The District Attorney strode to his table and picked up a large cardboard drawing of our apartment. He placed it on a rickety tripod stand and pointed to it.

"Officer Essex, this is a diagram of the apartment where the crime took place. Will you refer to it as you testify, please."

The detective left the stand. The back of his brown suit was creased and shiny. He pointed at the corridor. "The front door was slightly ajar. There was no sound of a struggle. I found them in the living room—right there—and his hands were still around her throat. It was weird."

"Weird? In what way?"

"After receiving the call from my dispatcher it took me about nine minutes to get there. When I found them, he was still choking her. It doesn't take that long to choke someone to death. There they were, neither of them moving and both naked. It was just weird."

Some people in the court whispered. Several jurors frowned. The newspaper people began writing on their pads. Two of them were artists and they were studying me as they drew my picture. The judge touched her eyeglasses. Someone behind us leaned over and handed my attorney a small cardboard box. He nodded his thanks. I listened to the detective explain his arrest procedure. When he had completed his report the District Attorney asked him, "Would you know that man if you saw him again, Officer Essex?"

"I sure would."

"Is that person in the courtroom?"

"He sure is."

"Would you please point him out for the jury and the court?"

"It's the man in the pale blue suit sitting next to the defense counsel at the counsel table."

"Your honor, may the record indicate that the witness has identified the defendant, Stephen Jerod."

"Let the record so indicate."

"I have no more questions, your honor."

My attorney stood up and brought the cardboard box to the witness stand. He faced the jury as he spoke.

"Officer Essex, you said that when you arrived at the scene of the crime, the defendant had his hands around the deceased's throat, and that they were both naked."

"Yes."

"By naked, do you mean they had absolutely nothing on?"

"They may have had something on."

"Then they were not absolutely naked."

"I suppose not—not *absolutely*."

"What, then, were they wearing?"

"I wouldn't know how to describe it. It was weird."

"I can accept that. Then let me show you what they were wearing at the time."

He opened the cardboard box. People leaned forward. I glanced down, suddenly ashamed.

He picked out the long purple velvet cape and purple beret. He held it before the jury. He turned and rippled it at the judge. He slung it across his arm and picked out the waist dagger and the

purple embroidered scabbard and belt. The newspaper artists began hurried drawings of the articles. He turned to the police officer.

"Do you recognize these?"

"Yes. They look like what he was wearing."

"What you meant to say, then, was that he was wearing a
replica of a fifteenth-century cape and a beret. And around his
waist was this dagger—or, to be more accurate—a stiletto similar
to those used in the fifteenth century, in Italy. And the only one
who was naked was Shara Medford. Who may have been strangled
by a fifteenth-century man named . . ."

The District Attorney jumped up. "I object, your honor. He's
asking for conclusions from a witness not qualified or expert in
that field." The judge agreed. "Objection sustained." My attorney
shrugged and said, "No more questions." He submitted the costume as evidence, Defense A, and returned to the counsel table.

The District Attorney began calling an array of police person-
nel. They read from their mimeographed reports. This was the
procedural portion of the trial. Their information qualified the
facts of the crime. Martin Lormer did not trouble to cross-examine
them. He would lean to me and whisper comments. "I'm not going
to waste my shots on a lot of flunkies." Or, "The judge is about
ready for her afternoon nap. Did you know she's into transcenden-
tal meditation? That works for us, you know." Or, "The DA thinks
he's got a winner. He'll be getting careless soon."

He talked to me for several reasons: to show the jury our relationship was amicable, and to trap me into answering. If I answered him, then my vow of silence was null and void. And
because he was a man who liked to talk, his ideas came not only
from his careful thinking. They came from hearing himself talk.

The only time the jury became interested was when photographs of Shara were displayed for evidence. She had been photographed naked.

When the District Attorney pointed to the dark bruises on
her neck, the jury and others in the courtroom viewed her lovely
breasts. Even in death they were upturned and lush. "Kiss them,
Stephen," she would tell me. "Your mouth belongs to my breasts.
Be the child I will never have." When the District Attorney indi-

cated the line of scars across her spine, the people studied her buttocks.

My attorney leaned to me and whispered, "Now there, Father Jerod, is a glorious piece of ass. Was it her ass that turned you on?" I glanced away, annoyed that he would try to provoke me to speech in such an obvious manner.

After Sergeant of Detectives Clinton completed his testimony, the judge announced that the court would break for lunch and convene again at two o'clock. My attorney picked up my journal of Barthelamo Vecchio and fitted it under his arm. People stared at me as the bailiff led me to a side door where I would then be escorted to the county jail. Martin Lormer walked alongside me. He patted the journal and smiled at me. "You know something, Father Jerod? You didn't know Shara Medford. You didn't know her at all. You're due for an education." He patted the journal again. "The answers are in here, and you never even saw them."

I stared at the journal, knowing every word I had written— wondering even now, as I had wondered a thousand times before, if I had really written that damned journal or if the life and spirit of Barthelamo Vecchio in me had written the journal through me.

Date: 1498   Month: April   Time: Evening
"Pravum est cor omnium, et inscrutabile."
The heart is deceitful above all things, and desperately wicked.
Jeremiah 17:9

Preparations for the examination of Cesare Borgia's wench were completed. We stood in another ducal chamber, enclosed within a compartment constructed of tapestries bound on slender wooden racks. Long tapers were held in brackets attached to the uppermost frames. The maiden, completely covered with white silks, lay on an ornately carved table. Only the rhythmic sound of her breathing revealed that she still contained life. Borgia had placed himself at her head and waited for me to begin the examination. He was pleased that I could not determine her figure.

I removed the silk wrapping from her left limb. It was well

formed, the contour smooth and soft to touch. There were no blemishes. I raised the leg much as I would elevate the lever of a machine. I could feel his eyes bore into my mind, trying to know if this was pleasuring me. I ignored his interest. He could not know my feelings, my thoughts. I hummed tunelessly, then spoke as though to an idle barkeep.

"In excellent condition. Without blemish or infection."

I covered the limb and undraped the other. There was no tension in her body. She was placid, but not lethargic. I wondered about her. Was she in devout prayer that I find some unsuitable portion so she could be free of his desires? Although not as famed a lecher as his father, the Pope, his sexual savagery, after the brutal pillaging of Capua, drove him to taking forty aristocratic maidens as increase to his already swollen concubinage. There were also several royal males he had dallied with. Though this was not unusual for the nobility. Inwardly, I sighed. The fate of this wench was not my affair.

I could feel stirrings of anticipation, and fear. This was no casual event tossed to me by chance. No opportunity presents itself without a deeper purpose.

I muttered to Borgia, "This limb, too, is in excellent condition. Without blemish or infection."

"Get on with it, Physician. The sight of her parts causes me to become anxious."

I covered the leg and quickly examined her arms, then shoulders, then stomach. I began feeling strange in sensation, and did not know why. Silently, I prayed that visions of my former existence would not now invade my consciousness. This Borgia, this prince of evil, though now in the throes of sensual lust, was also attuned to those auras which filter from the souls of men. If he suspected that there was more of me than appeared before him—that I contained corridors back into Time which he could not traffic in—he would think me bewitched, and this opportunity presented to me would vanish in his wrath.

I cursed the white companion within me. He demanded intrusion. "Bianco, Bianco," I silently begged. "Let me be."

Though I could hear the lisp of Borgia's breathing, only a portion of my mind examined the woman he would use for his evening's amusement. I was held by the vision of Bianco who was staring at a woman among the captives the warriors had taken. She was tall, her hair utterly black, its length flashing across her back as she was driven to where all the prisoners were penned. The Albino, garbed in his feathery cover and headdress, stood and stared at her. It was then he felt smashed in his sensations with a desire for her. And he was afraid.

He was not allowed to do to a woman what other men did. He was the son of the Great Cold Eye. The sons of gods did not need to birth for the strength of the city—to grow and become warriors or breeders of more children. Gods lived forever, unless they were killed for having lost their god-ness.

He stood and watched the captive woman being pulled along with the other women. Then she stumbled on the dry brown earth, and fell. A warrior on horseback rode to her and slashed his knotted lash across her lower back, cursing her to get up and walk. The Albino wanted to kill the warrior for abusing the woman he knew he would take for his own—though he risked losing his god-ness. She pushed herself up from the ground and again walked with the other women. The Albino could see smears of blood across the base of her spine where she had been struck.

I felt faint with the hatred Bianco was feeling, but Borgia did not suspect my mind was elsewhere. Thus, whilst I dabbed my fingertips to the maiden's flesh, I entreated Bianco to depart from my mind. But I had no authority over his appearances. He returned to my vision in another place in his village.

He was seated on the earthen floor of an abode of odd construction. The roof was made of coarse leaves and branches. The walls were of stone and smelled of fruit rinds. Crude rectangular holes were fashioned in the walls to serve as windows through which the dark sun entered. All about him were eerie symbols dangling from the walls—faces carved in jade, animals cast in thick gold statuary, skins of slain beasts, and many bone ornaments and human skulls, dried by time.

He was seated before a glowing fire. Pungent smoke and sweetly acrid aromas emanated as he dropped herbs and shrunken fruits upon the coals and chanted in an alien tongue. He was nude but for a leather loincloth that covered his privacies. Other than his blatant whiteness, he was without physical deformity. He was thinking about the woman captive he had seen. He reached to his loin cloth and fondled himself. He would make her his woman.

Before him, the curtained entrance was parted and a maiden, wearing only a wrapping about her waist and trinkets about her neck, stepped in and knelt before him. She placed a wooden bowl containing steaming foods at his feet. Her nudity did not arouse his interest. She was not the woman he wanted. The maiden did not look at him. She was afraid. No one ever looked upon his face. They saw only his bleached skin. He waved her away and dipped his hand into the succulents, and ate.

When he was done, he set the bowl aside and raised a jade container holding carved bones. He rattled them. He cast them to the ground and studied their design. Only he understood the meanings they formed. When the next full moon—his father's eye—looked down from the Above, there would be rainfall. The wells would be filled. The sacrificial prisoners would be properly bloomed and festering with fear. Their bodies would be painted blue and there would be seasons of abundance when their hearts were torn from their breasts and brought to feed the gods.

He stood up quickly and kicked aside the clutter of bones. The woman he wanted was among those to be sacrificed. He picked the jade container from the floor and smashed it against the stone wall. He must find a way to keep her life.

He was suddenly startled by a wheezing noise. He felt a brush of wind, then heard a heavy thud. He turned to the sound. The thick shaft of a long spear was sticking into a wooden mask. Feathers trembled from the quivering shaft. He stood, with fear bursting water upon his white skin.

His enemy, the son of the Great Burning Eye, had warned him that he wanted his death.

The vision was closed from my mind by Borgia's impatient voice. "Well, Physician, well? Is there to be no end to your prodding and poking?"

I sighed with proper respect. "I will not endanger you with my haste." I reached for the silk across her breasts and Borgia raised his hand, halting my action.

"Uncover each one, in its turn."

I shrugged, then bared the right breast. He murmured with lascivious delight. In a moment of frivolity I wanted to tap the rosy nipple and say, "Aha, so it is you, Angela." I restrained myself. One does not destroy himself over the sight of a breast.

"Perfectly formed and well balanced," I said. I concealed that breast and exposed the other. "This too, my Lord." Before he could protest or conduct a discourse on courtly proprieties, I quickly drew the cloth from her womanhood. We stared at it.

It was a common womb, not unpleasant to behold. Scrubbed and perfumed in preparation for royal entertainment. Borgia hummed, "A sight to cause excessive salivation, eh, Physician?"

A smooth pad of pubis was thick above her receptor and the orifices were ordinarily distant. Although there was no way to know if she, or any other maiden, was truly virginal, or if other males had found their way to her favors, I, as would any reasonable physician, performed the ritual of inquiry by inserting my fore and center fingers into the narrow aperture. She trembled slightly though I was not causing her discomfort.

To avoid Borgia's irritation, I looked up into his eyes as I appeared to gently probe. There were glints of amusement in them. He was interested in estimating my response. Did I envy the delights he would achieve from her? Was the utter obedience she would pay him what I, a man with a deformity, had always sought in a woman but could never attain? The maiden remained still and I admired her will of submission. Borgia frowned at me.

"You tarry in her womanhood for too long, Physician."

"Only in your interests, my Lord."

"Well? Your verdict?"

I could, by mere opinion, command this maiden to a life of common servility by declaring her to be spoiled—for Borgia's rage at her fraudulence would be a manic fury. Or I could state that she was without previous violation, and commend her, for a short length of time, to a life of luxury and lavish depravity. But she had been pliant, and silent. Attributes I admired in these sisters of Eve.

"Her maidenhead is secure, my Sublimity."

"Excellent. Will I also draw blood?"

"I cannot say. It is in the whim of the Fates."

"I'll suffer none of your blasphemies, Physician. God is ruler of the universe, not the Fates. Declare for me as other Physicians have declared. Will I draw blood?"

"I am not other Physicians and I cannot declare what is so unpredictable. Has my Lord always drawn blood upon entry as other Physicians have declared, or promised?"

Grudgingly, he shrugged. His thick eyebrows clotted together like a singed crust above his eyes.

"Physician, you must learn to speak the truth in such a way that it does not offend more than the lie. However, continue the examination, and be done with it."

Carefully, I drew away the silken scarf covering her countenance. Her eyes were open and she was staring at me and suddenly, as though I had turned liquid, my life's substances drained from me and I stared into her eyes, as certain that I had known and loved this maiden before, in another existence, as I was certain my life was now worth only a short time of breathing if I betrayed myself before Borgia.

Her long auburn hair lay in thick ringlets across her neck and her eyes, a dark, moody umber, flicked to my face. There was no recognition of me in them, while I was still all sensation for knowing I had once loved her. I had never beheld her face before but I had shared the essence of her. *Dio mio,* I had. Yes. There is a spirit, I heard my mind declare—as we stared upon each other—it is a motion, invisible but with substance, that moves from Time to Time throughout the vastness of Eternity, and those who love once, love again, and always, for all time—though this is not revealed to everyone. But I was cursed with knowing another existence, and this maiden, this nameless, lovely maiden whose privacies I had inspected, was in my other existence—and we had loved, deeply and for all that time—so deeply that we needed more time and another existence to conclude its fullness, its truth. And now I was blessed for possessing such recall.

Lying before me, silently staring at me, was the reason I had never loved another woman, and all women I have had have left me wanting, and devoid of affection and passion even as I released the ultimate of my sensations into them.

It was she.

This unblemished, no doubt virginal, maiden whose soul, and mine, were inextricably coupled throughout the fertility of Time. And where once my dreams were the nightmares of the damned, I believed them now to be the beneficences of a God I had always doubted.

God even used corruptions like Cesare Borgia to bring His gifts.

I was startled from my bewildering reverie by the grate of Borgia's impatient voice.

"Physician, you try my endurance. There are matters of court and state that require me. Get on with the examination."

I knew he must not have her. No man but myself would ever possess her. Our destinies were locked together. I was now afraid.

There were fleeting signs and remembrances in my other existence that had warned me of threat and jeopardy. And whilst in one depth I was stricken, in another depth of me I was calculating a method for deceiving Borgia so he would not use this maiden, yet not so despise her for his disappointment that he would designate her destruction.

I touched my fingers to her mouth and said, "Open." My tips trembled through her parted lips but I pretended to stare within while my mind devised a sequence of deceptions. Carefully, I covered her face, afraid to look into her eyes again, lest I stoop to touch our mouths and whisper, "I welcome you into my existence again, beloved." I looked at Borgia.

"There is no taint or infection to her, but . . ." I glanced away, frowning, knowing he would be quick to sense that I was in a dilemma. He tilted his head to the side and knit his brows.

"*Che succede?*" he asked. "Do you find an unwholesome humor?"

"No, my Lord. But I am disturbed. I must return to her womanhood again. There is a . . ."

"You have examined it. You are done with it, I say."

"My Serenity, I am troubled by a suspicion of her left side. There is a design to the veins, an implication in the vertebrae, a delicate curvature in her pelvis. I have seen it twice before. In a marchioness, from Lourdes, and a barkeep's daughter in Foligno. It is a strange condition of the womb."

"An affliction? A malady?"

"No, no, neither. A peculiar substructure partially within. It might well place his Excellence's member in danger. It would have the effect of a large stone dropped upon your eminent staff."

He touched his groin and shuddered. Though she was silent as we talked, I could sense her stiffening with fear. *Cara*, I wanted to whisper to her, I am lying for you. You are perfectly formed. Do not fear.

Borgia tapped his mouth and his eyes flicked across my face like beacons, searching for deceit. I did not look away. My ruse relied upon the irrefutable appearance of truth—while within me, in that depth of life I contained and which no other human but myself could know—I mocked him. Yes—I mocked this mighty tyrant, this conveyer of fratricide and incest and mass assassination. I would not let him have her. He desired her for a moment. I wanted her for my present eternity.

"Proceed, Physician. There is more in the balance than my pleasures. Your future, your life, are being weighed on my scales. Do not trifle with me."

"If to guard the source of my Lord's pleasure, I must afix myself to mortal jeopardy, I do it happily."

"Enough. I am covered with the dung of your diplomacy. Be on with it."

I uncovered her abdomen and womanhood and, feeling his angry gaze upon me, I tapped the graceful rise of her hip bone with my thumb while, with my other hand, I pressed hard onto her pubis. I felt her quiver. A gossamer gloss of perspiration formed upon her skin. She was grappling with her will, I knew. I was stigmatizing her. Causing her ruin.

Though I did not know her name in this existence, I wanted to murmur, I am saving your goodness from the outrages of a perfumed animal. I am protecting you, *carissima*, and in time, we will love. It is foreordained.

I tapped her thigh and said, "Raise." The leg was slowly elevated. I cupped my palm about the warm inner softness. Her pulse fluttered in frantic palpitation. Borgia moved closer to me. My hump began to bristle with anxiety. I depressed the leg and shook my head.

"It is, as I suspected, your Excellence. There is a malformation of the bones, within her. Upon entry, the royal member would be endangered. After the veil of maidenhood is penetrated, an arrangement of nerves and tendon would be provoked and—without her consent, or will—she would be sent into a sequence of apoplectic spasms that would embrace, with the power of a beast's jaws, and cause both agony and injury to any intrusion therein."

"She could cause my rod of divinity harm, you say?"

"Grievous harm, my Lord. Not through her choice. It is her anatomy that would rebel against such massive intrusion as you would present to her."

"But unless she is penetrated, how can you know this?"

"There, Excellency, is the value of my dissections. I risk my welfare in search of knowledge and now my search serves you. The most revered physician Galen did not dissect the human, therefore he makes no mention of it in his writings. Still, there is reference to such a condition in Jacques Despars of Turnai, and Avicenna's revelations in *Canon of Medicine*, and the work of Guy de Chauliac bears witness to my findings."

"*Fandonie!* It cannot be."

"This is not a common occurrence, but it does occur. Nor is it the work of the devil, nor a sorcerer's curse, nor a fault in her stars. It is a birth defect, not a sin. It would have gone unnoticed until the day she was taken and the bed of delight would be rent with the unfortunate male's screams of torment. If he were to continue the fornications, his member would be rendered . . ."

"*Ferma!*" he demanded. I stopped speaking as he shook his head, muttering, "*Peccato, peccato*," and looked at her covered form, then suddenly clenched his sturdy fist and cursed, "*Puttana!* Is this what the convent sends me? Does God frown upon my simplest pleasures, even from there?" Then as though his enraged disappointment were a gust of air blown from him, he sighed, "*Non importa,*" and sighed again.

I allowed my breath to ease from my throat, thinking, *finito*. It is done. She would be returned to the convent and in a short while, a month, two perhaps, when Borgia could no longer remember her life, I would seek her out and we would begin our time together in this existence. I felt dizzied with wonderment, faint with expectation.

Then Borgia laughed.

He struck his hands together in a violent clap and his huge body shook with his private entertainment. I looked to her on the table, still covered, and her limbs began to quiver because his laughter had become satanic, like a child scraping and crumbling the wings of a dove. I was filled with dread.

Then as suddenly as he began to laugh, he wiped tears from his eyes with his broad thumbs, and ceased his laughter. His mouth became a threatening slash of merriment.

"I will not have her returned to the convent. It would be judged that I have refused her and the ravenous *padres* would spoil her. No. I want her condition preserved, and unsuspected."

"Preserved, unsuspected, my Lord? For what purpose?"

"Hold yourself to purgatives and sacrilegious dissections, Physician. Do not probe about in Borgia's mind, or court. I'll suffer no attempts to cure her malformation. She is, as she is, valuable to me beyond your trifling logic. It may well be a year before I use her—it may well be tomorrow—but I will use her. Thus, I charge you with the preservation of her condition."

"I am profoundly puzzled, my Serenity. What am I to do with her? My house is small, my . . ."

"You will leave your present circumstances and serve in my attendance. You will aid the honorable Marius Vitto in his medical service to the House of Borgia."

He laughed again, and pushed aside a portion of the compartment, almost toppling the structure. She did not move, and slowly her quavering subsided. I watched him stride to the massive oak doors with nude *putti* gamboling in erotic caprice carved on the panels. I did not allow myself the disposition of joy, or despair. He was not done with us.

The moments of apprehension were a suffocating pause for

me. There was fire and then frozen rock carousing about in my deformity. It felt heavy on my back, and wild, as though it were a living animal wanting to tear free. I disregarded the pain. In a matter of hours I had achieved what physicians from all of Italy aspired and conspired for. Yet that was the least of my exhilaration.

It was she, lying covered on a table beside me, that gave me rare ecstasy.

Though we had been lost to each other in the opaque transferences of time and place, we were found now. *Dio mio*, we were found now. My vision of another existence would stop because she was of that existence, and our Times had been coordinated. We were found now.

Below me, I heard her shift on the table, preparing to rise. I touched her arm and whispered, "Be still." She was instantly immobile. I watched Borgia reach the doors, then turn to me. I did not breathe. Our lives rested on his impulse.

"Physician," he said. He drew the dagger from its hilt and pointed it at me.

"You are now in the service of the House of Borgia. Your allegiance to my court is final. I know only one sentence for acts against me. Death. Death for collaboration against me. Death for betrayal, death for deception, death for dishonoring me. It is simpler to destroy a man than to imprison him. I employ death in the service of my life—the life of Cesare Borgia."

Suddenly, he flung the dagger at me. I did not wince nor cringe. Motion seemed slowed and I could follow its flight toward my forehead. Slowly, it arched down and thudded into the broad edge of the table she lay upon. I heard her gasp. We stood, a long distance between us, but it was as though we were pressed to each other, gripped in a moment of strange intimacy.

When the blade stopped quivering, I allowed breath to enter me. Borgia waited, his wide mouth a patient smirk. Slowly, I bowed low.

"Your Excellence, my life is yours. My fortune is bound to your glory—therefore I am blessed."

He laughed derisively. I remained in my court curtsy until he left. Carefully, I raised myself and turned to the table, elated with a flare for living I could not recall ever feeling before. I touched her hand, lovingly, and murmured, "You may rise now—then come with me."

I sat on the edge of my cell bunk, trying to force more of Barthelamo Vecchio into my consciousness. The memory of all he had lived within me was more interesting than what was happening now. I wanted to think about the Albino and his dangerous courtship with the captive woman. I did not want to dwell on my grief about Shara.

I could not. Her memory and my mind were inseparable.

Yet we had known happiness. Happiness swelled in Shara's eyes when we agreed to live together. There was no doubt in us. I believed that our living together had been determined long before we met, in this lifetime.

"I love to cook, Stephen. You'll get so fat, I'll nag you to diet." I had laughed. There had been so little laughter in me, before. And my body felt electric with lust. Plain, direct, robustly heroic lust. It was as though I was trying to recapture all those years wasted on celibacy.

"You don't blame me for what happened, do you, Stephen? For causing your loss of—well, of virtue?"

"Blame you? I bless you."

"Stephen, look at the clock. Look at the time."

"It's a quarter after three. Why?"

"Don't you realize that you have been celibate for the last two hours?"

We studied our working hours and eliminated every moment that kept us from being together. We did not blur our identities with male chauvinism and women's liberation pretenses. My income from the university would be the main source of our economy. While I was not blatantly untidy, I was not fanatically neat. I was also an incompetent cook. Shara would keep her position and manage the housekeeping. My only demand was that we keep separate closets. I wanted a place in which to hide my journal.

Our life together became a pleasant routine. She would leave for her work in the morning. I would remain in the apartment, preparing my class for the day. I did not believe she was seeing another man. Until the night I asked her the question all men instinctively ask after making love. "Are you all right, darling? I mean did you—you know."

She pressed her face to my bare chest and murmured, "Oh, yes, darling. Marvelously." But hidden within her sigh there was a plaintive whimper.

"You're lying to me, aren't you, Shara?"

"No, darling, I'm not. I am very satisfied. More than that. I mean it."

"It's all right, you can be truthful."

"But I'm not lying."

"Confess it, Shara."

"Stephen, you're being a poor ex-priest and a foolish man. I am marvelously satisfied and, to be truthful, I don't really believe in the therapy of confession."

"How can you say that? It was through confession that we met."

"I wasn't there because I was desperate to confess. While it was true that Mr. Jimson was trying to go to bed with me, I wasn't afraid of him. He's rather a fool and can be manipulated. But I had to go to your church. It was very strange."

"I don't understand. Why was it strange?"

"Because I'm living in Berkeley and I am directed to go to confession in a church in San Francisco. I find that strange."

"What do you mean, *directed?*"

"I don't know what I mean. I was just directed. It was as though I was one part of a magnet being drawn to the opposite part. But would you like to hear something even stranger?"

"All right."

"I'm not even a Catholic."

Chapter 3

When I was brought from the county jail to the courthouse, there were newspaper and television reporters waiting to photograph and interview me. My wrists were cuffed and a slight steel chain was held by a policeman leading me into the massive gray building. Pedestrians were crowded behind the reporters and some of them called to me. A few held up papers they wanted me to autograph. Two other policemen walked on each side of me, keeping the reporters from getting too close.

I did not try to shield my face from the cameras and I never spoke. It was not the kind of celebrity I enjoyed. The questions they yammered at me were always the same.

"Tell us about those other lifetimes, Father Jerod."

"What is the church's position on reincarnation?"

"Why did you give up the priesthood?"

"What is the latest discovery that you're working on?"

"Has Martin Lormer discussed his strategy with you?"

"Are you conducting services for the other inmates?"

"Can you predict your own future?"

I knew they disliked me because I refused to speak. While the murder and the trial were good copy, my silence did not create excitement. And I did not like them. They were articulate barracuda living off the remains of tragedy. Many times I wanted to laugh at a remark one policeman made to another. "Let's keep a close eye on this priest. He's liable to snap his fingers and fizzle away, or disappear up in smoke."

The District Attorney called Mrs. Alice Hillman to the stand. She was the woman who attended the old priest in the Pinole church. She tidied his rooms and brought him food and cleaned him when he messed his clothes.

She was a short, nervous woman with neatly fluffed gray hair. When she sat down she fussed with her clothes.

"Mrs. Hillman, you were in the church at Pinole on the Sunday afternoon of April 9, 1977, were you not?"

"I was, yes. I came to put Father Gorman's dinner in the freezer. I would have to telephone him to remind him to take it out and put it in the oven."

"Yes, yes, very good. You were doing this on your own, weren't you? Not for pay, but voluntarily?"

"I was doing it for my beloved Mary, and her divine Son, Jesus. '*Whatsoever ye do for the least of Mine, ye do for Me.*' That is what is written, you see."

"Fine, fine, thank you. How do you, by the way, remember that day in particular?"

"It was my granddaughter Melanie's birthday. She was twelve years old. I wanted to hurry home to dress for her party."

"What other reason is there for remembering that day?"

"It was for the shock of it."

"The shock of it? Would you explain that, please."

"Yes, mind you, the shock of it. On my way to Father Gorman's rooms, I passed the young priest's rooms. I heard some funny noises. It's not my habit to pry, mind you, but I did become curious. The door was a little open, so I peeked in."

"That's most understandable. And what did you see?"

"Well, I saw the like of which I never saw before. It was the young priest and there was a woman with him and they were— well—without a stitch on and they were—well, you know what."

"They were what, Mrs. Hillman? Don't be embarrassed. We're all grown-up."

"Well, they were—they were intercoursing."

People began to mutter and some snickered. I was surprised to know Shara and I had been observed. People shifted in their seats to look at me. Bishop Carmondy crossed himself and bowed his head. The faces of the jury, as though all attached to the same lever, turned to me.

The District Attorney stepped to the witness. "Is that priest in this courtroom?"

"Yes, sir. He's there, in the blue suit."

"Let the record show that the witness has indicated the defendant, Stephen Jerod."

"The shock of it was awful, I tell you. At first I didn't recognize the young priest because of what was on his . . ."

"That will be all, Mrs. Hillman. Thank you. No more questions, your honor."

Martin Lormer stared at the woman while the judge said it was his turn to question her. He kept staring at her. She glanced down and squirmed and patted the skirt of her green flower-print dress.

Martin Lormer leaned to me, whispering, "I'm going to play a crazy hunch. Just to test the validity of your journal. If it works, then I've got an angle that is mind-boggling." He stood up and smiled at the woman.

"Mrs. Hillman, I know you are a truthful woman. I want to ask you two questions. Not to embarrass you, not at all. But because the Bible says 'You shall know the truth and the truth shall set you free.' Am I quoting that correctly?"

"Yes, sir. That's the word of God."

"Good. Now, why were you in church that Sunday afternoon? You had already attended the early morning Mass, hadn't you?"

"Why, yes, as a matter of fact, I did."

"Now, Sunday is the Lord's day, isn't it?"

"Yes. A blessed day of rest, thanks be to God."

"And, knowing a woman of your religious integrity, you would use that day for rest. And, since you were so devoted to taking care of Father Gorman, you would have prepared his dinner on Saturday and brought it to him—gotten it into his freezer and telephoned him on Sunday to remind him to remove it and put it into the oven. So you would not have to work at anything, on Sunday, the Lord's day. Does that sound reasonable?"

"That's exactly what I always did. He was getting a bit forgetful, you see."

"Yes. Still, Mrs. Hillman, you were in church on Sunday afternoon when you should have been home resting, or dressing for Melanie's party. Wouldn't you say that was peculiar?"

She frowned at him. The District Attorney drummed his fingers on the table. His assistants cleaned their fingernails. A short man on the jury put his hand over his mouth and yawned. Mrs. Hillman's frown deepened.

"I remember that day, yes. It was very peculiar. I don't know why I did it that way. You see, in fact, I recall my own daughter snapped at me. She said the old priest was taken care of and I . . ."

"What she meant, would you say, was that you had already brought him his food that *Saturday*. And you were—for some strange reason—bringing him more food."

"Goodness, yes. That's exactly what my daughter told me. But I had to bring him that food. I simply had to, you see."

The District Attorney raised his arm. "Your honor, I see no point to this line of questioning. I object to his leading the witness."

The judge looked to him. "The line of questioning does seem rambling. But I'll let it continue a while longer. Objection overruled."

Martin Lormer smiled at the witness. "Something drew you to the church that afternoon, then. Something you can't quite explain. Now, tell us what drew you to the room. Was it the sound of bedsprings, drunken laughter, someone shouting for help?"

"No, not a'tall. It was the howling."

"Howling? Did I hear you correctly? Did you say *howling?*"

She nodded several times. "Yes, like there was wolves in the room. Howling. It was a fright, I tell you."

Martin Lormer slowly turned his back to her and looked to the newspaper people as he spoke to her. "Do you know if there were wolves in the church, or on the grounds?"

"I not only never seen one in the church, but not anywhere in Pinole. But I know howls, and it was maybe no wolf howl, and it was no dog howl neither. Just howls the like of which I never heard before."

Martin Lormer looked to the jury and waited. Our lovemaking had been intense that afternoon. I could not remember hearing any sound. Martin Lormer grinned and spoke as if to himself. "I've heard of all sorts of sounds during that activity, but never howling." He shifted around to the woman.

"Before the District Attorney dismissed you, you were saying, 'At first I didn't recognize the young priest because of what was on his . . .' but you were interrupted. Would you finish that statement?"

"Well, when I looked into the room and saw them I was shocked, wouldn't you know. He was a priest, you know. There he was, and her too, in the all-together, on holy grounds. The sacrilege of it. I made myself not look at what they was doing. I wanted only to see who it was so I could report them to the Bishop. It was him, the young priest, Father Jerod—but I wasn't sure at first, you see. I wasn't sure until I saw his face."

"Why, Mrs. Hillman, why weren't you sure at first?"

"Well, now, while it was his face, mind you, there was an awful looking hump on his back, too."

I stiffened with rage. The woman had been bribed. I wanted to jump up and damn her lying soul. She had been prepared by reading my journal. Martin Lormer turned to me and smiled slyly.

The District Attorney began calling character witnesses to the stand. Martin Lormer leaned over the table and wrote on his yellow legal pad as a tall woman with short-cropped blonde hair testified that Shara was a cooperative worker, a cheerful and loyal friend ". . . who never used a vulgar word that I can recall." Martin Lormer pushed the pad and pencil to me. His handwriting was neatly small and precise. He had written:

He is attempting to prove that this particular killing was motivated by a long-standing hatred on your part. He will establish that while the motivation may not have been premeditated, the felony was so malicious and accumulative that it amounted to murder. I will have to cross-examine to prove any violence you took to the victim was provoked by her. I will have to dig into the dirt of your relationship. Can you, or Shara, stand the exposure?

I pushed the pad and pencil back. He was cunning. If I replied to his question, even in writing, it would break my vow of silence. I ignored him and watched the court clerk tap on his stenographic machine. I did not care about what the witnesses claimed to know. No one could know what Shara had caused to happen in me.

After three months of living together I realized that Shara had not menstruated. This observation became important to me. Was she abnormal, or blessed? I did not believe Shara was pregnant, yet she never used any birth control methods.

I waited another month, studying her for indispositions. Changes of mood. Physical discomforts. When there was no difference in her calm and amenable manner, I became intimidated by Barthelamo Vecchio's influence on my existence. I began thinking that Shara had brought spells and incantations into this life and she was doing something to her body that Letitia might have done.

In their medieval time the menstrual blood was believed to guarantee an assassination by poison—seven drops stirred seven full turns in a lethal potion would keep the victim from suspecting he was being poisoned. If a woman menstruated when the moon was in a descending slope you could not dance with her or speak with her while she was sewing. If the cloth she used to absorb the flow was nailed to the front door of your enemy, it would attract evil spirits into the house.

I began to wonder if Shara secretly practiced witchcraft. But I persuaded myself to believe it was merely a biological imbalance.

The District Attorney leaned on the wooden arm of the witness stand and spoke to the woman who had worked with Shara.

"Did she ever complain to you about the man she was living with?"

"Yes. I was surprised when she did. Shara usually kept things to herself. She came into the office one morning and asked to borrow my makeup. She wanted to cover up some black and blue marks on her arms. They looked awful."

"Did she say how she got them?"

"Yes. She said she didn't know ex-priests could be so violent—and suspicious."

"Did she tell you why he did that to her?"

"Yes. She said, 'He was trying to turn me into a liar.' He had accused her of cheating on him. That is, that she had another lover."

"Thank you. No more questions."

Martin Lormer walked to the witness. She poked her rimless glasses closer to her eyes. He rubbed the side of his nose thoughtfully.

"I'll just ask you one question, Ms. Hayes. Was this ex-priest successful in shaking the lie out of her? Did she deny or admit she had been cheating on him?"

"No. Come to think of it, she never said, either way."

"Then what was the lie she wouldn't tell him? That she was, or was not, cheating on him?"

"She never said."

"Do you know if she was cheating on him?"

The District Attorney slapped the table and stood up. "Objection, your honor. The question is calling for a conclusion and it is also irrelevant."

The judge nodded. "Objection sustained." Martin Lormer grinned, saying, "No more questions, your honor."

The District Attorney called a Frank Ferguson to the stand. I did not know him. He was a chunky man of about fifty-five. His complexion was so ruddy it seemed about to peel. He said he was a gas station attendant and worked for the Shell conglomerate. His station was on the corner of Bleech and Vanguard Streets—four blocks from where we had lived. I did not care to listen to the questions.

Shara did not menstruate, nor did she experience sickness.

I could not recall anyone who had not been touched by some illness over a period of five months. Shara never sniffled, never coughed. In the mornings she would rise from the bed and never ache from having slept in one position for too long. We were together just one month when the Asian Flu covered Alameda like an infectious blanket. I was in bed for nine days. The apartment complex in which we lived was a zoo of sick noises. Shara tended me, bringing me antibiotics and juices, covering me when I was chilled, cooling me when I was feverish. She bought a vaporizer and made me sit with my face in hot steam until my congestion cleared. She was the only one not affected.

Once she was carrying a heavy bag of groceries and had slipped on a pencil I dropped. She fell backward, her buttocks slamming to the floor in a spine-injuring crash—the side of her forehead struck the wooden arm of the couch—a large can of fruit cocktail thudded into her breasts.

She had jumped up and laughed. "I'm fine, Stephen. But that should convince me I'm not destined to become a ballet dancer." I held her and rubbed the places that were hurt. She kept laughing. "I'm fine, darling, really I am." I looked at her forehead and there was no bruise. I opened her blouse to massage the pain from her breasts. There was no welt.

I closed my eyes, not wanting to remember her. There was still too much I could not understand. Martin Lormer began drumming his fingertips on the table. I looked at the jury. Some were resting their chins on their palms, listening to this Frank Ferguson testify.

". . . and I didn't mean to listen to him arguing, only he got so loud, I couldn'a helped hearin'. He was callin' her names you hear in a low-class bar."

"What were some of those names?"

"They ain't exactly decent."

"Just reveal some of them, if you please."

"Bitch, and whore. Just them two. Only he said them lots."

"Do you recall the reason he was using such words to her?"

"Sure. He said she was steppin' out on him. You know, doing adultery."

"Did he do anything else besides call her those names?"

"Sure. He hauled off and whammed her across the face."

"You mean he struck her—actually violently hit her?"

"Pow, right across the mouth, twice't. Back and forth."

"Is the man you saw strike the victim in this courtroom?"

"Sure. He's there, at that table, in a blue suit."

"Let the record show that the witness has indicated the defendant, Stephen Jerod."

Martin Lormer leaned to me and whispered, "He's really pushing to brand you a sado-masochist. Let's see if we can turn you into a somewhat normal human being." When the District Attorney sat down, Martin Lormer left the table and smiled at the witness. The man stroked his gray hair. His fingernails were stubby and clogged with dirt.

"Mr. Ferguson, I want to ask you a question. Have you ever hit a woman?"

"No, sir. I have never hit a woman, and that's the livin' truth."

"Good. I believe you. All right then, what might cause you to strike a woman—say, like your own wife?"

"It'd take a helluva lot, I tell you. Ethel's the best and I don't have a temper a'tall."

"But what if you learned she was stepping out on you?"

"Well, that's another story all together."

"What would you do?"

"I'd beat the livin' piss outta the bitch."

"Thank you, Mr. Ferguson. No more questions."

Some people in the courtroom laughed. Several jurors grinned. The judge squinted at Martin Lormer, who returned to our table. When he sat down, he muttered, "A little here, a little there, and in a little time, no one knows what the hell is going on or what to believe." The District Attorney put the tip of his pencil to his pad and wrote a check beside a name. He stood up. "I would like to call at this time Marsha Jenner."

She was a chubby female with a tight-fitting pants suit that emphasized her contours. I remember Shara telling me, "I feel so sorry for Marsha. She just can't develop a meaningful relationship with a male."

I did not listen to the beginning of her testimony. Martin Lormer became occupied with reading a page of my journal. I glanced at the page. It was the portion where Barthelamo Vecchio began conducting his practice in the palace of Cesare Borgia. He could not prevent himself from being absorbed by the pathological madness that permeated a *palazzo* inhabited by nobility.

Men and women of all ranks and lineage summoned him to their chambers for examination or treatment: Ambassadors on business for their republics and emissaries come to settle disputes from foreign nations, deputies soliciting favors for their provinces and Cardinals haggling over Papal rights with legates concerned about their territorial revenues. In the first weeks he wore fatigue like a leaden cape.

They demanded his presence and complained of loathsome maladies. He cleansed the infections they believed were given them by the devil. He bound the sprains and injuries and demonstrated that their bodies could function while disorders caused them discomfort. His procedures for piercing boils and eradicating rashes and skin flakings were performed with garish theatrics. A simple cure made their infirmity seem less significant and his skills unworthy of respect. They began to believe he possessed medical alchemy and treated him with cautious awe.

The nobles became like children offering their welfares to a holy man who, because he was not engaged in worldly affairs, would not be tempted to conceive their ruin. In his company they stepped from behind their poses and babbled to him of misfortunes and expectations, of ambitions and collaborations they would otherwise contain in crafty silence.

He was also apprehensive about Letitia. When he lied to Borgia about the malformation of her womb, he had sensed her shock. He did not know if she wanted to scream, "He lies a devil's lie, my Lord," because she had already been deflowered by a priest visiting her convent, or a lusting bishop—or if her shock was from innocence.

Martin Lormer closed the journal and looked to the witness. Marsha Jenner answered the District Attorney. "No, I have never seen Shara drink," and looked to the press section as though hoping they would snap her picture. "She told me that the taste of liquor or wine made her nauseous." I frowned. Shara always had wine with her dinner. I wanted to tell Martin Lormer, "She's lying." I remained silent.

"When she discussed her relationship with the defendant, did she express happiness?"

"No, au contraire, unhappiness. She said she was afraid of him. She said he was wild. Wild, that was her word. He threw things. Très terrible, you know? He ranted and raved."

That too was a lie. How often I had prayed that I could scream and shout my fears at Shara. I stared at Marsha, studying her. Why was she lying? I had always been courteous to her.

"Did the victim ever discuss her social life with you?"

"Oh, yes. Many the times she would complain that he never took her anywhere. There was the King Tut—Tutankhamen, that is—exhibit that she wanted to see, but he would not allow it. When the Scythian gold exhibition came to San Francisco, she wanted to see them, but he wouldn't allow that either. Going to the *symphonie*—the symphony—is another. She said he hated music."

The District Attorney shook his head as though disgusted by what he was hearing. Martin Lormer seemed not to care about the testimony of this lying witness. He opened my journal and began reading. I glanced at the pages as he turned them. Held between the pages were long strips of white markers. He had written notes and observations on them. He fixed his attention on one page and studied the carefully written lines about Barthelamo Vecchio. He muttered, "Her testimony doesn't make sense, according to your journal. Why is she telling lies, and yet not lying?" The District Attorney crossed his arms over his chest.

"Did the victim, Shara Medford, ever come to your apartment for any unusual reasons?"

"Oh, definitely. Once a week, from August of last year 'til March of this year. She came to leave me some money. She didn't deposit all the money she earned in their mutual checking account. She held out twenty dollars every week and brought it to me. Sometimes she brought a hundred dollars. I have no idea where she got this money."

She opened her purse and drew out a white envelope. She held it up for the jury, then the judge. "I always put it into my savings account and kept careful records. I drew it all out two days ago." She handed it to the District Attorney. He opened the flap and rifled through the bills and deposit slips.

"How much is in here?"

"Three thousand, one hundred and eighty dollars, plus the interest accrued. There is also three weeks of her vacation pay included. She said he didn't know she was getting paid for her vacation time. She said she wouldn't go anywhere because he would not allow it."

"Why did she give you this money to hold for her?"

"Shara said he was *monstrueux*—monstrous—and a miser. He demanded all the money she earned. Even though they had a joint checking account, he was the only one who wrote checks on it."

"Did she give you any other reason for why she was saving this money?"

"Yes. She said she was afraid that one day he would do her serious bodily harm. She said the hospital insurance she had might not cover all her injuries."

"Was there any other reason?"

"She said that if he killed her, she wanted enough money for a proper burial."

People looked to me. They frowned and wrinkled their mouths. I was helpless. I wanted to stand up and declare that she was lying. Martin Lormer glanced at me and smiled slyly. "Makes you want to deny it, doesn't it, Father?"

I clenched my hands on the table edge. Silently, I recited, *"I believe in one God, the Father almighty, Maker of heaven and earth, and of all things visible and invisible. And in one Lord, Jesus Christ,"* and then I was calmed. While the money was counted and submitted into evidence I controlled my breathing. I had no reason to be enraged about the witness's lies. They worked against me. A mountain of lies had turned me into a man who killed—let it be another mountain of lies that fashions my tombstone.

"Did the victim ever discuss her physical relationship?"

"Frequently. She said the reason he was so vicious to her was because of his own guilt. Because he was having an affair with another woman."

I gaped at her. Shara was the only woman I had ever known sexually with one exception, which she provoked. I sat with my hands under the table and began rocking my body, wondering if this Marsha Jenner was actually being truthful. That it was Shara who had been lying about me. "Shara, Shara," I moaned in myself. *After knowing you for so long, how could I not know you at all?* Martin Lormer whispered, "Sit still. You're distracting me." I kept rocking and thinking about Shara.

So much of the time I was with her was confusing. I often cursed myself for being so unworldly, for believing love was the magic solution for each dilemma. Shara began asking me extraordinary questions. "Stephen, how long will I live?"

She began trying to find out what her future held. She brought home a deck of tarot cards and a book of instructions. I would watch her lay out the card patterns—place her fingers on the face-up cards while studying the face-down cards—and begin reading their meanings. I tried to sound amused when I said, "What are you searching for? Your lost keys?" Because there was no anger in her disposition, she had smiled. "This is an ancient method of prediction, and I really believe it has merit."

When the tarot cards did not please her she brought home a Ouija board, then abandoned that for the I Ching, which she found too symbolic and prissy to be accurate.

Letitia had the same spooky temperament. She would skulk about Borgia's palace, seeking out Messr. Vandelli, the astrologer. One afternoon she had seen a cat slinking across the north courtyard with a dead sparrow in its mouth. The right wing of the bird was broken. The cat had four white tips on its paws. That was her sign of pending misfortune. She wanted Vandelli to read her stars and discover a countersign to negate the forthcoming adversity. She met Teresa Luigi, a maiden in the service of Borgia's sister Lucrezia. She was told that the astrologer had become the victim of a fatal accident while charting the stars. He was taken with a dizzy spell and fell from a high parapet. Barthelamo knew that the astrologer had caused Borgia to lose twenty-three *condottieri* when he sent the mercenaries to raid a village near Urbino. Letitia became aggrieved because she would have to wait until another astrologer could be found.

The captive woman was always pressing the Albino to throw his container of bones and other objects. She wanted to know when she would be returning to her people. She would stroke his body and fondle him, then step from his reach when he wanted her, indicating he could not have her until he read her signs.

We were cursed. That was the only explanation. An ancient, impossible-to-trace-through-Time curse was imposed upon our lives.

When the District Attorney finished his questioning of Marsha Jenner, the jury looked to Martin Lormer. He edged around to me and smiled, but his teeth were clenched.

"Ms. Jenner, did you think it odd, or foolish, for the victim, Shara Medford, to continue living with a man who abused her so awfully?"

"I did. I even told her so. *Il t'amoindrit*—I told her. He is making you less than you are. Why don't you leave him? Do you know what she answered? She answered, 'I can't. He has done something to my soul.'"

"That is a curious statement. Did she reveal what she meant?"

"No. I didn't press her for anything further. It was too spooky."

"Being so close to the victim—her dear friend—would I be presuming to think that you had many talks together? You know, woman-to-woman talks. About life, universal events, your jobs, even about men."

"We did. Yes, we were talking all the time."

"Did you ever ask her if she loved the defendant?"

"No. I didn't feel it was my place to ask that."

"Did she ever volunteer it?"

"No, she never did."

"Tell me this, Ms. Jenner—were other men attracted to Shara?"

"They couldn't help but be. She was a beautiful woman."

"Did they flirt with her?"

"You might say they did. But she never flirted with them."

"Was it because it was not in her character to flirt, or because she was afraid of what the defendant would do?"

"She was deathly afraid of him."

"I see. Then what you are saying is, if Stephen Jerod were not in the picture, Shara Medford would have flirted with other men."

The District Attorney called out, "Objection, your honor. He's leading the witness." The judge said, "Objection sustained."

Martin Lormer shrugged. "No more questions," he said, and returned to the table and scowled at me.

Marsha Jenner left the stand and the District Attorney called a Bruce Mandel. My attorney looked at a list of names and muttered, "He's going to be a real bitch." I watched Bruce Mandel walk to the county clerk to be sworn in. He was wispy in physique and short. He was about twenty-eight years old and easily intimidated. Even his steps seemed to stammer. I could never understand why Shara had chosen him for her idiotic interpretation of my character—not even when she explained, "I even chose a man not dangerous to you." I clenched my mouth. Humiliation never fades. Bruce Mandel was the first man I could recall hating. Our one meeting was a scar in my memory.

Shara said she wanted to see the French film, "*Défendu.*" The director was booked to address the motion picture conference at the university and she would be responsible for programming his academic itinerary. She had never viewed his work.

"Why don't you come with me. *Défendu* means forbidden. The critics consider it a modern classic."

"I can't stand foreign films. They're so utterly, utterly symbolic. It's like watching life through someone's armpit."

"I must see this one, darling. It's important."

"What time will you be home?"

"As soon as the film is over."

I knew she was lying. Tonight she was going to have an affair.

If I accused her and demanded that she remain home, she would say I was paranoid and delusionary. I shrugged. "I'll wait up for you," I said, and went into the kitchen, pretending to cook some scrambled eggs. When she left the apartment, I followed her.

She drove to Berkeley. There was mist in the night air. When the windows fogged, I used the wipers. I learned on that drive that there is more to coincidence than blind chance. The arrangements of living, the pattern of alternatives we choose, are all designed before we act.

When she veered off the highway to the ramp, my car suddenly stalled, then stopped. I became frantic. I slammed my fist onto the steering wheel and cursed, "Goddamn," and struck the darkened dashboard dials. I stepped out of the car and kicked the front tire. Now she was gone. I began to sob, why, Shara, why? Not one day has passed without our making love. Am I so unsatisfactory? Don't do it, Shara, please don't do it. Give me one more chance to prove I'm the only one you need. I have been, throughout the ages.

Cars screeched by me. My clothes were becoming damp. I shivered. I returned to sitting behind the steering wheel, the tears of my helplessness blurring my vision while I idly turned the ignition key. Suddenly, the engine grated, then caught. The dashboard lights went on and the motor revved when I pressed the accelerator. I sped off the ramp, almost hysterical with despair for having lost her. Half a street up I had to brake quickly. Shara's car was parked beneath a lamppost. She was seated at the wheel.

Something had happened to her car, too.

I waited. I saw her dark outline lean over and her car started. She drove ahead. I laughed. "Oh, God, how good you are to me," and then remembered why I was following her.

She stopped on Shattuck Avenue and walked into the Allegory Bar. Again, I waited. A police patrol car drove toward me. It slowed and the policeman on the passenger side flicked a flashlight at my face. I smiled. "Good evening, officer." He nodded and the car drove away. I sat and tried to understand why Shara had gone into that bar. She knew that I was suspicious of her. Whenever we were apart and I could not account for her time, I always asked her to explain what she had been doing. Why would she commit this unreasonable act of going into a bar alone? A jealous man was so easily provoked. A jealous man, given evidence that his jealousy was founded, became dangerous.

The door of the bar opened. Shara, holding the arm of a man her own height, stepped out. His hair was like runny caramel and his face a pudge of dollop features. He wore a green checkered sports jacket and poorly fitting green pants. They walked toward a gray building with a pink neon sign, "Haste St. Apts," jutting from its side.

I left the car and slowly walked behind them. I whispered,

"Shara, darling, you're not doing this filthy thing, are you? You have a new life now—be different." They went into the building. I jogged to the doorway and listened to them climb a flight of stairs.

I heard them walk along a linoleum-tiled corridor. I counted their steps. Seventeen. Keys clinkled and a door opened, then closed. Before I could rush up the stairs a middle-aged woman carrying a fluffy brown dog shuffled down the steps. She cooed to the animal, "Tch, tch, Oswald, don't be a grumpy." Shara and that blob were kissing. The woman rocked the dog as it licked her fingers. "Want to have a bitty-witty, don'cha?" she murmured. Hurry, you bitch, I wanted to shout. His hands are clutching her breasts, his fingers are nibbling into her.

The woman stood still and looked at me. "Would you mind getting the door, please? I have my hands full, as you can see." I quickly pulled the door open. She nodded an array of pink curlers in her hair. "Thank you." She carefully dropped the dog to the street and walked after it. I raced up the stairs to find the apartment Shara was in. My rage screamed in me.

The District Attorney stood with his hands clasped behind him. Pinched between his fingers was a photograph of Shara taken when she had attended a retirement party for the senior coordinator.

"Mr. Mandel, on July 11, 1977, you were admitted to the Franklin Memorial Hospital in Berkeley. The emergency room. You were treated for multiple bruises, lacerations about the face, and a dislocated jaw. Would you tell the court how this came about?"

"It happened approximately one hour after I met this young lady at the Allegory Bar on Shattuck Avenue in Berkeley. After our meeting, we went to my apartment on Haste Street, the corner of Shattuck Avenue, just half a block away."

"Would you look at this photograph and tell me if you know this woman?"

He took the glossy photograph from the District Attorney's hand and studied it. I heard the shifting of bodies, the scrape of shoes on the floor.

"This is the woman I met in the Allegory Bar on July eleventh. Her name is Shara Medford."

"Thank you. Let the record indicate that the victim, Shara Medford, has been identified by the witness. Now, Mr. Mandel, why are you so specific about remembering that evening and Shara Medford?"

"First of all, I'm a certified public accountant and specifics are my business. Second of all, it isn't every day that I have to go to the emergency ward to be treated for having been brutally beaten. Third of all, my hobby or, as you might say, my avocation, is in remembering conversations, and ours was quite unusual. It was an unusual evening for me. I had never been to that bar before."

"Yes, thank you for that information—but would you please tell us how you met Shara Medford."

"I went to the Allegory Bar and a very attractive woman entered. All eyes turned to her, both male and female. She stood for a moment and looked about and then, quite boldly, she came to me. She asked if I would enjoy spending the evening with her. I was quite flattered, you can well understand. I am not exceptionally attractive to women. I was taken aback by her proposal, but quite delighted."

"What did you do then?"

"I paid for my drinks, naturally. We then walked to my apartment."

"And then?"

"Well, without any overtures or much conversation, we undressed and, as they say, we had at it. I was doing my utmost to perform properly. Then the door burst open. A man I had never seen before attacked me. I was too overcome to defend myself. He punched me repeatedly. I was knocked to the floor, striking my face on a metal magazine rack. Then I was unconscious for a few moments. When I revived he was beating the female and calling her filthy names. I pretended to still be unconscious. When they finally left, I called for a taxi and was driven to the hospital."

"Is that man who so violently and viciously beat you in this courtroom?"

"Yes. He's that gentleman in the blue suit."

"Let the record indicate that the witness has identified the defendant, Stephen Jerod, as his assailant."

I shifted to the side and focused my vision on a group of people sitting near the aisle. I began imagining them to be dressed in the clothes worn by the people in Barthelamo Vecchio's time. One wide-shouldered man with an angular, pouchy face looked like a Cardinal Morelli who had once staggered into Barthelamo's rooms, pleading, "Save me, I have been done in by a vile wench." He reeked of urine and excrement. He had accosted a lady-in-waiting for Lucrezia Borgia and tried to rape her. She was carrying a marble chamber pot. She smashed it onto his head, splitting a portion of his skull and befouling him with an evening's releases. I stared at the man seated on the aisle and smiled. Only Time and Place change. Faces remain the same.

"Tell me this, Mr. Mandel. After experiencing such a brutal beating by the defendant, why didn't you call the police and have him charged with—say—assault and battery?"

"I would have done that, I assure you. But I was afraid. After attacking me, he attacked the woman. One time he said, "Shall I kill this man the way you wanted me to kill Marius?" Before she could reply, he smashed her face. I was injured, yes, but not that badly. I was afraid of him. I did not want him coming after me when he was released from prison."

"Yes, Mr. Mandel, I do understand. Any normal person would be terrified after such violence. Thank you, and no more questions."

While this Bruce Mandel was being questioned, my attorney had been reading my journal and then writing on his yellow legal pad. He tore a strip from the bottom of the page and shifted it to me. "Please sit up straight. Your poor posture reveals despair and that is not a healthy picture to convey to the jury." Instinctively, I pushed my shoulders back and pressed my spine against the chair. My bones felt as though they were warping and my back muscles ached. I shrugged. I would sit comfortably.

"Mr. Mandel, you stated to the prosecution that 'My hobby, or, as you might say, my avocation, is in remembering conversations, and ours was quite unusual.' Can I presume that you are really good at doing that?"

"Yes. If modesty will permit, I am quite exceptional. I can

remember ordinary conversations, verbatim, for weeks. I can recall, exactly, unusual conversations for at least five years. Word for
word."

Martin Lormer slowly rose from the chair and squinted at the
witness. Bruce Mandel edged back. The flesh under his chin quivered.

"Prior to your meeting with Shara Medford, you stated that
you had never gone to the Allegory Bar before, a bar which is
notoriously a gay, or homosexual bar."

The District Attorney stood up, annoyed. "Your honor, I
strongly object. The defense is casting aspersions by association.
The witness's sexual practices or preferences are not in question."
The judge smirked at Martin Lormer. "Objection sustained." He
sighed, then shrugged.

"Did you feel comfortable in the Allegory Bar?"

"No, not at all. I had never been there before but I knew it
was a place where homosexuals congregate. In fact, the reason I
was in that type of a bar is the only thing that is not specific in my
mind on that—well—that eventful night."

"Then can you explain why this unusually attractive woman
came up to you and asked if you would enjoy spending the evening
with her?"

"Truthfully, I can't explain that either."

"What was your first impression when you saw Shara Medford?"

"I thought she was a dream come true. A vision become
real."

"All right. Now let's put your talent for recalling conversations to work. What were her exact words when she came to you?"

"She said, 'Thank you for waiting for me. It is necessary for
you to make love to me.' Those were her exact words."

I did not understand any of this. The people in the courtroom,
the press, and the jury, were leaning forward, avidly listening.
Bruce Mandel was no longer afraid of Martin Lormer. He sat in a
casual slouch, his mouth a smug arc. He was now enamored with
his own mental prowess. I rubbed my right hand, remembering
how my fist had smashed against his face. I wanted to smash him

now. He had been with Shara and though she was dead, I still despised him for having once blended his body to hers.

"What did Shara Medford mean by 'It is necessary for you to make love to me?' "

"I have no idea. I didn't much care. I was not going to pass up such an incredible opportunity."

"Would you describe what happened when you entered your apartment. For example, did you kiss?"

"Dear me, no. She pointed to my couch—which opens into a bed—and said, 'There,' and began undressing. I was truly startled and unable to move. She then said, in a rather snappish tone, 'Undress. Quickly.' I went to put off the lights. She said, 'No. Leave them on, please.' I was a little embarrassed, so I turned my back to undress. When I turned around again she was lying on the couch nude. I went to her. We embraced and we—well, we started to go at it. Then the door burst open and . . .' "

"One moment, Mr. Mandel. That is not what you stated when questioned by the prosecution. You said, and I quote you, 'I was doing my utmost to perform properly.' Would you tell us what you meant by that?"

He looked down at his hands. He licked his lips. Martin Lormer had the mind of a mystic. His intellect was like a multitude of groping antennae—sensitively detecting meanings others would ignore. He leaned to the witness and smiled gently. "Just describe what your lovemaking was like."

The District Attorney stood up but the judge motioned for him to sit. She frowned at Martin Lormer. "I fail to see where a detailed account of the sexual union will contribute to the edification of the jury." Martin Lormer moved closer to the bench and looked up at her.

"Lurid details do not provoke my interest either, your honor. The witness, however, has implied that he made love to the victim. I cannot accept that as a qualified fact. And there seems to be more here than has been said."

The judge leaned back and seemed to look toward me. "All right. Continue your line of questioning. But please be discreet." Martin Lormer returned to the witness.

"When you say, 'I was doing my utmost to perform properly,' what do you mean exactly?"

"Well, I may not be the most robust of men, but I do have all my faculties and they function quite normally. But from the moment we began, I was unable to perform properly. Because I was repulsed by her."

"Repulsed? Did you say *repulsed?*"

"That's the only word I can think of. Repulsed. There was a feel to her that was not healthy. Her skin was, well, it was quite coarse."

I did not want to listen to the muck of his passions. I closed my eyes, suddenly afraid that the glorious sexuality between us had been a lie. That I had been crude and inelegant. That she had permitted the congress of flesh because she was obedient to a force dominating her will—a force that was punishing her for some corruption she had committed in another century.

Martin Lormer said, as if to himself, "How strange, to find a young woman of Shara Medford's beauty repulsive." He flattened his palms together as though in prayer. "Was there anything else about her that you can recall that—shall we say—turned you off sexually?"

Bruce Mandel wrinkled his mouth and nodded. "Yes. There was a smell."

"Are you saying that she was not inclined toward the habits of cleanliness?"

"No, oh no. She appeared to be very neat. It was another type of smell. I've come in contact with it only once before."

"Could you be more specific about identifying the odor?"

"It was the odor of formaldehyde—embalming fluid."

Martin Lormer blinked his surprise. I grinned. The man was obviously insane. Lying next to Shara was like resting in a loved garden. Her fragrance was always heady, sexual. The District Attorney stood up to offer his objection, then sat down and shrugged. People began whispering to each other. The judge waited. The District Attorney's assistant, a slender man with a long underslung chin, reminded me of an elder in the Albino's village—a grim man given to selecting what the captives would wear when they were offered as a sacrifice to the Great Burning Eye god. His hands were thick and he had squat fingers, but the nails were grown at least seven inches long. He walked among the penned-in captives, touching them with his palms, prodding them with his elbows. He used his fingernails to scratch the areas of skin where the captive was to be decorated with a pigmented clay design.

When he reached the woman the Albino wanted, he had fondled her bare breasts and turned her around to dig the curled tips of his fingernails into her buttocks. The son of the Great Burning Eye, a fiercely tempered and thickly muscled man, shouted at the elder, protesting. The Albino, standing at another area outside the pen, was caught between hating the Great Burning Eye's son and his plans for freeing the captive woman he wanted. It would be more difficult now, and more dangerous. The other tribal god also desired her.

Martin Lormer stood near the jury box. He said, "She smelled of embalming fluid." He began to chuckle. "I'm not surprised that you were turned off sexually." Some people on the jury smiled.

"You stated in your testimony that while you and the victim were together, the defendant charged in. You were both in a state of undress. He attacked you. Punching you repeatedly. You fell to the floor, lacerating your face on a metal magazine rack. You were rendered unconscious. The defendant stopped beating you. In the time you lay there, pretending to be unconscious, did anything odd happen while he was beating the victim?"

"He called her a whore and a bitch. She pleaded with him to stop. She said, 'I did it because of you, Stephen. I know you wanted me to do this.' "

"What was the defendant's response to that odd statement?"

"He said, 'You did it for yourself. You were always an oversexed, treacherous bitch. Thousands of years haven't changed you and a thousand more will find you the same.' He kept . . ."

The District Attorney stood up and wagged his hand. "I object, your honor. This is irrelevant, highly speculative, it is a mass of . . ." The judge shook her head. "You opened this up. Objection overruled." Martin Lormer said, "Please continue, Mr. Mandel."

"He kept slapping her. She dropped to the floor, no more than a foot from me. He kicked her. Quite hard. She begged him to stop. 'I did this to help you, Stephen,' she said. 'You have been hating me from the first time we loved. You wanted a true cause for hating me. I know you have been following me. When your car stopped tonight I deliberately stopped my car and waited for you. I was not trying to hide this from you. I even chose a man who was not dangerous to you. Stephen, I love you so much, there is nothing I would not do for you. Even to staying with another man.' Those are her exact words. I was shocked beyond . . ."

"Thank you, Mr. Mandel. No need to upset yourself. Did she say anything else?"

"She said, 'I love you, Stephen. You have made me come alive again. You have given my life a purpose. Even if you kill me, my last breath will be taken in my love for you.' Then he dragged her out of the apartment. I never saw her again."

Martin Lormer turned his back to the witness. "Thank you. No more questions." The District Attorney stood up. His suit jacket was wrinkled. "Your honor, there are only a few minutes left before the lunch hour is called. Rather than bring in my next witness, could we break now?"

The judge glanced up at the circular courtroom wall clock. She tapped her gavel onto the wooden plaque. "Court will break for lunch. We will convene again at two o'clock." The bailiff came toward our table. Martin Lormer began pushing papers into his briefcase. He turned to me.

"Father Jerod, I've come to a serious conclusion—that reincarnation is a sin. Yes. A grave and quite lethal sin." I looked at him, not believing what he claimed. He was a genius at deception.

He smiled at me. "I know, Stephen. You think I'm trying to trick you into breaking your vow of silence. I understand." He reached out and touched my forearm. I was momentarily confused. It was the first time he had addressed me by name.

"I don't believe you are a reincarnated man. But I'm not defending what I believe. I'm defending what *you have* believed."

The bailiff stood at the table waiting. Martin Lormer said, "I have had my staff conduct a thorough and meticulous investigation of Shara Medford. I am afraid to use what they have found out. Would you like to know why I'm afraid to use it?"

I looked down at his hand gripped onto my forearm. I was surprised to see that his fingers were stubby. He said, "I cannot believe what I have learned about Shara Medford." He released my forearm and snapped his briefcase closed. The intensity of his stare hurt my eyes. "When Jesus said, '*A prophet is not without honor, save in his own country, and in his own house,*' He could have meant that for the courtroom too. If I use what I have found about Shara Medford, in your defense, it might get us all locked up in the crazy house."

Chapter 4

I stood in the holding cell, leaning against the wall, feeling buried in the shadows. I did not listen to the sounds of the prison as I usually did. When Martin Lormer said, " . . . reincarnation is a sin," did he mean that a belief in reincarnation was sinful, or that to be reincarnated was to live in total sin? The statement was confusing to me.

I rubbed my shoulder against the wall and wondered if all of this was only a corrupt dream.

What if I was not alive at all, but merely the creation of someone's dream? And when he awakened, I would disappear. And all that had happened between Shara and me—between Barthelamo Vecchio and Letitia—between the Albino and the captive woman—would fizzle as the dreamer gradually awakened.

Yes. That belief was as sensible or as ridiculous as reincarnation. Perhaps the one who was dreaming me would awaken before the murder trial was over.

I grinned. Maybe I could awaken the one who was dreaming our lives.

I began clapping my hands together noisily and jumping up and down. The deputy assigned to attending me stepped closer to the cell and studied me. I smacked my hands as though applauding an actor's performance. I jumped high and crashed my shoes on the floor. Wake up, sir, I'm tired of being dreamed.

The deputy said, "Hey, Father Jerod, are you all right?" I nodded to him as I clapped and jumped. Wake up, will you, damn it, wake up! I kicked the metal bunk, trying for a more clashing noise. I pulled my right shoe off and began beating the heel onto the metal sink. The noise thunked in my head, dizzying me. The deputy yelled to me, "If you don't settle down, Father, you'll force them to sedate you."

I stopped making noise, thinking, perhaps I could pain the dreamer into awakening. I smacked my face and pinched my cheeks hard. The deputy rushed to a door and shouted, "Get someone on the priest. He's upchuckin' his cookies." I stopped hitting myself when my teeth ached and my eyes watered.

Perhaps I was wrong to do this.

If I awoke the man who was dreaming me, what guarantee did I have that when he went to bed again, he would not pick up the same dream again?

Why did the woman who brought the old priest food hear howling when Shara and I first made love? Was it the sorrow of God crying at our demonic union? It is written in God's Word: *They have cast fire into thy sanctuary, they have defiled by casting down the dwelling place of thy name to the ground.*

Why was Shara's skin coarse to Bruce Mandel's touch, and why did she smell of embalming fluid? Was I the only one meant to be bewitched by Shara?

Someone came rushing to the cell. He wore a gray business suit and carried a black bag. The deputy opened the cell door. The man stepped in and flashed a small light at my eyes, making me blink. "Are you all right, Father?" I let him study my eyes. Perhaps he could see into my soul and sedate the torment. He lowered the flashlight and held my right wrist, feeling my pulse. "Is the excitement getting to you? Would you like something to calm you down?" I shook my head and stared at the wall.

Why did Shara give Marsha Jenner money to put away for her funeral?

The doctor stepped out of the cell and the door was locked. "He's all right. Just keep an eye on him."

I lay down on the bunk and stared up at the bleak gray ceiling and thought about Barthelamo Vecchio and the Albino. I thought about all that I had not written in my journal, the hurtful insights about Letitia and the captive woman which were too elusive to record through the written word.

Letitia assisted Barthelamo with his practice—she was the mistress of his surgical instruments and medical paraphernalia. She never intruded with startled sighs or gasps at the sight of a festering wound or when, at the tyrannical demands of the foolish nobility, Barthelamo opened the veins of the feverish and bled them. She was quick to predict his needs but never hasty or given to presumptions. She was amenable to changes, but not docile. And he could sense, at times, her amusement at his grumbling impatience at the whining nobles who imagined bodily disasters with each belch: the bursting of blood vessels after each cough. He taught her to prepare poultices and purgatives—the work of apothecaries he would not trust because they were either stupid or indifferent to proportion. She was adept at learning the balances of ingredients and dependable in recalling the formulas to prepare for him.

One day a page in the service of Marius Vitto had come to summon Barthelamo Vecchio to the elderly Physician's rooms. Barthelamo's deformed back, his lean face and brooding eyes caused the page to believe he was in the presence of an evil sorcerer who could turn him into a bat with a reptile's tail. Barthelamo had pointed at his chubby face. "Convey to the revered Physician that I will attend him immediately." The page rushed from the room almost crying. Barthelamo told Letitia to bring his medicines and accompany him. The page, a nephew of the Borgia house, recently arrived from Spain, hurried ahead.

The Physician's suite was a clutter of bottles and vials. Along one wall was an assortment of knives and pincers fixed to the mortar with metal pegs. A young goat was tethered to a table leg. Pigeons fluttered in wooden cages hanging from the domed ceiling. Marius Vitto lay on a great bed with a black canopy stretched over the carved posts. Except for his thin face and long white beard, he was hidden under feather-stuffed quilts. At the base of the bed the quilts were raised and held up with a formation of sticks. His feet rested on the warm bodies of ten sleeping kittens. His thin frame shook with spasms.

Barthelamo did not speak to the elderly Physician. He began mixing a sedative of mint and bezoar. He was certain the old man would not remain alive to attend Lucrezia Borgia's wedding. Then the rush of convulsions passed and he lay still and sighed. He smiled at Barthelamo. "Will you blow hellebore into my nostrils that I may sneeze away this damnation?"

Barthelamo answered softly, "I think not, revered Physician.

Sleep is your true remedy. Your affliction is not of the mind."

The old man squinted thoughtfully. "A purgative then. Antimony infused with pigeon dung and mint, perhaps? To clear my bowels of this dread."

Barthelamo whispered, "We shall see," and told the people attending the Physician to remove all the coverings but one. "Take the kittens away. They will distress his sleep."

Letitia touched his arm and motioned for him to come to her. He frowned at this unusual boldness. She pointed to a vial of viper venom used to draw field infections from the skin. "He is past his reasons of living," she whispered. Barthelamo was momentarily confused. She hissed at him, "You will be the Duke de Valentino's physician then. You will gain fortune, and honor. A title, no doubt." He edged to her, controlling his sudden rage. "*Assassino—sozzura*—you filth! Go about your duties before I slit your vile throat!" She bowed her head and shuffled to the bed to help the page.

Although he would not forget her covetous urging, he did not let himself remember it as meaningful. In many ways Letitia was still a child. Children do not kill. They merely eliminate inconvenience.

And there was no will, no character depth within him that could impede his loving her. She was in his history, she was inherent in his eternity. Each day she worked beside him he became familiar with her longings. She could not conceal her ambition when she gazed upon the finery of the ladies inhabiting the *palazzo*. Envy narrowed her eyes and made her mouth tremble. Several times when helping a noble disrobe, she would bring the garment to a closet and Barthelamo would observe her holding a sack of ducats the way a child would clutch a precious sweet.

She became moody and grimly silent when she touched a silver urn or fingered the golden threads of a tapestry.

A count, wounded in a clandestine duel, was carried into the castle. He wailed in agony and terror for his life. Barthelamo removed the blade that had snapped in his chest. He stanched the bleeding and cauterized the wound and the count's gratitude was so extreme he drew a costly emerald ring from his center finger and demanded that Barthelamo accept it. Letitia could not stop staring at the ring. Barthelamo whispered, "One day I will give it to you." It was then, for the first time, that she looked steadily into his eyes, boldly calculating if he would, one day, keep his promise.

He no longer probed his mind to understand why he loved her. He was immediate, and unthinking. But his love did not bear happiness—did not cause him laughter and caprice. His desire for her was agonized by his deformity. His desire was tormented by his fear. Were he to consummate his craving to brand his body to hers, she would know he had lied about her physical malformation. Her rage at his deception, swelled by her ambition, might overcome her reason and she would betray him to Borgia.

He was infuriated by his predicament. This woman he had loved through Time, and loved now, was barely sixteen, and she was causing him an intimacy with unholy hatred. He consoled himself with the hope that her dependency upon him would incite her trust—but he could not overcome his perceptions of her character.

There were, it seemed, hundreds of cats and dogs roaming about the palazzo—mongrels and pedigrees—and it was reported to him that Letitia, when loitering in the several kitchens, awaiting the foods that Barthelamo prescribed for the ulcerated nobles, would pick the hairs from her head and roll them into balls and drop them into the foods fed the dogs. She would kneel beside the cats lapping goat's milk and stroke their coats, only to slowly work her hands beneath their soft bellies and suddenly pinch their teats and send them screeching through the halls. And she would clap her hands and laugh.

In a short time she had become a court curiosity. A lovely phantom, always mannered and proper, always silent. Dutifully servile but without the fawning obedience of the spineless.

The contingent of nobles Barthelamo attended were, at first, cautious about her presence. While he treated their ailments—often requesting that they disrobe so he could trace the origin of their skin eruptions—they were intimidated by her presence. "She sees, but she does not see," he would inform them. They would undress and stand naked before her. There was no interest or impression of them in her eyes. But he sensed her breathing quicken when she viewed their privacies.

When the lecherous nobles inquired about her, he would tell them the truth about her past. She was without a family—her mother and father having met their demise by one of the pestilences that ravaged Tagliacozzo, the city of her birth. She had been sent to the convent of Romagno where Cesare Borgia first glimpsed her beauty and she was now in his service. One noble, a slender Frenchman suffering from enlarged boils under his arms, told Barthelamo in a whispered confidence, "I would give many florins to bed with her only once." Barthelamo quickly reminded him of Borgia's irrefutable edict concerning Letitia. She was inviolate. Certain and terrible ruin awaited any person who tampered with her virginal condition. He then lanced the boils of the noble with deliberate harshness, making him scream with pain.

One night Letitia startled him.

He had been accorded three rooms in the northern portion of the *palazzo*. He slept in the large room as befitting his station. Her bed chamber was separated from his by the spacious center room used for dining and as his laboratory. One evening he had returned from quieting the attack of palsy of an elderly Cardinal. He was stooped with fatigue and almost asleep in his steps. Letitia went to him and helped him remove his upper garments. His exhaustion rendered him indifferent to his deformity. When his torso was bared, he remembered.

She did not gasp with disgust or run in horror from the fleshy mutation. She placed her hand, cool and soft as newly spun silk, upon the mottled skin, and slowly rubbed the ache from the gnarled tendons. She is a child offering a pleasure to her father, he thought. Though within him there were gentle tears because her touch, light and without passion, was lovingly sympathetic to his body. She pressed her cheek to the veiny contour and whispered, "Had you but asked, I would have done this sooner."

He remained still, feeling her cheek warm his flesh. His eyes were wet with tears. "You are so kind, my Letitia." It then became their nightly ritual. He hurried through the day to bring the evening sooner. He would sit upon his bed and she would stroke and caress his deformity. She has touched me, he would think. She is touching me. He believed there would be more. One night he would be touching her. And then one night, one extravagantly glorious night, they would be touched together in passion.

But when she was done with her ministrations she would return to her room and begin another nightly ritual.

He would listen to her undress. Her garments whispered from her body and dropped to the floor. She opened vials of cosmetics and perfumes he had seen her steal while accompanying him. Her nudity was glaringly defined in his memory. There were no blemishes on her skin to be covered by powders. He believed he could hear the strokes of her hand, the dab of her fingers as she rouged her breasts—using violet on the nipples, green on the rims, as the titled women did. Then she would adorn herself with other objects she had pilfered—agate earrings, a linen kerchief bordered with lace, satin gloves, a fragile gold tiara long forgotten as being lost. She posed in her incomplete finery, examining herself, delighting in her own image. Barthelamo lay on his bed, agonized between craving her as a man lusts for a woman, and hating her for gilding her unquestionable beauty for someone—someone—and his hatred deepened in knowing that her beauty was being gilded for an imaginary lover whose figure was not burdened with a deformity.

In those nightly intervals he writhed on his bed, trying to ignore her presence by concentrating on his own ambitions. Cesare Borgia, a prince incapable of trust, was beginning to rely upon his skills and his intelligent candor. But Barthelamo's desire to feel exalted with his good fortune was continually disrupted by the agitation of the Albino's life revealing itself in those nightly intervals of anguish over Letitia.

"Bianco, Bianco," he would plead in whispers. "Will you never be gone from me?" He was afraid that one day the Albino, like a poisonous fluid, would gradually spread through his mind and body and overcome him, and he would become the ancient creature and Barthelamo Vecchio would be absorbed.

He wanted to dig his fingers into his skull and blind his inner eyes and not see Bianco raising a large headdress from a niche in the wall of his home. It was the ornamentation of a great beaked bird with dark jade eyes and flares of bright plumage that would cover his entire head. A fine filigree of human hair was woven across the sockets to protect his eyes from the sun. He drew the feathered garment from its place on the floor and shrouded his alabaster skin.

He moved among the communal residences like an immense flying creature lazily moving along the ground in search of prey. The people touched their hands to their hearts when they crossed before him. He carried a knobbed staff with a leathery sac on its end. A dried heart cut from a sacrificial captive. Within the stiffened flesh were objects that clinked and rattled when he tapped the ground.

Though he was aware of the son of the Great Burning Eye following behind him, he never turned. He was not in terror of being attacked. The children of gods could only cause their own destruction. The other god was fierce, but not clever. He tyrannized young maidens to enter the Albino's home and pretend they were taken by terrible spirits. They stood before him and shook themselves in the motions that would free them from evil. They wanted him to touch their places only the warriors could touch. He wailed and chanted and fanned smoke from his healing pots, until they could not breathe and would leave his home.

Barthelamo hated the treachery of the son of the Great Burning Eye as he hated the presence of the white creature living in him. The Albino's existence was only a series of weightless images, but they were like stones pressing onto Barthelamo's mind. While he followed Bianco in his restless walks about the village—his lower body covered with feathered garments, his bleached face hidden beneath a fierce headdress—Barthelamo shuddered as he received Bianco's feelings and understood his thoughts.

I am near the place where the captives are always held. The child of the Great Burning Eye is still behind me. He knows I am as one with the captive woman. He has seen my arousings. There is joy in him for he knows I will labor to save her. He believes I will fail. Then we will both become food for our gods. But I cannot stop myself.

We have only looked upon each other and yet we are touched so true that if her heart is torn from her to feed the starving gods, my heart is torn from me. She will be fed to the beasts that circle the village. I will remain to feed other maiden hearts to the gods, but I will never be as I once was. As I am now. I will always be alone. As in death.

There is wind and many roars of storm in my mind as I come closer to the place of the captives. I do not know why. I have plunged my knives into maiden hearts and as they screamed, I spoke to my father glowing from the Above. When her life was silent—for her spirit was no longer in her—her life had returned to the village of her people who were in wild dance and sobbing so the lives of their dead could be brought to the loving of their gods. I grasped out her heart with the claws of the god-bird. I sang as I held the red food aloft for all to see before I placed it upon the table of the gods. There was always joy in me, and in the people. The gods were fed. Food would grow and water would fill the deep wells. In war we would always conquer.

If I do not save her, I will become as stone. But my heart is fearful. In saving her I will do with her as no God should do. And my god-ness will be gone.

Yet the god of the Great Burning Eye has coupled with maidens of the village. I know this. I have looked into his shelter when I walk about the village. The maidens cannot speak of how he has coupled with them. They would be struck down for spoiling the glory of a god with their woman filth. I do not tell of his couplings.

In the day, from my shelter, I am always watching him as he does his god-ness. He is doing against me. He stands in an alone place in the field, touching stones of color, tearing leaves from the tree that gives us white ointment, making soundings of his voice that are the beasts of the day, telling the people of how he will turn me to clay, to dung, to sand—to fire. I guard myself against his castings and cursings. But his power, each day, lasts longer. He can be looked upon by the villagers. Thus I am a lesser god.

Having now seen her and being seen by her, she is now in me. I am stirred to a hardened spear beneath the cloth that covers my parts when I see her. I want to walk high and proud for all to know the largeness she makes in me. But I must hide myself from the eyes of the other god who is always watching me. I am afraid, but to know her makes me strong. We have looked into each other's hearts and *though we have not spoken or touched she has told me she will let me place the stirrings of my joy into her. Though our coupling will cause the gods to rage and thunder, we will not fear. There is in us what cannot die—her heart has told me this.*

I look to the Above in which all things happen. I want god-gifts to show me how to save the captive woman. I stand without motion and raise my face to the Above. I shake my staff until the casting bones and dead beasts' teeth tell my god I am calling him. I wait. But the Above is silent to me and soon my eyes are wet with sorrow.

I see only fiery specks. First one, then another. They flash into the dark, then vanish. My father is in another place. He sends only bits of fire that fly about me. They glow, then darken. I know this tiny fire. They come from a valley beyond this village. The fire specks sleep in the day. They awaken in the dark and bring it light. They sit upon my skin and flash. Why have they come now? They belong in another place. Is my father giving them to me? I feel them taste my flesh as they flash and darken.

One night, Barthelamo cried out in his sleep. He awoke to see Letitia sitting on his bed, her face squeezed into a frown, her hand clutching the black cross she always wore about her neck. When he sat up, keeping himself fully covered, she asked, "Are you in pain, Master Vecchio?"

"No, Letitia. It was a dream I was having."

"You were speaking so strangely. I could not understand."

"The mouthings of a foul dream. No more than that."

"I would swear by the beloved Virgin it was a language you spoke. There were no words in it, but it was a language."

"I speak only the language I speak. You are mistaken."

"I am inclined in languages of foreigners. I have heard such speaking like it before. From the good sisters who came to the convent from a distant land."

"You are mistaken, Letitia. Return to your bed."

"The witch, Maria Montasucci, spoke in such a way before she was put to stake. I have heard that . . ."

"Letitia," he shouted at her, angry and wanting to strike her for sitting at his bedside like a common snoop, listening to his dreaded dreams. "Go to bed, Letitia. I'll hear no more of this."

Dutifully, she stood up and returned to her room. He could hear her muttering to herself, and he became afraid.

And in the darkness within his mind, the Albino gleamed white. He was standing before the towering temple cresting the heights of the village. His legs and waist were covered with thick swaths of varicolored feathers. His upper torso was naked. He held a thick staff with a human skull fixed to its end.

The people were lined in regular intervals on the wide steps below him. He was calling, in a rhythmic chant, to the war gods to look upon them with favor. To be joyous in the sight of their courage during battle. He moved and danced and shook his body and there was a jangling and chiming in his motions as his golden ornaments struck each other. His alien skin glowed with eerie whiteness as moonlight bathed its surface.

The women standing below him held torches that shifted and shimmered in the wind. The men waved their spears in ritual gestures and sang throaty sounds. In the height where he stood the wind was stronger and lashed and hooted about him. The metal symbols laced about his arms chilled his skin.

Barthelamo felt his own body shudder with fervor of the Albino's prayer. The words seem to be without verb or vowel, but he understood it was a prayer to bring great abundance as their time for sacrifice began. Then there was a wailing and yelling noise that intruded upon the prayers as captives were brought up the temple steps for his inspection and sanctification.

They were pulled and prodded with sticks to climb the steps and stand before him. While he shook the skulled staff at them, he was grateful for the feathered hood he wore. He did not want them to see his rage. The son of the Great Burning Eye, covered with a hollowed-out animal's head—the sacred beast that hides in caves, which Barthelamo identified as a strange tiger—was standing among five naked warriors. They glared and twisted their faces and clawed their hands. The other god kept stroking a golden disc with carvings on the surface. He was causing a curse to the Albino.

The prisoners were forced into an irregular line before him. Flat sticks with stones bound to their ends were used to strike the captives until they knelt. Their bodies, already bruised from beatings, were partially swollen and discolored. They knelt huddled together. All except the woman the Albino wanted. She remained separate.

I quake within me for I am beginning to know a way to save her.

We stare at each other and she knows she will not lie upon the stone that is soaked in the blood of other captive people.

She does not tremble from seeing me. Her eyes hold my whiteness. I am like the blankets that cover the distant mountain peaks. In the darkness she is colored as the gentle brown in the leaves that lay berries on the earth. Our warriors have dragged her from her village, beaten her with shafts and hardened hands, but the dust and soils and marks of striking do not hide the golden quiet that glows from her flesh. Her hair is wild and strayed but the black longness is thick and conceals the mounds of her front. She stares at me. She is showing me her heart, telling me that while she will not be taken, she can offer herself.

I want to beg my father in the Above to place a dark cloud upon only us, to hide us. In that aloneness I would tell her, "I am no warrior, no chieftain. I have not been with a maiden as other men have been. Those who have made me a god believe my god-ness must remain pure. Still, I can save you, for I am a god. But my want of you has drawn my god-ness from me. Still I can save you. Her eyes that grip my eyes know what I am thinking. She is not afraid.

When the ceremony was done, Barthelamo watched the Albino raise the skulled staff and move it from side to side as he descended the steps. He wailed and moaned and shook his shoulders. The people shifted aside and formed a wide aisle. He walked toward the village while the captives were abused on the path back to their prison.

The wind was softer in the lower land. The Albino slowed his walk and soon a golden dot Barthelamo knew to be a firefly flickered in the night. Under his hood, Bianco smiled. He remembered a time when he was a boy in his own village and the strange insects carrying bits of fire had come into the air. His people ran from them. They believed the day-god was angry and had killed the night-god and was now spitting fire poison at them. He ran too.

While trying to hide in some brush he had stumbled over the Holy Man's tall jars of colored juices. His white skin was splashed. He sat, dazed, and wanted to cry. Then the fire insects swarmed to him. He beat the air to chase them. But one flit upon his chest. It did not burn. He sat still. Another dabbed onto his hand. There was no sting. He began to giggle as the bugs lighted themselves, then went out, then lit themselves again. He was no longer afraid. More settled on him. He laughed at how their lights sparked and died, sparked and died. The juices covering his body smelled sweet. The golden dots enjoyed the taste that had spilled on him.

Barthelamo was startled when the Albino skipped a step and danced a pattern of steps, and laughed with cackling joy. He understood how he could save the captive woman.

I was taken from the holding cell. My hands were cuffed behind my back as I was escorted toward the courtroom by another deputy sheriff. He was an impatient man, easily agitated. Passing along the corridor I heard the sound of people shouting somewhere in the street. A series of whistles blew, a siren screeched. I wondered if some dignitary was going to attend the trial. The deputy sheriff muttered, "Creepy Jesus freaks," and looked at me.

"You see what you started with this reincarnation crap?"

I frowned at him. He pointed to the street windows. His thick arm was like a beige railroad signal.

"There's Jesus freaks out there. Picketing. They say this trial's an advertisement for the devil. Did you ever hear crap like that before?"

I did not believe what he was saying. His meaty face dented with a smirk. "You think I'm horsin' you, huh? Okay, go on, take a look."

He held onto the chain attached to the handcuffs and followed behind me. In the street below there were about twenty people parading before the courthouse steps. They looked small in the distance, but I could read one sign that a chubby woman carried on her shoulder. "Put On The Whole Armor Of God."

The deputy sheriff pointed to the tallest man, a redhead wearing a pale green suit. His head looked like a bleached raddish.

"That's Reverend Calvin Cooledge Jones. He runs some kind of kookball church in Oakland. Like the Holy Rollers. He's one big pain in my tired ol' ass."

Four uniformed policemen stood on the street, their arms crossed on their chests. A patrol car with its colored lights flashing was parked near the courthouse entrance. A green and brown panel truck drove up and stopped across the street. "KPMC Television" was painted on its surface. The doors opened and a cameraman stepped out. When the Reverend saw the camera point at him, he suddenly raised his arms and shouted, "Get thee behind me, satan. Thou art fallen. The blood of Jesus Christ against you!" The pickets stopped and jiggled their hands high, shouting "Amen" and "Hallelujah." The deputy sheriff tugged the handcuff chain. "Let's go, Father. That phony crap makes me wanna puke."

A woman's voice was a shrill current coming into the corridor. "Christ is the Way."

I walked beside the deputy sheriff. I looked at his face, trying to know if he resembled anyone in Barthelamo Vecchio's or the Albino's time. He was just a face.

I stopped before the door leading into the courtroom. I wondered if, upon entering the courtroom, my appearance would awaken the man who could be dreaming my life. I closed my eyes and muttered a quick prayer to God to please awaken the man—I am tired of this dreary and frightening dream.

The courtroom felt strange to me now. It was like sitting in itchy air. The judge fussed with her robe and papers. The District Attorney was whispering in argument with his assistants. Martin Lormer kept clicking the clip of his mechanical pencil. The lean-faced court clerk could not properly insert paper into his machine. People shifted and stirred on the benches. Jurors fidgeted with their clothes. The men and women in the press section were writing or doodling on their pads. The newspaper artists were scowling as they drew my picture.

Martin Lormer jiggled his foot, opened his briefcase and began arranging his papers. He muttered, "I have some experts coming in from the east and the sons of bitches aren't here yet." The judge tapped her gavel. "Is the prosecution ready to begin?" The District Attorney looked up at her. "If it please your honor, I need a few moments more." Martin Lormer placed his hand on the binder of my journal and ticked his thumbnail on the corner. He frowned at me.

"Did you know that there were stacks of documents found among the art treasures Borgia had hidden away? Documents that were not written by Borgia. I've gotten special permission from the National Museum in Italy to have photocopies made and flown in. They might be interesting—I've got my fingers crossed that I can use them for a theory I have."

I shrugged. Cesare Borgia had been a meticulous saver. I tried to recall if Borgia had saved any of the documents Barthelamo had written. I heard the District Attorney clear his throat and saw him stare at his clipboard.

The District Attorney called a John Graybor to testify for the state. I recognized him as a former student in one of my classes. He was a youth of twenty who walked with short, hesitant steps. His narrow shoulders were hunched in. I remembered that we had once met in the men's room of the university. He was washing his hands. I saw the long, deep scars on his wrists. I wondered if Martin Lormer would notice the slash scars and use the attempted suicide against him. I hoped not. He had been a pleasant student.

Martin Lormer shifted to me and poked my elbow with his thumb. He was annoyed. "Damn it, Father, will you please sit up straight. You look half asleep." I moved my shoulders back and sighed. My attorney could try a man's patience. The District Attorney glanced at the clipboard he held.

"Mr. Graybor, you are a student at the Calvin Coolidge University in Alameda."

"Yes. I'm a junior."

"What are you majoring in?"

"Comparative religions and doctrinal theology."

"Were you a student in the defendant's class?"

"Yes. I was."

"While you were in the defendant's theology class, was the subject of reincarnation ever discussed?"

"Yes. Frequently. Mr. Jerod was most emphatic about its impact on Christianity."

"Did he approve of reincarnation?"

"No, sir. He was conducting a class in doctrinal differences and he was quite condemnatory about anyone who believed in the possibility of reincarnation."

"Indicating that he, himself, did not believe in reincarnation?"

"I believe so. In fact he compared the doctrine of reincarnation to playing roulette. You are born in the condition of a chip fixed on a number. The wheel of life turns and that is the life cycle. When it stops, your life is over. If you are on the winning number, you go to the Godhead. If not, you become another chip and are put onto another number, and the wheel is turned again. It goes on and on, until eventually, by some luck, you are born on the right number."

"Did he ever inquire as to the possibility of someone in the classroom being reincarnated?"

"He did, as a matter of fact."

"Did anyone declare that they were in a state of reincarnation?"

"No."

"What was his response?"

"He said, 'Thank God that no one in this class is afflicted by that demonic madness.' It was a confusing statement but . . ."

Someone's voice boomed in the courtroom. "This trial is a farce. You are leaving out the power of the Son of the living God." The entire courtroom stared at a stout, balding man who stood with his arms stretched upward. His face quivered with feeling. The people beside him shifted away. "We must pray for this man," he shouted. "We must pray for him. He was used to bring attention to demonic powers." He clasped his hands and swayed fervently. "We must stand against these evil spirits, in prayer. This poor soul doesn't need a trial—he needs deliverance."

Two bailiffs hurried to him. The man took a Bible from his jacket and shook it at the judge. "I am an ordained and bona fide pastor of the Risen Lazarus Church. I am not trying to disturb the peace—I am calling for communal prayer. We must join hands and pray for him." His voice vibrated through the large room. Some people, their faces squinted with seriousness, called to him, "Yes, Pastor," and "Amen." The judge raised her voice to instruct the bailiffs. "If that man is not out of this court in two seconds, I'll . . ."

She was interrupted by his boisterous warning. "Do you think that ousting me will be your protection? There are greater forces at work here than you know. This defendant is a good man, but he's being oppressed, and he must . . ." He stopped speaking when the bailiffs grabbed his arms and pulled him into the aisle. The tall officer called to the judge, "Do you want him charged, your honor?" People shook their heads and some spoke out, "No," and "He meant well." The judge closed her eyes and rubbed her forehead. She sighed resignedly. "No. No, just get the old fool out. Get him out."

The man wagged his Bible at her, pleading, "Hear me, your honor, please. Carnal trials have no sway over spiritual matters. "*We wrestle not against flesh and blood, but against principalities, against powers, against the rulers of the darkness of* . . ." He was shoved out the doorway.

The judge drummed her fingers impatiently. "Now that the disturbance is over, the prosecution may continue his cross-examination." The District Attorney glanced at the page on his clipboard. He said, "I have no more questions, your honor." She looked to Martin Lormer. "You may cross-examine."

He nodded, then shifted to me. "I've seen his wrists, Father." He patted my arm consolingly. "Don't worry, I won't bring up his attempted suicide. It's liable to call attention to your own attempts." He left the table and moved to the witness.

"Mr. Graybor, while attending the defendant's classes, did you find him to be an interesting instructor?"

"Very. His classes were always interesting."

"Were there any areas, in particular, that provoked your interest—that kept you more attentive than usual?"

"His lectures on primitive and Renaissance theology were the most interesting."

"Did he cover Puritan beliefs—and pre-Renaissance, Asiatic and Oriental theology as well?"

"Yes. It was required that he do so."

"Did you use your text for those areas you found most interesting—the primitive and Renaissance areas?"

"We had a text."

"That isn't what I asked you, Mr. Graybor. I asked if you used your text."

"Oh, I see. Not very much. Much of what he talked about was not in the text."

"Did the defendant use lecture notes? You know—a book, three-by-five index cards, any material that served as a reminder for him?"

"Now that I think of it, no, he did not."

"Did you use your text, and did he use notes or reminder materials when he taught in the other areas?"

"Yes, I believe he did. Yes. I know he did. I remember he was not always organized in those areas, now that I think of it."

"But those lectures were not as exciting as his talks on primitive and Renaissance theology—is that correct?"

"Yes. Those were the most exciting."

"Would you tell the court why you found those classes to be the most exciting?"

"He was fascinating. He talked about tribal customs and how they were founded on religious themes—on god worship. He knew the gods and their particular functions. He covered material we had never heard about before. When he brought the class to the time of the Renaissance—it was, well, it was just fascinating. He covered the Inquisition in such detail that some students were actually frightened. Witch hunts, burnings at the stake, persecution for religious convictions—the medicines and kinds of surgery that went on in that period—my God, he was fascinating. It was almost like he had been there himself."

Martin Lormer leaned close to the witness. His face was near the highly polished chrome microphone. "Did you, deep down, at any time, believe what you just said?"

The young man frowned. "What I just said?"

Martin Lormer's voice became a careful whisper which could be heard through the courtroom loud speakers. "That the defendant had actually been there."

The student licked his lips and glanced at the jury. They leaned closer, listening. He said, "Yes, to be truthful, I sometimes actually believed that he had been there."

Martin Lormer stepped back and grinned. "Thank you. No more questions."

The District Attorney did not allow the people a chance to react to the student's confession. He quickly called Albert Klauss to the stand.

I turned my head and looked out the large street window. The afternoon was bright with clear air. I heard the witness say, "I have investigated many claims of reincarnation. Not one person was without a long history of mental disorder or deep-rooted neurosis." I stared at the witness. He was a gawky-looking man with shaggy gray hair. An expert witness for the prosecution—an investigator who was debunking reincarnation.

"There is no scientific method for proving reincarnation. It is a philosophical conjecture. The only proof that could be acceptable is corroboration."

"But what about the two important discoveries the defendant was responsible for? Surely that could be considered corroboration."

"I have studied both the finds of the defendant, and I cannot agree that this is corroboration. His locating the hidden Italian art treasures and the pre-Mayan city merely indicates that he knew of their existence. That knowledge could have come from other sources. That is not proof that he was alive during those centuries."

"Then what type of corroboration would be satisfactory?"

"If someone from those former centuries were able to appear and verify his existence in those former centuries."

"But that's impossible, and ridiculous."

"Yes—I agree. As impossible and ridiculous as the doctrine of reincarnation is. However, in the psychic realm, imagination and contrivance is a major form of . . ."

He was interrupted by the court reporter, who began slapping the side of his stubby gray machine. Martin Lormer said, as if to himself, "Something really strange is going on in this courtroom."

The court reporter jiggled a lever and checked an arrangement of knobs, then shrugged. He looked up to the judge. "I'm sorry, your honor. My machine just went out. It's never happened before. It just won't work."

The judge leaned forward. "Isn't there anything you can do about it? Have you got a spare?"

He shook his head. "I didn't bring my spare today. It's being cleaned. I'll need another machine."

The judge stood up and smoothed her robe. "Ladies and gentlemen, we will recess for fifteen minutes. The defendant can remain in the court during that interval. Thank you for your patience."

People stood up and stretched and yawned and began leaving the courtroom. The people on the jury walked through the side door to another corridor where they would be served coffee. The judge left for her chambers. Three newspaper reporters went to Martin Lormer, who shook their hands and smiled, then said, "I'm sorry, I won't answer any questions now."

A woman reporter with a yellow pencil poked into her blonde hair asked, "Who is your client reincarnated from? Napoleon? The Wizard of Oz?"

Martin Lormer laughed. "Come on, fellas, and ladies, give us a break. I'd like to have some time with Father Jerod. All right?" They stepped back and he shifted closer to me. He spoke in low, secretive tones.

"I know you've thought about what I said during the lunch break—about reincarnation being a sin. I believe that, Father. I believe it is against the will of God. I'm on your side, you have to know that."

I flattened my hands on the table and stared at my fingers. He was a devious man who would say anything to gain his purposes. If I were freed, what would I do with the remainder of my life? Join a circus and stand before hordes of people who would gawk at "The Reincarnated Man?"

A newspaper reporter stepped to the table and spoke to me. "Father Jerod, what is the reason for your vow of silence?" A paunchy bailiff lumbered over and poked the newspaper man's shoulder. "Come on, Johnson, you know the rules. Take off, and I mean it." The bailiff stationed himself at the table, guarding us.

Martin Lormer traced his finger along the binding of my journal. "You haven't the slightest idea of what I'm trying to do." He sighed, sadly. "I've been sitting here, letting that asshole of a District Attorney make point after point. I'm trying to let him prove that reincarnation cannot exist so I can establish the impact of its unreality." I stared at his hand now resting on my journal. "You win a jury not with logic or reason. You win a jury by involving them in the life and mind of the defendant. When they become you, then they doubt the logic of reality and want to be found not guilty themselves." I wanted to believe him. I wanted to believe in something that was real.

I wanted to stop wishing that I was Barthelamo Vecchio or the Albino. They had been faced with life and death decisions and they had been able to choose, to act. There was a section in the journal, in Barthelamo's life, in which he was forced into situations where, if he had remained passive, undecided, he would have provoked his ruination or death.

It was in the early part of 1499, while Borgia was still infuriated at having been defamed as the "bastard son of the Pope" and then rejected in his attempts to marry Carlotta of Naples, the daughter of King Federigo. A serious political alliance had been thwarted. The Duke de Valentino would soon be negotiating for another advantageous marriage and many European monarchs were agitated over the prospects. Rather than deal with Borgia and his powerful Papal support, it was simpler to assassinate him.

Date: 1499   Month: February   Time: Day
"Nolite confidere in principibus." (Put not your trust in princes.)
Psm. 146:3
My prince, the illustrious Borgia, seems always to seek my company. Because I do not curry his favor, it is given to me. Because I do not contrive for higher position, I am elevated.

Borgia was a regent of extremes and excesses. A noble whose

heritage began centuries ago could not feel as other men might feel. The higher their office, the lonelier they must live. The greater their ambitions the more lurid was the shadow of death following after them. Borgia was utterly, inherently ruthless and without love for anyone—though he did experience an urge for affections and facile friendship.

He was never alone during court affairs. Before a minister, a visiting duke, an avaricious cardinal could approach him for an audience, the notable had first to pass through a cordon of six *bravi* who constantly surrounded his presence. In the passage of only three weeks at his court, I learned of plots against his life that were so diabolical and bold that my comprehensions were awed by his genius for remaining alive.

One afternoon four mercenaries, armed with sword and pistol, had been apprehended as they waited in Borgia's bed chamber, prepared to murder him and the maiden he was using. They were of French origin. Their heads were decapitated and sent to the court of King Charles as a memento of his failure.

My first clash with my Prince came when a trio of Germans attempted to destroy him during a boar hunt. His life, guided by the benevolent Fates, had been spared when his steed stumbled and threw him from the saddle. The assassins' arrows flew over his body and lodged in a nearby tree. They were taken. I was brought to the dungeons where they were imprisoned. They were bound on tables naked. He instructed me to sever their genitals, which he would then have fashioned into a necklace to be sent to the German monarch. I had refused.

"Do such matters render you squeamish, Physician?"

"No, my Lord. The command is illogical."

"You are not to question my purposes. You are to obey them."

"Shall I allow my revered Prince to appear foolish before the German court? Am I to allow your exalted presence to appear as a braggart puffed with great rumblings, yet without evidence of statesmanship?"

"Physician, you exceed your limits. Your reasoning befuddles my mind."

"Genitals, my Lord, are genitals. They are without nationality. Are they German genitals, or French? They are rods and sacs, my Sublimity, no more. Genitals, my Worship, are not the extraordinary possession of assassins only. Until you can devise a more suitable method, continue sending recognizable heads."

Grudgingly, he conceded to my reasoning. "Saints preserve me from the logic of Physicians." He strode from my presence, laughing. "I shall instruct all monarchs who desire my murder to stain the members of their assassins—"

Two court tasters, in two successive days, had suddenly died. They were brought into the small room I used as my apothecary chamber. Borgia, terrified that a pestilence had killed them— though I had diagnosed their deaths as of poison—insisted that I dissect them.

"Is my Lord requiring that I dissect human cadavers? Would you have me blaspheme against the Church? Would it not offend the dedications of the Pope, your father?"

"Your humor does not amuse me, Physician. Open them!"

I performed the autopsy, exposing throats and bowels to disclose how the fatal doses had coursed through their systems to destroy them. His mood was bland as he studied the bared bone and naked tissue, though the tic beneath his right eye vibrated fiercely, belying his amused smile as he shrugged. "It is to be expected. This marriage I propose for Lucrezia is not welcomed in Ferrara."

The men who tried to assassinate him, their wives and mistresses, were quickly absent from court. Nor did they ever appear in society again. Borgia was devoted to his belief in the *vendetta*, in which his revenge was as barbaric as that of the families of Dattiri and Chiaravallesi who, when one of the opposing families was taken, was often decimated into small parts which were distributed and cooked and eaten by the family temporarily triumphant. There were many mornings, just as dawn was brightening into another day, when a carriage of somber hue, drawn by two massive horses, could be seen leaving the castle walls through an obscure portal to roll along the ribboned countryside road leading to the remote fields of Romagna where Borgia allowed the men who had failed to murder him a heathen burial.

After each slaying he would reach to me and rub the deformity upon my back and shoulder and laugh. "Physician Vecchio, you are a boon to me. A blessed talisman." We would stroll, with Letitia following behind, about the vestibules and foyers of the palace, and he would speak of his plans for great conquest.

At night, knowing that Letitia was merely steps from me, I slept fitfully. Patience, I urged myself. I had position now, and soon I would be gaining influence. Patience, and you will have her.

These were my nightly delvings into expectation, into glorious hopes and calamitous despairs, until one dark hour I was awakened by Borgia, who stood over my bed, holding a small torch. I sat up with startled haste, fearing Letitia had informed him about my dream ravings where I was in the life of Bianco. He touched my bare shoulder. There was a muted urgency in his voice. "I have need of you, Physician. My beloved sister requires your skills."

"An unexpected illness, my Lord?"

"No. Worse, I fear. A strange malady. Her time of blood has not arrived for three months. She wants it brought forth from her."

I almost shouted, "*Stupido!* She is with child," but occupied myself fastening my stomacher. Was the child his, I wondered. The promptings of lust are without discrimination. His plans for Lucrezia's marriage into the Este dynasty were being threatened by a phenomenon he could not command away.

"You will help her, Physician."

"My Lord, there are many causes that may be hindering her flow. It need not be what . . ."

"Enough of this prattle, Physician. I know the cause. The cause has been chastized and dropped into the forest where the *animali* are having sport with him. Now I must deal with the result."

"This is a dangerous enterprise, Excellency."

We looked upon each other and he knew my meaning. To deliberately destroy a life that God had placed into a woman was a depraved blasphemy against church canon. If it was learned, he would lose his Duchy. He could be exiled or executed. My deformity pained me and I was afraid.

If Lucrezia died my life would be spilled with her blood. My deformity became a stone taken from an oven and strapped to my back. Borgia changed the torch to his other hand and studied my face as though penetrating a shadow.

"Physician, I do not delight in your hesitation."

"My Lord is requiring the impossible of me."

"If I required less, I would seek it elsewhere. We do game with life, and death, you and I. Were we ordinary men we would not be where we are or as we are. Nor is it title or birthright that renders us uncommon. You know this, Physician, you know this."

"Yes, my Excellence, I know this."

"I have felt this about you from the moment you stood in my presence. A less loving Prince might deem you bewitched. There are qualities in you which elude my comprehensions. But I do not care. You serve me well—though I know you serve only yourself. I would expect no less. We earn our destinies, you and I. My beloved sister is not a simpleton, but she is most unwise. The Este family is cluttered with mathematicians. Thus she cannot marry in this condition. But marry she must. You will therefore alter her condition. In doing so, your condition will be altered."

Suddenly I wanted to laugh. Yes. It might be that there was no ruin for me. That I, like the old physician, Marius Vitto, would be allowed to live out my age.

"Excellence, I will need one hour of preparations. Letitia will assist in what I must do."

"She cannot know the purpose of your . . ."

"She will not know, Sire. I will need strong leather bindings, many clean sheets, several empty buckets and chamber pots, much boiling water. Also a stout oak stick and several large stones. Some which are too heavy for your beloved sister to raise and carry."

"Those are odd preparations."

"You are concerned only with the consequences, my Lord. Not the procedures."

He chuckled. "True, true, Physician," he said, and strode to the door, placing the torch in a wall bracket. He turned to me. "I will command my sister to do your bidding without question." He opened the door and I could see his escort of *bravos* outside, alerted to set their purchased loyalties in the path of any danger to him.

I hurried to the entrance of Letitia's room and called to her. "Letitia, awaken." She stirred, then gently muttered, "Yes, Master Vecchio." In the dimness I could see how her hair swayed between her breasts. She rubbed her eyes and stretched. Though the rooms were cold she slept in the thinnest of gowns. I did not want to see the marvel of her form. Not now.

We had to pass through a cordon of twelve *bravi* who stood in the vestibules and foyers at Lucrezia's suite. They were fully armed. Letitia, carrying my medical container, did not appear to notice them, but I sensed she intuitively observed their physiques. Silently I cursed their marvelous forms and damned her for believing that perfect bodies mattered in the meanings of love. One *bravo* opened the door. I heard him whisper to her. She did not reply. We hurried in and Borgia was standing at his sister's side, his thick arm about her waist.

She was almost as tall as Borgia, but curvaceous throughout her height. Her long blonde hair, combed back and without adornment, was spread across her shoulders and flowed down her back. There was an aura of innocent passion about her. A longing to be held and pressed seemed to emanate from her. She stood beside a large chair and her hand stroked the stout arm as though caressing a sturdy thigh. Her full mouth, tinted with dark cosmetics, was partially open like a maiden about to inhale a lover's sigh. There was a sensuous subtlety about her even as she remained still. Her eyes, as blue and clear as her brother's, looked upon me, but there was no desire in them. I was a Physician and deformed. Whilst I smiled I cursed her. She would bed with any man the moment lust itched her senses, and I was a man, and for Letitia's awareness, I wanted Lucrezia to lust for me—to cause envy and jealousy in Letitia. I bowed low.

"My Lord, m'Lady."

"Are your preparations concluded?"

"Yes, Excellence. But you will leave us and I will not abide any interruptions. You may post your *bravi* outside, and some porters to assist with cleaning, but they must remain outside, no matter what they hear issuing from this chamber. There will be much noise of unwholesome origin. Letitia will be giving filled chamber pots and buckets to be emptied and returned—but I cannot do my work with your barbaric *idiota* charging in and out at will."

He strode to the door, muttering. Lucrezia wandered to the bed and sat upon the covering, her hands limply clasped on her stomach, her eyes staring with glazed indifference at the floor. I took my medicine case from Letitia's hands and began preparing a purgative—a concoction of wine of dates, benzoin, camphor, and cubeb. The odor was foul, as though a gorgon had belched in the room.

When I was done I held it to Letitia, instructing her, "Hold her nose whilst she drinks it." She shook her head and quickly crossed herself. "I will not, Master Vecchio." I frowned at her, annoyed. "Have you abandoned your senses? Do my bidding." She shook her head again and again crossed herself, and though I loved her, wanted, even now in the openings of my anger, to clasp her to me and tell her we are absolutely one, even though not yet brought together, I hissed, "You will do my bidding or be severely punished."

She held the cross settled between her breasts and licked her lips. "It is a mortal sin what you do. God will desert us—the devil will suck our hearts. We will be cast into . . ." I stopped her by placing my hand across her mouth and pulling her to the corner of the room. I demanded, "What do we do? Do you know?"

She nodded. "She is *incinta*."

"Are you also a Physician? Have you examined her to know that she is with child?"

"I know what I know. She is *incinta* and you will destroy God's work."

"If I do not know the cause of her illness, how can you?"

"If you do not know the cause of her illness, how can you know how to treat her?"

"Medicine is learned by learning. I treat her to learn how to treat her."

"Borgia would never permit experiment with his beloved."

"The nobility are people and they fear as commoners do. Fear causes them to go contrary to their titles. You will do as I say."

"I cannot. God will punish me."

"God does not know you are alive. His interests are else-where, where it matters."

"God knows of everyone. Even the fallen sparrow has . . ."

I suddenly smashed her face with my opened hand and she fell to the side, huddled and cringing. I could not endure her disregard. Because I loved her I would not let her turn me into her carpet. She cuddled her face and wept. I reached to her and pulled her up by the hair. She moaned and clutched at my hands, and though I loathed myself for abusing her I could not live within myself if she did not obey me. I shook her head as though to tear it from her neck.

"*Stupida!* You are chattle, *villana*, you are less than a flea. You have no tomorrow, no destiny, unless I decree it. You are female and low-born, a *fuorusciti*—an exile between church and state. Your life is nothing unless I give it value."

She stared at me and the fear in her eyes was not as deep as the hatred burning through them. She is hating me, I thought. *Dio mio.* A moment of life has finally happened between us. I smiled with joy. Love often begins by the turning around of hate.

"How am I to take this dung that you are and fashion your life into a prized jewel? If sin is being committed, I am the agent of that sin. God has heard your protest and He has shackled the devil from grasping your soul. You are now without evil and beloved to Him. And now you will do as I say, Letitia, or I will demand that Borgia have you bound between two stallions and torn in half. You are—only because I allow you to be—and you will become what I make of you. We must do our work, this instant."

She rubbed her cheek where I had struck her. I moved to her until our faces almost touched—the odor of her was heady and sweet. Her eyes narrowed and I could sense her cunning. "Will she live? I have seen such things in the convent. The cellars were soaked with blood and discardings. Will she live?"

I held the vial to her. The thick liquid shimmered. "Live? Why should she not live?"

She continued caressing her bruised cheek. Her voice was a narrow tone of anger. "If she does not live, you will never have me, Master Vecchio. You will lie in your bed in hell and be tormented for never having had me." The vial trembled in my hand. She knew.

I muttered, "There is a tumor in her, nothing more. My treatment will rupture it from her organs. She will carry stones until she falls, then I will beat her a little, and it will be done. It is only a tumor, not a child."

She knew that I was lying. Her hand darted to my side and she grasped my arm. "If she dies, I will tell Borgia of your dreams. That you are bewitched. I will not be exiled for your sin. I will save myself."

Her fingers softened on my arm. Her fingers were lips moving to my hand. Her fingertips stroked my flesh. "If she lives, your nights will no longer be torment. I will come to you."

Softly, as though lullabying a child, I told her, "She will live. History needs her. Now do my bidding." She drew the vial from my fingers and went to Lucrezia. I did not let myself think. It was time to begin the sacrilegious ordeal.

Chapter 5

The court reporter returned with another stenograph machine and the trial was resumed. The judge reminded the prosecution's witness that he was still under oath. The gray-haired man acknowledged her admonition and waited for the District Attorney's question.

"In your experience with people who claim to be reincarnated, what has been the most striking similarity between them?"

"They were unsuccessful in whatever their occupations or interests happened to be. That was the one constant factor they shared. They had not been successful in achieving personal fulfillment, thus they had become involved in an intense fantasy life. In time their constant preoccupation with ludicrous imaginings prompted them to believe they were not really themselves. They were other people. The need for this convenience is obvious."

"Obvious to you, perhaps, but not to the court. Would you please explain?"

"If these people who believe they are reincarnated are not really themselves, then they cannot be held responsible for what they do. It is not their failure, but the failure of the person they have reincarnated from. They become superstitious and begin to believe that the bad luck of their lives belongs to the person they reincarnated from. Reincarnation provides them with an excuse for not being held accountable."

"Thank you, Professor Klauss. No more questions."

Martin Lormer left the table and walked to the witness stand. I studied the calm, untroubled countenance of the witness. How splendid it must be to be so expert in the phenomena of mystery. How marvelous it must be to live and to know. I sat and stared, yet all I could see was the agonizing method Barthelamo Vecchio had used to abort Lucrezia Borgia. The pain and hurt she suffered carrying heavy stones from wall to wall of the large bed chamber. How she pleaded with him to let her rest. I wondered, even as I visualized that memory, what this expert would say if I described it to him. Martin Lormer made a thoughtful steeple of his fingers.

"Professor Klauss, do you have any idea of where the soul of a person goes after he dies?"

"If you believe in the human soul, there are many theories to offer that destined location. If you do not believe in the human soul, none of these theories apply. I do not believe that there is such an entity as the human soul."

"I appreciate your forthright answer. Thank you. However, believing in the human soul does not create the existence of the human soul, does it?"

"That is correct."

"Yet if the human soul does exist, a disbelief in that doctrine will not destroy it, will it?"

"If proven to exist, that is correct."

"What then, Professor Klauss, is your proof that reincarnation does not exist?"

"I don't quite follow the question."

"You offer corroboration as the only proof that reincarnation does exist. The prosecution has determined that this corroboration is impossible to acquire. All right then. What specific and tangible proof do you offer to determine that reincarnation does not exist?"

The witness stared at Martin Lormer. He rubbed the side of his nose with his thumb. I could sense his distress. Some people on the jury smiled. The District Attorney scowled. Martin Lormer tinted his voice with a snide tone. "I have no more questions for the prosecution's witness." He returned to the table and winked at me.

The District Attorney called Althea Jackson to the witness stand. People watched the tall, casually moving woman dressed in a tight-fitting pants suit that emphasized her lush figure. Her complexion was walnut black. Long gold pendant earrings swayed against her slender neck. Her hair, a moderate Afro, was an encasement framing her circular face. Her teeth glittered brilliantly as she smiled and swore to ". . . tell the truth, the whole truth, and nothing but the truth." I knew who she was and I did not feel afraid. She would only tell so much and either evade the remainder, or she would lie. She had her own public image to sustain.

"Ms. Jackson. You were a close friend of the victim, were you not?"

"We were very close. Shara was a remarkable person. I truly respected her."

"Were you close enough to share confidences?"

"We were close enough for that, but our relationship was not based on petty confidences, such as clothes, food, entertainment, and the like. We confronted ideas. She was a brilliant person."

"You were a political science major when you attended the University of California in Santa Cruz—is that correct?"

"I have a masters in political science. My secondary was in psychology."

"Did the victim, Shara Medford, ever confide in you concerning her relationship with the defendant, Stephen Jerod?"

"Yes, she did. She was troubled about his growing domination of her. His tyranny. The first time he had beaten her, I advised her to leave him. When she revealed to me that she believed he wanted to kill her, then I really pressured her to leave him."

"When she said she was afraid he would kill her, did she ever indicate that she would either defend herself or cause him bodily harm before he could put his plans into effect?"

"No. She was utterly without violence toward anyone. She was a most defenseless woman. She was a good and loving woman."

"Then she never indicated that before she would let him kill her, she would kill him instead."

"That's ridiculous. I remember her telling me that she hated to tear up weeds because they had life in them—the same as did roses. There was no violence in her. Not one bit."

"You do not know of one single instance then when she was ever violent or threatening to anyone?"

"None. Not one instance that I can . . ."

She began coughing suddenly. Shrill air burst from her throat.

She cupped her mouth and shook her head and huddled over. Her large eyes bulged. The District Attorney looked about the courtroom while she continued coughing. The judge raised her chromium carafe of water and poured some into a Styrofoam cup. "Here, give this to the witness."

Martin Lormer studied Althea Jackson, how she was crouched over, her shoulders tensed, the dark ligaments in her long arms straining, unable to stop coughing. He shifted to me and whispered, "Father Jerod, would you break your vow to answer one question for me—then you can return to your vow to be silent." I looked at him steadily, silently. He tensed his mouth, asking, "Are you using any psychic power to cause these disturbances?" I sighed. The man was a fool.

I studied the scratches on the table's surface. His voice hissed at me. "Barthelamo Vecchio and the Albino had psychic powers. Why couldn't they have been transferred to you?" I turned to him and grinned. He had just betrayed himself into the admission that he did believe that I was reincarnated.

The witness stopped coughing and edged her face upward to be able to breathe. Her large breasts heaved. The men on the jury watched her. She was sexual—lavishly sensual. I sat and smiled. This interrogation would be a waste of time. Althea would preach and polemicize about women's liberation, but the bitch would never disclose what she was really like.

One night Shara snuggled against me and I knew she wanted to make love. She was warm and there was a quickness to her breathing. I moved against her and began kissing her neck. Her hand was a warm feather moving along my bare thigh. All other times in our lovemaking I was immediately responsive. That night I was numb. It is nothing, I assured myself. I began a concentrated effort for sexual arousal. I was unable to stir my body to interest. When I lay back, tired and depressed, Shara hugged against me, loving, kind. "It's all right, darling. Those things happen to men now and then."

I pushed her away. "How do you know so damn much about men?" I went into the living room and slept on the couch.

My impotence continued. Shara pretended to be understanding, patient.

"It's only a phase, darling. There are probably hundreds of reasons why something like that happens. It could even be some sort of virus. Worry and guilt will only prolong it. Instead of retreating and losing contact with each other, why don't we force this thing to pass by really going at it?"

She said this with her face pressed to my face. I did not believe her. She was a woman who contained centuries of superstition and spells and, in secret, she had cast a hex onto my sexuality because I was tiresome to her. She wanted me to leave her. But I could not deeply believe what I believed. Panic was making me more primitive than the Albino in me. I submitted myself to the process of having my virility provoked back into me.

She brought home a chart imported from India. It demonstrated the thirty-six basic lovemaking positions. We clasped ourselves together and many of the positions were straining exertions that bruised away the pleasure. We decided that visual stimulation accompanied by theatrical effects would generate sensations I had never experienced. We used mirrors and odd lighting and stagey music. She would pose upon the bed and I would stand and stare at her.

"Think of how marvelous it was before, darling. Remember us together."

Only once in six weeks of experiment and trial did I feel a slight hardening. We dramatized a newspaper headline. She lay on the bed in her sheer nylon nighty. She was on her side, reading by lamplight. Silently, I opened the door, and, barefoot, I sneaked to her. I deliberately coughed. She turned and was startled by my presence. She saw my ski mask, the leather jacket and jeans with opened fly. She screamed. I leaped on the bed, my hand clamping her mouth. She struggled and kicked and flailed her arms and legs. She tried to beat me off while I forced apart her legs and jammed myself against her—she kept fighting and trying to scream and I threatened to kill her, to cripple her, scar her, while I thrust myself at her until I stopped because the hardness would not remain and there was no reason to keep thrusting.

I stopped trying.

Her nakedness began to repulse me because I could not recall ever having been her lover. My body had been limp and cold for so

long it could not recall her flesh. I had run my course with the
energies distributed to me in this particular lifetime—used them
up—and now I was in an existence but not totally alive. Shara
continued urging me to try again but I shrugged at her. And then I
felt a growing fear. Was this the structure of betrayal that Barthelamo Vecchio and Bianco had experienced with the women they
loved? Was impotence the opening stage of their destruction?

I could not recall, in all the days and nights they had revealed
to me, if there was any interval of impotence. Because I had great
portions of their lives, I had their consciousness at those times, and
there was no memory of sexual deficiency, or fear. Their betrayal
began for other reasons. Letitia because she was ambitious, the
captive woman because she wanted more power than the Albino
could provide. The answer to my impotence was somewhere in
their pasts, but I could not reach it.

When we returned home from our employments we would sit
and read or pretend to watch television. We had been separated
by our efforts to be brought together again sexually. I could feel a
constant anger at her. How could she, at the age of twenty-three,
be so unabashedly uninhibited about her body? Is it because she
may have lived through centuries and, though she was unaware of
her death and reappearance, her depths no longer regarded the
moral and sexual proprieties as important?

Then one night, in bed, she told me she had spoken to her
black friend, Althea Jackson, about the sexual problem we were
experiencing. That angered me.

"Damn it, Shara, why? What the devil was the point to doing
that?"

"Because Althea knows about men. She has an exceptional
mind. She also has a degree in psychology."

"I don't care about her damn mind. She's just some political
activist bitch who cares only about herself. She must have been
gloating and laughing at you. And me, as well."

"She's not that way at all. She really cares for me, and she's
worried. She wants to help us."

"What am I supposed to do? Lie on the couch and confess my
soul to her? Tell her about my mother and father and that I was
toilet trained improperly?"

"Please, Stephen, don't be so absurd. She wants to help sexually."

"Sexually? Now how in God's dear name can she do that?"

"She believes your body is being used as a weapon against me. It's being directed by deep-rooted resentments in your mind. Resentments that aren't caused by me but are directed toward me, because I am in your life now. I'm not sure I understand all of it, but what I do understand makes sense. She believes that your mind, in some psychosomatic way, is directing your body to become indifferent to me. That your mind, for reasons not even you can understand, wants our relationship—our love—to be stopped."

I wanted to fix my hands to my ears and shut away her voice. It was not my mind that wanted our relationship to be stopped—it was the intercession of God. The way we were now, and why, was displeasing to Him. He was rendering me impotent, speaking to me through the failure of my body, so I could turn to Him for help, for guidance. God was trying to encourage the awareness that my love for Shara was outside of His divine will.

I breathed deeply, to calm my feeling of helplessness and anger.

"Your friend, Althea, is either an idiot, or she's sick in her own head. All I can tell you is this—I don't want any women's liberation freak playing around with my soul."

"Being into women's liberation has freed her from the inhibitions that most women experience. It's because she's a liberated woman that she can offer us help. And she so absolutely sexual—so desirable."

"What the hell does her being so desirable have to do with the help she's offering?"

"Because she's agreed to go to bed with you—in fact, we'll both go to bed with you."

"Are you crazy?" I sat up and though I could not see her I still stared at where her head would be on the pillow. "Are you crazy, Shara? Or just teasing?"

She sat up and her voice hushed against my cheeks. "I'm not crazy or teasing. I'm serious. You're the one who feels the pressure and humiliation of not being able to make love. Not me. I can live with your impotence for as long as it's necessary. But your brooding, your agitation—it's begun to hurt what we have for each other. What we have is being threatened. Do you think I care if you have another woman—in a relationship of sex, and nothing more? That might be just what you need to bring you out of this. I don't like it, but I'll be damned if I allow some provincial morality to cause our love to die."

"But it's—it's, it's just wrong."

"Please, darling, don't be an old fuddy about this. My concerns are for our lives together. I couldn't possibly be jealous. Not over Althea. Sex without attachment, without involvement, without obligations, that's her premise. It will be only sex. Pure physical, pleasurable, exciting sex. A woman can always forgive a man's sexual encounters. She can't forgive his love relationships with another woman."

I could not believe what I was hearing but I could not deny its logic. I felt her hand touch my knee. "Darling," she whispered, "it will be all right, I promise you. Althea is a good and understanding woman, for all her political affectations."

I shook my head. "It's wrong, Shara."

Her hand went to my genitals and she held me. Her voice tensed with anger. "What good are they to you, and what good are they to me? I have them in my hand and they're dead to both of us. If I held another man the way I'm holding you now, he would be all over me and in me and doing what he was born to do to a woman. But I can touch you, swallow you, spend hours trying to arouse it, and absolutely nothing happens. I don't give a damn if what I'm proposing is not conventional. Didn't Sarah agree to bring Abraham a slave girl to bear him a child? If it was proper for the people of the Bible—God's chosen people—then it can't be that horrible or perverse if we do it."

I could not answer her. I had been a priest long enough to know that in all emotional crises the first restraint to be abandoned was morality. But I could not understand why she would do this, and I became excited. She was the only woman I had been with. I suddenly felt like giggling and Shara laughed. "You have feelings down there, darling. I can feel them."

I wanted to push her down and quickly try again, but she

shushed me. "No, lover, we'll wait until tomorrow. If you try now and fail, there's no telling how long you will stay depressed." She drew her hand from me. "We'll wait." My groin felt chilled. She lay back and I settled beside her. I put my arm under her head and she turned to cuddle her face against my muscle. She sighed.

"Did you know that if you shift the letters in the biblical name of Sarah—by moving the H before the S—you get Shara. Isn't that interesting?"

I could not remember the day that passed, as I lived it to reach the evening with two women. Shara said, "Althea has a fetish for promptness," and our doorbell rang at exactly nine o'clock. Shara opened the door. They hugged and grinned their greetings. I looked to the black woman and she nodded to me. She's Shara's friend, I told myself, and almost laughed, wondering how it would be done.

Althea held up a dark brown brandy bottle and wagged it at me. "This will warm the cock-les in your heart, and yes, the pun was intentional."

Shara stared at the bottle, saying, "Let's not bother with dialogue and overture. Let's get to the purpose of the evening." Her tone was surly and I wondered if she was regretting her solution to my impotence.

Althea said, "I'll play bartender," and went into the kitchen. I thought, how does she know where our kitchen is? Has she been here before? Shara stepped to me and touched my hand. "I want this to be effective, but try not to enjoy it too much. I'll not let it become a habit."

I caressed her cheek and whispered, "Why is she doing all this? Will you have to reciprocate in kind with one of her black male friends?"

She wrinkled her mouth. "Don't be silly. Althea doesn't like black men." Althea returned with three glasses. She poured them to the brim and tucked the bottle under her arm.

We didn't speak. We looked at each other. She is beautiful, I thought. Her eyes were charred marble fixed on my face. She was my height. Though she stood in relaxed ease, I could sense the vibrance, the excitement she was feeling. She brought the glass to her lips and nodded to me. We drank the brandy. The liquid burned my throat. Shara coughed. Althea took our glasses and filled them again. She raised hers and grinned.

"I quote from the father of our country, George Washington. 'Our cause is noble, it is the cause of mankind! And the danger in it is to be apprehended from ourselves.' "

Shara said, "I'll quote from Ernest Jones. 'Man's chief enemy is his own unruly nature and the dark forces pent up within him.' " They smiled at me. I was feeling sleepy and that warned me that I was afraid. I pointed the glass at them. "I quote from Terence. 'Homo sum, et humani nihil a me alienum puto.' " They frowned at me. I interpreted for them. "I am a man, and nothing pertaining to man is alien to me." We clicked our glasses and drank again.

Shara went to the record player and put on Ravel's "Bolero." Althea began moving to the slow, muted rhythm. Shara sidled to me and began unbuttoning my shirt. She whispered, "Give yourself over to being loved, darling. Give up on hating yourself." I closed my eyes and wiggled my toes on the carpet and watched Althea sway and shift and remove her blouse.

She tossed away her blouse and twirled her body and there were no garments beneath her flair skirt. Her breasts swung in cadence to the throbbing music. I watched as Shara slowly undressed me, stroking my body. I felt like a child being attended by baby-sitters. Althea squinted and stretched her mouth and spoke in a clench of passion. "Honey chile, I'm goin'tuh take you'n drain you dry." I grinned at her. Shara drew down my pants and I stepped from them. Althea looked to my groin and hummed, "Hung like an ape, yeah, yeah," and I laughed, and shuddered.

She shook her body and moved to the wall and snapped down the light switch. The room was brought to shadows. She pivoted in tempo to the music and suddenly tore off the skirt and I saw her naked before she flung the cloth around my face, blinding me. I struggled to pull it from my head so I could see and breathe. Shara began kissing my feet and stroking me. I finally unwound the skirt and breathed and Althea was before me, pumping at my face. "Git you head on me'n do me, honky mutha," she said, and grasped my hair and pushed it to her front.

I felt smothered between her quivering thighs and she laughed and moaned and Shara's mouth bit into my stomach, her breasts hugging my groin, and then we happened into a blend of three and I could not recall the sensations the instant they arose in me as other sensations hurried through my nerves as I kissed and touched and moved and I was partially drunk and laughing and the music rolled and rumbled in my hearing and their voices were hushed melodies as fingers probed me and mouths absorbed me and I tasted flesh scented with savage aromas and Althea's black body was a snake coiled about me, a fluid shadow encompassing me, and I was dizzy and she became the other half of my soul, the black and wild and violent portion hidden from my knowledge and I lay on my back and howled into Althea's womb while Shara gulped me and there was no softness hanging from me now and there was no time or other men living in me, there was only me, only me, Oh God, only me. . . .

. . . and then we were another way and I was thrashing into Shara while Althea's face was burrowing between our parts and suddenly I yowled and roared as I burst into her and though I wanted them to fall upon the floor and sleep Althea would not let me rest and feel glory in my returned virility as she suddenly slapped my mouth and cursed me. "Honky pig, you come too soon!" and she grabbed my crotch and wrestled me to the wall, jamming herself against me as her mouth bit my mouth and Shara jumped against us and bit my neck and chest and I wanted them to stop and I began struggling against their weight and shouted, "I've had enough, I'm all right. . . ."

. . . but Althea scraped her nails down my chest and laughed. "You commin' off again, honey," and I was weak and let them bring me to the floor and while Shara moved her opened mouth along my body Althea sat on my chest and brought her knees upward and I inhaled her and the music whirlpooled to a beginning crescendo and the shadows flailed and slashed and I was erect again and her black body was a shroud of flesh and I felt a beast's rage and I clenched her buttocks and ground my face into her and she shrilled her laughter and I could feel Shara settle onto my groin and I thumped and bucked while Althea flowed and I was twirled into the darkness and I thought, I am drinking of evil, I am giving away my grace and vestiges of God, all is blackness, blackness, I am in the black abyss, Oh, God, don't let me leave you, and as

Althea constricted I convulsed and Shara clutched me and wailed as though falling through space and all of me became a glorious torrent as I screamed into the depths of Althea, and then I was done, emptied, lying in a cushioned passion that hummed and rocked and I wanted to sleep as they left my body. . . .

. . . and I half slept and listened to the accelerating music and I was drunk and drained and resting in a yawn of Self and through the music I heard their sounds and I forced open my eyes but all seemed viewed through mist and warp though I could see Shara on the couch and Althea seemed to be upon her like a glistening puma and I thought, my love is tired and her friend is ministering comforts to her, what a good friend is Althea—how pleasant it is for one woman to kiss another woman in affections of friendship. They are joyous of my victory, they are playful with pleasure for my superb virility—and I yawned and closed my eyes and let myself sleep so I did not disturb their play. . . .

The courtroom felt cold and bright. I looked at Althea, who had recovered from her coughing and was now reveling in the attention of the courtroom. Newspaper artists were sketching her. Women were envying her. Men were secretly seducing her. I had no energy, no feelings in me to hate her. She was just a lovely, vibrant black woman who had helped me back into virility. I would not allow myself to think beyond that. I did not care that she was lying in her statements that I planned to kill Shara. The District Attorney rubbed his palms together and stood away from her as he asked questions. He wanted the jury to watch her as she answered.

"When you say that the victim feared the man she was living with and you advised her to leave him, would you tell the court why you offered this advice?"

"From all she said about him I was able to determine that he had all the symptoms of a classic sadomasochist. He was given to prolonged depressions, he gained stimulation from his abuse of her, he required that she abuse him, he doubted himself as a man, etcetera, etcetera. The symptoms are too plentiful to go into. I do remember that she was shaken—emotionally shaken—by my analysis of him."

"Was there any particular portion of your analysis that was responsible for shaking her up?"

"It was when I told her that she had better leave him because in most cases of extreme sadomasochism, the disturbed person is unpredictable. They plan and conceive fantasy situations that are often homicidal. You can't guess what they're going to do next—they don't know what they're going to do next. There are no signs to determine when they might decide killing is a solution to their problems."

"Why did this shake her up?"

"She said that there were times during the night when she would catch him staring at her in a manner that made her feel he was planning to kill her."

"Thank you, Ms. Jackson. I have no more questions."

My attorney remained seated. He studied Althea. She was not troubled by his careful appraisal. I no longer believed that Althea had been lying. Shara had been telling her friends that I intended to kill her. Shara had been partially right. I had worked to contrive a way of keeping her alive after I had killed the Letitia and Captive Woman existing in her. I did not think this ridiculous. When you are victimized by an infirmity originating in the supernatural, the natural procedures for a cure are no longer useful. Human logic is of no value in the unhuman realms.

I realized the courtroom was unusually quiet. I could hear the hush of my own breathing. Martin Lormer stood up and walked to the witness stand. I sensed that he was annoyed.

"Ms. Jackson, it is not my intention or desire to embarrass you. However, there is one fact that I must know. Are you a lesbian?"

The District Attorney jumped up and shouted, "Your honor, I strongly object to this outrageous attack on the character and morality of . . ."

The judge interrupted him. "Objection sustained." She scowled at Martin Lormer. "Counselor, I warn you not to impugn the dignity of the witness or the decorum of this court. If you do, I will hold you in contempt."

Althea Jackson raised her hand. "Your honor, I will answer that question. Yes, I have had lesbian relationships. If I had cause to be ashamed of them, I would never have become involved in them." Some people in the courtroom edged to each other and whispered. The District Attorney flung down his yellow pencil. It dropped to the floor. Two women on the jury watched the pencil roll under the table. Martin Lormer placed his hands behind his back and paced toward the jury, who shifted between watching him and Althea.

"I appreciate your candor and integrity, Ms. Jackson. Were you interested in Shara Medford for reasons other than the remarkable intellectual compatability you shared?"

"If you are asking, did I desire her—yes. She was a fantastically beautiful woman. I did not desire her in the cheap way you seem to be suggesting. I desired her friendship, her mind, her love."

"But you were interested in her sexually?"

"How can any relationship deepen and grow if the sexual dimension is missing? Shara was murdered before we could develop that dimension."

"She did not smell of embalming fluid, as a previous witness testified?"

"She did not."

"Nor was her skin coarse to the touch?"

"It was not."

"Why did she dye her hair from blonde to brunette?"

"I was not aware that she had."

"Oh, yes. Shara was a natural blonde and decided to dye her hair and let it grow long."

"I thought her hair was naturally dark."

"Why was that?"

"Her hair was brown all . . ."

She stopped speaking and sat with her mouth clenched, realizing she had admitted to seeing Shara in the nude, implying that their relationship was also sexual. The women on the jury smirked. Two men smiled knowingly. Martin Lormer fingered the end of his solid gray tie. He had demonstrated to Althea that he was equally clever and probably more cunning than she was. He flattened the tie against his white shirt and smiled.

"I'm not interested in your relations with men, or women, Ms.

Jackson. My concerns are in another area. Why did Shara Medford tell you that she believed the defendant was planning to kill her?"

"She trusted me. When she told me he was planning to kill her, I admit, as I have already testified, that I did try influencing her to leave him. Not so I could have her. I was afraid for her safety."

"I believe you, Ms. Jackson. She told you once, and you . . ."

"Not once, she told me repeatedly."

"Why repeatedly? Wasn't once enough to frighten you both?"

"The feeling was always with her."

"Then it was a feeling, not a fact. Did she say how he would kill her—did she know the method he would use for killing her?"

"She would spend hours trying to guess but never reached a conclusion. It was only when I decided to tell her a more exact way that he might do it that she stopped speculating."

"Would you tell the court what you told her?"

"He would do it in a personal, intimate way. He was a sado-masochist and would not use a weapon that would render the killing objective. He would do it with his hands in some way, because that is an intimate and personal way to kill."

Several people on the jury instinctively nodded. Martin Lormer pushed his hands into his pockets and looked toward me. He stood as though waiting to be photographed. He walked to our table and turned his back to me, blocking Althea from my view.

"Did Shara Medford ever explain why she continued living with a man who was going to kill her?"

"She said she could not stop herself from loving him or from remaining with him. Not even with the threat of death hanging over her. She said that something more powerful than her own will was compelling her to live with him. She used the word *compel*. What really astounded me was her compassion for him."

"Compassion for him? In what way?"

"She said that Stephen Jerod was not anxious to kill her. Someone inside of him wanted to kill her. I told her that was metaphysical crap. He was only a man. One man. A man who was flesh and bone and blood, like any other man—like any other sado-masochist."

"Tell me, Ms. Jackson, do you know how to kill a werewolf, how to kill a vampire?"

The District Attorney raised his hand. "Objection, your honor. I fail to see the relevance of a discussion of science fiction at this time." The judge toyed with her white lace collar and studied her slender gold wedding band.

Why was he talking about vampires and other mythical creatures? Had he recognized something in my journal that I had written but not understood? I could not recall a black woman in Barthelamo's life. I smiled. Why would she have to be black? Perhaps Time had colored her.

The judge said, "I'm going to overrule the objection. I want to see where counsel for the defense takes this line of questioning." Martin Lormer shifted aside and I could see Althea. She was frowning.

"I'll repeat the question, Ms. Jackson. Do you know how to kill a werewolf, how to kill a vampire?"

"From what I can recall of fiction and myth—you kill a were-wolf with a silver bullet and a vampire by driving a stake through its heart."

"That is correct. Now, how do you kill someone who is reincarnated?"

"I haven't the slightest idea."

"Neither do I, Ms. Jackson. But perhaps we know now. If Shara Medford was, as the defendant believed, reincarnated . . ."

The District Attorney shouted, "Your honor, I . . ." but Martin Lormer completed his statement. ". . . perhaps choking her to death is the only way you kill someone who is reincarnated."

The District Attorney hurried from the table and strode to the bench. "That is a ridiculous and theatrical conjecture. I not only object but I ask that counsel for the defense's remarks be stricken from the record."

The judge struck her gavel onto the wooded flat and nodded.

"Objection sustained." Martin Lormer shrugged. "I have no more questions of the witness." He walked toward our table, then stopped. He pivoted around, surprising the District Attorney.

"Your honor, I have a statement to make outside the presence of the jury. Could the jury be excused?"

The judge turned to the jury. "You will be excused and remain outside the courtroom until notified to return." They stood up and a bailiff hurried to the door and opened it for them.

"Your honor, at this time I respectfully request that the court declare a mistrial in this case and discharge the jury."

"On what basis do you make such a motion?"

He stood in a relaxed pose but his voice was almost atonal, ritualistic, as he offered his reasons for a mistrial. "This trial does not belong in a court of law. Stephen Jerod should be tried by the church." I heard some snickers. The District Attorney yawned. "This is no longer a courtroom, your honor. It has become an arena where supernatural forces—Good and Evil, God and the devil—are warring for the soul of the defendant."

His timing was perfect, I thought. Althea Jackson's testimony was damaging and he was trying to distract the jury from its effects.

The judge licked her lips and stared at him hard. "Although the reasons cited by counsel for the defense seem somewhat unprecedented, they cannot be taken lightly. The court is not prepared, at this time, to decide upon the motion. The hour is late. I will indicate my findings when the court convenes tomorrow morning."

Martin Lormer came to the table and smiled. "Whatever points our beloved opponent made have been muddied over. Tomorrow we'll hear your confession. That will be a toughie, believe me." He began putting papers into his briefcase. A bailiff stepped to the table and waited. Martin Lormer picked up my journal and held it toward me. "I'm sure you have read what you've written, Father. But have you *examined* what you have written?" He knew I would not answer him. He fitted the journal into his briefcase, then stepped to the bailiff and whispered to him. The uniform guard nodded and edged back. I waited to be handcuffed and hobbled.

Someone called out, "Hey, Mr. Lormer, what's in your surprise bag for tomorrow?" He raised his arm and waved without looking at the person. He moved closer to me. "The trouble with you priests is that you believe in God but you have no faith."

He turned away and I watched him walk toward the aisle, nodding and smiling at people who talked to him. I heard the metallic rattle of handcuffs. The bailiff cleared his throat. "Eh, Father Jerod, I'm ready for you." I admired his courage. Only heroes would touch men crawling with demons.

There were tears in my eyes and I did not know why.

Chapter 6

I have been drugged. Now I am in a dark cell and isolated. I was the cause of a riot.

The court recessed and I was escorted to the jail. At my approach, the prisoners began flinging their food and roaring, "Get that devil lover'n his demons outta here!" They smashed furniture and shattered toilets and when I was not quickly removed they smashed bed frames against the bars and burned their mattresses and the smoke billowed to the ceilings and through the windows. The riot squads could not stop them until I was taken to maximum security—but the killers and the crazies screamed, "He'll bring the devils and the demons—get him outta here!" The drugs they fed me made me sleepy first, then sorrowful, and I huddled over and wept and begged satan to leave me be. But he would not pity me. And while the prisoners cursed and smashed their belongings and urinated through the bars and flung feces at the guards and bellowed, I began slapping myself to clear away the demons clinging to me, crawling on me, until I was exhausted into calm and they walked me through corridors and down long flights of stairs and then put me into a basement cell, like the dark dungeons of old. Then I was alone again, a monk, a recluse, a priest in penance—alone with the demons and waiting for the devil, or Shara, to visit me.

Shara, Shara, Shara, Shara. . . .

I do not have demons on or around or in me. I am a man of God. I gave my life to Him. He spit it back into my face. *He* abandoned me. Oh, God, let me sleep. I do not want to pace this cell they have put me in.

The long narrow door-window to the cell opened and a face poked against the bars. "Hey, Father, you all right in there?" and he kept watching me as another voice yelled, "He's on a vow of silence, I told you. He don't talk." The face watched me. I stood below the caged fifteen-watt ceiling bulb and let him see me. I kept rigid and did not sway. The bars sectioned his face. His voice came to me in parts. "We don't like your being here, Father. Only it's the only place where you won't cause a riot."

I let him observe me. He was a good guard. He could see there were no demons hanging from me.

"Tomorrow you get tried in a high security courtroom, Father. It'll be nicer'n the one you're in now," he said. The face drew back and blurred. He did not close the door-window. He wanted to hear my sounds. He was trained to suspect all prisoners of an interest in suicide. "I'll never commit suicide!" I wanted to yell at him. All I had ever tried was partial suicide.

I yawned and wanted to sleep. Yet tiny pulses of song began to throb in me. It was the fatigue of the trial and the drugs they had fed me. I knew now what Martin Lormer had whispered to the bailiff before the court had convened. "Have the defendant sedated. Put the stuff in his food. I don't want him trying to hurt himself."

I looked at the darkness of the cell and the shapes became interesting. Drugs and fatigue can turn the common form into a fascinating contour. Some shadows were ghosties and others were ghoulies. They flitted and wiggled through the spray of light and began chatting about me.

I stood and held my hands over my eyes. I was becoming a sequence of cubicles leading back and forth through time. I was a man of three dimensions, alternating and simultaneously. I could not sort one from the other. I was part Barthelamo and part Bianco and part myself.

In one walled cubicle Barthelamo was concentrating on causing Lucrezia an abortion. She was bound, ankles and wrists, to the bedposts. Huge feather pillows were fixed to her stomach and he was crouched above her, beating the pillows with a stout oak stick. Letitia was cringing in a dark corner, whimpering, *"Mamma mia, Mamma mia"*—touching her beads and kissing her cross.

In another cubicle the Albino was performing the human sacrifice to his Great Cold Eye god. He had already torn the hearts from four captives. The night was dark. The hearts were taken into the stone temple and placed into an elongated jade bowl. It was their gift to him. When the god awoke and burned in the sky, he would see the hearts and know he was worshipped and feared.

The people stood in crowds before the long rise of steps, holding torches and muttering and swaying while their son of the Great Cold Eye stood before the next captive and dipped his hands into the bags of powder and cups of ointment held in another elongated bowl, fashioned from gold. He stroked and rubbed the terrorful captive, smearing his skin with blues and reds and livid greens and then the attending warriors beat and dragged him to the massive stone table. They lashed him still with thick viney ropes. The captive woman he wanted would follow. He had strutted and danced and shaken his hands before her, only to whisper, "When it is your time, do as I do. You will be spared."

He crabbed his body, he scurried about the sacrificial stone, flitting and swooping and leaping while he flashed and clanked his hooked knives above the victim. He stopped suddenly, then loped like a crippled wolf and the captive shrieked as the knives were plunged into his chest and Bianco's white flesh tensed and bulged with strain until he stood up, holding the blood-wet organ in his hands. The people screamed their joy and struck their weapons to the sky while he strode into the temple, holding the heart before him—the knives still jutting up from the dead captive's chest.

The other captives waited in horrified crouches. Only the woman he wanted stood in an untroubled, poised stance.

"Filthy savage, filthy savage," I kept cursing as the Albino in me dropped the heart into the bowl before a large grotesque statue. I hated that vile, barbaric creature in me. I wanted him destroyed. I would kill him, and then kill Barthelamo.

The guard's face was at the door again. I let him watch me. He lit a cigarette and turned to blow the smoke into the corridor.

His face filled the small space. He grinned, asking, "By the way, Father—you gettin' any cut on that book Lormer's goin'ta write on your case, huh?" He turned to where the other guard was seated. "How much the papers say Lormer's goin'ta get from them publishers? For the book on the Father here?"

I waited, silently feeling the drugs they had fed me oozing

through my veins and nerves. Would they cause me to sleep or merely render me tranquil? I heard the other guard say, "Lormer got four hunred thou, was what I read. Yeah. Four hunred thou— man, *that's* money."

Oh, the treachery of Martin Lormer, I thought. I'm his carnival, his stadium. Hurry, hurry, step right over here, come one, come all, look at the priest—he's a genuine bona fide, real-life reincarnation. Is he here, really? Is he there, really there? Guess what century he's in and you win a prize. Oh, the treachery of that demon Lormer.

What will he write about me? Would he have been frightened, or puzzled when I had skipped like a child as I saw Barthelamo seated at Lucrezia's bedside, studying the rhythm of her breathing? Letitia had picked at a lute and was softly chanting a church hymn, praising Jesus Christ. Her voice was frail but melodic. She is so gentle now, he thought. But when the dark and clotted blood had flowed from Lucrezia's body, he had attended her while Letitia, almost rigid with fear, knelt and did her beads before a black and gold tapestry depicting Christ burdened by the cross He was forced to carry to Calvary. Barthelamo thought of what she had told him. *"If she lives, your nights will no longer be torment. I will come to you."*

He was startled from the caress of his expectations by a pounding on the door and a *bravo* demanded, "Physician Vecchio. Open. You are needed. Borgia has been slain."

Letitia swooned upon her chair. Lucrezia awakened and tried to rise but fell back. I undid the door latch and the *bravo* burst in, his clothes in disarray, his eyes wild. "An assassin's crossbow found Borgia. The arrow is lodged in his heart. He is dying. He calls for you to save him."

Letitia quickly arranged my medical container. If Borgia was not finally dead then I would not allow death to take him. My need for him was too great. I went to Letitia. "I shall not require you. Attend Lucrezia."

She closed her eyes and spoke as though in prayer. "Will she live?"

I stroked her cheek. "She will live. She will bear many children. Your promise—does it still hold?"

"I will do as I have said. When you are done with Borgia, I will come to you."

I hurried from the chamber and along the chilly corridors, following behind the tall *bravo* who carried my medicine cabinet. I could hear shouting and the clanking of metal as guards rushed about the vestibules, searching for the assassin.

In the chamber where they had carried Borgia, there was no solemnity of dying. There was a crowded furor of shouted advice and the scurrying about of nobles and ladies suffering to understand and be counseled of the change in their fortunes now that their Duke had been struck down. Somewhere in the center of delegates and ministers, courtiers and prattling women, Borgia lay on a green velvet divan, an arrow piercing his chest. There was no grief that I could perceive—no sorrow for this pillager of provinces who sanctioned rape and torture as amusement for his soldiers; this genius of intrigue and corruption who ignored negotiation in favor of murder as a resolution to threats against his ambitions. I noticed three counts and a marquis whispering cheerfully. They were no doubt saying, "I will take his lands and manors, and you, Ottaviano, will be my Minister of Finance. You, Messer Gasparo, shall have the armies."

Cardinal Minutolo, his red hat tipped forward as he prayed, was pushed by a squat courtier as he reached to the elderly Physician, Marius Vitto, entreating, "You must at least try to remove the arrow." The beleagured Physician, being shouted at by others as well, stroked his silken white beard with a palsied hand and cackled, "His life will spill from him if I do."

A stout friar who had traveled from Milano, earning a minor fortune along the way by hawking indulgences, chips of wood he claimed were parts of the cross Christ was crucified upon, anxiously urged the people near him to pray for Borgia's soul. "His time is upon him, we must bring his troubled spirit to the beloved Father," and stood with head bowed whilst one hand under his robe fingered his purse fat with coins.

The *bravo* swung my medicine cabinet in a wide arc, striking the thighs of the people as he shouted, "Make way for the Physician, make way!" The clusters of spectators dispersed and I heard a foppish noble tell someone, "It is the hunchback. He can work miracles." Cardinal Minutolo hastily grumbled, "Only Christ can work proper miracles."

Borgia's head lay to the side, his torso shuddering as he breathed in difficult gasps. His hands were flattened near the slender arrow shaft protruding from the center of his chest. It appeared to be nearer his lungs than his heart, which was hopeful. Deep grimace lines were rutted into his usually stoic, calm expression—though there seemed a slight tilt to his mouth, as though he was amused with his misfortune and pain. I sensed his pleasure in this event. The subtle jousts for greater position, the cunning bargains for more valuable holdings that were being conducted about him in the possibility of his death, or recovery, offered him pleasure. He thrived on hatred and fear—affection and sorrow for his plight would have angered him. Borgia looked to me and moved his lips to speak and there was no blood in his mouth, and I was cheered.

"Physician," he said throatily, "I must not be allowed to . . ." but I silenced him with a gesture, saying, "If I am to save you, I need command. Give it to me now." He slowly raised his arm to Don Domenico Borghese, his Minister of Finance, who hurried to his side. They whispered and the Minister, a small man with puffed gray earlocks and the eyes of a frightened ferret, nodded many times. He left Borgia's side to stand with his arms upraised.

"By order of the Duke de Valentino, we will depart from this chamber at once. It will not go kindly with those who tarry."

While the people quickly dispersed, I tapped the bravo on the shoulder. "I will require a brazier of flaming coals and a cauterizing iron. Quickly."

He grinned. "Immediamento!" he said, and rushed to the doors to do my bidding. Many people looked at me, annoyed at the favor and importance I was being accorded. The back of my hand was touched by Bishop Bibbiena, who smiled modestly. "May I remain? I am troubled about his salvation."

I shrugged. "Your concerns are misguided. Survival now, salvation later." The bravo returned carrying a deep platter of smoldering coals supported by a tripod. A stout porter waddled behind him, clasping a bucket and a long, thick iron with a cloth-encased handle. They placed it near the divan and left. Borgia stared at the smoking coals that were beginning to burst forth small flames.

I stooped to my opened medicine container and began preparing a *spongia somnifera* to ease his consciousness when I extracted the arrowhead. While I saturated the sleeping sponge with the juices of mandagora and opium and blended them to a mixture of conium and hyoscyamus, I listened to his breathing that seemed like the thick tail of an obese rat scraping along a mortar floor. "Physician," he called to me. I stepped to the divan. "Lucrezia, is she . . ."

I gestured for his silence. "She is no longer burdened by her infirmity. She is now suitable for marriage."

The edges of his mouth tilted upward, then he lay back with his eyes closed. "If you save me, what shall be your reward?"

"None. I need no reward for fulfilling my profession. Now be silent, your Excellency."

"I will speak, Physician. Dead, dying or alive, I will speak. I demand that you be rewarded. A rejection could mean your very life."

"If my Lord cannot be silent, at least be wise. Is my hand to be shaken by your information of my peril? Are my wits to be addled by your promise of my horrible fate?"

Though my impulse was to declare, "Free Letitia from your authority so that I may have her without fear." He would think a moment—consider the innocence and inexpensive simplicity of the reward, and grant it to me without agitation or rancor. But when he was recovered and again thriving with power and ambition, he would reflect on the reward and believe I had forced it from him, then realize the deception I had used to prevent his taking Letitia to his bed—and his rage would be beastial. Letitia, Letitia, will there ever be a time of peace to my loving you?

I set the sleeping sponge onto the table and picked a long, sharp scalpel from my cabinet and held it at my side. "We will speak of rewards at another time, my Lord."

He raised his face from the cushion and glared at me. "Your reward, Physician. You will not place a hand upon me until I know."

I set myself over him and used the scalpel to cut away the clothing covering his wound. He placed his hand on mine and stayed my motions. "I will have you thrown to the rackmaster's amusement unless you name your reward."

"As you wish, Excellency. Let my reward be your lifelong loyalty in my cause. Give me your oath that you will not betray me in my time of need, though my need be in conflict with your interests."

"My interests are nations. No man is worth a nation."

"Nations will never rise or fall on behalf of my welfare. I am a mouse in the affairs of circumstance. The beasts of history do not notice me."

"I have never before given such an oath."

"Then do not give it, my Lord. Be silent and let me do my work."

"Very well, Physician. You have my oath. I shall never betray you. What do you require as a binder?"

"Your word is sufficient."

"Fool—an oath is useless without a binder."

"If I fail in saving you, then you are officially slain and your oath is of no value. When I am done with this work, you will devise the binder. Now please, I beg of you, be silent and still."

I placed my hand on the shaft of the arrow protruding from his chest. He stared at me, his mouth turned to a smirk, questioning my courage while displaying his own. He whispered, "Do your bloody work, Physician. We live only once and die only once." Instantly I thought, you fortunate fool. To live and to die and be done with living and dying only once—*Dio mio*, if that were only so. Suddenly, without warning or compassion, I tore the arrow from his chest.

He kicked his legs and flung out his arms and shrieked and I hurled myself onto his torso lest he lunge from the divan in a madness of agony. Great convulsions wracked his body and his bucking was so powerful I was almost heaved from his chest and the divan threatened to topple over—but his shrieks quickly subsided to a wet gargle and the constrictions of his muscles and tendons softened and though he gasped to breathe, I could feel the hurried pulsations of life returning to him. I raised myself and tossed the

arrow toward my medicine cabinet and pried open his mouth to
know if there was blood gushing up from his innards. If so, he
would soon be dead.

His tongue was swollen and his teeth doused in bubbling sa-
liva, but there was no tincture of blood. Hastily, I pressed wads of
white cloth onto the now bleeding wound and waited for his startling pains to cease and be replaced with a constant pain that could
be endured.

Behind me, heavy fists pounded upon the door and voices
shouted, "Open, you devil—we want to see the Duke," and "What
are you doing to our Prince?" Slowly, I cleansed the blood from
Borgia's wound while tingling sensations crept through me. I
tensed myself, unwilling to allow Bianco to invade me now. I
pleaded to him, "Bianco, go from me now. I will give you my fullest attention when I am done with this surgery." The sensations
immediately ceased. Suddenly I laughed. Was Bianco some obedient demon I could dismiss or call upon when needed? No. Demons were bodiless spirits—Bianco was a man within me.

Borgia's breathing was a staggered rush of harsh gasps. I drew
the iron from the coals. I fixed my knee upon his chest and drove
the tip into the wound and held it. He woke from his coma and
screamed and tried to fling me from him. His shrieks became a
wail and he returned to his coma. The iron smoldered in his flesh.
The stench was rancid. I drew the iron back.

The boisterous pounding continued. I looked at Borgia's
wound that glared from his whitened skin. It was roughly gouged
with crusted flesh and without the seepage of blood. The skin was
shriveled and bordered with livid blisters. I placed the iron onto
the glowing coals and prepared an ointment. I listened to the
voices, demanding that I open the doors. They were the nobility
but I despised them.

I turned back to Borgia. There was drying spittle on his wide
mouth. A flutter of nerves in his thick cheeks. Conqueror, I
thought. Where is your power now? His breathing was blurred
now. I placed the pad onto his wound.

I was startled when Borgia whispered to me, "Is it done? Will
I live, Physician?" His voice was a sound filtered through dense
smoke.

I nodded. "You will live, my Lord. The scar will design your flesh more interestingly. The wenches will be joyous."

"You are a target now, Physician. Restoring me from death's corrosions has signified your allegiance. Do not stand in the shadows for too long. Do not linger in the light a moment more than needs be. To side with The Bull is a dangerous affiliation."

"I side with no one, Eminence. I stand courageously in the middle."

Painfully, he shifted on the couch and drew a ring from his finger, the surface as an egg yolk, bordered with diamonds of rare quality. In the center was the Borgia signet, a golden bull, poised to charge. He smiled. "Your love for rituals is most curious, Physician. Often it is the doing of witchcraft."

A shock of cold fear thrust through me. I stood as though unable to hear. He held the ring to me, chuckling. "If my father learns of this he will damn me, before my natural time of damnation."

I made myself chuckle. "Your father is a kindly man, my Lord. I hear he is the only Pope who does not eat little children."

Borgia glowered at me, then quickly grinned. "In time, he will cultivate the taste. Here, this is my binder to you. Wear it always. You are secure in my oath."

Knowing the stoutness of his fingers, I fitted the ring onto my thumb. He lay back and closed his eyes. "Leave me now. I will sleep."

I bowed low and quickly left the chamber. Nobles and ladies rushed to me, calling questions and jabbering speculations—men grasped my robe and tugged for my attention. Women fluttered perfumed handkerchiefs and poked fans at me. "Does he live, tell us!" They grasped at all parts of my clothes except those covering my deformity, believing that if their fingers touched the monstrous hump they would acquire infections. The feel of them disgusted me. I raised my arms to silence them. Count Ponzio Beccadello pushed his girth forward and smirked with sinister understanding.

"You wear our Prince's ring. Are your fees so exorbitant, or do you rob the dead?" The count stroked his beard and studied my eyes. All others about us were silent.

"I cannot rob the dead who are not dead, my beloved Count. I rob only the ambitious of their perverse plots. Cesare Borgia lives."

His eyes were a hating squint as the others muttered and whispered. A gaunt Cardinal called out, "The Physician is an instrument of miracles." Another replied, "The shaft was in his heart, I tell you. I saw it. How can he still live?" A buxom lady who had once been Borgia's mistress claimed, "Had the shaft gone lower, he would have been truly slain. That is where his heart is." The Count turned from staring at me and smirked to a noble of lesser importance. "Physician Vecchio had best save some miracles for himself," and pushed his way clear to stride along a corridor.

I pointed to a *bravo* in Borgia's guard. "Attend your Prince," I said, and stepped ahead. The nobles and ladies parted to give me passage. Their chatter continued whilst my fingertip flicked on the rim of the ring I had taken from Borgia.

The cell felt like a steam chamber. Sweat was sticky on my skin. I could not hear the guard talking. I hated the drugs in my body. They tried to drug Christ when He was on the cross but He had refused them. I opened my shirt and fanned myself. A white shadow began screaming in my mind.

I had been indifferent to the miracle Bianco had cunningly devised. A miracle the villagers believed had come from their god, the Great Burning Eye. I stood up and undressed. I enjoyed my nakedness as I watched his miracle.

He had strutted from the temple to plunge his hands into a squat tub of water to rinse the blood from his skin. The hundreds of people standing on the great rise of stone steps were chanting in unison, hitting the ends of spears and sticks onto the stones. They struck metal discs and shook ornaments, their torches flashing in the dark. The moon was a snowy globe in a star-littered sky. Bianco began stalking before the captive woman. He shook his body and flailed his hands while within him he spoke to his father, the Great Cold Eye that watched from the Above. He was prayerfully asking his father to send the strange insects.

He poked the captive woman's breasts. He pulled her long black hair, he stroked her bare thighs, then forced her to turn and caressed her full buttocks in ceremonial gestures. She did not cower away from him as the two other women had done. The people were dissatisfied with her display of courage. They shouted that he must beat her into submission. He promenaded around the sacrificial table and began screaming at them that she was not like the others. She was also the child of a god—a god unknown to him, but who was powerful.

The son of the Great Burning Eye strode into the sacrificial apron and wagged a heavy staff with a boar's head fixed to the end. His face was covered with the mutilated head of a spotted jaguar. His thick torso was draped with animal pelts. A wolf, a sleek dog. He shook the staff at the people and announced that he would take the captive woman's heart, that he was not afraid of her god. Bianco knew that his enemy did not want another god to have her.

While he ranted at the people, he pounded his chest to emphasize his strength. Bianco stood near the captive woman, knowing what to expect. The other god jumped to her and swung the staff at her head. Bianco instinctively brought the long hooked knives together, catching the thick wood in the apex. They scuffled, then stood held in a rigid strain. The eyes behind the jaguar's sockets were furious. He hissed at Bianco, *"I have cursed you."* He drew back the staff and again ranted at the people.

While the other god tried to persuade them, Bianco was dipping his hands into the bowls of special ointment he had prepared. He stood behind the sacrificial stone, partially concealed, and rubbed the ointment onto his skin. He edged back until he was beside the woman and smeared her. He was not afraid of the other god. His father was in the black sky of the Above, watching and pouring power into his god-ness.

The people cried out their disapproval at the son of the Great Burning Eye. His god-ness was in the sunlight. Bianco suddenly leaped before the stone and waved his arms and loudly damned the other god and the people did not know he was also spewing the ointment's aroma into the air. His voice heaved and pitched above them and the other god stopped speaking. The dark air began to carry bright flickers. Bianco pirouetted before the stone, then roared his declaration that the captive woman's god did not want him to take her heart. Her father/god was friendly with their god. They will see the sign of this friendship.

He began a rhythmic chant as he darted from the stone table and stood swaying and jerking before the captive woman. He stroked her body in more ceremonial gestures, smearing the ointment over her breasts and shoulders and face.

The fireflies became a thickening stream, their lights flickering like a rush of celestial fragments. The people quickly quieted. The other god shuffled away as the insects began circling about Bianco and the woman, then timidly touching onto their skins. He told her, *"Do not fear,"* as the flies landed on her cheeks and arms. The other captives began screaming and falling to their knees and jabbering their terror. Bianco edged to the ointment bowls and sneaked them into the waist of his feather skirt. His white skin glowed and darkened with tiny lights. He held her hand and spoke softly, *"Do as I do."* He slowly raised his arms and she imitated him. He paced to the edge of the temple level and posed on the topmost step. She stood beside him. The fireflies were clusters of luminous, animated pocks on their bodies.

He lowered his left arm and pointed to the other god. Her left arm performed the same motion. The other god cringed back. Bianco condemned the son of the Great Burning Eye who had disobeyed and defied his father/god by wanting to destroy the favored daughter of another god that burned powerful in another place. Their arms, layered with insects, sparkled with glistening arrows. *"He must be punished!"* Bianco demanded. *"He has shamed our people!"* He held his arms out straight and began descending the long column of steps. She walked behind him. The fireflies followed them like a trailing bridal veil waving in the darkness.

The people shoved from their path, reverently allowing the children of the gods to pass. Bianco felt faint with happiness. Crowds began charging up the steps to where the other god stood. They struck him with sticks and arms—he had spoiled this night's sacrifice, had disobeyed his father/god. Bianco hissed to the captive woman, *"Hurry!"* because the aromatic spell of the ointment would fade in the cool night air. They strode ahead to his abode.

I applauded my Albino. I stood in the cell slapping my palms onto my thighs and stomach. Oh, Lord, what a heritage of genius I bear within me. I am blessed, I am a conveyor of miracles. I kept applauding, pounding my hands onto my chest. . . .

. . . but the pounding now was the jail guard striking the cell door and calling to me, "Hey, Father, you doin' somethin' kinda magic with the lights? The lights're gettin' screwed up." I noticed the grimy light in the ceiling blink erratically. The guard's face at the door-window flashed dark and gray. He pressed harder against the bars to see if I had rigged some device to interfere with the current—if I was scheming to electrocute myself. He turned to the other guard. "He's okay. Nothin' goin' on in there."

The other guard's voice was irritable. "I don't trust those mother-humpin' demons he's carryin' around."

The guard left the cell window and I was alone again. I liked being drugged. I could drift through my life and my Time and the Time of anyone I chose.

I stood up and slowly paced the cell. I could hear the crackle and scrape of radio static at the door. I suddenly struck my fist against my palm, repeatedly, wanting to give myself pain. I would not accept the devil's gifts and gratuities. I had abandoned the grace and presence of God to find my own reality in the world— not to become a child of satan.

I was stronger in character than Barthelamo. I was facing death now, as he had once faced it. But I would not give in to the temptations of satan, as he once did. It was not I who was damned with demonic ingredients—it was Barthelamo.

When he left Borgia recovering on the couch, he was both anxious and fearful of returning to Letitia. Though Letitia would not dishonor her oath to lay with him, there was no happiness in his expectation. They would perform the rituals of love but she would not love him. The beginnings of his pleasure would be the conclusion of her obligation. If she was not virginal his rage would damn her. He would feel betrayed. Yet, if she was virginal, he would be so timid and softened to her that he might not fulfill her.

He walked along the cold vestibules. Shadows were flashed about from the torches fixed high in wall brackets. The thick tapestries along the walls, soiled at the bottom from many hand wipings, were curled up like drying parchment. Fatigue was a warm lead slowly draining through his sensations. He moved so slowly his steps were soundless.

Somewhere along the remoter corridors I heard voices and wondered if the crowds of nobles had dispersed now that Borgia's life had been restored. I sighed and continued walking to where Letitia was awaiting me.

"Damn her," I suddenly cursed, and kicked a thick stone urn, bruising my toes. I did not want her orifices, I wanted her womanhood.

I heard a scraping sound, like the lisp of a sad baby. Then a thunk and some whispers. It was not the noise of apparitions scaling about me. It was the sound men make when they stealthily approach an enemy. I turned and saw three *bravos* moving toward me. I knew them to be Count Beccadello's assassins. By rescuing Borgia from death I had destroyed Beccadello's opportunity for rule. If he did not manage my death, the court would mock him. His ambitions would be thrust into ridicule.

They moved toward me in a strategic arc so I could not elude them by sudden running. Each had his weapon drawn, each man's beard was cleft with a menacing grin, though there was no hatred in their faces. They were not passionate to kill. They had been set upon me by their Lord. I was a mere interval in the employment of their profession.

I remained still as they drifted still closer. The shadows about us flailed slowly, like languid snakes. I did not tremble as I watched their burly forms come nearer. I was cognizant only of the premonition that it was not yet my time to die. But I could feel fear tingle in me. Premonitions were wishes that were not always fulfilled. I did not want my death now. Letitia was awaiting me.

The arc they moved in widened. Slowly, my fright deepened. The burden on my back throbbed with rapid pokes of pain. They did not look to each other as they edged to me. They had no need to debate on who would restrain me and who would do the murder. Killing was their procedure. Gently, I raised my hand and they stopped.

"Do you have business with me?"

The tallest *bravo* with the spade beard as black as death's eyes nodded. "Your life is our business, Physician Vecchio." The center *bravo*, a mercenary I recognized from a battle in which I had served as a Surgeon, shuffled forward and grinned. "You ply your skills too well. Borgia's gain of life makes your life forfeit." The shortest assassin, with a cast in his eyes that made him seem to be viewing me through a murky glass, leered. "Are we to awaken the nobles with your screams whilst the floors spill with your blood?" His tone became kindly, like a parent urging a silly child to behave. "Resign yourself, Physician. You are done with. Honor us with a silent death, and a hasty one, so that we may return to our wenching."

I moved back until I was against a wall. I glanced about the halls and corridors, ferret-eyed and breathing heavily. My deformity began to thrash upon me as though an animal were trapped within the skin. The outer *bravo* chuckled wickedly. "Can you work your miracles now, Physician?" He drew his blade and held it toward me, playfully swaying it before my face. Another cutthroat laughed. "Now, mighty doer of mystery, work a miracle for yourself." Their laughter and the perfection of their physiques angered me, dispersing my fear. Suddenly, I raised my hand and, though I did not know why, I spoke in an incantational booming rhythm as I spread my fingers so the radius of tips pointed to their eyes.

"Will you dally with a man who is not a man—you fools. Your blades will stab the air. Your swords will cleave the space I stand within. Your hands will strangle the wind. You cannot kill what has been killed but which was never killed. Come, my fools, kill me and bring upon yourselves the torment of hell."

They stopped moving toward me and looked at each other. They were touched with slight alarm for there was no pleading, no fright in my speech. The spread of my fingers were blunt darts at their faces.

"Shall I part the ground upon which you stand? Am I to draw a bolt from the heavens to strike you down? I am the center of all Time—born on the rim of Eternity."

I laughed heartily at their widening eyes. Obscure depths opened in me and sayings of the church were brought into my mind—sayings couched in the language of the church I attended when a child. I pointed to the center mercenary. "*Aut insanit homo aut versus facit,*" I said, and chuckled with sinister tones. "*Cantabit vacuus coram latrone viator.* Place a hand upon my person and it will be burned from your body. Your mothers will rot in their graves to be held from God in the stillness of eternity until the devil takes them."

The *bravo* at my left side leaned back to avoid the poison in my voice. He hissed to his companion, "It is not as the Count said it would be. He is more than a Physician. There is blackness to his medicine." The center assassin shook his head in heavy dilemma. "I have seen the bewitched. He does not froth and bubble. Smoke spills from their eyes, their flesh has a green cast."

The other ruffian pinched his beard in worried hesitation. "The bewitched are not always alike. Their art is deception and demonry. Perhaps we followed the wrong one. Perhaps he is not Physician Vecchio but only a pretense to lure us from Vecchio?"

I leaned to them and pushed my fingers at them. "Shall I command your feet to take root and turn you into stone so the castle beasts can bespoil you with their leavings?" They shuffled back, intimidated by my fingers.

I knew the minds of these simple men. Long ropes could become dragons and slight string turn into worms for them. Their ignorance made them believe in the powers beyond common wisdom. A green gem could be the eye of a gnome, a swarm of bed vermin, a colony of people doomed by an evil fairy.

I would not be deprived of Letitia. Madness or cunning was my only weapon. I raised my hands above my head and struck them together, startling them. "*Frustra laborat qui Omnibus placere studet,*" I said, as though moaning through an infection. I pretended to interpret the Latin phrase. "I have just evoked the powers of the dark to aid me." They wet their lips and fluttered their eyes.

"*Gravissimum est imperium consuetudinis,*" I cackled. "Oh mighty Lorius who controls the shadows. Enfold these three destroyers of an accursed Count who have come to slay me. They are curs, low mongrels. Blind them so they may nevermore see the wenches they adore."

I strained to subdue my laughter when each, in turn, touched a cross upon his chest.

"Oh everlasting *Demrota*, god of entrails and ligaments—palsy their arms and bellies and befoul their loins with a maiming malady."

They cupped their groins to protect that glory they believed was all of manhood. And they were momentarily spellbound. I was a magus plying his black science against them. Then, behind the *bravi* who gaped at me, awed by my nonsense incantations, I could see other uniformed stalwarts approaching from a distant vestibule. The blades in their hands glinted and I knew that if they were not for my aid, then they were for my death, and all that I believed of Destiny and its endless chains of lifetimes was a lie.

I stepped to the *bravi* and they edged back, afraid to be touched by my hands. I felt enormous, welled with power. "*Gutta cavat lapidem, non vi, sed saepe cadendo,*" I spoke, breathing my words as though through swollen lips. "*Magna est veritas et praevalebit,*" and I could see fear making them perspire.

The men approaching moved on tiptoe, their weapons pressed against their bodies to mute the sound. I pointed to the nearest villain. "I cast onto thee fifty-four demons. What you drink will be turned to the urine of vultures—the children you have spawned from the bellies of whores will become sores on the carcass of sheep," and I stamped my foot and huffed my breathing to the *bravo* at my left, hooting words at his long face. "Each wench's breast you glimpse will darken your vision, each limb you stroke will deaden your limbs—and on the day they entomb your corpse in the filth of cattle, demented children will find your bones and scatter them so distant that the God you have forsaken will not learn how to find you!"

Then the other *bravi* behind them, nine in all, suddenly rushed forward and the leader, the chief of Borgia's cutthroats I knew as Mario, shouted, "Hold fast," as my attackers struggled to fight free from the holds restraining them. They were quickly disarmed and struck heavily with the weighted hilts of knives until they hung like disjointed dolls. They let the three bodies slump to the floor and began kicking them. Mario grinned at his men.

"Hold. It is done for now. When our Prince recovers, he will want his amusement."

Slowly the terror I had neglected to feel in the rush of my trickery returned, and I stood trembling. Mario stroked his scruffy black beard and waited. I clenched my thighs and squeezed my buttocks taut to stop from releasing myself. He reached out to place his enormous arm across my shoulders, but stopped his companionable gesture to avoid touching my deformity. He laughed heartily. "My Prince expected this to happen. In saving his Excellency, you have made enemies."

I could only nod and whisper, "*Grazie*," and he thunked his blade against his thick thigh with finality.

"It is good that you have saved our Prince's life."

"To save our Lord's life, I could incur the enmity of the devil himself."

"You seemed engaged in just such an affair as we approached you. My men heard you and believed you were a demon come to life."

"It was the dark, and some trickery. I was entrancing Beccadello's brutes whilst waiting for rescue. A simple trick for simple minds."

"It appeared most genuine. We crossed ourselves before our charge."

"There was no need of it. It was only trickery."

"Return to your apartment, Physician. You'll not be troubled again. My men are posted in your behalf."

"Extend my gratitude to my Lord."

"I will tell him. I will tell him *all*."

"All?"

"Yes, Physician Vecchio, all. The attempted slaying, the trickery—all."

I shrugged, muttering, "As you will," and turned my back to him as he ordered his men to drag the assailants to Borgia's rooms where, when he was recovered from my surgery, he would devise macabre methods for questioning them. Count Beccadello would then go into flight, losing his estates, until he could align with another prince who would plot to overthrow Cesare Borgia. I shrugged again. It matters little. Destiny predisposes, but Fate pre-determines.

I listened to the guards laughing as they pushed and dragged the three bodies along a corridor. The chief of Borgia's *bravi* would tell him all that he had seen and heard. " . . . the *attempted slaying, the trickery—all.*" Borgia would be amused. Were he foolish enough to believe me demonic—a warlock disguised as a Physician—he would not cause my ruin. I pressed the ring he had given me and laughed. A Prince's honor is his life.

"Hey, Father Jerod, hey. I'm talkin' to you. You got a visitor."

I made myself turn to the guard and look at him. I could not focus my eyes. I hunched against the cell wall. He had called me Father Jerod. Yes, yes, yes. I was a prisoner and drugged.

"Your lawyer must've given this newspaper columnist the right to interview you. He's Johnny Vickers, you know, the feature writer."

I edged along the wall, trying to hide from his sight. I wanted to think. Barthelamo's trick to save his life had also doomed him. Bianco's prayer to a god to bring on the fireflies had unknowingly established a pact with the satanic world. They had called upon evil spirits to aid them. Later, these demonic spirits would demand their payment. "I am innocent, my God," I laughed within my mind. I am innocent. Yes. An innocent bystander at the accidents of Time. If I am the residue of a reincarnational sequence, I am not accountable. I am innocent.

"Do you want to talk to Johnny Vickers or no, Father? He's important. He can do you some good. He could have an influence on the—well, you know who."

I stooped over and hurried across the cell. I wanted to hold the Bible they had given me. The guard followed my movements. I picked the Bible from the bunk blanket and hugged it against my chest. All priests have the minor order of exorcist. I would conduct a quick exorcism and cleanse myself of this demonic dust sprayed onto me through Time. The guard stepped away from the door. "Sorry, Mr. Vickers, he's incommunicado, as they say. If you ask me, he's also gone fruitcake."

I heard the guard walking to the door. A tray thunked on a ledge and the leather flap was lifted from the small cutout in the cell door. He said, "Here's a snack for you, Father. We know how hungry a guy gets just waitin' around."

There was a Styrofoam cup of milk and a paper plate of watery applesauce. I was suddenly hungry. The guard said, "It's all clean, don't worry, Father. There's nothin' ground in it." I believed him. You do not lie to a priest. You lie only a little to an ex-priest. I took the food and held it to the ceiling light. He smiled at me. "It's clean as a nun's bikini, honest. It's my milk'n sauce. I can't eat it 'cause it gives me the runs."

I bent the plate and drooled the applesauce into my mouth. It was cool and pulpy. The guard said, "Sorry we don't have napkins, Father. This ain't the Plaza, you know." He removed the tray and left. I drank the milk. They would drug me at breakfast. And I would accept the drugged food happily. I crushed the cup and plate and tossed them to the corner. I yawned and rubbed my eyes.

There was a tapping noise on the door. "You look kinda sleepy, Father. Why don't you sack out on the bunk?" I tried to see his features clearly. He was smiling. "What're you sleepin' on your feet for?" I made myself move toward a low, long shadow hovering above the floor.

The other guard called out, "What's the priest doin'?"

The guard kept looking at me. "He's asleep on his feet. The shit they put inta the sauce must'a just got to him. What'll I do?" I had to lean against the wall again. "Don't go in there. Let'm sleep where he falls." I sighed. Even those trusted men of the law had betrayed me. The guard chuckled, "Nighty-nite, Father," and left the cell door.

I yawned again. Slowly I drifted to the floor. I cuddled my face on my forearm and kept yawning until I could no longer feel my face.

Chapter 7

They had shifted the trial to the high-security courtroom. Seven tough-faced, uniformed bailiffs stood by the door. Outside were four special security guards. I had awakened feeling hunger pangs and though I believed they might want me drugged again, I had to eat. After eating three eggs, seven strips of bacon, four slices of whole wheat toast, and several cups of coffee, I was feeling comfortable and drowsy and did not worry if I was drugged. If I could sleep through this trial I would not be tempted to speak, to protest what was said about me, or the lies of the witnesses.

While the deputy sheriffs were walking me through tiers of cells and long corridors I was followed by people asking me questions, pleading with me to give them autographs. The deputies told them I would not answer and I was not allowed to write. A long chain was attached to the chain about my waist—another to the chain on my wrists. I was sad for myself, and feeling like a child in a charade of cops-and-robbers. I moved slow-footed and lonely. Shara was not among the people. She had not visited my cell last night.

Heavy doors were opened for me. Faces fixed atop uniforms gawked at me, then stepped aside. Though I tried to think, flickers of questions and conversations kept distracting me.

"They say he caused that pileup of cars on highway four—as a warning to go easy on him."

"They were sleeping on the lawns and in cars so they could be early to get into the trial."

"Father Jerod, where was your Shara Medford born? We can't find that in her records."

"I never seen so many television people since that slasher got taken. How many'd he slash? Twelve?"

173

"I think it's all a crock of shit. Just another one of Lormer's setups."

"Rumor has it that you were kicked out of the church for embezzlement. Have you anything to say about that, Father Jerod?"

I had passed street windows and saw lines of people carrying signs I did not stop to read. Television panel trucks were on the street, waiting for a dramatic event. Heavily armed policemen were stationed in strategic positions before the courthouse.

I was brought into another courtroom. There were wire screens on the windows. The doors had thick steel locks. The witness chair was bolted to the floor.

Martin Lormer was wearing a gray suit and looked neat and relaxed. When they brought me into the courtroom he winked, asking, "Did you have a pleasant night, Father?" I sat at the table. He opened his briefcase and turned to the District Attorney. "And good morning to you, counselor," he said. The District Attorney smiled. Soon they would be snarling and performing their ritual of anger and disrespect for each other and the jury.

The courtroom seats behind me were fully occupied. The people were noisy and restless. I did not turn to look at them. They were faces intruding into my life. By ignoring them I kept my deeper life secret.

Martin Lormer drew my journal from his briefcase and put it onto the table. There were long marker strips between the pages. I glanced to my right to see if Bishop Carmondy was there. He was staring at me. His eyes seemed glazed with his disgust. An opened Bible was on his lap. There were nuns seated behind him and beside him. One of the nuns was his mistress, I was sure. I wondered what his testimony against me would be. Two rows before him were Althea Jackson and Marsha Jenner. They were looking at me and holding hands.

Suddenly I was thinking thoughts that were not my own. Experiencing sensations that were not originating in my feelings. Grim loneliness and anger. Martin Lormer was wishing he could be in his studio in his Pacific Heights home, working on the sculpture of his twelve-year-old son Jason. He was feeling hatred focused on him—hatred for the personality they believed was his character. He was lonely and yearning to allow his authentic character to appear in his profession—not ruthless, flamboyant, unpredictably brilliant—but the gentle, serious, compassionate lawyer he was when he first began practicing. And was a financial dud and obscure.

My God, I thought. I was reading Martin Lormer's thoughts. I was interpreting his feelings. I gripped the edge of the table and cursed the devil for trying to compel me to believe I had the gift of mental telepathy.

No, damn you, satan, no. I will not accept delusions or your demonic gifts. I despise you. Take your supernatural filth and stuff it back up your ass.

I shook my head and breathed deeply, wanting my mind and sensations cleared. The people in the area nearest me became quiet. They were watching me and wondering. I kept gasping in breath. I would not know another man's life, I would not accept his life into my own.

Martin Lormer touched my arm. "Is something wrong?" I looked at his face. He was cursing the incompetence of the prison medical department for giving me such a mild dose of drugs. The small muscles at the sides of his jaw twitched. Then the telepathic knowledge passed. I stopped breathing heavily and turned from him. I sat with my eyes closed, praying to Jesus Christ to please interpose Himself between me and the demonic forces working on my life. I clasped my hands and began the Lord's Prayer. "*Pater noster, qui es in coelis, sanctificetur nomen tuum: adveniat regnum tuum: fiat voluntas tua sicut in coelo, et in terra. Panem nostrum quotidianum da nobis hodie: et dimitte nobis debita nostra, sicut et nos dimittmus debitoribus nostris. Et ne nos inducas in tentationem. . . .*"

The door of the jury room opened and the twelve men and women of the jury walked to their seats. I wondered if the devil would again try to trick me into believing I could read their minds—if I would know the verdict before the court did. They looked tense and uncomfortable. The door to the judge's chambers opened. A tall bailiff stepped out and strode to the left of the bench. He announced, "All rise." Everyone stood up. Martin Lormer poked my arm. I made myself stand. The judge entered and stiffly walked the steps to her place behind the bench. Two golden dots were fitted into her earlobes.

She shifted forward and scraped her index finger on the surface of the microphone. The noise scratched through the loud speakers. She said, "Good morning, counsel; good morning, ladies and gentlemen of the jury." She nodded to the people. "Please be seated."

She patted her lace collar and spoke to the court reporter. "Let the record reflect that both counsels are present, the defendant is present, and the jury is seated in the box." The court reporter's fingers skittered over the keys of his machine.

"And after much deliberation and advice from the presiding judge, this court has come to its ruling. I would be derelict in my duty if I were to stop the trial at this point. The motion for mistrial is denied. Ladies and gentlemen, the court will now resume the trial of this case. But I must first apprise you of certain allowances. If any one of you cannot continue as an impartial juror in this case, it is mandatory that you bring this to the attention of the court. It will then be my duty to examine you on that question and decide if you are, in truth, unable to remain as impartial jurors. I ask you now—is there anyone who feels unable to continue as a juror?"

Two women raised their hands. I silently cursed satan. He was giving me his corrupt merchandise and not telling me the cost.

The judge nodded to the chubby woman with two long front teeth. "Juror number five—without going into the facts of the matter, is it your belief that you cannot be fair and impartial in this case, at this time?" The woman began blinking her eyes and scratching the scars on her arm. Her voice was whiny.

"Yes, your honor. I honestly mean that."

"Do you base this on events since the outbreak of this trial?"

"Yes, I really do. Honestly."

"Do you feel that under no circumstances you can be fair to the people and the defendant?"

"I mean it, your honor. There's no way I can be fair. I'm just plain nervous on all this. I don't even want to talk about it. Or anything. I just want off this and to be someplace else."

"Very well, juror number five is excused. Alternate juror number one will be seated to take her place."

Her walk to the door was awkward. Martin Lormer looked to me and frowned. "Father Jerod, I would like you to do me a favor. *Please sit up straight.* You look ridiculous." I ignored him. He sighed, deciding to be friendly. "How are you feeling?"

I let my eyes settle on his eyes. Silently, I concentrated on telling him that I wanted him to continue having me drugged. Wordlessly, I told him, "This is an ugly world to me. All about me is despair and ruin. I do not seek its company." His eyes narrowed. Because he now realized that I wanted him to continue the drugs, he believed he was reading my mind. I almost smiled.

Juror number seven, the woman with the dark complexion, was dismissed and alternate juror number two sat in her place. The judge said, "The trial will now continue. Will the prosecution please call its first witness?"

I leaned my head back and closed my eyes. A doctor, Albert Jenkins, was brought to the stand. I did not care to listen to his statements about the fallacy of reincarnation, the delusions and psychoses people undergo when believing they are reincarnated. I began yawning and drifting, but I did hear an amusing declaration that caused even Martin Lormer to chuckle.

"I can produce records proving that Joan of Arc has been reincarnated four times during the same month in 1973 in different areas of the world. Each case was written up and authenticated by a different university in each of the different countries. Each university, I might add, is highly respected throughout the world for its psychic research programs. As an aside, let me also add that I have had people come to me who believed that they were reincarnated from Robin Hood, the Pied Piper of Hamlin, and the Lone Ranger."

I dozed a little while Martin Lormer asked his questions of the same witness. Three more people were brought to testify—friends of Shara—who told of her fear that I would kill her. When Martin Lormer questioned them he had them repeat Shara's fear that I would kill her. One said I planned to shoot her, another said she was afraid I would take her to a high place and push her off, the other said I would choke her to death. I did not know why he kept pressing them to dwell on Shara's fear that I would kill her. Why didn't he, instead, interrogate them until they admitted that they were lying—or that Shara's sense of humor had become warped during our life together.

Outside the courtroom I heard the droning chant of Hare Krishnas. The judge and other people looked out the window. They did not know the religious cult was calling upon some of their gods to intercede and stop the trial. A human was going to be destroyed by the judgments of men, before the time chosen for him by the gods. They were probably moving in a circle and passing glossy pamphlets while intoning their esoteric phrases. Then the clangor of fire engine bells and a pitched siren dominated the melodic wave of prayers.

The District Attorney waited for the noise to fade before he continued questioning a sergeant of detectives who was testifying on the prevailing characteristics of the many sadomasochists he had dealt with. "One thing you don't do is ignore a threat by a sadomasochist. It may take a long time for him to keep his promise, but you know eventually he's going to bring it to bear." I wondered who he was talking about.

I looked at the judge and I knew her thoughts. She wanted to smoke a cigarette. I imagined her cursing her father, who made her take up gymnastics because he had always wanted a son. Poor sad woman, I thought. Then she jumped, as if suddenly pinched, when a large tomato hit the side window and spattered on the clean pane. People shifted back and some began looking at me. I continued to ignore them.

Other people were brought to the stand to testify about me. They were various and odd. Some knew me personally, others were experts using their professions to define my character, my existence. Where do these people come from, I wondered. Though some looked familiar, I could not recall knowing or ever meeting most of them. It was not the drugs misting the sharpness of my memory. My present circumstance were causing them to leave the recesses of their world to appear in mine.

I had committed the serious crime of murder.

Ordinary people can forget other people they will never meet again. They can ignore the secret information strangers have learned about them. They can become indifferent to the impressions their former behavior caused in past relationships. It is only when they commit the crime of murder that this trivial information becomes dramatic with dreadful meaning.

My ordinary past was being turned into a deadly weapon against me.

A priest about my age was called to testify. Who was he? I squinted my mind, trying to remember. Was he going to claim that I had once cursed God? Was he that peephole priest who stood at my door, watching me masturbate and listening to me loudly damning God for causing me this humiliation, this sin? Bring me a woman, damn you. Letitia, the captive woman, or the woman I will one day meet and who will try to destroy me. No. That was another priest—not this thin, wispy one. The other priest was fat.

"Father Elgin, would you tell the court what urged you to contact the District Attorney's office to proffer information you believed relevant to this case?"

"Stephen Jerod, and myself, were assigned to the church in San Francisco at the same time. We were both young and inexperienced. After the first communion we attended, I filched the bottle of wine that was placed under the altar. Father Jerod saw me and followed me out of the sanctuary. We went into the lounge and began drinking the wine. We became quite tipsy. I have never again, by the way, done such a shameful thing."

"The court understands, Father, rest assured. Please continue."

"It was during that unconventional time that Father Jerod began admitting that he had an inordinate craving for fame. He became quite excited. He claimed that he would not remain an anonymous priest all his life. He claimed that the reason he was not famous—at that time—was that he did not have the right angle. At first I thought he said angel. I told him that modesty, humility, and anonymity was the true goal of every priest. He laughed at me. He became insulting and abusive."

"Is that all that happened?"

"No. He said that when he found the angle he wanted, he

would become more famous than the Pope. If I had not been—let us say, under the influence—I would have been more tactful. I told him that satan fell from Heaven for similar reasons. For wanting to become greater than God. Then he struck me. He's a very powerful man."

"Did you report the incident?"

"No. We had been drinking, you understand. I was afraid of the censure that would ensue. I merely, as they say, turned the other cheek. It was when he was credited with locating the Italian art treasures that I remembered his boasting, and I understood."

"You understood what?"

"That he had succeeded in finding the angle that would make him famous. Reincarnation."

"Thank you, Father Elgin. No more questions."

While Martin Lormer questioned him I thought, that if I wanted to live—if I was not carefully allowing myself to be convicted of first-degree murder—I would expose this hypocrite and liar of a priest. Look at him, I would say. Look at his frail pose, the delicacy of his gestures, his carefully cultivated lisp. Why does a black suit and turned collar blind you? Don't you know he is a malicious homosexual?—that he would wander about the corridors of the church, carrying a canvas gym bag in which he had his cosmetics and dainties and wig. When he was allowed into another priest's room he would don his female costume and perform his pleasures. It was the night he tapped on my door and entered my room and pleaded with me to "do him"—swearing that he would become my darling, my faithful lover—that I punched him.

The District Attorney called Bishop Carmondy to the stand. He was dressed in an expensively tailored suit that concealed his lumps and sags. Except for the six-inch sterling silver cross he wore on the slender chain, he appeared a used-car salesman about to persuade a farmer that an elaborate Porsche was more suitable for his fields than a grubby tractor. He caressed the binding of the Bible when he offered his oath of truth. He did not look at me.

"Excellency, you are the Bishop of the Church of St. Francis, in San Francisco?"

"Yes, I am."

"You are personally familiar with the former priest Stephen Jerod, who is sitting at the defense table, are you not?"

"Yes. I have known that man for many years. At one time he was directly under my supervision."

"Excellency, would you tell the court your impressions of the defendant when he was affiliated with your church? Was the defendant in any way different from the other priests? More outstanding, or perhaps less effective?"

"In the initial phases of his service he was effective. He was devoted to the parishioners and quite sensitive. He was well versed in history, particularly medieval history. He also demonstrated a remarkable memory and a brilliantly analytical mind. However, that first impression proved to be false."

"What kind of person did emerge from this first impression?"

"He became noticeably eccentric, preferring his own company. He eventually became indifferent to prayer, to meditation, to services, to the people. He would not use the name of God. It saddened us to recognize the exceptional torment he was experiencing."

"Did you do anything about it?"

"Not until he brought scandalous attention to the church with his public proclamations about reincarnation. Then I decided to censure him. He chose to ignore my suggestions that he desist from such occult beliefs. I was forced to again censure him after his second claim for public attention. By that time his involvement with pride and vanity and a need for fame had become more than he could resist. And so he resigned."

Although I could not fault his testimony, I knew that soon he would begin warping and distorting. Martin Lormer whispered, "This Bishop reminds me of an advertising con man. He'll really damage us. I won't be able to hurt him, but maybe I can blind him with some fancy footwork."

The drugs were altering me again. The District Attorney drifted to our table and smirked at us. His face became balloon large—then was quickly swept back to become a glossy peach pit. He used a somber and respectful voice that quivered with seriousness. "After the defendant voluntarily resigned, was there an occasion when you met him again?"

Bishop Carmondy leaned forward. The large silver cross dangled over the prayerful steeple of his hands. "Many months after his departure from the church, I was surprised to receive a telephone call from him. He wanted to meet with me. I was somewhat fearful. I had always suspected he had a violent temper. I knew that he had leased an apartment and was living with the woman he had seduced while still a priest. I could not, in all conscience, reject his request to meet with me. He was living in mortal sin and I speculated that he wanted to confess his . . ."

I had to breathe deeply and concentrate to remember the time he was telling about. Yes. Yes. I did meet with him. It was just before I had tried to commit partial sexual suicide—when I had become frantically troubled about Shara.

After the misery of my impotence had been resolved, I was almost rabid with sexual needs. I would not allow Shara to sleep until I was utterly exhausted. I was like an open furnace being fed great logs of lust that were converted into inflamed passion. I had gone berserk with lust. Shara was always accepting of my demands. She did not—not once—claim fatigue or disinterest. Even when I was without fervor or desire, I would not rest. I was performing a ritual, desperately afraid that if I allowed a day to pass without sexualizing, my capacity would atrophy and impotence would return.

During those passionless intervals of lovemaking, I would occupy myself with predicting Shara's responses. If I kissed her there, she would touch me thus. A caress to this part of her would cause her to move in this erotic manner. My skill in estimating her reactions was almost perfect. There were evenings when moonlight was an intense glow illuminating the bedroom. I began opening my eyes while making love.

I did not want to be deprived of visual pleasure—visual stimulations. I was startled to see that Shara made love with her eyes open. But they were not observing my body—using my contours and shapes to heighten her arousal. Her eyes were without focus, and glazed. She was remote from me. She was engrossed in a realm of herself I could not enter. I was penetrating only her body.

I would not allow this realization to diminish my desire. But I was heavily troubled. She was enduring me. She loved me and was submitting to a sexual chore like a dutiful mannequin. This pushed me to become more demanding. I had to drive her from that inner life that was excluding me.

I became imaginative, versatile. I even returned to the East Indian chart of thirty-six basic lovemaking positions she had once brought home. I would compel her from the dead past of Time. Even when I could not complete a sexual session I would keep dallying and fondling and using her. But the glaze in her eyes did not change. I could not enter her depths.

I wanted to talk to someone about women, about sex. The name of Bishop Carmondy kept appearing in my thoughts. Talk to him about the problem. It seemed ridiculous to me, to favor him as the man I should confide in. But I was not searching for reasonable solutions to my dilemmas. They were not reasonable dilemmas.

Bishop Carmondy had lived with one woman in an anonymous residence for over twenty years. His oldest son had recently graduated from high school. That connoted sexual experience. The woman probably believed in his sexual fidelity. While I was in service at his church he had acquired the stature of a sexual legend to the good sisters. That indicated sexual cunning.

He was not a handsome, boisterously virile man. His appearance was sedentary, piously flabby. But within the church and several convents he had founded a reputation for being a high-caliber sexualizer. I had often heard the sisters telling each other what a gloriously satisfactory lover he was. Having sex with Bishop Carmondy would not cause them difficulty with their Mother Superior, for she had been the second of his continually changing mistresses.

I wanted to speak with Bishop Carmondy because I was living in sin and did not know how to accept its effects. It was our sin that was drawing Shara into a remote realm of self when we made love. While fulfilling my needs she was suffering in her own shame. And only someone who had learned to absorb constant sinning could advise another man living in the same circumstances.

I knew also that when I spoke with the Bishop, I would reveal all my life to him, and the lives of Barthelamo and Bianco. Their existences were reaching me with greater frequency. While I loved with Shara they began revealing portions of how they conducted their love affairs. The belief that I was sinning seemed to intensify the impact of their lives on my vision. I not only feared for myself, I was troubled about them.

Barthelamo was relieved of his impatience to become as one flesh with Letitia, but woven into his joy were the barbed strands of distrust.

She was suspect to him for two reasons. There was ease and comfort in their lovemaking. He had expected groanings and pain and troublesome timidity—and virginal blood. In the months of his anticipation that Destiny would bring their flesh together, he had counseled himself to be gentle. No sudden grasps and savage embraces—no brutal thrusts into her softness. He would not be bedding with a casual wench used for relief of agitation. This time of love would be the culmination of past centuries brought into an immutable bond, to make them one. He had rehearsed, in his fantasies, again and again, how carefully he would offer himself. He would cultivate her shyness with his doting fervor, stroking and adoring, until her comfort freed her to become erotic.

After he had entered their rooms to undress and bathe the stink of intrigue and the blood of Borgia from his hands, he had called her to his bed and smiled.

"You need not share my bed this night, Letitia. You were in grievous distress. You are not bound to the oath you have given me."

She touched his arm, her voice a demure whisper. "My oath was also my wish, Master Vecchio." She could not know his joy. Only God could perceive his ecstasy. She reached for his hand and fondled the ring Borgia had given him. "Cleanse my mind of one fear, Master Vecchio. Do you have powers to save and destroy? Powers that other men do not possess? I must know the truth."

She trembled and he feared that she would cry. He drew the ring from his thumb and held it in his palm. "Inside this ring, there is a saying. 'Fays ce que dois, advien que pourra.' Its meaning is, 'Do what you must, whate'er betide.' Long before I understood this, it was my creed."

The circular border of diamonds glittered with light from the lamps on the wall. The precisely carved bull, though in miniature, seemed to shudder in an anger to charge. He shook the ring in his palm.

"My powers are those of a Physician, no more. I am no apparition sprung from the bowels of a toad, nor an agent of the devil tempting maidens from the compassions of Jesus. Other men fear knowledge, thus they attribute all fortune or misfortune to the divine, or the demonic. There is no magic in me beyond the amazements given me by my medical knowledge."

She touched the ring. Its size would seem to encircle her wrist, he thought. Her pale blue gown, frilled with lace and sweeping along her body, quickened his breath. She smiled and put her thumb through the ring. "Borgia does not give this to common men."

He drew the ring from her thumb and cupped it in his palm. "It is only a jewel. It has no power. Come, Letitia, let us talk of love."

His first surprise had been to learn that she had bathed. It was not a usual practice and he had not told her to do this. How could she know that aroma and scent was a heady disposition during love? She had placed him into her with unashamed boldness and though his passion was not distracted, he was alarmed to know she was leading him into loving wherein he had planned to master. And because she was without fear for her supposed vaginal malformation he believed she had been used before. A fleeting thought had twinged in his mind—perhaps she did believe she was malformed and was using it to destroy his manhood.

When they were done, she had slept. He did not want to ruin her satisfactions with abrupt questions. He did not despise her for having been used by other men. Those fornications had happened when they were absent from each other, when Destiny was still bringing her to him and she was beyond his rule. But she was, now, consigned to him by Borgia for his service. He would protect what Destiny had finally determined for them.

He left the *palazzo* and traveled to Tagliacozzo, where he was not known. He purchased a Girdle of Venus which he would demand that Letitia wear. He would thus prevent the possibility of an infidelity. The contrivance, brought in from the province of

Bergamask, was in flourishing use by nobles who affixed them to their wives before leaving for military campaigns. The mechanism was of thin dark metal with a proper size and spacing for releases through the female orifices. On the right side, at the hip bone, were two links through which a sturdy lock could be attached. He was given the only key.

When he informed Letitia that she must wear this belt of chastity at all times, she wept. Her sobs were muffled behind her hand to keep anyone outside their rooms from thinking she was more than his servant. "Why must I wear this vile thing, Master Vecchio? It will cause me cankers. I will clank as I follow you about."

He used her ignorance of worldly behavior to soothe her misery. "Borgia's favor has given me a range of power and privilege others now covet. Rivalries and jealous factions will seek to distract me. One attempt has already been made on my life. You are now part of this aggression. It is not inconceivable that you might be set upon and your violation be blamed on an innocent. This belt of chastity will protect you against such barbaric intrusion."

"My protection is Borgia's command that I remain untouched."

"If not even the commands of God can calm the lusts of men, can the rule of a mere Prince do so? The Duke's edict is a fleeting measure."

"You lied to our Prince; would you not lie to me who is so much lesser?"

"Your question proves my principle. A man, inflamed by desire, is given courage beyond his reason. No, *carissima*, you cannot persuade me otherwise. You will wear this. I will chain the key to my heart. We will remove it at night."

He caressed her and they loved again and upon awakening she silently allowed him to place the metal protection about her privacies. When she moved along the room to learn a motion that was comfortable, he thought, I am a fool. My distrust of her will not prevent an infidelity—it will force it upon her. He wanted to suddenly rush to her and unlock the monstrous metal confinement and smash its form. Tell her, *it is not you, my beloved Letitia, that I must control. It is Destiny.*

He sensed that she was hating him. He would not relent. *Her hatred is nothing. A slave for her master, no more. Time will teach her my wisdom.*

She turned to him, softly pleading, "Let me remove this, Master Vecchio, I beg of you."

He strode to the door, more angered at himself than at her pleading. "I must attend our Prince's wounds." When he left he could feel her hatred follow him like a corrosive mist.

I saw Barthelamo now, closing the door and pressing his hump against the carved wooden panels, damning himself for having forced the brutal mechanism onto her body. His eyes burned with tears. She now held his life in her honor. All she need do is seek an audience with Borgia and raise her gown to show him the belt of chastity and Barthelamo would be brought before the Duke—bound in chains and judged for punishment.

I knew that when I wrote this incident in my journal, my hand would tremble, sweat would sting on my forehead. I did not want in my life now what had happened to Barthelamo then.

I had telephoned the church and asked to speak with Bishop Carmondy. "On a personal matter." His secretary told me, "One moment, Father Jerod." I was pleased her memory was failing. She was a past-middle-aged woman so ugly and arthritic she was protected from the Bishop's lecheries. I was feeling taut and foolish. This was going to be a serious mistake. The Bishop was too clever for me. I heard him clear his throat. "Hello? Is that you, Stephen?" His voice was calm and without resentment.

"Yes, Excellency. I'm calling because I need your help. I'm having some serious problems."

"That is regrettable, Stephen. Perhaps I can find time for you in, say, a month or so."

"No, Excellency, it will have to be now. Tomorrow night, in fact."

"Stephen, I do have a rather busy schedule, as you well know. Could you be good enough to tell me why you called. I'm quite busy."

"It's about sin, and life, and probably reincarnation. I won't come to the church to talk about it. You'll have to come here, to Alameda."

"Impossible. I never go to Alameda."

"Bishop Carmondy, I'm not in the mood for games. You be at my apartment tomorrow night, at eight-thirty, or I will contact the news media and inform them about your private residence on Kirkwood Avenue, about your illegitimate progeny, and other matters pertaining to . . ."

"All right, Stephen. Give my secretary the details."

The connection was broken and I stood with my hands gripping the telephone, feeling a strange moment of realization. There were no superstitions, no authorities or reasons to prevent me from eliminating my circumstance of sin by marrying Shara. Yes. Dear God, yes. I would marry Shara.

When Bishop Carmondy arrived tomorrow night, I would tell him, "Monsignor, I want to apologize for my cruelty to you, and my stupidity. Forgive me for threatening you in such a vicious manner. I want to confess my sins and receive absolution, then I want you to arrange your schedule so you can perform a marriage."

Yes, dear God, yes. Life is simple when you abandon your guilt.

The remoteness in Shara's feelings, the glazed look in her eyes when we made love, did not happen because I was an inadequate lover. My sexual frenzy was not stimulated by a psychological abnormality. We were both experiencing the absence of God's protection. He would not protect fornicators. He was most stubborn and prudish about His attitudes. He demanded marriage.

I told Shara the Bishop would be visiting us. I could sense her annoyance. "Why would you ask an enemy into our home?"

I reached out and caressed her cheek. "I'm going to confess my sins, and I'll have a surprise for you."

She stepped back, as though confused. "What sins have you been committing?"

I brought her hand to my mouth and kissed her fingers. "That will be between my confessor and myself." I winked slyly, unwilling to reveal that we would soon be married.

I became agitated while waiting. I went to the medicine cabinet and took a Percodan to help me relax. The agitation would not diminish. I took another pill. It was an hour before he would appear. Perhaps I could nap. Shara came into the bedroom and frowned at me. "Why are you so upset? You're no longer under his authority." I would not answer her. She went into the living room and returned with a glass of whiskey. "Here, darling, this will ease the waiting." I drank the liquor and coughed.

I told her, "I'm going to lie down for a while." When she left I swallowed another pill and in a little while I felt sleepy.

Shara came in to wake me up and saw I was not asleep. I was staring at the ceiling. Shara shook me gently. "Stephen, he'll be here in a minute."

I giggled and tried to raise myself. My shoulders were nailed to the bed. Shara said, angrily, "Damn it, now I'm stuck with that pompous asshole." The doorbell rang. She left and did not completely shut the door.

I heard Bishop Carmondy introduce himself and Shara apologized for my absence. She said, "He isn't feeling well this evening. His class schedule has been very heavy this term."

The Bishop sighed. "How unfortunate. I did so want to speak with him. He sounded so troubled." Only a furry slat of light came from the living room.

I sensed, instantly, that he was attracted to her. I tried to get up, but the blanket was a mysterious adhesive clutching me to its surface. Then my mind began to fill with the images of Barthelamo holding a lighted torch as he accompanied Cesare Borgia along a dank vestibule in the lower portions of the castle. They were going to the Duke's private treasure vault.

I wanted to force the visions from my mind, to shout a warning to Shara. Be careful, darling. Don't stand too close to Bishop Carmondy. He has a magnetism, a lecherous charm. Hold onto your fidelity. I'll be up in a moment to rescue you. But Barthelamo, wearing a long black cloak with an ermine collar, kept following Borgia to the vault, and while he listened to Borgia tell him how many paces north and then fourteen paces south, he was being troubled with scenes of the Albino in his abode with the captive woman.

Later, later, my strange Bianco, he pleaded with the view of the Albino who was gesturing to the woman to undress so he could rinse her skin of his ointment. Later, Bianco, later. I will see your conjugal joys later.

Borgia had just returned from his successful attack on the small state of Forli. He was carrying three paintings by Paolo Uccello which he had taken from the citadel of Caterina Sforza. They would be placed in a secret chamber that only three other men had been shown. The men had been assassinated.

"I trust no man," he told Barthelamo. "But some I distrust less."

He was revealing the vault to Barthelamo because he did not want these treasures to be lost to the world. "I believe that my departure from this world will be most sudden. When I am dead, whether I soar to the heavens or plummet into hell, these treasures will purchase me nothing. What I cannot have belongs to the world."

But the Albino persisted in revealing himself to Barthelamo and I lay on the bed, unable to concentrate on listening to Shara and Bishop Carmondy as I saw Bianco through Barthelamo's vision.

It was when he brought the captive woman into his abode that he believed she would seek to ruin his god-ness. He had saved her. It was the way of her people that she must become his woman. She would begin to take care of him. She would make herself into the darkness that walked behind him. His people would look upon her as a bringing from the god of All.

He was in sadness.

When he told her the ways of his people, there would become an animal inside of her. It would hunger and scream for a feeding from him. He knew that when he told her the animal must starve, it would then grow bigger from starving. It was forbidden to bring his flesh upon her flesh. Then the animal would make her want to ruin his god-ness.

She had stood naked before him. He slowly rinsed her skin of the ointment that had drawn the insects with burning in them. She had pointed to herself, saying, "Onadyh." He nodded. He could not tell her he was without a name. The hurt of his wanting to feed her animal became so unendurable he would not finish cleansing her.

She told him, "I am your woman." She began rinsing his skin of the ointment. When she rubbed down his chest he had to turn again to hide the hardness of his animal. She laughed and touched the feathers he still wore to keep it hidden. She drew her fingers down his skin and looked at the tips to see if the whiteness came off. She reached around and touched his hardness again. He slapped her hand and stepped away. "It is forbidden."

She stared at him, curious. He pointed to a straw mat covered with a dark blanket. "Sleep." She squinted. He could feel her animal awakening. He strode to the opposite side of the abode and stood by his mat. "I sleep." She shook her head and stepped to him. "No. I am your woman." While he stared at her, he asked his father in the Great Above what he must do. If the people learned his flesh had been upon her, he would have no god-ness. She held her hand out, pointing at the lift beneath his feathered garment. "I am your woman." He suddenly smashed her face. She staggered across the dirt floor to fall at her bed. He would do this each time her animal cried for feeding. He towered over her, shouting, "It is forbidden!" She cowered against the wall.

He would not let her make him lose his god-ness.

Bianco and the captive woman diminished into a shadow when Borgia stopped at a solid stone wall that formed an ell leading into another corridor. The cold air was like the tongue of a wolf licking their hands.

Borgia withdrew the elaborately carved parade sword from its ornate scabbard. "Remember this well, Physician. If death is to cut me down abruptly, you will show the world my history. The artist Da Vinci created this vault for me."

He reversed the sword and held the tip. He tapped the hilt against the uppermost stone. He brought the hilt to the left and tapped the fourth stone away from the adjacent wall. He looked at Barthelamo and smiled. "There is a mechanism within a mechanism. Within that mechanism, there is another. It is controlled by weights and balances. Da Vinci is quite mad—but he is a genius."

Slowly, the wall began to separate. It opened in the manner of an immense volume. Barthelamo brought the torch forward. He was stunned by the amassed treasure the vault contained.

The walls were draped with lavish tapestries depicting many of Borgia's military conquests. There were paintings by Giotto, Orcagna, Masaccio—a portrait of Lucrezia Borgia composed in such madonna-like innocence her virtue throbbed in the beholder's vision. Beside that angelic vision was one of Cesare's younger brothers, Giovanni, who had been murdered—some claiming it was Cesare who, in a convulsion of jealousy on learning that the youth was the incestuous lover of Lucrezia, had arranged for his assassination.

At the north wall were the many colored flags he had won at tournaments. Dangling from the beamed ceiling, like massive insects, was an array of weaponry pillaged from foreign armies. There were high stacks of volumes he had collected from the monasteries he had sacked. Tiaras, rings, bracelets, diamond and pearl necklaces were in long golden casks. The floor was crowded with urns and candelabra and sculpture. Barthelamo did not allow himself to feel envy at such wealth. He knew that if Letitia were with them, she would not restrain herself from stealing.

Borgia brought an inkpot and quill to the carved teak table. He unrolled a parchment. "Physician," he said, "I have no patience with the keeping of records. Write this for me." Barthelamo leaned over the table and dipped the point into the silver filigreed vial. Borgia paced as he dictated.

On this eve of January, in the year of fifteen hundred, of our merciful Lord, I place within my vault three masterpieces by the artist Paolo Uccello. Acquired from the citadel of Caterina Sforza.

Barthelamo completed the record. Borgia took the quill and carefully inscribed his name. He returned the plumed instrument to Barthelamo. "I require your witness. Place your mark below mine. *Your mark only.* I will endure no other man's name in my history." Barthelamo printed the initials B. V. on the document. Borgia powdered the writing and nodded.

"*Finito.* Let us now return to the business of the world. My beloved father, our revered Pope, is preparing to appoint me papal vicar of the cities I have conquered."

Barthelamo held the torch high to light Borgia's way. Before leaving the vault he looked at the precise arrangement of levers and stones balanced on pegs and secured with chains. The mechanism was a design as well as a function. He believed what Borgia said about Da Vinci—that he was a genius with mechanisms—though he doubted that the artist was mad. Borgia hummed as he moved through the shadowy corridors. Barthelamo moved beside him though in his mind he was watching the Albino, who was standing beside the captive woman's bed, staring at her.

She lay on the mat, her eyes closed. Tears glistened on her cheeks. He turned away from her. His hands were clenched.

She did not know that until he had been captured by this people and given god-ness because of his strange skin and eyes and hair, he had been the lowest slave of the village that was conquered. They had fed him their throwings. When the fields did not grow the life that filled their bowls, they kicked and struck him with sticks. They tied his long white hair with vines and let the children drag him along the earth. When the god who gained joy from weeping did not spill his water to the ground, the people drove him through barren stretches of land and allowed the hot eye of the day to burn and swell him into screaming. While he loved the captive woman in a magic of lust beyond his knowing, he would not give away his god-ness.

Now she would do against him. Her animal would not have his food. Her anger would make his god-ness less. He had shamed her.

Slowly, he went to her mat and knelt. "Onadyh," he whispered. She did not look at him. He touched her hand. He squeezed the fingers. She sobbed. He edged closer and began telling her of how their happiness would become a long laughter. The other women would want her joy. Because she shared his god-ness she would have the first foods of all the cookings. When the warriors went to overcome other villages, she would be with him and do prayers to the god in the Great Above. When his father looked upon them with his cold eye, she would wear the story blankets that spoke words to the gods. They would leave their abode and the people would stand to touch them. To give them offerings.

As he talked he stroked her hand and then her arm. His animal began changing in him. She breathed hard and swayed beside him. He leaned closer as he spoke. Her hand flattened on his bare thigh, the fingers dabbing to him. He could not make himself smash her and shout, "It is forbidden!"

She held his animal and he became silent. He sat with eyes closed, struggling to breathe. He let her caress him and hug herself to his chest. He reached to where her animal was hidden. He heard a sound outside the abode. A touching of bone to bone—a shaking of metal. He jumped up and hurried to his mat before the son of the Great Burning Eye could find a looking space in the wall. He hissed to her, "Sleep." She nodded. He could see her slow smile. She would take his god-ness, she knew.

Their images faded in Barthelamo's mind as he stepped into a corridor and glanced about to see if there was danger. He nodded to Borgia. "We are alone, Excellence." Borgia grunted and strode ahead. Barthelamo touched the ring Borgia had given him. It did not matter if he was not in Borgia's total trust—he had the Duke de Valentino's oath.

I lay in a paralyzed stupor trying to regain Barthelamo's image to avoid hearing Bishop Carmondy talking to Shara. His voice was basso and rhythmic. Her voice was faint. "You seem so troubled, my child. Shall I pray for your peace of mind?" I opened my mouth to yell and warn her but there was no sound in me.

"Thank you for your interest, Excellency. But I know we will find a way out of our difficulties."

"Of course you will. You are a lovely person and your heart is clear. Let me serve as your confessor that your heart may be right in the eyes of God."

"I'm not a Catholic."

"Then speak with me as a friend—a confidant. Stephen is a very troubled man—you realize that, don't you, Shara?"

I did not hear her answer in my anger that he was calling her Shara. How dare that sonofabitch be so familiar?

"Do you know that in another day and age—forty or fifty

years ago—Stephen would not have been allowed on the streets? He would have been locked away."

"Monsignor, I don't want to . . ."

"I know I sound most cruel, Shara. Nevertheless, it is true. Stephen is an exceptionally troubled man. There is no telling what he might do. If I were to tell you some of his activities while he was a priest, you would be horrified. I speak this way only for your protection, not with malice. He is quite unstable and . . ."

"Stephen is an emotional man. That does not mean instability."

"He was a pathological masturbator. That sin eventually affects your mind."

" 'Pathological' pertains to a disease. I doubt if masturbation could be judged that forcefully."

"You're too young to understand how it does affect a man. The act itself is sinful, and offensive. The consequences, over a period of years, can be extreme. You should have him looked at by a psychiatrist."

Now I knew what he was doing. Planting a seed and persisting to make it fertile. Impose the idea of insanity on the vision of a woman and during stress she will look for its existence. Don't listen to him, Shara. Wait for me. The drugs will soon wear off and the whiskey will lose its effects. I'll leave this bed and kick that treacherous sonofabitch out of our home. Don't listen to him, darling. Please don't listen to him.

"You claim you love Stephen, but you can't explain why."

"Why do reasons for love always have to be understood, Monsignor? Why do we have to be able to explain what we feel? You love someone, sometimes—because you love him—and there is no way to make that love reasonable to other people."

"Yes, my dear, yes, I understand. But aren't you sometimes afraid that Stephen might—you know, might become *violent*. Or has he already? Ah, he has. I can see in your eyes that he has."

She was silent and I waited for her to call him filthy names and demand that he leave. His voice was soothing, a hushed pleasantry flattering her. She did not answer. Then I was astonished by a remembrance, and tried to lunge from the bed. Dark hands grappled me back to the bed. I fought the hands, I strained against them while I remembered overhearing a nun talking to another nun about her Bishop. "He's rather amazing in bed. He never stops talking while he's going at it. At first it was distressing. After awhile, it's rather pleasant. Soothing. And he's tremendous at what he calls *relieving your burdens of the day*."

Now I understood Shara's silence. He was hypnotic, entrancing. He was telling her, "The weight of souls placed upon me is so wearying. There are so few comforts for someone wearing the mantle I must wear," as he was undressing her, fondling her. She had become engaged in his charm and she was helpless.

They were locked together now. "Yes, I would rather be as I am now, a humble servant of God, than a corporate executive with wealth and power untold."

I could feel my heart thrash within my body as I struggled to lift myself to leave the bed and stagger into the living room where he was violating her. I would smash his skull. When he recovered he would have me brought up on charges and locked into an insane asylum, but I didn't care.

I heard him chuckle, "Now, now, you mustn't concern yourself with the burdens of a Bishop. We are really ordinary men and . . ." I lay as though in a coma. His voice chatted away time and then I heard him sigh and I cursed his sexual release and contentment and I could not hate Shara and—though I wanted to damn her as wanton and whorish—I could not hate her and I knew we would never marry. There was no marriage in Barthelamo's life, nor in Bianco's life. Why should there be in mine?

I heard the door slam. Shara went into the bathroom and ran the tub water. Yes, darling, clean his filth out of you. It is our love, in Time, that matters. Not our piss-ant flesh. Don't have me locked away. I have been alone for so long.

I did not breathe until she was finished bathing. I was ashamed. I should want to kill her for the gross infidelity, the outrageous dishonoring of our love. In that long, unbreathing span, I persuaded myself to know that my lack of rage was not unmanly to me, but it might be to Shara. She would not want to live with a weakling. Bishop Carmondy had planted an idea in her: Lock him away.

Shara walked into the room and whispered, "Stephen?" She smelled of soap. She knew I was awake but unwilling to speak. She placed her hand on my shoulder and laughed softly. "The Bishop really hates you. He also envies you—the notoriety you once gained for your discoveries." Though my eyes were closed I could see her sly smile.

"He kept asking me about your background in medieval history. I told him a few lies. Actually, I told him what he wanted to hear."

I managed to sigh. She touched my forehead. "You feel feverish, darling. Let me bring you some aspirins." She left the room. I lay in the dark, unmindful of the lies she had told Bishop Carmondy—afraid only of the lies she might tell when she wanted to have me committed to an insane asylum.

Sitting in the courtroom now—listening to the District Attorney questioning Bishop Carmondy, I thought—Shara is dead. None of this matters anymore. Let the dead past bury its dead.

But the dead past was still alive in me.

There was a world outside the courtroom. A world I never really knew. There were people using my life and Shara's death for their personal causes. They were picketing to stop the trial while others were picketing in a demand that the trial be continued. Newspapers were publishing my photograph and writing about me. People were being interviewed on television and radio programs, discussing the reality of reincarnation or the psychotic fallacy of it. Preachers were sermonizing and priests and nuns were crossing themselves and parishioners were praying for me, or against me. Yet they did not know me. I was a figure, a symbol, they needed to use so they could become more intimate with their own lives.

And why was satan being so passive now? Why wasn't he acting up and disturbing this trial? Why wasn't he setting the District Attorney's pants on fire as he paced before Bishop Carmondy and asked him questions?

"You say that on the evening you visited the apartment of the defendant, you did not have the opportunity to speak with him, even though he was most frantic about getting you to visit him?"

"Yes. I did not speak with him. The woman he was living with—the victim, Shara Medford—said that he was indisposed and was in another room sleeping. I was rather annoyed with him."

"While the defendant was in the other room sleeping, did you talk with the victim?"

"Yes. We had a long conversation. She was a charming person. Quite direct and honest, for someone living in—let me say, a state of sin. She was deeply troubled and I tried to comfort her. At one point she seemed on the verge of tears concerning a lie she had been forced to live with."

"A lie, your Excellency? Did she tell you what it was?"

"Eventually. This was spoken to me in confidence, but not under the seal of confession, you understand. She said that her lover, the defendant, Stephen Jerod, had misled the public and certain authorities into believing that he was a reincarnated person. His discovery of the Italian art treasures was determined through deduction, not through some supernatural phenomenon."

"Did you ever learn how he managed to determine the location of the Italian art treasures?"

"Yes. Apparently there are many detailed pictures on a particular sword that Cesare Borgia carried. It is called, if I recall correctly, his 'parade sword.' The surface of the sword and scabbard are covered with engravings that depicted the life of Julius Caesar. By an analysis of their positions, the classic meaning of the symbols, and the mathematical arrangement of the frames and their sizes, he was able to conclude that the treasure was in an unknown vault in the Castle de Cite. She said it took him two years of study to accurately deduce its location."

I did not flinch or shrug when he said this. I knew that people were looking at me with their mouths crimped with contempt. I did not dislike Shara for what was happening now. She could not have known that the lies she had told Bishop Carmondy would become savage weapons against the credibility of my life, just as she could not have known that I would reverse the continuity of our many lives together by killing her.

"That is hard to believe, your Excellency. Why couldn't the professionals do this? Surely their resources were far greater than the defendant's?"

"This is not uncommon. Amateur astronomers are always finding undiscovered stars. Apparently the professionals in archeology made some simple mistakes. They applied contemporary interpretations to medieval symbols. They did not credit Cesare Borgia with a mathematical sense. They also assumed that certain scratches and indentions of the top of the sword hilt had no meaning. The defendant deduced that it was used for striking against stone. It is very complicated and I don't understand it all. I do know that the Italian art treasure vault was not found by reincarnation."

I sat gripped in rage and helplessness. I hated that man. His face was an animation of smirks and sly smiles, resentful pouts and hostile grimaces. His conceit was changing Shara's lies into the truth. I wanted to shame him, bring him down. Now I wanted power from satan. God would not give me power to cause injury. I closed my eyes and listened to his testimony.

"You understand, of course, that I do not have the proper background to qualify as an expert. But I was shocked by what the victim told me. You see, I have never been involved in anything pertaining to reincarnation. Her statements were serious charges and I felt loath to bring them to the attention of the . . ."

I could feel myself tingle as I listened. I was being reached by a strangeness of disposition that rendered me airy and limp.

"Did the topic of the defendant's other discovery come up during your conversations?"

"It did. The victim disclosed that his other discovery was predicated, not on his imaginary reincarnated life, but on his remarkable analytic talents. An exhibit of pre-Mayan and Mayan artifacts was brought to the Winfield-Smithman Museum, in San Francisco. All pieces, except three, were dated and explained. They were stones with a type of writing carved on their surfaces. Although they had not been deciphered, they were displayed because they were part of the collection. Apparently the archeologists assumed the writings to be a language—an unknown dialect or tongue. Stephen Jerod determined them to be mathematical symbols. He was able to . . ."

Martin Lormer slowly turned to me. I could sense that people were watching us, waiting for an outburst. I could feel the curiosity, the interest in each of the jurors. I could sense Martin Lormer's excitement.

". . . and the victim said that she had been carrying this burden of lies for too long. Fortunately, she chose me to tell them to. I was glad to have given her some comfort before he killed her."

"Did she tell you anything else about those discoveries?"

"Only that the defendant was bitter because the societies and foundations he gave this information to did not give him any financial reward."

"Thank you, your Excellency. No more questions."

Martin Lormer remained seated. He opened a manila folder and seemed to be reading from a document. I knew he was deliberating on how to question the Bishop. The judge spoke to him. "Defense counsel, do you have any questions to ask of this witness?"

He nodded and stood up. "Yes, your honor. I do." He walked slowly to the stand, trying to appear respectful and kindly.

"Bishop Carmondy, do you believe in reincarnation?"

"I do not. It is a ludicrous blasphemy."

"Have you ever believed in reincarnation?"

"I have never believed in reincarnation. To my mind, it is profane."

"When you took the oath of truth, I noticed that your hand lingered on the Bible longer than is usual. Was there any reason for that?"

"None, really. Only that I love the Bible. It is the inspired Word of God."

"Then you have not only sworn to tell the truth, but by your commitment to God, you are dedicated to upholding the truth."

"Yes. You put that exceedingly well."

"Thank you. Now, Bishop Carmondy, I would like you to be patient with me while I take you back into the past—your past."

The District Attorney raised his hand, saying, "Objection, your honor. I fail to see where the past of his Excellency has any relevancy in this trial." The judge looked to Martin Lormer, who smiled at her.

"Your honor, I am in complete respect for the Catholic office of the Bishop. However, I am dealing with a man, now. His testimony has cast the character of the defendant into a negative light. I am attempting to establish the credibility of this witness. I do not intend to abuse the integrity of his office."

The judge poked her glasses closer to her eyes. She looked to the District Attorney. "I can understand and accept the defense counselor's purpose. Objection overruled."

Martin Lormer turned to Bishop Carmondy. His tone of voice was genial. "Does the name of St. Francis call any response to your mind?"

"Yes. He is a most revered saint. He was born at Assisi, in 1182. He was rather much of a roustabout until divine grace transformed him."

"Wasn't he also the saint who experienced the stigmata—blood coming from his hands and feet the same way it happened to Jesus Christ—except that St. Francis was not pierced?"

"Yes. It happened to him on October 3rd, in 1226, on Mount Alvernia. He received the stigmata there."

"Do you actually believe this supernatural event, this stigmata?"

"I most certainly do. St. Francis was not the only one this has happened to."

"Then you do believe in the supernatural."

"I see what you are leading to. I believe in the supernatural when it comes from God."

"Do you believe in the supernatural when it comes from satan?"

"I do not."

"I see. Then there is a good and true supernatural, and a bad and false supernatural. All right, then tell me, Bishop Carmondy, are the acts and works and disasters caused by the devil mentioned in the Bible?"

"They are."

"If, then, as you have testified, the Bible is the inspired Word of God, and the Bible says satan exists, then satan does exist, doesn't he—because the Bible also says, 'God is not a man that He should lie.'"

Bishop Carmondy shifted on the chair. He did not appreciate the canny disregard Martin Lormer held him in. His smile faltered and he squinted. He fingered the cross that hung down and lay on his dark blue tie. The people in the jury were scowling at Martin Lormer. The newspaper reporters were writing down the questions asked and the responses given. I was absorbed with this testimony. Bishop Carmondy cleared his throat.

"Yes, satan exists."

"Has God killed satan?"

"No."

"Then satan is still active in the world, isn't he?"

"Yes."

"Doesn't every priest have the minor order of an exorcist?"

"Yes."

"When the priest exercises the authority of this order, what does he cast out of people?"

"Demons."

"Then demons also exist."

"Yes."

"Would you say that reincarnation, which you termed as blasphemy, could be something that the devil would cause to happen in the mind of a human being?"

"I can't speak for what the devil might or might not do. I can only give testimony for what God has done."

"You believe in the supernatural phenomenon of stigmata, but not in the phenomenon of reincarnation. However, I will let that pass."

Martin Lormer walked to our table and drew a paper from a manila folder. He brought it to the witness stand and flattened it against his thigh.

"When you were twenty-six years old and still studying for your doctorate, were you ever censured by the authorities in the seminary?"

"Not that I can recall. It was so long ago."

"Take your time, Bishop Carmondy. It was in the last phases of acquiring your doctorate."

Martin Lormer stood and drummed his fingers on the paper he held. The District Attorney frowned at his associate. Bishop Carmondy glanced at the paper Martin Lormer held and edged back as though trying to disappear. Martin Lormer asked him again, "Were you ever censured by the authorities in the seminary?"

The Bishop blinked and tried to smile. "Yes. But it was a misunderstanding. It was for a paper I had written."

"Would you tell the courtroom the title of that paper?"

"Truly, sir, it was misunderstood. The board believed I had written it in all seriousness. I had composed it as a philosophical conjecture—an abstraction."

"What was the title of the paper?"

The Bishop glanced down and cracked the knuckles of his soft hands, muttering, "I Am the Reincarnation of St. Francis of Assisi." I could feel the tension of surprise whip through the courtroom. People looked away from the Bishop. He sat as though huddled in his suit. The District Attorney flicked a file folder with his blunt thumb. Martin Lormer raised the paper he held and waved it at the Bishop.

"There was another incident for which you were censured. I believe that has to do with the supernatural. Would you tell the court about that incident?"

"It is much too far back for me to remember."

"Let me help you a bit. It was on the third day of October, in 1952. A day that Catholics commemorate the anniversary of the birth of St. Francis of Assisi."

"That incident was nothing more than a childish prank. Nothing but misguided zeal."

"A twenty-six-year-old is not quite a child. He is a full-grown man. He is accountable. Please tell the court the reason you were censured."

The Bishop muttered something that was not received by the microphone before him. His face was ashen and sagged. Martin Lormer said, "Louder, your Excellency, if you please."

The Bishop nervously licked his lips. "I claimed to have received the stigmata."

I heard someone behind me say, "Dear Lord," and other people shifted in their seats and someone called Martin Lormer a disgusting bastard. The judge tapped her gavel and the courtroom was silent.

Martin Lormer's voice boomed like a loudspeaker suddenly

turned to full volume. "That's not quite all, is it, Bishop Carmondy? Didn't you also deliberately pierce your hands and feet and run through the campus claiming the blood as proof of your stigmata—and when you were then censured, you stated, 'The devil made me do it!'"

The Bishop placed his right hand around his eyes. His shame seemed to have emptied his body of life. I was thrilled to witness the Bishop's humiliation. Martin Lormer sighed. "Thank you. I have no more questions."

He returned to our table. The Bishop left the stand as though in a coma. I could see how the people pitied him. Martin Lormer turned to me and winked. "Good lawyers work hard and try to cover all angles. But it's the lawyer who does his research thoroughly who achieves brilliance."

He turned away, and I could not deny his feeling of pride. Softly, I allowed myself to be taken over by the drugs still flavoring my bloodstream. In the lulling, furry torpor I laughed at the pleasure of knowing Bishop Carmondy was a fallen man. Shara was avenged for the mean way he had used her sexually.

I sat as though slumped within an enclosure of veils and all about me was gauzy and indistinct. I heard a clacking sound and assumed it was the judge hitting her gavel and making an announcement.

I realized that the court was convening for the lunch hour and that I was being brought to the cell. People's faces, like misty globs, spoke to me and then were annoyed that I did not answer them. I was, in truth, afraid to speak. My voice would sound squeeky, *castrato*, from lack of use. I sat in the cell, deciding to think. There were grand and monumental meanings to think about. I sat and thought about thinking and had no thoughts.

Chapter 8

A tray of food was moved through the slot in the iron door and I was alert enough to know that it was probably drugged. I began eating hurriedly, pushing the food into my mouth with my fingers.

I would sleep awhile and then be brought back into the courtroom where I would sit and listen to more testimony and then be subjected to hearing the tape recording of my confession. The court clerk or bailiffs would distribute photocopies of the confession and the judge and jury and District Attorney and defense counsel would sit and read the words while I spoke them.

I made a shell of the paper plate of apple sauce and dribbled it into my mouth. I dabbed my lips with a napkin and squinted and frowned and pressed my mind to make myself remember why this feeling in me was familiar. I sighed, then smiled. Of course.

I felt now as I had felt the night I tried to commit partial suicide. I did not want to kill all of myself. Only two-thirds of me.

That night, like a month of other nights, I had not been able to sleep. I stared up at the dark ceiling, listening to the hush of Shara's breathing. I was troubled about the condition of my life. Where other men might ask themselves, "Who am I?" I was compelled to ask myself, "How many who's am I?" or "Who is the one-third of myself that I am?"

The two other lives residing within me had become intolerable. They were demanding that I keep seeing them, that I know them. They were dragging me from an interest in myself—in today. I wanted to be rid of them. Only by destroying those alien lives within me could I ever become complete.

In an instant—as though the genie had snapped his fingers in my mind—I understood how I could destroy those other lives in me.

I would commit myself to the act of partial suicide. Killing only their influence on me. I would kill, in myself, what these men were making me feel and do.

They were men who had died centuries ago, yes. But I was carrying the core of what caused these men to be destroyed. They had both loved women with such dominating intensity that they had become neglectful of their own lives. I could not know the true origin of their love for these women, but I could know that it was through their sexuality, through their passions, that they felt their love, and revealed their love.

Their sexuality had caused them to love without a governing reason. I was carrying their sexual fervors. If I destroyed that sexual corruption in me, then I would rid myself of their lives. I would be released to live my own total life and experience my own full sexuality.

Yes. Yes. And I suddenly became anxious. I must be careful. I did not want to commit complete suicide. That was the utmost of sacrilege. Yet, I must be heroic.

I waited until the next night. Shara would not be coming home until late. I was too excited about my partial sexual-suicide to care about what she was doing with her friend Althea Jackson.

I began swallowing the Ephedrine pills I used to relieve me of sinus distress. One at a time. Then drinking the brandy Althea had brought the night we overcame my impotence.

I kept swallowing pills, feeling like a sharpshooter sending lethal pellets at a target—the sexuality of Barthelamo and Bianco, that was in me.

"Suicide, suicide, suicide," I chanted and struck my hands together. "Barthelamo, Bianco," I shouted. "I am committing you into this suicide so that I may be free of you—both of you!" I jumped and touched the ceiling, I punched the shadows, I spit at the dark living-room corners. The pills and brandy had led me into the washing machine of Time. When Shara returned home my partial suicide would be complete and she would see a man soaped and rinsed clean of heart, squeezed of impurities of soul, laundered in spirit. Without the stain of two other sexualities soiling my own. I would be her immaculate man. Our love would be spotlessly white.

The pills were making me feel swollen while the brandy sifted a sleepiness through me. The shadows were solidifying into specific shapes. They were the forms of Bianco and Barthelamo, come from former times, trying to stop me from destroying them as living memories.

I became angry and swallowed three more pills. I poured brandy into a glass and drank it quickly. I understood what I must do to commit partial suicide, and I became afraid. "Shara, Shara, help me," I pleaded. She should be with me, standing before me so we could embrace and she could shield me from the sinister forms trying to stop my sexual salvation.

But suddenly I began to doubt. A man lived through his sex. He loved through his sex. I did not want to endanger my own. "God, God," I prayed. "Tell me what is happening to me." Maybe I was the hallucination Barthelamo was having. Maybe Stephen Jerod had not yet been born and Barthelamo was hating me for being a future person who was imposed on his present time.

Then I strode clumsily to the closet and dressed in my priest's clothes. I began crossing myself and offering blessings to the shadowy forms still clutching at me. The sign of the cross was power. It would cause the hallucinations to vanish. At the bottom of the closet was the journal I was writing. It was hidden in a locked suitcase where I kept my ceremonial clothes. I touched the soft linen amice, patted the long white alb, muttering, "*Make me white, O Lord, and cleanse my heart; that being made white in the blood of the Lamb, I may deserve an eternal reward.*" I carefully moved the maniple, the stole and chasuble. I untied the cincture I had bound around the journal. While the sexuality of the two men in me was dying, I would burn this journal and destroy its recorded remains in the present.

At the other side of the closet was a gallon-sized can of paint thinner I used for cleaning stains from my hands. I brought the journal and can to our outside terrace. The floor was concrete. I touched the can to unscrew the cap. I suddenly snatched my hand back and yelped with pain. I blew on my fingers, cursing my stupidity. I had placed the metal can on an exposed electrical wire. I rubbed my hand and frowned. There were no wires anywhere. I shuddered. I had just been shocked. I grasped the cap and twisted, then jumped back, again yelping with the pain of current bolting through my arm.

The telephone began ringing. I rushed to the telephone table and swallowed three pills before answering. "Stephen, darling." It was Shara—she always called me "darling" to conceal the guilt she was feeling. I laughed.

"If you want to see them die, you better hurry."

"See who die? Stephen, you sound drunk. Have you been drinking?"

"I am not drinking, my dearest. I am undergoing a partial sexual suicide. Yes. The pills go to the white sex, and the brandy goes to the medieval sex. I have it all worked out. But something is wrong with the paint thinner. It won't let . . ."

"Stephen, what is wrong, what are you talking about—what are you doing to yourself?"

"You're with Althea, I know you are. You are having a to-do—I don't mind, my lover. When the white and the medieval are destroyed and I am all my own, I will destroy your Letitia and Onadyh and you will be all your own, and God in heaven will be at peace. Bianco is occupied at the moment, but would you like to say goodbye to Barthelamo?"

I held the phone to the ceiling and laughed. I wanted Barthelamo to materialize from me like a gooey apparition wiggling into a full-blown man, and then ask me, "*Vuole avere la gentilezza di presentarmi a questa signora prima di andarsene?*" and I would answer his request for a proper introduction with "*Con piacere. La presenterò immediatamente,*" and then tell Shara, "This is someone who has lived inside me since I was twelve. You knew him several centuries ago as Barthelamo Vecchio, the Physician." And the Letitia in her would chat with the Barthelamo in me until they were ready to say "*Arrivederci,*" and then he would die in me, and the partial suicide would be partially done.

I placed the telephone to my ear and grinned. "Shara, my love, isn't he a charming man? I have no right to believe he is driving me mad." There was no answer, no sound. I slammed the phone down. Inconsiderate cold bitch. Would not even say a common *arrivederci* to someone who had loved her so desperately he had defied the grandest, most violent noble in Italy. I grabbed the telephone and flung it across the room, smashing a hole in the plaster wall.

I returned to the terrace to burn the journal. I felt sad. How desolate and alone I would be without those lives in me. I stood by the journal and can of paint thinner and was suddenly afraid. Would I kill two sources of insanity in me, or an irreplaceable two-thirds of myself?

I touched the can and was pleased that I was not electrically shocked. I unscrewed the cap and tried to raise it to pour. It would not move. I curved my fingers through the metal handle and used all my strength but could not lift it. Some dust and paint had gotten onto the can and formed a tight bond between the metal and concrete. I tried pushing it with my foot. It was rooted firm. The pills and brandy had weakened me. I brought the journal back to the closet and again bound it with the cincture and hid it beneath my ceremonial clothes. I stood against the closet door and let myself sleep a little.

In the drowsy comfort of reverie and peace I began to understand what had caused Barthelamo and Bianco's ruin. The wisdom of the church and its demands for celibacy made me know. The weakness, the evil, was contained in the genitals. It was not the source of male power, it was the stimulus of his mindless stupidity. It was the devil's lever, the satanic instrument of self-destruction. Adam had not been duped into eating the fruit from the Tree of Knowledge. He wanted to screw with Eve. He used the eating of the fruit as his deception for getting her onto her back.

I was right. Absolutely right. I struck myself above the groin and shouted, "I wear the devil's lever." I clutched myself and squeezed. "This is the satanic instrument of self-destruction." It had caused Bianco's catastrophe, it had inflicted ruin upon Barthelamo, it was smashing my sanity.

Get rid of the foul thing. Yes. Eliminate the evil and live in constant goodness. "To the pure, all things are pure."

I was naked then. My realization caused me to jump and skip for joy about the apartment until I stopped before a mirror and cupped myself and held it out to my reflection. "Filth," I shouted at it. "Without you I could have peace. I would be my own man."

Other men would cringe to consider losing their parts. They had never been a priest.

The room was misty now. Shadows hung under the lights like ghostly vultures waiting for a tidbit. I moved to the bathroom as though sloughing through emulsified sand. Barthelamo and Bianco were in my genitals. Get them out—get those fornicators out.

I drank some brandy and swallowed another pill, knowing that when I did this brave thing Shara would worship me.

The mirror jiggled and the walls shuddered. The floor shook. I was centered in the volcano of myself. I would do the bravery now, before the fury and violence I felt burst me into a coma of sleep. I swung around, hiding myself from the mirror. If the reflection I had left inside the glass was watching me, I did not care.

I opened the medicine cabinet and picked a razor blade from the white shelf. I felt myself weave and slowly stagger back to the living-room mirror. I wanted to see what I would do. No act of bravery is done in secret. I heard a voice—it was my own inner voice, I presumed—telling me, "Yes, that is your salvation. Rid yourself of that filthy appendage. God will honor and love your sacrifice." I stood before the mirror and grinned.

I heard a hand strike the door. "Stephen," Shara yelled to me. "Stephen," and then she turned the key in the lock and I touched the razor to my flesh. She opened the door and I spun to face her and laughed. "Now we'll be free!" and she shrieked, "No, don't do it!" as I pushed down on the blade and I screamed with pain and she flung herself against me, pushing me to the wall, making me drop the blade. I looked in the mirror and saw blood gushing from my groin. She rushed to me as I began to faint in horror.

I awoke in a hospital bed. Shara was there. She was crying. My mouth was dry. My tongue was a chunk of leather laying heavy on hollow teeth, and I did not feel alert. I wanted to ask her if she still loved me. She placed her fingertip to my lips and whispered, "Don't try to talk, darling. You will be all right. I stopped you just in time."

I closed my eyes, wanting to understand what she meant. She leaned over and kissed my forehead. I could feel myself sleeping even while I remained awake. Someone else came into the room. A man's voice said, "You might as well leave, Miss Medford. He'll sleep for at least eight hours." Their steps moved away from the bed.

"Will he be all right, Doctor?"

"He'll live, if that's what you mean. However, his sexual relationships with women should drastically change. Do you have any idea of why he did it?"

"I'm sure it was an accident. He was drinking, you know. I imagine he was trying to shave at the time, or something like that."

"That isn't very plausible. However, I'll put that on the report. Has he ever had psychiatric treatment?"

"No, not that I know of. I never realized his problems had taken such an odd inclination. Will he be able to . . ."

"Perform sexually? Yes. There was only partial—well, let's say, partial injury, you understand. Primary reanastomosis—the sewing—was accomplished in—well, let me avoid the medical terminology. In time he will be able to accomplish an erection, but his penile sensation will be markedly reduced. He will also have great pain upon seminal emission. I'm sorry. The damage was repairable, but considerable, nonetheless. I would strongly advise that he be given intense psychiatric aid—or he might do it again. And succeed."

"Thank you very much, Dr. Steirman. I do appreciate your kindness."

I began to sleep and in the quiet of my mind I was pleased that I had not eliminated my manhood in the effort to rid my life of Barthelamo and Bianco. But the peace of mind I felt was only momentary. Shara was now compelled to destroy me.

By eliminating those former lives from my present existence, I had endangered Shara's continuity in Time, and her future lifetimes. Having destroyed my past, I was now fully myself, and would never again become another lifetime upon my death. When Shara's next lifetime was due, and I was not there to find her or to be found by her, she would be alone and without purpose. Her loneliness would be unbearable.

Yes. Yes. All of this was as real and as true as God.

Shara would not allow this supernatural calamity to happen. She had to destroy me while I was alive so I could be reincarnated anew when she was brought into her next lifetime. Or she would live in an everlasting and purposeless repetition of lifetimes, doomed to wander about in a barren eternity like a troublesome ghost.

Oh, God, I thought, as I pressed my face into the pillow. How complicated it is. How befuddling it is to disbelieve what you believe and to believe what is unbelievable.

I could sense that Shara had returned to my bedside and was studying me. I pretended to be asleep though I was more awake than asleep. Our life together as people who loved had passed. We could not be the same to each other. I was no longer burdened by her lifetimes and yet she carried my death. While the total of what I had now become still loved her—all of what I was now feared her.

I could feel her staring at me. Let me sleep, God. Take her eyes from my soul. And when the drugs they had infused into my body wear off, let me feel the pain. I am penitent and repentent, I forgive and want forgiveness, and where there is pain there is life.

I was awakened. I hadn't known I was sleeping. Someone was rinsing my face and straightening my clothes and telling me that my posture was getting weird and that I must not appear like some back-alley bum. Through the mist over my vision I could see Martin Lormer smiling at me. "We've got to hear your confession, you know." He patted my shoulder as he held me. "Don't worry about how you sound on tape. Confessions aren't as damaging as most people believe they are."

I was led back into the courtroom and I sat and watched as the detective who had recorded my confession placed a large reel-to-reel tape recorder onto the evidence table and then sat in the witness stand. Under questioning, he explained how the confession was given voluntarily, "without any persuasion." Copies of the confession were passed to the jury and the tape recorder was turned on.

> My name is Stephen Jerod. I live at 345 Chelsea Street, in Alameda, California. I have been read my legal rights by the detectives present with me now and I am confessing of my own free will. I killed Shara Medford by choking her to death. I was defending myself because I knew that the time had arrived when she was going to destroy me. I did not want to choke her because I loved her. I still love her. We have lived together, you see, in other lifetimes, and in other centuries, and in those former times she had been responsible for having me killed. In those times there wasn't much that I could do about it. In this present time, I was stronger—perhaps you get that way over the centuries—and I was able to . . .

My confession was not interesting to me.

Martin Lormer sat leaned over, pinching his earlobe as he read the pages and searched for the keys to his defense. The judge sat back and listened with her eyes closed. Some jurors used their index fingers on the pages to follow the words I spoke. There were other voices on the tape—the detectives who asked me questions. "Did she have a weapon?" and "Had you been drinking?" and "Were you using any form of drugs?" and "Did she refuse to have sexual relations with you?" and I explained that it was most peaceful that evening. Shara had begun to read the Bible.

"I actually tried to discourage her from reading it. I did not like her reasons. I had quoted something to her, about the devil, and she wanted to check the accuracy of my interpretation."

"Do you recall what part you quoted?"

"Yes. It was from II Corinthians, eleven—fourteen and fifteen. 'And no marvel; for Satan himself is transformed into an angel of light. Therefore it is no great thing if his ministers also be transformed as the ministers of righteousness; whose end shall be according to their works.' Shara didn't believe it when I said the 'ministers' were the demons of satan."

"Did she get violent in her disagreement?"

"Oh, no, it was nothing like that. I explained that satan often appears in the guise of an angel. Everyone attributes war and disaster and other horrors to God. Why did He let it happen, they ask. They never realize that satan is the ruler of the world and that satan causes the disaster, not God."

"And Shara didn't like your saying that, did she?"

"No, she didn't. Shara was of the devil herself, you see. I've always known that but I would never allow myself to honestly believe it. I loved her, you see."

"But you became worked up against her, didn't you?"

"I was upset, but not irrational. It was then that I told her about our lifetimes together. During the fifteenth century, and in a very ancient, probably pre-Mayan time. She laughed at me. That still didn't trouble me. Then I gave her my journal to read. When she read what I had written—although only my hand seemed to be writing it—my consciousness was taken over by Barthelamo who just about dictated what I wrote, as he lived it in me."

"Barthelamo? What was his relationship with the deceased, Shara Medford?"

"He had no relationship with Shara, in this lifetime. His relationship with her was when she was Letitia, during the time of Cesare Borgia."

"Cesare Borgia? What was his relationship with the deceased, Shara Medford?"

"I was a Physician in his court, when I was Barthelamo. He had given me—Barthelamo—Letitia, who later on became Shara, as the woman to assist me in my . . ."

"Hey, man, hold on. Slow it down a minute, you're gettin' us all mixed up. You were *who* when you were *what*, and where was that again?"

"I do not believe in reincarnation, although I have lived as though I do believe in it. But that was all part of satan's doing, you see. When I was twelve years old two men appeared in my mind and they began revealing their lives to me and . . ."

I no longer listened to myself confusing the detectives. Though I had to strain to keep my eyelids from closing, I could see the people in the courtroom absorbedly listening to the confession. I looked to my journal at the left of Martin Lormer's elbow. Shara had been horrified by what she had read. Once, she had exclaimed, "My God, Stephen, you must be mad to believe this! Are you trying to convince people that Bishop Carmondy was right about you?" I believed her, saying that was the clue to revealing that her time to destroy me was drawing near.

How could she believe the journal was the writing of a lunatic? What those pages contained were more interesting to me, now, than what I was confessing through the tape recorder. In this lifetime I had achieved celebrity for the act of murder—but Barthelamo, deformed in body, without a noble heritage or material possessions of importance, had acquired celebrity by his intelligence, his skills.

He had become, not only physician to the House of Borgia, but the Duke's confidant. He was appreciated for his wit and perception, for the way he listened and allowed the military mind of Borgia to hear the imperfections of his own war strategies. Even the nobility solicited Barthelamo to become a voice in their behalf when their personal interests were in opposition to the Prince's. Many wanted Borgia to wait for winter to pass before conducting his attack on the city of Faenza. Barthelamo remained aloof from the lavish rewards offered him. He could not be certain if the proposals were genuine or if they were prompted by Borgia as a test of his loyalty. He knew also that not even the fierce freeze or snow that assaulted Northern Italy could hinder the obsessive ambitions of this feared warlord.

When Borgia was not with his mistress, the Florentine courtesan Fiammetta de Michelis, he was in his military chambers studying the huge maps that covered the stone walls. "There!" he would suddenly shout. "There!" He would strike a portion of the map with his sword and place the tip on the area he coveted. "I will mount an army that stretches from the Lamone valley to the Marzano river. Soften them with mortar fire, then bring forward basilisks and . . ."

Barthelamo would listen, though in another depth he was thinking of Letitia. He would compel her to wear the girdle of chastity for only one month more. He could not endure the chaffing bruises and welts he saw raised on her delicate flesh when he removed it at night. Her displeasure had intensified to anger. No, he thought. I will remove it when Borgia returns to the battle-field—be it a month, or on the morrow.

When Borgia finished the articulation of his strategies, he would turn and laugh. "All of the Papacy's opponents will go down like weeds beneath the power of the Bull, eh, Physician?"

Barthelamo would gaze thoughtfully at the map and slowly nod. "It is a daring plan, Excellency. Yet to accomplish this cam-paign, in such formidable weather, you will require the finances of twelve sultans."

Borgia would turn back to the map, muttering, "Yes, yes, I require additional companies of archers, two thousand more arba-lestiers—ordinance must obtain thousands more matchlocks be-fore the . . ." Borgia was cunning and ruthless. He would gain the finances he needed—through negotiation, though he preferred as-sassination. Killing was less tiresome than compromise.

Date: 1500   Month: January   Time: Evening
"Cretenses semper mendaces, malae bestiae, ventres pigri."
(The Cretians are always liars, evil beasts, slow bellies.)
Titus 1:12

It was on this day that the balance of my life has fallen toward evil, and to death. My soul is no longer pleasing to God. All that is left me is my love for Letitia. It has become a possession I clutch with such desperation I endanger its existence. I curse the Destiny that has chosen to reveal a portion of its plots and schemes to be used in the rule of my life. I have labored to alter its unkind con-clusion. Until this day, I believed my will had accomplished this.

I am a curious tragedy.

I left the Duke's presence to attend the nobility with winter ague and fever. When I returned to our rooms I was comforted to see Letitia preparing philters and nostrums. Furious gusts of wind shook the leaded windows as I went to her. "*Amato*, you have done enough for this day." She dabbed her soiled fingers on her apron and moved to the fireplace. "*Grazie*, Master Vecchio." There was no affection in her voice. I was sorrowed by the fragile, balanced way she moved.

"It will please me greatly were you to address me as Barthel-amo."

"Whilst I wear this vile metal about my parts, I am your servant, not your *amato*."

"You must not despise me for protecting you."

"These monstrosities are for preserving my fidelity. I have given you no cause for doubting me."

"My faith in you is absolute. It is the lechers that abound in this castle that I fear."

We were startled by a sword hilt thudding against our door. I called, "Enter," anticipating the summons of a noble believing himself stricken with a lung disease. A *bravo* pushed open the door. "His Excellency would have words with you."

"Inform my Lord that I am . . ." Borgia strode past the guard. His eyes were narrowed with humor. "Physician, I have need of you." I bowed low. "I delight in your need of me, Sublimity." Borgia placed his hand across his mouth and stared at Letitia. She could not curtsy. She stood with eyes lowered. Borgia turned quickly. His great ermine cape flared as he left the room. I followed him. Four heavily armed *condottieri* were stationed in the corridor, alert for danger.

"Physician, I will use the wench this night."

"The wench, my Lord?"

"Yes, the wench who mixes your potions, who has become your shadow. I have use for her this night. I desire to maim Count Finiguerra."

I could not gasp with the shock that crushed my soul. I looked into the blue eyes that were cold with the pleasure of his plot. I groped for a cunning plan to thwart his intentions, but horror had left me addled. He crossed his powerful arms on his chest.

"The Count sups with Lucrezia and Cardinal Vera. He has seen your wench and desires her. I cannot, in all conscience, deny the good Count his dalliance."

"Is his offense of such a loathsome character that he is beyond your mercy?"

"The filth intends withdrawing his finances and influence. Such action alone is of meager consequence. *Diavolo!* His greater intention is to persuade others to follow his treachery. Were I to deal with him in the usual manner, my revered father would disapprove. The Count is highly favored."

I could not answer him. Were I to tell him that Leititia was not malformed in such a way as to endanger the Count's manhood, his rage would be monumental. He would kill me where I stood and, perhaps on the morrow, remember his oath to protect me. Were I to humble myself before him, confessing my love for Letitia—that we had been lovers in centuries past—he would put me to the stake for sorcery. Yet I could not allow Letitia to be used by another male. My soul screamed from the offense. Count Finiguerra enjoyed applying the lash. There was no end to the screams that resounded from his rooms. His wife dragged about the palace, a pathetic cripple.

"You are silent, Physician. Your silence troubles my amusement."

"What am I to say, my Sublimity? Your method for entertainment, and vengeance, leaves me *affascinato*."

"Fascinated, hah. Wisely spoken. You will prepare the wench with spirits to enliven her appetites. Her imperfection will destroy him in a way that cannot be called my doing."

I bowed with respect though within me I was suddenly aburst with joy. Borgia had provided me with the cunning I could not discover in my own wit. I would not administer an aphrodisiac to my Letitia. *I would drug them both.* While they slept I would use a strap across Letitia's buttocks to produce the evidence of his pleasure. I would then mercilessly injure his manhood. When he awoke—and Borgia would believe he had swooned from his calamity—and raised the castle with his agony, Borgia would know. The Prince would conduct a mock investigation and, in time, Count Finiguerra would become the butt of international humor.

Borgia raised his arm, signaling his guards. They hurried to him and formed a cordon about his royal presence. He leered to me. "You will inform the wench of my wishes. The Count will be in your rooms within the hour." He turned from me and strode down the dark and cold vestibule. The armament of his mercenaries clanked as they shielded him from assassination.

I hastened to our suite. Letitia frowned at me. I loosed the key from the chain about my neck. "Master Vecchio, what did he desire of you?"

I gave her the key. "Free yourself. Borgia has ordered that I allow you to amuse Count Finiguerra." So serious was her astonishment, she could not speak. Our eyes held each other's souls. I knew the hatred she felt. She was chattel, without choice. She knew my anguish. Another man—a plump bag of filth—would contaminate my love. I whispered, "I am not a fool, beloved. You will not be defiled by that scum."

Tears flooded her eyes. I pressed my mouth to each one, kissing the sweetness of her despair.

"You must both drink the wine I shall prepare. It will cause you to sleep. When you both awaken you must express your enthrallment in the mastery of the Count's lovemaking."

"He will surely know."

"He will know only what his vanity informs him. I will leave, that his guards may observe my departure. When sufficient time has passed I will return through the small door to your room. I shall undress each of you. On my sacred oath, beloved, you shall not become the amusement of that scum."

"Borgia has spies everywhere. I am afraid he . . ."

"*Rapidamente!* Attire yourself in your grandest allurements."

She hurried to her room and quickly undressed whilst I prepared the drug. I mixed a philter of water lilies and the syrup of poppies, then some coriander. While I added other ingredients to form the potion I heard Letitia drop the Girdle of Chastity to the floor. I completed the drug and waited until it became a clear, almost indiscernible liquid. Recalling that Count Finiguerra favored an abundance of Sicilian wine, I poured it into a *fiascone* of *fior d'arancio*. The drug disappeared into the pale wine.

Letitia stepped from her room. Her hair was netted with frail silver strands. She wore the gown I had given her—a pale green velvet, brocaded with delicate golden webs. Around her neck was a string of precious seed pearls she had pilfered. I hoped she remained awake long enough to rob the Count. The contour of her figure revealed she wore no undergarments.

I damned Borgia and cursed the Count. Her bosom heaved with her distress. I pointed to the *fiascone*. "Drink from this. The bottle need not be emptied. One glass will be sufficient." I heard the tramp of mailed feet echo through the corridor. I touched her cheek, whispering, "Trust me, beloved. We will hinder doom and turn it to triumph. Trust me." I left her.

Outside I walked more huddled than was required by my deformity. The Count, portly and bearded, hailed me. "Ha, Physician—your charge awaits me, I pray." He laughed and caressed his groin. "As she is *bella*, so will I adorn her with my skills of love."

I thought, *bestia*, as I bowed. "I am honored in contributing to your royal pleasure." He did not detect the sarcasm. He wore a jeweled dagger against the bulge of flesh on his side. The two guards shortened their steps to keep behind his shortlegged waddle. He pinched his mustache and entered our residence. The guards stationed themselves at the door.

It was while I pretended to leave on a serious purpose that I was inconvenienced from my disposition of hatred by a sudden visitation from Bianco. I cursed, *"Diavolo!"* I would not have him within my mind. I would not. I clasped my own head and strained to force him from my inner vision. He would not leave.

I hurried to a dark apse in the wall, concealing myself from curious passers and the chill of the night. To determine the passage of time I stared at a slow burning torch held in a distant wall bracket. I was now grateful for Bianco's appearance in my mind. Observing his life and dealings with the people of his village would prevent me from the torment of envisioning how—before the potency of the drug overcame them—Count Finiguerra was mauling my Letitia with his sensual fervor.

Bianco believed the captive woman had accepted the way they would live. Although his flesh would not cease burning to be upon her, he was eased to know her animal no longer hungered.

She stayed with him while the day burned outside their abode. She left only to walk about the village and ask the people what they wanted the son of the Great Cold Eye to bring them. He would also cure the illnesses that came to them in the darkness.

The days passed. The Great Above darkened and then be-

came fiery, to darken again—his father's Great Cold Eye had
opened to its widest many times. When the fiery time passed to
become darkness again, the people left the village center for their
fires and eating, and he left the abode. Onadyh walked with him at
his side. His speech was not always in her words but there was
pleasure in their saying to each other. The children of the people
looked to her and shook arms and called until she saw them.

The son of the Great Burning Eye now feared him. The spells
and castings he did were now weak. The women who served him
cursed Onadyh. They had killing in their hearts for her. It was
their master making this happen. His animal still hungered to leap
upon her flesh.

She was joyed to lead Bianco to the wide digging in the earth.
She told him how the women sat by the holes and brought their
weavings to be placed in the swimming colors. He had not ever
cared to know this before. He placed her hand into his and guided
her to the ovens where the warriors made their weapons. They
shaped gatherings of earth into a hand. They placed them into the
mouth of the oven. When they were drawn from the fires they
would fit into the long leathers they whirled over their heads.

Bianco's wanting was to become as the elders, without an animal, and not having fear. Sitting near the fire and speaking in a
knowing only elders can have.

Then his sleeping brought a knowing that made him scream
awake in hatred. He saw Onadyh leave the abode to sneak along
the village side to where his enemy waited. The women he had
used in a way that was forbidden him were made to leave. Onadyh
danced before him. On each passing he grasped a covering from
her. When she was without coverings, they leaped upon his mat
and their animals began feeding.

His screaming into wakeness did not disturb her. He looked
upon her and his hatred to kill the son of the Great Burning Eye
changed to a blacking fear. Her skin, so shaking as she walked, now
lay tight. The mounds his mouth pained to taste were greater.
What he thought had given her fullness by many eatings was a
carrying of his enemy.

He sank to the floor and placed his face on the earth and it
became wet from his eyes. The village would shout he made her

full with a carrying. He saw what they would do to Onadyh. Beat upon her with heavy staffs and drive her from the village. She would walk into the land where there was no drinking. When she fell, the great beasts that flew would eat upon her. He could not again save her.

He saw what they would do with him. He beat the floor and shrieked.

She awoke. She went to him. He placed his hand upon her carrying. She said, "If I did not, he would do your death." She placed her hand onto his animal. "You will save me." He sat and rocked as he trembled with knowing what the people would do in his punishment. She moved herself to sit upon him. She drew his long white hair to her mouth and whispered, "I am your woman." She placed his hand where her animal was hidden. Slowly, he became stilled. Before he fled with her and lived without god-ness, he would do the forbidden.

"Bianco, Bianco," I murmured. "You were such a fool."

My eyes ached from staring at the torch to determine the passage of time. I drew my cape tighter about me to ward off the wintery chill. Though I was impatient to do my work with Letitia and the Count, I did not want to leave until I could know what would happen to my troublesome, and now pathetic, Bianco. I could not know the terror he felt for what awaited him—yet I prayed I would never know it for myself. But the torch that was my calculation had burned down. Enough time had passed.

I left the dark apse and entered Letitia's room by the narrow vestibule door. I was without pleasure for what I must do. Maiming the manhood of any mortal caused me repulsion. Better a man be dead than without manhood.

The scent of Letitia's perfumes was a caress to my disposition. The darkness exaggerated her presence. I moved stealthily toward the door that had been left open to my rooms. I heard moanings and sighs. The Count sleeps noisily, I thought.

I moved soundlessly to the broad arras stretched across the entrance to my bedroom. There was the sound of a muffled voice breathing lazy pleasure. I slowly drew the material aside—and I was smashed in soul at seeing the Count moving above the inert nakedness of Letitia. His bulk thudded into her, his black face lacerated her neck and breasts. God, oh my God, I wailed in my depths, and cursed aloud, "Pig, you filth, you pig!" and lunged to him. He drew apart from her, astounded as I gripped his hair, pulling up his head and shattering his mouth before he could cry out. He fell to the floor and quickly rose, holding his face. I was without reason as I pummeled his gross body.

He toppled to the wall and I rushed to him and clutched his neck, choking him in a madness of strength. His eyes bulged and blood smeared his beard and he was able to shake free to fall onto the bed, sprawled across Letitia, enraging me further. I saw the jeweled dagger among his clothes and snatched it from the sheath. He gasped in horror and cried, "Physician, no, I beg you, by God, no!" and I stabbed the blade at his face, plunging it into his neck. He whined and convulsed and I released the hilt. He tore the dagger from his flesh. Blood burst over him. He struggled to rise. I stepped back, knowing he was dead. In a spasm of motion, he fell to the floor and crawled to the door.

I rushed to Letitia. She stared at me but there was no sight in her eyes. I placed my fingers to her lids and closed them. She was innocent. The Count had duped her. In the suspicions of his character, he pretended to drink the drugged wine while she drank fully. "Cara mia," I whispered. "Sleep, my beloved. Awaken without fear. This will be a mystery to Borgia." I drew the sheet over her naked form. The Count lay huddled at the wall, blood still dribbling from his neck. The dagger was in his hand.

I stepped over the bulge of his form and hurried to the wine bottle. I concealed it beneath my cloak and again left by the narrow door in Letitia's room. I felt no sorrow for the Count's death. I was troubled only about how I could explain it.

I was jolted from the painful recollection of Barthelamo and Bianco by Martin Lormer pinching the back of my hand. "Wake up, you damn fool!" he hissed at me. "The jury thinks you're a lunatic." I did not move my hand, though I did look at the jury. Many of them were shaking their heads while they listened to my tape recorded voice and read the confession.

". . . Okay, let's get back to last night's incident. When did you decide to kill Shara Medford?"

"I never *decided* to kill her. It was determined for me. Her intention to destroy me had finally become manifest. I was only protecting myself."

"What made you think she was going to kill you? Did she have a weapon?"

"You've asked those questions before and I have already answered them. I did not want to kill Shara. I loved her. I still love her. But there is an instinct for survival that I had which Barthelamo and Bianco did not seem to have. The instinct for survival transcends reason, and even love. Yet it was more than even that. I was *urged* to kill her by a power, an inhuman entity, that was in me, although it was not, in fact, *me*."

"Now what the hell does that mean?"

"It means exactly that. There is nothing more to say. I confess, in truth and as God is my witness, that I killed Shara Medford and I will sign a statement attesting to that fact. I have now finished my confession and there is nothing more to say but God forgive me."

Only a wordless hum came from the tape recorder. The court clerk put down the copy of the confession he had been reading. I glanced about the courtroom. The silence was like a jelly of thought. People were remembering what I had said. Their faces were soft, their eyes staring ahead, their bodies relaxed. Some jurors were looking at me. I was sad for them. They had to do what God had determined they must not ever do—judge another man. The District Attorney stood up and walked to the tape recorder. He placed his hand on the side and spoke to the jury.

"There it is, ladies and gentlemen. The confession of the defendant. 'I confess, in truth and as God is my witness, that I killed Shara Medford.' He confessed willingly and clearly. 'I confess, in truth and as God is my witness, that I killed Shara Medford!' He killed Shara Medford. Not in the heat of rage, but coldly. Not through impulse, but deliberately. Not by her overt provocation, but for his inner purpose. He killed her in cold blood—in full possession of his faculties—and he has confessed to the crime."

He turned to the judge. "Your honor, the prosecution rests." He walked back to his table and sat down.

The judge looked to Lormer. "Defense counsel, are you prepared to proceed?"

Martin Lormer leaned to me and whispered, "If you have any respect or affection for me, sit there and pray for me." I felt sad, knowing what he meant. That he was afraid. That he was not the same man he was when he began this trial. He walked to the county clerk and said, "I want to borrow your Bible." He stroked the worn black binding.

I wanted to pray for Martin Lormer but there was no feeling of prayer in me because I also wanted him punished. He was opposing the devil while he served him. He placed the Bible under his arm as he moved to where the jury was seated.

"Ladies and gentlemen of the jury, I begin my opening statement in the defense of Stephen Jerod with a *fact*. He did kill Shara Medford. His claim is that he killed her in self-defense. No evidence has thus far been presented to uphold that claim. Therefore, is it a lie, or merely a truth that has not yet been revealed? Here is another *fact*. Not everything about human behavior is completely understood, or has been completely documented. Is there anyone in this courtroom who would not defend himself, or herself, when someone intends to kill him? Of course not. It is instinctual. The defendant, in his confession, has declared that his instinct for survival 'transcends reason and even love.' Here, then, is a puzzling contradiction. You are to judge him on the visible, tangible, and discernible facts. Yet instinct, which is an invisible cause for behavior, *is also a fact*. This, then, ladies and gentlemen, will be your greatest difficulty. You will have to accept that which is invisible. You will have to accept as believable that which is impossible. You will have to approve that which is unbelievable as being that which is possible."

I heard someone say, "Now that's layin' it on the line, only I don't know what he's layin' on the line." I glanced to the jurors and some were frowning. He drew a white handkerchief from his pocket and dabbed it on his forehead.

"We have come to know a great deal about Stephen Jerod. But before a man is to be convicted, or vindicated, of a crime so grave that another person's life is taken, then something must be known about the victim. Who was Shara Medford? What was the character of this woman? We know, from the coroner's report, that she was approximately twenty-three years old. Witnesses have testified that they were present at her twenty-third birthday party. We can accept her age as a *fact*. She was a lovely woman. Far above average intelligence. She appears to have been imaginative, interested in cultural activities, and was gainfully employed by a noted university. But who was the woman known as Shara Medford? Where was she born? She told the defendant that she was born in Philadelphia. Yet her employment application states her birthplace as Stockton, California. One witness for the prosecution, under questioning, informed us that she claimed to have been born in Palm Beach, Florida. Still another declares that her place of birth was Council Grove, a small township in Kansas. These contradictory *facts* fail to offer us suitable information about her background. Who was Shara Medford?"

He paused to drum his fingers on the Bible. He glanced down and slowly shook his head. He hummed thoughtfully, then looked to the jury.

"I find another *fact* to be strange about Shara Medford. Where are her parents, or relatives? We must presume them to be dead, or else they would be here, serving as character witnesses for the prosecution. This trial has been given not only national, but international coverage. Isn't that strange that everyone in her family is dead—or that they do not care to attend this trial? Why are there no photographs of Shara Medford as a child? Testimony has been offered stating that she believed the defendant intended to kill her. Why, then, did she continue living with him? Did the defendant threaten to one day kill her, did the victim imagine that he intended to kill her, or were there deeper motives for her telling people that he intended to kill her? Those motives will be revealed—and proof will be offered to substantiate them."

He paused. There was no sound or movement in the courtroom. I began to feel closed in. I did not like the questions he was asking the jury. Not even I could answer them.

"If Shara Medford was so afraid of being killed by the defendant, why didn't she report her suspicions to the police? The love affair between Shara Medford and the defendant began in a church. Why would a decent, respectable woman solicit the ministrations of a priest when she was not a Catholic? And then consent to having sex with that priest *in the church*. A witness, Bishop Carmondy, testifies that she revealed to him the true source of the defendant's discoveries. Not through reincarnation, but by analysis of ancient artifacts. I believe Bishop Carmondy was telling the truth. Shara Medford did tell him that. In my defense of Stephen Jerod, I will prove that she lied. Why did she lie? Shara Medford consents to having sex with a man—Bruce Mandel—not to please herself or the man, but because she believed that this was what the defendant desired her to do. Can a woman love so deeply that she would fornicate so coldly, merely to please the man she loved? Here are some other *facts* that are most puzzling. There are no records, in any of the states Shara Medford claimed to have been born in, to indicate that she ever went to a doctor or a dentist. There is no record, in any of those states, of her birth.

"Stephen Jerod is a man who lived most of his life trying to disbelieve the reality of reincarnation—even as he was being destroyed by its effects on him. Is reincarnation real? Can it be proven? Ladies and gentlemen, here is a weighty and ironic paradox to consider. I am defending a man who has killed because of reincarnation and I state flatly and unequivocably that *I do not believe in reincarnation*. It is a sequence of vivid impressions and visions imposed on the natural mind of man by the supernatural forces of the devil. Even as I state that, I feel ridiculous. Answer this question yourselves, then. Two jurors left the jury box because they were afraid. What were they afraid of? They were afraid of the devil. Why, then, hasn't anyone questioned their sanity? Great universities and scholarly institutions and foundations support and sponsor investigations of ESP and other parapsychological activity—all of which originate from a dimension that is supernatural. Yet no one damns them as crazy. Then why not accord reincarnation *and what it might cause people to do* the same validity and respect? Can you give credibility to only some of the supernatural?"

I enjoyed his voice. It was unhurried and rhythmical with the calm of logic flowing into the stress of conviction. The jury was listening to a strange tale their minds were gradually transposing into a mystical adventure that pleased them. Only the District Attorney was not entranced. He sat in a casual pose. He was waiting.

"Thus far, the prosecution has presented information and facts about the life and death of Shara Medford. I will do the same. But the information I present, and the *facts* I offer, will not be the same. My investigation into the background of both defendant and victim has been thorough and costly. Each fact, by itself, is believable. But bring these facts together to form *information*, and all becomes incredible. I tell you this, in all honesty. What I have learned stuns me. I am the defense counsel for Stephen Jerod and I cannot understand what I know, nor can I believe what I have learned. But my role is to present this information, and your function is to give it meaning. I tell you this now—although what you learn will be impossible to comprehend, it is genuine fact and the only ground allowed you for disbelief is if you actually deny *fact*."

He drew the Bible from under his arm and slowly stroked the binding. The black plastic cover was dried about the edges. He held it against his thigh.

"Here are some interesting aspects of the mystery you will be required to solve. The prosecution, for whatever reasons they felt acceptable to their consciences, failed to inform this court that lying under the naked body of the victim was a razor blade. Just an ordinary, double-edged razor blade. Why is it important enough to bring to the attention of the court? I'm not really sure at this time. I will, before this trial is over, learn the reason. There is also a journal written by the defendant—a personal record of the two lives from which he claims to have been reincarnated. The prosecution will declare this journal to be a fabrication—the literary dabblings of someone pretending to have lived twice before. I will prove only two facts contained in that journal and the proof of those two facts will authenticate not only the journal, but Stephen Jerod's reincarnation. I now close this statement with one comment that I must make, though it places my entire defense of Stephen Jerod in jeopardy. While all of what I present is absolutely and without a shadow of a doubt true—in order for you to maintain your sanity—*you must not believe it*."

He clapped the Bible against his thigh and held it up, then kissed it. As he walked to our table, people began to applaud. The judge gently tapped her palms together in admiration, then blinked, surprised at herself. She struck the gavel onto the desk top and the applause ceased. She pointed to Martin Lormer, forcing her voice to sound stern. "I will not tolerate any cheap theatrics or flamboyance, Mister Lormer."

He smiled at her. "I accept your admonition and appreciate your indulgence, your honor." He glanced at his wrist watch. "Your honor, although it may seem irregular or unstrategic, the hour is approaching when court would ordinarily recess for the day. I will admit to some fatigue. If it is acceptable with the prosecution, I ask that the court be recessed at this time."

Chapter 9

I am in the cell again and they passed a paper plate of food through the cell-door slot. I placed it onto the floor beside the bed. I will not eat their drugged dinner. I do not need drugs to influence me. What Martin Lormer had said in his opening argument was fixed in my mind. I had loved a woman I did not know through the ordinary facts that comprised a woman's history. I did not recall, clearly, seeing Shara enter the church the first time we met. She had just appeared.

I wanted to believe that she had been sent by the devil who had instructed her, "There's a man, Stephen Jerod, I've been gaming with. I've warped his mind by making him believe he's reincarnated. Now I want to really lay it on hard. Go to his church and meet him. He'll believe you've been reincarnated too—that he knew you before in other lifetimes. Then stand by for additional instructions."

And though I would not believe that to be the reason for our meeting—I wanted to believe it. That explanation would help me feel sane. I was tired of thinking.

The cell was cold. There was a strange ache tightening in my back, keeping me bent over. I moved about the cell, holding my pants from slipping down. I became interested in what former prisoners of the cell had scratched onto the stone walls. The fifteen-watt bulb in the ceiling spread a poor light. I read with my fingertip. "Mom, I'm sorry." I almost laughed aloud when I touched the words, "Nobode dys 4evah." I did not know that serious criminals had a talent for irony.

I heard someone walk into the corridor. It was probably Ernie, the short and white-haired trustee who shambled about in wrinkled prison clothes. The last time I saw him he had winked at me. I did not need strange powers to visualize what was happening outside the cell. The slump-shouldered sheriff's deputy was frowning at him. "Hey, Ernie, what're you doin' down here, now?" I stood against the wall and listened to their chatter.

"I come tuh give the priest a paper tuh read."

"He don' need a newspaper."

"Come on, Jimmy, let'm read on himself. He's front page."

"You passin' him somethin'?"

"Yeah, it's a big Russian tank I'm passin'm. It folds up an' flattens out an' makes believe it's a newspaper."

"Yeah, yeah, okay, piss-ant, give'm it, then split."

"Thanks, Jimmy. Maybe the priest'll make you a novena."

They laughed. The folded newspaper slid through the slot. A hand smacked the cell door. "Hey, Fatha, here's somethin' for you. You got your name on it. I don' think you're jinxed, see."

The newspaper looked like a thick slab of wood lying before the door. Without opening it I knew the headline. "Priest's Attorney Blames Devil!" I shrugged. I did not need psychic powers to know that.

But I had been thinking about my possible madness. If the devil did not exist, then all I had done was of my own doing—and that was the tally sheet of a lunatic.

I began pacing the cell, realizing that I was on the verge of a drastic decision. If I was insane because of the content of my own character, then I must commit suicide. Yes. If I determined that I was an unquestionable lunatic, and committed suicide, God could not hold me responsible. I would not be condemned to an everlasting hell. Only when a human is reasonable, and sane, does God consider him accountable for his life—or his death.

A metal object tapped on the door and the deputy sheriff called to me, "How's the food, Father? Did our chef roast the beef jus' right?" I did not reply. The deputy sheriff grumbled, "Still not talkin', huh, Father?" I heard him walk from the cell door. I smiled. I knew exactly how I would commit suicide.

I would stand against the cell door, facing the opposite wall. I would quickly stuff the drugged food into my mouth and swallow frantically, knowing that it would glut into the wrong channels and begin choking me. Before I could cough it up, I would charge across the cell and, in full force, smash my head against the stone, knocking myself unconscious before I could throw out the food. In unconsciousness, I would quietly choke to death.

I crossed my arms on my chest and hugged myself hard, enjoying my cleverness. Then I was startled when a voice within me said, "You are a fool, Stephen. People kill themselves only because they can't endure their sanity." I shook my head. I would stop this intrusion into my mind by thinking of Shara. My feelings for her were still so intense that not even the devil of my mind could push them aside. I knew that I would enjoy remembering the peace I felt after succeeding in committing partial suicide.

We were going to a party proposed by her friend Althea. This would be the first time we were being social since I wounded myself. Beneath my underwear I wore a packing of ointment-treated bandages held by a slender elastic belt. Except for having to walk slowly, no one could suspect I was injured.

We still slept together but we were not yet lovers again. It would be at least three more months before we could bring our bodies together to become one flesh. The doctor warned me that while I was capable of responding with a full erection, there was danger in losing it as my sensations intensified to the point of ejaculation. There would be pain and a loss of pleasurable sensation as my body intuitively responded to avoid discomfort, by withdrawing from its cause. "You will, in all probability, lose your erection, Mr. Jerod."

Shara was present when he told me this. I did not look at her. The doctor began writing a prescription for tranquilizing pills. "However," he said, "if you can build up a tolerance to that discomfort, you can overcome the—well—the handicap, so to speak, and conduct a fairly normal sex life."

I thanked him for his counsel and did not tell him, or Shara, that I would rather endure a physical pain to which you could acquire a tolerance, than to have the lives of two dead men resurrected in me, trying to persuade me to believe I had once been them.

A month had passed since that drunken and drugged night and I had not had one further experience with Barthelamo or Bianco. Eliminating them from my existence was worth the sacrifice of some of my sexual capabilities. They were gone from me now—

terminati, perfetti, finiti—but my sexual capabilities would be returned. Shara and I were now happy. We were going to a party and I had promised her that I would not drink and that she would be overcome with surprise at how I could exude charm.

There were seven people in the long rectangular studio apartment. I recognized some of Shara's friends. Haitian straw scatter rugs covered the hardwood floor. Lighting was accomplished by long steel rods angled toward the ceiling, creating the feeling of moving below a dense morning cloud. Prints of artworks were framed on the walls. I smiled when I recognized Da Vinci's "Madonna and Child," which Cesare Borgia had once hoped to acquire after he attacked Florence. He had told Barthelamo, "It contains a glory and power all its own. The child Jesus lives in your sight. It will dominate my vault."

Shara introduced me to the young man who hosted the party. I shook his hand and thought him effeminate. Except for another woman—stout and wearing a murky black dress with green fringes like mold—I was the oldest person there. The woman, Mrs. Wildolfsky, wheezed when she breathed. I was annoyed when Shara whispered, "She's a mystic. There'll be some sort of a séance." Althea wore a cowboy shirt and jeans that were absolutely pink and skin tight. With her dark complexion she looked like candy. I was not provoked by the sexuality that blared from her.

I did not join the chatter of conversation and after half an hour Althea turned to the woman, asking, "Are you ready for the séance, Mrs. Wildolfsky?" Her fleshy face shook when she nodded. I said, "I'd like to observe rather than participate." The woman shrugged. They moved to a five-foot circular table with a pure white formica top. I stood behind Shara's chair while the woman set her large glass globe onto the table.

It contained clear liquid and a sediment of white and black granules and was fixed on a curved wooden base. She said, "There is no magic to that which will occur, if the spirits are cooperative. They live beyond our awareness and they possess their own temperaments. They will appear in the images they choose."

Shara turned to me and looked up, whispering, "Isn't this fun, darling?" I nodded, because I had promised to be charming. Althea reached for Shara's hand and caressed the fingers. "It's all a lot of crap, but it's eerie."

The woman held her thick, veiny hands above the globe. Her words droned through wheezes. "The spirits of our affections live in Space and Time and do not adhere to our limitations. Ah, but they can be controlled by our will. Faces, words, images, shall be formed within the glass—they shall appear for those who desire their appearance, fervently, and with extraordinary need."

I did not listen to her pitter-patter. I was slightly happy. I had destroyed the two men who had once lived within me. I had freed myself from a supernatural curse. I was myself, only, and that self was worthy of Shara's love.

"There are secrets in this room," the woman said. "There are vibrations reaching me. Bring them forth and do not fear. What is hidden must be disclosed. Only by seeing those you once have loved will you know the truth. Someone here is terribly troubled."

Her chubby face had become elongated. Marsha Jenner giggled. Althea whispered cutely to Shara, "How's 'bout choo, honey chile? Youse got you sum black folk in yo pass, huh?" Shara smiled. The woman began swaying her hands far above the globe and the granules at the bottom stirred, their tendrils flaring up. Someone said, "Look, they moved, and without her touching it."

The woman continued swaying her hands and the white and black particles roiled and shifted. "There is a force present among us. I feel it. A troubled soul now present yearns to view someone long dead. The desire is concealed in trepidation. The spirits know your hidden desires. The spirits know that which you will not reveal to yourself."

Her voice was a slow drone, gritty with vibrato. The people glanced at each other and quickly looked back to the globe. A clump of granules suddenly burst upward and sprayed along the curved contours. I waited. Perhaps Shara was calling someone from the past to appear now. Her dead parents—a sister or brother, perhaps. The flecks began to group and edge into an appearance while suspended in the liquid. It became a blurred sculpture gradually defining itself. The woman intoned . . .

"We are friendly to your presence—we welcome you into our midst—how kind of you to bring yourself into our places—we are ever so grateful—would you now turn to the dear soul who called you before us."

It was a face, slightly warped but distinguishable. The black flecks settled into lines and shadings that emphasized the clotting white grains, casting it into specific features. It was ghostly as it slowly turned and stopped before Shara. She shifted back, startled, while the others gawked their amazement. "Who is it, Shara?" someone asked, and Althea whispered, "Is it some lover you never told me about?" Then, in a minute motion, the gritty apparition edged upward and the dark hollow eyes and lean mouth seemed to study me and oh God, oh dear, merciful God, it was the face of Barthelamo.

I gripped the back of Shara's chair and closed my eyes and stood rigid while they tried to guess the identity, and someone said, "It's moving again! It's starting to change again," and I would not open my eyes until the image of Barthelamo was gone from me. I felt Shara's hand touch mine and she asked, "Are you all right, darling?" I did not answer and Althea said, "Doesn't that blow your mind. Another face. I don't believe it," and I opened my eyes and did not have to look to know it was the face of Bianco.

I suddenly shoved Shara aside and shouted, "No more! I don't want to see them!" and I grabbed the glass ball and flung it against the wall. Someone screamed while I rushed to the shattered globe and stamped on the pieces, crushing them and grinding the granules under my shoes to be sure they could not form again, and someone grabbed my arm, pulling me back as the mystic woman said, "Do not be afraid of him. This happens sometimes. We all have dark secrets." Althea snickered, "Look at what that crazy bastard did to the wall!" while I kept grinding the black and white particles into the wicker rug. I heard Althea tell Shara, "The smartest thing you can do is leave him. He's dangerous."

I began crying and I looked at Shara, pleading, "Help me, please help me." She cringed back and her eyes were wet with tears as she whispered, "What else can I do? I've done all I can do."

The chilled air in the jail cell made me shiver. I felt vicious to myself. I began pacing the cell to keep warm. My shoe brushed against the newspaper by the door. My picture would be on the front page, of course. On the editorial page there would be a hastily written commentary concerning my sanity. Articles by reincarnationists would speculate about my character. There would also be "Letters to the Editor" calling me slanderous names; other letters would support what they believed was my legal or moral right to kill Shara—there would also be a complaint from a local minister appealing to the public to know that vengeance was not in the province of the courts, but in the judgment of God.

Angrily, I kicked the newspaper aside. I turned my back to the flair of opened pages. I was being destroyed daily, and no one knew it. Those nights I wanted to make love to Shara—willingly causing myself sexual pain to give her gratification—were refused. "I don't want you to hurt yourself, darling," she would say.

"I don't care about the pain. You have needs."

"I'm in no hurry. Perhaps in a little while the pain will be reduced."

"I'll never be able to build up a tolerance to the pain unless I begin experiencing it."

"Be patient with yourself, darling. There's plenty of time."

"We can't live like this, Shara, sexless, amiable companions."

"If you won't wait a little while longer for your own sake, Stephen, then for my sake, wait a little longer. I can't stand to know you're in pain. Let me adjust to it."

Her consideration became my anger, my suspicion. She was using my pain as a pretense for refusing me. She was giving herself a cause for leaving me. But I would not let my anger become noticeable. We would lie in bed, reading and talking. I recall one conversation which, even now, I cannot really understand. I had asked her, "Shara, did you ever think of committing suicide?" She put down the book she was reading and stared up at the ceiling.

"No, not really. It always seemed to me that suicide was bad for your health."

"Be serious, Shara. Didn't you ever consider it? Even fleetingly?"

"No. Suicide holds no meaning for me. I cannot commit suicide. It would do me no good, and only make matters worse."

"What does that mean?"

"I'm not sure I can explain it to you, Stephen. But one day it will all be clear to you."

"You're being very abstract and mysterious."

"I suppose I do sound that way. There's a famous quotation from Shakespeare. 'There are more things in heaven and earth, than are dreamt of in your philosophy.' "

"That sounds impressive, but I'll take my quotations from the Bible. It covers a greater range of human behavior."

We kissed in a gentle way and she turned to her side and began reading again. I thought about what she had said, and because I did not understand it, I knew it was important. I promised myself to memorize the conversation and then analyze it. Because I knew that unknowingly she was hurting me, I began to think of how Barthelamo too believed that, unknowingly, Letitia was hurting him.

Borgia had gone to the Count's suite, expecting to find the noble in pain and horror for what using Letitia had caused in his privates. The Contessa Finiguerra, a woman who limped and carried a paralyzed arm at her side, informed the Duke that "My husband is elsewhere. Throwing the dice, or wenching, no doubt." Borgia hastened to Barthelamo's rooms, exhilarated with anticipation for the grotesque condition imposed upon the Count. The guards, still stationed at the door, stepped aside to allow him passage. When he found the Count dead on the floor and Letitia in a senseless drugged state, his rage was beyond control.

He smashed vases and ripped tapestries, gutted sofas and beds with his blade. He beat the guards with fists and roared curses at the dead body while he kicked its bulk. Borgia's *bravi* charged in and the two guards were struck with sword hilts and staves and dragged unconscious to the dungeons, where they would be tortured until they revealed who had rewarded them for entry into the rooms where the Count was fornicating. Oil would be poured on their heads, and ignited—sulphur spread under their armpits and burned—their feet would be put into thumbscrews and the mechanism tightened until blood burst from their toes.

Borgia had Barthelamo summoned. He went directly to Letitia and performed an examination of her skin, then her breathing.
He wet his fingertip and placed it on her lips, then tasted the
impression. "Drugged, my Lord," he said. "She was given a sleeping potion."

Borgia scowled down at the dead Count. "Why drug a willing
wench?"

Barthelamo shrugged. "It is easier to impose violence upon
the sleeping. I have prescribed for the Contessa on those times the
Count would use her for his brutal whim." Three *bravi* were
called and they carried the Count from the bedroom.

Suddenly, a spasm of rage overtook Borgia and he dragged
Letitia from the bed and flung her naked to the floor. Barthelamo
made himself remain without expression while Borgia kicked her,
demanding that she awaken. "Bitch! Who did this vile atrocity?"
he roared at her unconscious form. "When this is voiced to Rome,
my father will disown me!" Barthelamo restrained himself from
grabbing a soldier's blade to decapitate Borgia. "Revive the
wench," he bellowed. "Revive her that I may kill her again, till she
tell me the truth."

Barthelamo forced a medicine into her throat until she
coughed. He told Borgia that she would awaken in one hour. Borgia left the rooms to begin a rampage of investigations to find the
assassin. "This is a calamity, Physician. A calamity of monstrous
proportions!"

Count Finiguerra's presence in Borgia's court was an assur-
ance of three thousand foot soldiers, five hundred squads of arbal-
esters—enough to ring a city and flood the skies with crossbow
bolts—and an endless train of wagons carrying armor and pikes
and long swords tempered in the German furnaces. These addi-
tions to Borgia's army were vital when he renewed his attack on
Faenza.

The Pope, in his efforts to bring all Italian cities under the
domain of the Papacy, had entered into an expedient alliance with
Germany. Count Finiguerra, whose family line extended beyond
the time of the first Holy Crusade and whose estates were equal
almost to a monarch's, had served as envoy for the Pope. He was
introduced to Borgia's court for entertainment to overcome the

rigors of negotiation. His stature in the Pope's favor had caused him to believe his value to be greater than the Duke's. Foolishly, he had boasted to Lucrezia Borgia and Cardinal Vera that not only might he withdraw his finances and influence from Borgia's military thrust through Italy, but he contemplated a campaign to persuade others to do the same.

Hastily, Borgia had informed his father of the Count's aggressive attitudes. The Pope responded through his fleetest courier. "Be clever, my beloved son. He is no champion, he is but a challenge. Bring no aspersion to the house of Borgia or cause impediment to our interests." The Duke's method for chastisement had become a military and political disaster.

Barthelamo comprehended the inconvenience his crime had caused Borgia, and Pope Alexander. The ruling houses of Germany would forward their statements of censure to the Holy Church and all secret agreements would be nullified.

To recoup the funds he would lose through the death of Count Finiguerra, the Pope would have to antagonize carefully established alliances by confiscating the estates of recently deceased Cardinals. He would begin an "open offering" of Papal offices to be purchased by the nobility. A cardinalate usually brought 10,000 ducats. He would retract strategically pronounced excommunications by allowing the penitents to pay for their return to God's affections. Justifications for divorce would have to be created to sanction marital disruptions in the houses of the aristocracy. The Pope would now have to consent to an annulment between King Ladislaus of Hungary and Beatrice of Naples, at the probable fee of 30,000 ducats. But first the Pope would reveal his holy disfavor to his son, Cesare, by withdrawing his influence from Borgia's realm, until the Count's assassination was avenged and the affair turned to a gain for the Papacy.

Barthelamo was not afraid when Borgia began his inquiry with, "Physician Vecchio, what is your lineage—your past?" He stood before the Prince in an attitude of such innocence that he responded with mild indignation.

"Have I fallen into the range of your suspicions, my Lord?" When Borgia did not answer, he shrugged. "My lineage is obscure.

I am the spawn of a vague citizenry. My past, until my service to you, was most common. Without alliance or affiliation."

Borgia gazed at the ring he had given Barthelamo. He was remembering the day when Barthelamo pulled a crossbow bolt from his chest, rescuing him from death. "Had you known the Count previous to my mention of him?"

"Only in passing. I entered his rooms to minister to the Contessa. Beyond that, nothing. My Lord, I would ask you this. Can you find without your knowledge of me, any profit or gain, or pleasure brought me by this murder?"

"None, Physician, none. Yet I am troubled by the quality of your innocence. It is so unsoiled. I have found that such purity is always a contrivance concealing a beastial nature."

The deformity on Barthelamo's shoulder began to rasp and itch. He did not fear Borgia's suspicions. He feared Letitia's character as a woman, and the Duke's whim. He decided upon boldness. He bowed low and smiled.

"My Sublimity, I ask that you use me as you are using others in your quest of the truth. Put me to the rack, the thumbscrew, place me into your spiked cylinder and roll me down a steep hill—I ask this of you. I cannot serve you believing I am an object of distrust."

"Enough, Physician. You prattle like a hag. You do not enter into the realm of my reasoning. Assassination is done for gain of place and profit, of which you have no interest. *Vendetta* is the mother of murder and you are without family, or cause. The bloodthirsty and demented kill for the joy of it—you are not one of them. Your life serves me too well to misuse it. Tell me about the wench who serves you. What is her character?"

"She is simple. Her pleasure is in finery and decoration. She is without political interest. Because she does not think, she has become useful. She is dutiful to my needs and is most obedient. Her great skill is in remaining unnoticed."

"What is her sympathy to my cause?"

"Her loyalty and devotion to your house is unquestionable. She reverences her great prince, Borgia. When she learned you would not use her because of her malformity, she was inconsolable nigh unto death. If she possesses any interest contrary to your pleasure, it is her great penchant for kitchen gossip."

"Yes, yes, I cannot myself contend with the likelihood of her involvement. I will give her to Lucrezia to deal with. The castle must know there is none who will avoid my scrutiny until the assassin is found."

Letitia was taken to Lucrezia Borgia, who had her flogged. When Borgia saw Letitia's bloody back and deeply welted buttocks, he believed her cries of innocence and released her into Lucrezia's service, telling Barthelamo, "My beloved sister will care for your wench. She will be returned to you when I have unearthed the assassin."

He had treated Letitia's wounds and assured her there would be no scars. He would have said, "When we are together again, I shall kiss each place and that will hasten the healing," but Lucrezia was nearby watching. Her blue eyes were hardened with hatred. His method for eliminating the burden of an obscure *bravo's* child so she could marry into the Este line had been too debasing for her. He had caused her to beg him, a commoner, and still he had not ceased the abuse. Her pride would not allow her to forget that he had seen her debased. Though he had tried pleasantry and even servility with her, Lucrezia's hatred would not be eased. She had threatened to ruin him and she was honor-bound by the tenets of her nobility to fulfill that threat.

Borgia's temperament veered from exhilarated rages in which he struck and cuffed anyone whose attendance to his presence was not perfect, to depressions so gloomed with despair he would not speak. His investigations were gradually becoming fruitless punishments.

Date: 1500   Month: February   Time: Evening
"Ne glorieris in crastinum, ignorans quid superventura pariat dies."
(Boast not thyself of tomorrow; for thou knowest not what a day may bring forth.)
Prov. 27:1

Seven hundred French lances had already departed from his

army, taking with them the costly wooden saddles he had given them as inducements. Squads of crossbowmen had deserted. The skies roiled with dark clouds and thundered with inclement weather. Borgia's ambitions to conquer Florence and Venice were becoming as idle as the snow-covered cannons rusting in the fields. His father would allow him no peace. Couriers arrived daily at the castle, their pouches bulging with messages of complaint and threat. I sorely missed the presence of Letitia in my rooms. My sensations were barren, my moods as foul as Borgia's. This pleased him. Anger cannot tolerate the proximity of cheer.

I became anxious for Borgia to settle the crime in his inimitable cunning. I had been without my Letitia for too long. My nights had become dark and becrawled with creatures that mock and terrify. Love had released new passions in me. Without this love, they had become tormenting lusts—and unrequited lusts oozed into suspicions. Whilst I sought Letitia she appeared to avoid me. Her garments were now costly, her manner most aristocratic. She had become anxious in her eagerness for finery and Borgia's diabolic sister was glutting her with adornment. I feared Lucrezia, who, when not dallying with lascivious men, was a most beguiling and intelligent woman. Though her station in the house of Borgia demanded that she be discreet, the nearness of her marriage to the house of Este was causing her womanhood an unbridled craving. I did not want her to influence Letitia. Were I to learn that Letitia was being trifled with, I knew that I would kill again.

As the days passed, my vexation increased. Destiny had arranged that I meet with Letitia and that we should love. We were now, what we had been to each other in other times, in other lives. I did not believe that we were Bianco and Onadyh reappearing in other forms, in another place. No. They were our sources, our causations. Were I able to know and understand all the other lives and the events occurring in that interim between Bianco and Onadyh and Letitia and myself, I would then know where our escape from doom could be found. But Destiny had left that depth of Time blank, and I was afraid. I did not know Letitia's loyalty to me. She had never confessed her love.

One afternoon I chanced upon Letitia in a corridor. We

skulked to a dark vestibule. Though she seemed troubled, I spoke in endearments and we were able to touch. I gave her the gift of a ruby necklace a *contessa* had presented to me for alleviating a foul rash from between her thighs. Letitia blessed me for my attentions and I asked, "Does Lucrezia press you with questions on the Count?"

Her eyes deepened with fear. "Daily, Master Vecchio. I have been clever thus far. But she has begun to listen to my sleep. Does the Duke suspect me?"

I stroked her cheek and whispered, "If he does, it will not continue. It is time for me to dismiss his suspicions."

Her fingers became frightened talons on my wrist. "You reach too high. You cannot control the Duke. He cannot be controlled."

I kissed the fingers till they softened. "Does Lucrezia speak against me?"

The fingers again became harsh. "She is more to be feared than the Prince. I heard her tell him it was you. Was it, Master Vecchio? Are you the assassin?"

I put her hand upon my hump to know if she would withdraw it in repulsion. She caressed the contours and the folds. "Be at peace, beloved. The true villain will be found. We will be together again."

We parted, and I was overjoyed for her reliance upon me. With trust there is the certainty of love.

When a fortnight had passed since the murder of the Count, I was called to Borgia's rooms to administer a sedative. He sat in his great chair designed to appear as a throne. He had before him a parchment containing the names of those he believed would profit from the Count's murder. The purple plume in his velvet cap wagged at the chandelier as he shook his head, grimly bewildered. "There is no one who cannot account for himself at the time of the atrocity. Each one on this list is crucial to my cause." He was speaking to himself. There was darkness within the rage narrowing his eyes. "What have I overlooked? Who is it that makes a fool of Borgia?" He drank the sedative and angrily flung the golden goblet across the room.

"Who could have done this crime, and why? My father has given me an ultimatum. Find the assassin or suffer a loss of his support. He holds in waiting another commander, General Vitoria Fracassini, whom he believes can do what his bastard son cannot. Physician, delve into your store of mysteries and learn the cause of this offense to my interests."

My impulse was to deny that I understood mysteries. But contradiction to his thoughts was not now suitable. I had begun to perceive a corruption in his character. His fear was not of men, but of disaster to his ambitions. His hunger for power had deprived his boldness of its cunning. He was doubting his Destiny. In this weakness of soul I believed he could be manipulated. He stroked the ornate scabbard resting on his long muscular thigh. I stepped to him and stood in respectful courtesy.

"To satisfy the discontent of the Pope is all. My beloved Lord, finding the true assassin is not as necessary as persuading your illustrious father that the assassin has truly been found."

"You are requiring that I send an innocent to his death?"

"Has not my Lord often remarked that there are those born with the gift of innocence that they may serve those who command the eye of history?"

"Physician, you remember too well. Yet I find the thought intriguing, *incantatore*. Who is there in my court who can serve such a glorious purpose? There is not a noble who is not indispensable for my cause."

"When the entire body is in danger from the infection of a limb, it is expedient to remove that limb. Painful though the sacrifice may be."

I understood my words were thoughts he had long ago considered. My attempt was to distract him from the murmurings and rumors of Lucrezia. When Lucrezia was married and out of his presence, she would no longer remember the deformed Physician she had sworn to cause harm. Borgia touched his cheek and appeared pensive.

"I am wearied with thought, Physician. Create this assassin for me—that I might find him quickly."

"He must be one without exceptional lineage, my Sublimity.

Yet not so lowly that his rank be ignoble. A personage of sufficient use, though your cause not be placed in jeopardy by his absence. Whose loyalty is unquestioned—that others will be convinced of your devotion to honor. Someone who's zeal in your behalf has caused dissent in others less zealous. His loss must be felt, though not inordinately missed. He must also be known to have found your favor and thus his betrayal of you will be judged as an indication of his secret ambitions. His sacrifice must also serve to issue warning to others who might betray you."

He smiled and plucked his lips. "Your reasoning is *estatico*. The difficulty is in finding such a one as you have described. He is a jewel among the excrement which surrounds me."

He breathed as one tasting a savory aroma. "I am so weary of clever plans, of *l'intrigare*. I am a simple man, desiring only love." How simple it would be to slit the beast's throat, I thought. He then spoke as though in lament. "Solitude, Physician, I require solitude."

I bowed. "Your Excellence," I said, and silently left his presence. I stood outside, pressed against the door, listening. I heard him leap up and laugh and begin his thoughtful pacing.

I was suddenly afraid.

I touched the ring he had given me—the binder for his oath to protect me. "*Create this assassin for me—that I might find him quickly,*" he had requested. "*Dio mio,*" I moaned. Hurried cunning is the wit of a fool. In describing the perfect assassin for him, I had cunningly created myself.

"Hey, Father—Father Jerod, you in a trance or somethin'? I asked if you want seconds on the food."

I had to shake my head to become aware that I was in a jail cell and not in the cold corridor of a castle. I looked at the paper plate of food I was hungry. The deputy sheriff put his face at the four bars on the door and looked in. He frowned. "Hey, Father, how come you're not eatin'?"

I walked to the opposite wall. I could not tell him that a man cannot determine if he is sane or a lunatic when he is drugged.

The deputy called to his associate, "The priest's not eatin'. Should I take the food out?" I smiled at the answer. "If he don't eat, he don't eat. You gonna go in there an' shove it down his throat?"

I pressed my back to the wall and closed my eyes. If I could be certain that Martin Lormer would lose this trial and the court would sentence me to death, I would eat the food just to be in a tranquil coma until the time of my execution. "Don't be such a worrier—such a hysteric," a voice in my mind said, and I calmly thought, Lord, Lord, here he is again—and of course that must mean I am insane, else why would I be hearing that voice, and believing it was the devil chatting with me.

It was more rewarding to be insane, more interesting—than to be just a normal bore.

Bianco, Bianco, what were you doing while Barthelamo was beginning to fear for his life? Beloved Bianco, poor sad Bianco. White as unsipped milk and odd as a square moon. You are being driven mad with hate and love, aren't you? She is pregnant by another god/man and she told you it was forced upon her—that she fornicated with him to save your life. Bianco, dear Bianco, if you believe her then no man deserves so magnificent a love. If she is lying, the deceit is enough to make you want to kill.

Bianco had not panicked when he knew Onadyh was pregnant. He thought only of their survival. He was patient when he explained why they must now leave his people. When it was learned that she had been to a god/man as other women were to other men, the Elders would call the village women into a screaming crowd and they would beat her with thick staffs until she was without life. If they allowed the carrying within her body to be born, it would be a fierce monster who would bring great wrong to their people. Then the warriors would drag the god/man from the abode and lay him upon the earth that never saw water. They would tear the hair from his eyes so he could not close them. They would push the crawling creatures into his body and while the Great Burning Eye flamed him into death, the crawling creatures would eat all the evil from him.

Onadyh would not believe that this would happen. She knew only the ways of her own people.

In the village where she was taken from, carrying a gift from the Life-god was her honor. When she missed the time of her blood, the entire village brought her gifts and the women of the Elders began their ritual to the Life-god. They knelt before the stone and sang to the Life-god to inform him of their joy.

Bianco tried to make her know that this people also honored a woman who was carrying a gift of the Life-god. But she was not a woman of this village, and she had become the god/daughter of the Little Fires that fly in the dark. To do as other women did with their men was to lose her god-ness. If the people believed he had caused her to be carrying, he would lose his god-ness. The loss of god-ness brought punishment.

When Onadyh would not believe him, he beat her about the shoulders and legs. She would not submit to his fury. She mocked him. Why did he not punish the son of the Great Burning Eye for making her carry? While he beat her again he told her he would punish his enemy before they left the village. He put on a cloth garment that covered all parts of his white skin and head and brought her to a part of the village concealed behind the great stone temple. His purpose was to reveal how this people used women who did not obey the ways of their Elders.

She saw four naked women bound to thick wooden posts. Their heads were covered with hoods on which were woven the figures of coiled snakes—the Death-children. Their flesh was mottled with long black scabs and puckered with deep lacerations. They were completely soiled with drying blood. Insects crawled over their skin. Onadyh cringed back in horror and fear.

These were the women who had brought their flesh to the animals of men who belonged to other women. Their punishment was to be roped to the posts while the offended women beat them with a thin, pliable staff. The punishment was finished when the offended woman could no longer raise the staff. Many women were beaten until they were bloodied to death. If they did not die when the offended woman was unable to lift the whipping staff, they were made to stand bound to the post until their blood dried. The man whose animal was fed by the women went without punishment.

"Your people are not this people," Bianco told her, and she understood his fear and agreed to leave the village before it was known that she was carrying. "Where are we to go?" she asked. He told her he must first look upon the Story-Stone on which the ways of the All-god were shown. "I will know from his telling."

He brought pieces of cloth and showed her how to bind them into another garment that covered his skin so it could not be touched by the Great Burning Eye. He made her do this because it was the way of his people to have the son of the Great Cold Eye hang his garment outside his abode. The people then knew he had not gone to his father, leaving them unprotected. While the garment was before his abode, it was wrong for the village people to enter.

At night, when only the sounds of sleeping sang through the village, he entered the Temple and stood before the great Story-Stone and gazed upon the doing of the All-god. The large, precisely carved stone was sectioned into squares depicting the beginnings of this people. Each frame had a long finger at the top, pointing into the square and showing how the All-god had created them—guided their lives. Nightly, he knelt before the Story-Stone and asked to be shown which direction he should travel when they fled the village. The All-god did not speak, though his sight was always moved to stare at one square. It was the carving of the first village woman the All-god made. She was unclothed. Her front bulged and both carvings of her sides were swollen with a carrying. Bianco knew this to mean that he should allow Onadyh to decide his direction.

"We will go to my people," she told him. Though they would have to cross the great burning land which the All-god never watered, she believed she could find the place of her people. He asked if he would be the son of a god to her people. She had laughed. "They have never seen one like you."

They left their abode when the great Above was dark and walked about the village. They entered into the households where they were asked to do a ritual for curing a sickness that came during the dark. Onadyh stood beside Bianco and sang and smiled at the people. She knew that soon her body would swell and her tallness would make her bend. She was not afraid. The son of the Great Cold Eye would save her again. He would bring her to her people. When they saw him, they would give her honor. She did not know what the Priestess of her people would do when she saw this man who was not a warrior and not a worker, who did not have color in him as other men had. No one had ever captured someone like this strange god.

Bianco did not tell her of his hatred for the son of the Great Burning Eye. The hatred was a fiery hurt that was always in him. While Onadyh fashioned the cloth of his other garment, he began weaving a small basket which he would use for the death of his enemy. He knew the other god was always watching them. He was waiting for her carrying to become large and then he would cause the people to bring their killing. Bianco let himself be watched. He sat on the floor and rocked as he weaved one strand of wicker through other strands. He worked, knowing his enemy would tire of watching them.

When he finished weaving the basket he fashioned a cloven stick with a pull string. He dressed in the cloth garment Onadyh had bound for him. He told her that he would soon return. He began sneaking to the Temple, hugging the basket and stick to his side. The night air was cool. He looked up and saw the cold eye of his father watching him. He hurried up the long stretch of Temple steps and became a whisper passing the two guards sleeping at the entrance.

He moved through the long, shifting corridors. Torches burned from the walls, lighting his way. Grit from the stone overhead dropped onto his hair. The abode of each god had a wide, circular disc over the entrance. Their history and power was etched on the surface. The picture of the god was always fixed on the surface. The picture of the god was always shown with green and red jewels. He went into the room where the Death-god's children were asleep in a stone well-pit. He stared at the long slick bodies wound into separate coils. The red and black markings on their skins told the tale of the deaths they had done.

Carefully, he prodded the cloven stick into the Death-child closest to the edge. It flicked open its eyes and stirred. He fitted the string loop over its blunt head and pulled it quickly before it could snap the death bite at his face. It writhed and sounded its anger for being caught. He picked it from the pit and dropped the slithering length into the basket. He smiled.

He moved through the shadows so silently that the animals

who ate the village throwings remained asleep on the ground. When he reached the abode where his enemy lived, he edged aside the painted cloth draped before the entry. He listened to the harsh noise of the other god's sleep. He stepped in and moved past the woman who served and placed the basket near the son of the Great Burning Eye's side. He poked open the basket lid and quickly looped the Death-child's neck and raised it to gently ease it under the cloth warming his enemy's naked body. Soundlessly, he moved to the abode entrance and carefully flung the basket at the other god's face, causing him to jerk awake. When he screamed a pain and leaped from the sleeping mat and began trying to tear the Death-child's teeth from his flesh, Bianco raced from the abode before the village awoke.

He went to Onadyh and shook her. "The other god will die." She was startled and urged him to reveal how this would happen. He did not speak. It was not the way of this people for the men to tell the women their doings. He went to his mat. He knew there was rage in her heart for not avenging her. Before he died, he would speak the secret. She went to her mat and lay down.

Softly, he told her that they would leave the village when the people brought the body of the son of the Great Burning Eye to the Temple to clothe him in his god-ness garments. He was the son of the Great Cold Eye and could not enter the Temple while the Great Burning Eye watched them prepare his son to be taken into the room he would never leave.

I stood in the center of the jail cell and stretched. The ache drained from my body and I sighed. I wondered how Barthelamo felt when he had witnessed the killing Bianco had accomplished. Was he grieved to know he had been spawned from a heritage of murder? Did he admire Bianco for the caliber of his savage honor, the integrity of his love?

I strode to the bed and bent over the plate of drugged food, wanting to grab handfuls and shove it into my mouth, jam it down my throat until I could not breathe, then lunge at the wall and bash in my head.

I touched the cold mashed potatoes. They were like the bleached excrement of a dying animal. I wiped my fingertip on my pants and shrugged. There were moments when I did not love Shara. Not when she had begun inching out of my life and moving to destroy me.

I did not love her when she lay in bed, staring at the dark ceiling, stubbornly denying that she did not want sex enough to cause me the pain I would undergo to please her. And when she asked me, "Why did you do such a terrible thing to yourself, Stephen?" and I would not tell her, I knew she was crying though I could see no tears. "Stephen, darling," she had whispered. "Why don't you let yourself be helped?"

"I don't want to talk about it."

"A man doesn't do that to himself unless he has a serious problem. Why not let Althea Jackson find someone who . . ."

"I can't stand that bitch! And I don't need any damn psychiatrist. What will he do for me? Niggle into my past with stupid questions that lead to moronic symbols and idiotic assumptions? I won't explain why I did it, but I did have my reasons. And they were not neurotic."

"How can you say that and believe it? When a man tries to emasculate himself, he is either neurotic or he's—he's *seriously* neurotic."

"But you wanted to say, he's *crazy*, didn't you?"

She had shifted on the bed, lying near the edge. Her body was tense. I could feel no warmth coming from her. I did not move.

"You know something, Stephen—I'm afraid of you."

"Don't be ridiculous. You don't mean that. I know you don't mean that."

"I'm being very honest and truthful. I am afraid of you."

"In what way are you afraid of me?"

"I'm afraid that you are going to kill me."

I laughed and rolled onto my side to hug against her. I placed my mouth to her neck and chuckled softly. "Rather than abuse one of your fingernails, I would rather amputate my arm."

She edged away. Her voice was toneless, resigned. "You will try to kill me, Stephen, I know you will."

I became annoyed. I sensed an evil intention. "You're talking like a fool."

She sat up, covering her breasts with the sheet. "If you try to kill me, I'll understand."

"What the hell are you talking about?"

"I have become a threat to you. You have made me into some unobtainable goal and because you don't feel up to conquering me, you will want to kill me."

"Shara, darling, you sound positively moronic. You're spouting off like some freshman from a psychology class. You must be getting such nonsense from that bitch, Althea."

"Don't be angry with me, Stephen. I have the feeling you think I'm not like other women—that there are depths, or meanings, in my life that are not usual."

I felt small pushes of hatred for her then. She was convincing me of what I had zealously refused to accept. That we were reincarnated people.

Althea Jackson, that super-sexed, lascivious black bitch was causing this to be provoked in Shara.

Perhaps Althea Jackson was a reincarnation of Lucrezia Borgia who had caused such a vile influence over Letitia.

I put my hand on her shoulder and squeezed her hard to make her aware of my controlled rage. God, how I wanted her then. How I craved to have her body flushed and throbbing below the fierce and passionate ramming of my body. But I was afraid of the pain.

"Shara, listen to me. Don't ever think of leaving me. If you believe that I intend killing you, get that foolishness out of your mind. If you think that what I did to myself was insane, then imagine what would happen in my head if you start acting as though you'll leave me. If you love me—and I know you love me—don't consider leaving me, I mean that."

She stiffened and lay as though not breathing. I released her shoulder and I wondered, then, if she had become involved with another man who was pressing her to leave me. No. That was not in her history.

Admitting that she had a history in her genes—a history of behavior brought forward from the lives of two other women—was openly admitting that she was reincarnated.

Then I grinned and was pleased that she could not see my grin in the dark. I was not like Barthelamo or Bianco. They had killed for her. If Shara ever packed her belongings to leave me for the love of another man, I would most certainly kill her.

I wanted to sleep.

I looked to the barred window. There were no stars or moon in the sky. I recalled a line from "The Ballad of Reading Goal," "That little patch of blue that prisoners call a sky," and smiled, and then I heard the voice in my mind say, "Aren't you tired of all this self-pity? When will you give up your need to be insane?" I blinked, almost speaking aloud in surprise. I flattened my hands over my ears and shook my head to shut the sound from my mind. But the voice was inside my mind.

It had to be my own inner voice trying to stop me from believing I was insane. To stop me from killing myself.

But for every logical lie you tell yourself there is a more logical truth to deny it. It was not my own inner voice and I was not afraid to know it was the voice of satan. My fear came from realizing that satan had befriended me.

Why?

What did that diabolical son of a bitch want from me?

I heard something sharp click on the cell door. The deputy sheriff called in, "You eat your food yet, Father?" I remained still, waiting. I heard him call down the corridor, "He still ain't eatin'." He looked inside the cell. "If you're not goin'ta eat the food, Father, how's about passin' over the plate?" I could see that his eyes, squinted under slim brows, were pale green. We stared at each other. Look into my soul, my son. Cans't thou see I am troubled by the devil. Good must triumph. He winked at me. "You do your own thing in there, Father. We got all the time in the world." His face left the square cut out in the cell door.

I grinned. I understood what was happening to me.

The longer I remained in the cell, the stupider I became. I was not insane. And believing that I might be insane was stupid.

I stared at the newspaper and nodded. I was certain that somewhere on the pages there was a statement, made by an authority in the field of psychiatry, stating that I was obviously insane. The devil had prompted the inmate to bring me the newspaper. The devil wanted me to destroy my life and lose the great value that would be given to other people if the state destroyed me. The devil did not want people to believe that he was real. He corrupted through deception, subterfuge, confusion.

I stood and nodded until my neck ached.

When satan plunged his hands into our minds and played patty-cake with its substances, he could shape it into any of the kinky and weird devices he used to dominate our lives. Telepathy, clairvoyance, conditionability, external disinhibitory stimuli, levitation—all of the cutey-pie gimmicks contained in the pandora's box possessed by the psychic sciences. If I could believe in reincarnation then it was not fantastic—and I was not insane—to believe that satan was using my mind for his demonic purposes.

In time, I would become the splendid example of what happens to a man when he allows himself to believe in reincarnation. He will eventually become insane and, if he is not locked away in time, he will kill.

Blessedly, the state would kill me before I became insane—unhappily, I had already killed.

I intertwined my fingers and squeezed them hard. I would not commit suicide because that's what the devil wanted me to do.

Thank God, and bless you, Jesus Christ—I am not insane.

I could not laugh aloud because I was vowed to silence. I began patting my palms together and grinning. I snapped my fingers and thought of the swarthy-skinned Spanish dancers in their tight pants, clicking their heels and clacking their clackers, and I stood up and began to dance. I twirled and spun and snapped and clapped and my throat hurt from silently laughing. My breathing harshened. I kicked my feet and tapped on the concrete floor.

I was not insane.

I swung to the bed and did not stop dancing as I grabbed up the plate. There was no madness in me. I swayed and skipped to the slot in the metal door and quickly shoved the plate through. I was imprisoned and being tried and I would be convicted, but I was not a lunatic. My life was more than a grim little murder to be punished and then forgotten.

The devil had served to show me sanity and now God could use me by my conviction—by my death.

If only I could find a depth in my mind the devil could not read.

A deputy sheriff called to me, "Hey, Father, what're you doin' dumpin' your food?" The man was a moron. He knew I would not answer him. He said, "Now we have'ta clean up this crap!"

The deputy moved his face to the door. I glanced at him as I twisted and smacked my hands and sang a quick song in my mind.

> I'm not insane,
> I say again,
> I'm not insane . . .

And I snapped my fingers and clicked my heels in a fandango. "Joe," the deputy yelled. "Hey, Joe. The priest's gone ape-shit."

My laceless shoes flopped as I imitated a Bojangles shuffle-dancer. The other deputy's face appeared at the barred window. He said, "Hey, Father, what's with you, huh?" while in my mind I sang:

> Oh, Lord, I'm glad
> I was never mad.
> I sing this tooney,
> 'Cause I'm not looney,
> Oh, but life is fooney. . . .

While the deputies pressed their faces together so they could see into the cell. The green-eyed deputy asked, "What'll we do? Maybe we should call it in." The brown-eyed deputy drew back. "What for? So what if the kook's dancin'? So what? That's what kooks do—they dance."

My breath caught in my chest. I was dizzy from the spinning and leaping. A deputy said, "See, he's windin' down." I hop-skipped to the bed and flopped onto the mattress, my legs sprawled, my head against the cold stone wall—I was panting.

While I tried to inhale slowly, I concentrated on not thinking. I did not want satan to read my mind. My allegiance was still to God. I wanted to be convicted and the devil wanted me freed by causing my suicide. If, because of reincarnation, certain crimes were legalized, then satan would laugh and give the dirty finger to God. People would steal and kill and have their attorneys claim, "My former lifetime made me do it."

I gripped my hands on the metal bed frame and pulled myself to sitting. Unless I lost this trial, all the years of believing I was becoming insane would be wasted.

I grinned. You are never too old to become a martyr.

A deputy said, "Look, he's grinnin' at somethin'," and the other said, "That's what kooks do—they got their own brand'a laughin' gas." They withdrew from the door. I breathed a heavy sigh. Go in peace, my watchful children. I raised my hand and silently blessed them with "*If God be for us, who can be against us.*" I yawned. It was sleepy to be happy.

Chapter 10

All the seats in the courtroom are occupied. The jury is placed and waiting. The newspaper and other reporters are patient and alert. The principal players are at their stations, bearing their authority. The legal passion play is about to begin again. Except for two film projectors and a screen erected near the county clerk's table, the stage setting is the same.

I did not eat their dinner last night. I would not eat their breakfast this morning. I could not even trust their coffee. I am hungry and dry, but I am not drugged.

I intend to sit and listen to the trial and enjoy my thirst and hunger and not think. In my depths I am a gentle and loving man. I worship God, respect the Law, believe in the goodness of humanity. There is now no violence in me.

The only confrontation with reality I will allow myself will be with Martin Lormer's large thermos of coffee. The cylindrical body is dark green, the cap polished metal. It is an eight-cup container. After I see him drink some and observe that he does not become simple or sit in a drugged stupor, I will begin conniving to get some of his coffee.

The first witness Martin Lormer called was the manager of the apartment complex where Shara and I had lived. He was an organized man and his primness showed in the sniffy expression on his face. His testimony would be used to put my journal into evidence. After he stated that he had found the journal within the niche I had cut into the wall of our bedroom closet, he was asked, "Why didn't you bring it to the police?"

He fidgeted with his tie and patted his hair and explained that it was two days before he could enter the apartment to clean it and when he had informed the police that he had found a *book* written by Stephen Jerod, the sergeant of detectives told him, "Any book that killer ever wrote, we can get a copy of from the library. "He then hung up on him. Martin Lormer thanked him and held the journal up to the judge.

"Your honor, I offer at this time, into evidence, this journal of the defendant, Stephen Jerod. And, if it please the court, I will want some portions of it read to the jury before it is given to them to examine on their own."

The District Attorney stood up and shook his head. He was wearing a muted gray-checked suit. His black hair was parted at the side, showing a white line of scalp. "Objection, your honor. All that has been established is that the journal was found in the apartment where the defendant once lived. It has not been established that the journal was written by the defendant."

The judge nodded. "Objection sustained." She looked to Martin Lormer. "The journal will first have to be established as having been written by the defendant before being admitted into evidence." Martin Lormer tucked the journal under his arm and called Edward Jorden to the stand.

He was a tall man with thinning brown hair and eyeglasses that glittered when he recited the oath to speak only the truth. Martin Lormer asked him to state his qualifications and background in the study and analysis of handwriting. Martin Lormer handed the witness the journal.

"Are you familiar with this journal?"

"I am. You brought it to our office and requested that I authenticate it as a journal written by the defendant, Stephen Jerod."

"Were you able to establish that fact?"

"Yes, I was."

"How did you accomplish that?"

"While the defendant was in custody I spoke with him and asked him to write portions of the statement he offered as his confession. I did that to acquire a recent sample of his handwriting. Knowing that he would not have a fountain pen while in custody, I let him use my pen to write with."

"Why was that important?"

"Each handwriting contains individual characteristics. Yet

there are many factors that mislead or disguise handwriting. A different state of mind produces alterations or modifications in the handwriting, which is why I wanted him to write a longer piece, rather than only his name or some meaningless statistics. Spaces between letters, spaces between words, the nature of the line, the pen-lifts and sizes of letters, are all identifying characteristics. They show up better and more consistently when the person does a lot of writing. If the opportunity to observe the writing as it is composed exists, then it is advisable to be present at the time."

"What did you conclude?"

"That the journal you brought into our office—the one I am now holding—was written by the defendant, Stephen Jerod."

"Thank you, Mr. Jorden. Now, would you turn to the first page and read the opening entry. I want you to . . ."

The District Attorney interrupted by standing up and speaking as though impatient with trivial chatter. "Is this court going to be subjected to listening to the entire journal?" Martin Lormer drummed his fingers on the wooden railing, exaggerating his impatience.

"Your honor, I want portions of this journal read into the record before it is given to the jury to examine. Since it is the defendant's journal, I intend using it—*not for the truth or untruth it contains*—but to establish how completely the defendant believes it has influenced and directed his life."

The District Attorney said, "Before this masterpiece, referred to as the defendant's journal, is offered into evidence, I would like to examine it."

The judge nodded. "That is your privilege."

Martin Lormer brought him the journal and waited while he and two assistants studied it.

I began to feel that it would be good if the jury, if the whole damned world, read my journal. They would study a portion of my life in intimacy, and I would not be ashamed. The journal had its own life, its own power. At first, the jury would be hearing and reading the perverse logic of a lunatic. But then the self-life, the mystery within the pages would gradually influence them and they would begin to determine that I had planned to kill Shara long before I actually killed her—and they would then be compelled to find me guilty of murder. Bravo! Martin Lormer, I thought. Bravo!

People began shifting on the benches while the District Attorney turned the journal pages and kept shaking his head. I was becoming hungry. Small fingers with coarse nails were groping in my stomach, grubbing for the remains of other dinners. I looked at Martin Lormer's thermos of coffee and licked my lips. The District Attorney closed the journal and held it out to Martin Lormer and grinned. "If the defense wants to use this fiction, I have no objections."

The journal was marked as evidence and returned to the handwriting expert.

"Mr. Jorden, would you tell the court what you did after ascertaining that the journal was written by the defendant?"

"I focused my attention on authenticating the age of the journal and an approximation of the dates it was written."

"What were your findings?"

"The opening entry was written approximately fifteen years ago. Through the age of the paper and the watermark I was also able to determine that this paper is no longer manufactured—but it was in circulation at the time."

"But old paper and old ink is easy enough to acquire, wouldn't you agree, Mr. Jorden?"

"Yes. But there were other factors that led me to conclude that there was no deception."

"Would you reveal your findings to the court, please?"

"This binder, you will notice, has bulk. The indentions made by the pen being pressed onto the paper are quite distinct. As the binder is opened and closed, pressure is placed on the pages by the weight of the other pages resting on them. This pressure flattens the early indentions. The later indentions are flattened less by the fact that they have fewer pages weighing upon them. In this particular binder the indentions are progressively flatter. Indicating a constant opening and closing over a period of years. Thus, the age of the paper is not as important or as revealing as are the indentions pressed onto the paper."

"How very logical. Yet couldn't someone apply the pressure that is necessary to fake it—over a short period of time?"

"The chemical structure of the ink rendered my analysis conclusive."

"Really? Would you also explain that?"

"The brand of ink that the defendant used cannot remain after one year. After about a year the ink dries in the bottle no matter how tightly the bottle is sealed—even if the bottle is never opened."

Martin Lormer and the judge looked to the District Attorney, who sat pursing his lips. He wanted to raise an objection and was evaluating the consequence of his action. The journal had already been accepted as evidence. He would not be able to create doubt about its authenticity or when it was written. I watched his resigned shrug. Martin Lormer turned to the witness and smiled.

"Mr. Jorden, would you now turn to page eleven. I want you to read the section where the defendant is in the mind of the Renaissance physician, Barthelamo Vecchio, who is having a vision of the lifetime he once lived when . . ."

The District Attorney stood up and scowled. "Your honor, I most emphatically object. Defense counsel is assuming facts not in evidence. A journal has been put into evidence, not a factual report. This is a courtroom, not a kiddie program for television tots who want to hear bizarre fairy tales."

The judge stroked the side of her cheek with her thumb. "The court is patient, as long as not too many liberties are taken. Objection overruled." Martin Lormer looked to the witness.

"The part you will read deals with the Renaissance doctor who was, in his other lifetime, a—well, call him a witch doctor, who was also an Albino. His tribe has just conquered a village and is marching the captives away. They will be used as slaves, and some for human sacrifice. Among the captives is a beautiful woman . . ."

I did not want to listen to his telling about Barthelamo and Bianco. They would be mocked, they would be pitied. I sat and thought about myself. I might have had a normal childhood. Chasing the woods in search of unicorns and sniffing beneath rickety bridges for pixies. And there would have been a round-faced girl with splayed teeth whom I adored and wanted to marry if only she would have noticed me. God, God, are we born mad and live to become sane? Why was I not like others?

" . . . and the Albino, now overwhelmingly and desperately in love, wants to rescue the captive woman from the barbaric rites of human sacrifice so . . ."

The District Attorney raised his arm and shook his hand for the judge's attention. "Your honor, must we listen to this television treatment of that journal? Can't we just get on with the portion he wants read?" I could see that the judge, like the jury, was intrigued with the story Martin Lormer had been telling. She was annoyed by the interruption. "What counsel for the defense is doing seems appropriate." She looked to Martin Lormer who stepped back from the witness.

"All right, Mr. Jorden, please read the portion I have marked in red brackets, on page eleven. It is Barthelamo Vecchio using the defendant, Stephen Jerod, as his medium."

The witness opened the journal and wet a fingertip before turning the pages. He adjusted his eye glasses.

> I observed this white creature from whom I originated. He was chanting a tribal litany in a tongue I did not comprehend. His eyes were upon the woman in his favor. Whilst she was being conducted along a dry and rocky land, she stumbled and fell to the earth. A warrior of muscular proportions strode to her. He slashed a knotted whip across her lower back. He forced her up and drove her to continue walking. The white creature, whom I refer to as *Bianco*, when he appears to me, desired to kill the warrior. His whip had lacerated her flesh at the spine, drawing blood.

The handwriting expert stopped reading and closed the journal. Martin Lormer said, "Now turn to page forty-three and read until you . . ." and the District Attorney again objected. Martin Lormer moved closer to the judge's bench and spoke loud enough for the jury and the people in the press section to hear.

"Your honor, it is my intention to prove, irrefutably, that

Stephen Jerod is a reincarnation of this man Barthelamo Vecchio and the man referred to as Bianco."

"Mr. Lormer, are you telling this court that you intend proving what others, all over the world and in our greatest universities have failed to prove—that the doctrine of reincarnation is *fact?*"

"I am concerned only with proving that Stephen Jerod's belief that he is reincarnated from Barthelamo Vecchio and Bianco is founded on fact and not imagination. However, if in the course of this trial, I prove the doctrine of reincarnation to be realistic, and satanic, then let the universities reap the benefits of our efforts."

The District Attorney waved his arms at the judge. "Your honor, again I object to . . ." She raised her hand, silencing him. "Overruled. It is in the nature of the defense's case to do this. Mr. Lormer, you may proceed."

The District Attorney pouted and sat down. Martin Lormer slipped his hands into his pockets and though he faced the witness, he spoke to the jury.

"On page forty-three, there is an entry which reveals when the infamous Cesare Borgia began to trust the Physician, Barthelamo Vecchio. After aborting Lucrezia Borgia—who then became his deadly enemy—Barthelamo then saves Cesare Borgia, who is almost killed by an assassin's crossbow. The woman, known only as Letitia, is not present when this . . ."

While he spoke, the witness slowly turned the journal pages. He was told to begin reading again. His voice, coming through the microphone at the witness stand, was without theatrics. I sensed that the court was visualizing this humpbacked Physician following after the tall and majestic Cesare Borgia as they moved through the dark castle corridors to his secret treasure vault—then the description of Barthelamo Vecchio writing the receipt for three paintings to be deposited in the vault.

The District Attorney began a series of objections that were logical but which were obviously meant to disrupt the mystic and mysterious mood caused by the reading of the journal. "This is not fact," the District Attorney declared. "It is fiction until it is established as fact," and Martin Lormer countered with, "If it is not yet fact, it will be." The judge was patient and asked him to justify a further reading from the journal. He said, "Where does history come from? It comes from those sources still undiscovered but which are, nevertheless, history—once they are discovered." The judge allowed the reading to continue.

I sat and concentrated on soliciting the powers of satan so I could secretly levitate Martin Lormer's thermos to float under the table and open itself to pour me a cup of coffee. Then I smiled. Perhaps Martin Lormer had learned that I had not eaten the prison food or had any liquids and, to keep me in a tranquilized condition, had drugged the coffee. Perhaps he was doing what Shara had once done to me. Martin Lormer was a devious man, and sly.

Then I heard a stirring in the courtroom. The air had darkened and I noticed that people were looking to the ceiling rows of neon-encased lights, waiting for them to flicker on. The county clerk's electrical machine would not function. No sound came from the loudspeakers. I looked to the judge, who clapped her gavel and spoke with slow clarity. "This is a *mechanical* failure, nothing more. The court will remain in session but the proceedings will be suspended until electrical power is restored." I wondered if this was the work of satan or the fault of defective wiring and fuses. I could see by the expressions of other people that they were wondering the same.

Martin Lormer walked to our table and smiled at me. "This is a good day, isn't it, Stephen?" It was the first time he had ever called me Stephen. He patted my arm.

He put his hand on the thermos and frowned. "If shutting off the electricity is the work of the devil, then he's got something planned which I'll have to deal with." He uncapped the thermos and winked at me. "If you can clue me into what the devil will be doing next, I would appreciate it." I looked at the thermos, feeling hope. He shook his head. "Before this trial is over we may all be booked into the nut house." He poured black steaming coffee into the metal cap. I looked at my hands as he sipped.

Several people on the jury shifted on their seats and stared at us. The ceiling lights flickered but did not go on. Martin Lormer set the coffee before me. "Stephen, you haven't had anything to eat or drink. Have some coffee. I promise you it isn't drugged." I tensed my hands to keep them from moving.

My mouth felt like the inside of a sun-bleached water bottle.

The judge began studying some papers. The District Attorney spoke in cautious whispers to his assistant. Four jurors leaned back and closed their eyes. Two newspaper reporters chatted and glanced at each other's pads. I avoided reaching for the coffee and scanned the faces in the courtroom.

I saw Shara's supervisor, Franklin Jimson, sitting at the aisle. Beside him was Marsha Jenner. They were sneaking frowns at me and speaking softly about something. He had lusted for Shara. But I had been his impediment. I was Shara's predestined object—Franklin was inconsequential to her life. Men like him could be used, exhausted, and quickly destroyed. I was more interesting. To destroy me required many lifetimes. And Shara was always concentrated on her object.

She would awaken while I slept. She would roll onto her side, facing me, and begin whispering, "Suicide is only a bridge into another life." Her voice was a carefully spoken sigh. Never varying. "This life is tedious. The next will be fascinating."

I knew she had been doing this for weeks because my dreams had become macabre. I saw myself standing on high bridges. The night wind beat against my body, flapping the cloth of my pajamas. The water below was a stretch of black steel. I would climb the railing and sit blowing breath onto my hands to warm them. My feet were hardened by the cold and thunked against the metal girders. I did not want to jump. A huge, invisible hand was gripped onto my hair, pulling me forward. Each time I tensed myself to be yanked forward to be flung into the air, I screamed and awoke.

Shara was always facing me in the bed, the pillow fluffed about her cheeks, her eyes closed as though asleep. She pretended that my screams awoke her.

One night, while I was feigning sleep, Shara edged close to me, her mouth near my face. "You want to kill me, don't you?" she said. The words were caressed into my mind. "You want to kill me, don't you?" she repeated. I was awake—I was certain I was awake—and trying to understand why she wanted me to kill her—but the monotonous flow of her voice began to lull me and I drowsed. From that night on, I always placed flesh-colored cotton

dollops into my ears so I could not hear her trying to destroy
me.

Martin Lormer touched my hand. His fingertips were warm
from holding the filled coffee cup. "Stephen, I want you to sit up
straight," he said. His voice was gentle, his mouth was tilted into
an affectionate smile. I decided that sharing a man's coffee was not
the same as communicating with him. I reached to the filled thermos cap and drank some. The liquid was a hot caress stroking the
wrinkles from my throat.

Then the ceiling lights suddenly flicked on. People blinked. I
drank some more coffee and felt refreshed.

Martin Lormer told the judge that he had no more questions
to ask of the handwriting expert "at this time." She waited for the
District Attorney, who was leafing through some papers. Martin
Lormer shifted closer to me and spoke in low tones. "A lot of surprising information is about to come out, Stephen. I don't want
you acting foolishly. If you won't contribute to your defense, don't
distract from it."

He called Arnold Lazarus to the witness stand. The District
Attorney frowned while he skimmed his finger down a list of
names in his records. I studied the man as he recited the oath. He
looked like the average senior citizen and seemed in good health.
There was a slight dullness to his brown eyes. His gray hair was
carefully combed. His face was broad and tapered to a narrow chin.
He had a stiff, ten by twelve inch manila envelope tucked under
his arm. I wondered if he was another expert or a character witness
who once knew Shara. When he sat down, Martin Lormer leaned
to him and spoke in a casual manner.

"Mr. Lazarus, would you tell the court how old you are?"

"Sixty-three. Born in 1918. April 11th. In Baltimore. Lived
there all my life. I still live there."

"What kind of business are you in?"

"I'm retired. I had three photography shops."

"Are you married?"

"Not now. I was married, in 1937. My wife, Belinda, left me. I
never married again."

"How long were you and Belinda living together before she
left you?"

"Almost four years. She left me the day World War II started. On a Sunday morning, in 1941. A lot of people remember that day, December 7th, but for different reasons."

"Had you ever abandoned her before that day? I mean, could she have been retaliating?"

"There was only one time when I was forced to leave our home. When I entered a mental institution. The Babalyn Mental Institution. I was there for three weeks. Belinda stayed with me all that time. It was the day after I was let out, on a Saturday, that she left me."

"Why do you use that point of time for your references?"

"Because it was Belinda who was responsible for causing me to go to the institution in the first place. I almost killed her and I didn't want to. She was making me want to kill her."

"In what way did she try to . . ."

The District Attorney raised his arm. "Your honor, I fail to see the relevance of this testimony." The judge looked to Martin Lormer. He nodded. "I realize this seems unrelated testimony, your honor. But I assure you that his testimony is an integral part of the proceedings."

The judge stroked the lace collar on her robe and smiled at the District Attorney. "I'm going to allow this line of questioning a little longer." Martin Lormer stepped to our table and picked a glossy photograph from an envelope. He returned to the witness stand, holding the picture against his thigh, face down.

"When your wife left you, what did you do?"

"I offered a reward of one thousand dollars to anyone who could help me to find her. I put the notice in the *Baltimore Inquirer*. I let it run in the newspaper for one month."

"If, as you say, she drove you into a mental institution, why then in heaven's name would you go through the expense of trying to find her?"

"I loved her. She had quirks and twists in her, sure. But she was a good woman to me. I never stopped loving her. She was strange, and most beautiful. And special. But she kept doing things that drove me crazy with jealousy. I got to thinking about killing her—so no one else could have her. Which is why I went to the mental institution to take some tests. To see if I was crazy or safe to live with. After three weeks, they said I was fine. It was an inter-reaction of personalities, they said. But I didn't care. I loved her."

"Mr. Lazarus, I want you to look at a photograph for me. Then tell the court if you recognize the person in it."

He handed Arnold Lazarus the photograph. The man's eyes stiffened in the sockets. His mouth trembled. The hand holding the photograph shook. He moaned a sound that had meaning unto him. Martin Lormer turned to the jury as he asked his questions.

"Can you identify the person in that photograph?"

"Yes. It's my wife, Belinda."

"Mr. Lazarus, I want you to look at that photograph carefully. Now I mean *carefully*. A great deal depends on your identification."

"I'd know her anywhere. That's my Belinda."

"Even though thirty-seven years have passed?"

"The ones you love stay young in your mind. No matter how long a time passes, you don't forget the only woman you ever loved."

"Then you are certain, without a doubt, that this is the woman you were once married to and who left you in 1941, forty years ago."

"As certain as my own name. That's my Belinda."

Martin Lormer eased the picture from the man's hand and stepped toward the judge. "This photograph is a duplicate of the one marked as evidence three. I now proffer this photograph to be marked as evidence D, for the defense. Although it has been identified as the former Belinda Lazarus—*it is actually the last photograph taken of Shara Medford.*"

I edged forward, not certain I had heard him clearly. People began whispering. The jurors shifted and frowned at each other. The District Attorney stood up and huffed his words. "Your honor, I strenuously object to such ridiculous allegations on the part of the defense counsel." The bailiffs shifted from their at-ease stances. Their eyes flickered over the courtroom. The judge brought the photograph close to her face and studied it. Someone in the rear laughed. She put on her glasses and kept looking at the photograph as she spoke to Martin Lormer.

"Mr. Lazarus has testified that he was married to a woman named Belinda, who left him thirty years ago. He has now identified this photograph of Shara Medford as a picture of that woman. The court would like a more reasonable explanation."

"I am aware of how impossible it seems, your honor. Yet what else can I do but present the facts as they relate to the defendant's interests?"

"Are you trying to pass off what is obviously a case of either mistaken identity or a remarkable resemblance to the victim as a fact?"

"No, your honor, I am not. If you allow me to question the witness and then offer to the court the same material that I was offered, I will then accept any decision the court chooses to make in this matter."

"All right, Mr. Lormer. But let me caution you. You are trying not only the credulity of this court, but also its patience."

"Thank you, your honor."

I was sorry for the witness. The woman he had loved bore a resemblance to Shara—probably. But it was his dream, his delusion, that saddened me. Every man, everywhere, who had an inclination for love, wanted a woman like Shara. This poor man was more distraught than rational. Martin Lormer had overplayed his talent for drama. The man would be discredited.

He went to the witness and smiled. "I know this is an ordeal for you, Mr. Lazarus. But it won't continue much longer." The man blinked and looked to me. I glanced down.

"Mr. Lazarus, you stated that at one time you were the owner of three photography shops. Was there any particular reason for choosing that type of business?"

"Photography was my hobby. When I left college I decided to turn it into my business."

"Did you ever photograph your wife, Belinda?"

"All the time. She was beautiful."

"Did you ever photograph her in the nude?"

"Many times. She had a beautiful figure, and she also had

some vanity of it. She didn't like her front taken, though. Said it wasn't as good as her back. Though once in a while I was able to catch her in a semi-frontal shot. When she was waiting for me to set up my camera. I cheated on her, you might say. One of the pictures I took won third prize in *Photography Art* magazine. I caught her full face only once. That was the picture I used in the newspaper."

"Do you still have the art magazine and the newspaper photo?"

"I have them with me."

I did not allow myself to view the materials placed into evidence. I was—strangely—lonely to think about Barthelamo and Bianco. Was it because their existence in my life had become integral? I made a bridge of my hands and stared at the fingertips.

Barthelamo was living his days in loneliness for Letitia, and felt that unknowingly, or foolishly, she would betray him to Lucrezia Borgia. Though Lucrezia was of the nobility and Letitia a common servant, he believed they would become companions in secrecy. They were women, and they would gabble. Lucrezia would boast of the men she had bedded with—confiding intimate actions and amusing quirks. Believing Lucrezia to be a loving mistress, Letitia might tease, "Our great Prince, your beloved brother, is not as clever as my Master Vecchio. Of a truth, the devil could learn a wile and ruse from him," and then confess that she did not have a vaginal malformation. That would be enough for Lucrezia. She did not want him punished. She wanted him killed. And Cesare Borgia was in a killing disposition and his desire for violence and death had spilled a terrible fear throughout the castle.

All levels of the ducal palace—from the catacombs of economy to the military—had become guarded provinces, loyal only to their own. The stable servants no longer fraternized with the tanners—the tailors were afraid to speak with the barbers. Even the chisels of the masons and hammers of the carpenters seemed less talkative while making repairs. Blunt-faced *condottieri* were wary of exchanging gossip about their superiors with the foppishly uniformed mercenaries. The ground troops, placed in quarters according to their specialty—archers, crossbowmen, pikemen, cannoneers—would not trade memories of former campaigns in which comrades heroically died. Townspeople who were hired to empty the drainage ditches labored at hacking frozen debris from the clogged channels, and all wondered if there would be a feast, a scandalous celebration, a fortnight of games and orgies, when Count Finiguerra's assassin was found.

In one of the many communications sent to his son, Pope Alexander had written, "Cesare, my adored, the eyes of Italy are upon us. The assassin you discover must be the true assassin. I will come to you when he is found. Only my presence at his trial can establish the truth of his crime. Do not fail me." Borgia's power and title were in jeopardy. Barthelamo had to find an assassin who would convincingly confess to having murdered the Count. Quickly. But carefully. Before Letitia weakened. Before she confided to Lucrezia that he had drugged the Count's wine, thus causing Lucrezia to believe the crookbacked Physician was the true assassin.

Bianco was pleased that he had caused the death of the son of the Great Burning Eye. When the people asked the Elders how such a powerful god could die, the Elders stood together and held hands and chanted in prayer. Their wrinkled skins and sagged flesh trembled as their voices sang upward. When their speaking to the All-god was done they told the people that the son of the Great Burning Eye had been doing evils and his father became angry. He would soon send them another son.

The women who lived in the dead god's abode burned scented smoke pots and used oils and drying powders to keep his body. They placed the castings and garments and carryings of his power into the skin of the animal that dragged stones for their temple. They walked, one behind the other, wailing their sorrow, until they reached the place of waiting. The women of the Elders prepared cloth wrappings to be used for covering his flesh so it did not smell. He would be brought into the Temple and remain until the Elders were shown who was to become another son of the Great Burning Eye. Only this son could return his dead brother to their father.

Bianco and Onadyh were secretly preparing small animal skins and filling them with water. He was afraid to steal food from the stone houses where the warrior guards watched. He left the abode at night and walked to the edge of the village where the people piled their food leavings. In the darkness, when all the fires were smothered, the god of the beasts sent his children to the mounds of waste. Because they were fed, they did not attack the people. Bianco picked among the leavings for food they could carry on their journey across the vast land of rock and unwatered earth to find Onadyh's people.

They were waiting for the Elders to find the next son of the Great Burning Eye, before they left the village. The ceremony would continue for two darknesses and two lights. When the next son was given the markings that would never leave his flesh, he would be adorned in his powers and brought into the Temple to send his brother away in flame and smoke. They would leave then.

Bianco was not afraid of the terrible dying that happened to others who were made to leave the village. He had read his castings, he had read the signs on the creatures that sneaked to the wells and drank before the people awakened. They would not die. He feared only what the castings did not show him. Did Onadyh let the son of the Great Burning Eye use her flesh so she could save him from his enemy? When they found Onadyh's people, would she tell them of his god-ness—would she tell them he had caused the growing in her so the child could also become a god?

Each darkness, while she lay in the abode, making the soft sounds of her sleep, he would read the castings and speak to his father, to know what she would do.

I closed my eyes and strained to bring their faces into my mind. Barthelamo was a dark, undefined impression. Bianco remained a gauzy white blur. But I was able to feel the pain they were enduring. Their lives were being changed into ruins because of the women they loved. I shuddered. I heard Martin Lormer's voice telling the judge, "Your honor, this is the photograph Mr. Lazarus has identified as his former wife, Belinda. It is, of course, the photograph of Shara Medford, taken before her autopsy."

Shara's face was projected onto the screen. Her eyes were closed. I looked away, deliberately staring at the furled flag standing in its socket to the left of the judge's bench. Martin Lormer said, "This is the advertisement issued by the witness to identify his wife, Belinda. It was taken thirty-six years ago."

He placed the newspaper clipping onto the other projector. Like the other people and the jurors, I was startled when comparing them. Shara's face was framed in an odd hair style. Slight bangs across her forehead and curls puffed on top. Full lips and long smooth neck. The eyes were open. Their faces were identical. The copy below the picture read, "Reward: $1,000. Paid to anyone who can reveal the whereabouts of Belinda Lazarus. 23 yrs. old, is 5'2", weighs 117 lbs. Last seen in vicinity of Trackton." I heard a scraping noise at my right. The District Attorney stood up.

"Your honor, the prosecution accepts the similarity between both women. The resemblance is so remarkable, his misunderstanding that Shara Medford was his wife is understandable. But it is only a coincidence. I see no point to continuing this type of proceeding. I vigorously object."

"Mr. Lormer, will you reply to the objection?"

"Your honor, I agree with the prosecution. It is no more than a remarkable resemblance. What else could it be? It can be determined as nothing other than the appearance of a double, someone who looks exactly like someone else. It is more than a look-alike. It is an exact-look-alike."

"Your honor, so Shara Medford had a double. So what?"

"Your honor, my office was brought into this case the very morning after the crime. I even had my own pathologist present at the autopsy. I have gone through . . ."

"Your honor, must the court be subjected to this?"

"Mr. Lormer, please get on with it."

"When it was finally announced that I would be defending Stephen Jerod, the press and television began grinding out copy and it also published and showed the photograph of Shara Medford. My office was contacted by Mr. Lazarus and other people. I can assure the court that our investigation was most thorough. At first, Mr. Lazarus's story sounded ridiculous. And I would not place the defendant's case in jeopardy by bringing shoddy material before the court. However, no matter how peculiar or strange my materials may be, if they are relevant, I must bring them forth.

The question that must be answered is when does a coincidence stop, because it can be explained—and when does a coincidence continue to become something more, because it cannot be explained? When does it become strange or, perhaps, supernatural? And if your honor will allow me to continue, I will demonstrate that none of this is without a purpose."

He walked to our table and opened his attaché case and took some photographs from a file compartment. I sipped some cool coffee from the thermos cap. He leaned to me and whispered, "This is where it starts getting hairy—so control yourself." I continued sipping my coffee. He went to the evidence table and picked up a photograph.

"It is my intention, your honor, to now demonstrate how coincidences can cancel out coincidences, to produce even more baffling coincidences."

He placed a photograph onto one projector slide carriage and we saw the nude picture of Shara taken before the autopsy. She was lying on her stomach. I would not let myself remember the sensations that once flowed from that body into mine. He placed another photograph onto the other projector. It was the same pose—a woman lying on her stomach. The picture was clearer and more interesting in tone and shading. I heard some lascivious whistles. The judge struck her gavel. "I'll have none of that or I shall clear the courtroom." Martin Lormer said, "This is the photograph taken by Mr. Lazarus, of his wife Belinda. It should be noticed how exactly alike they are. You will recall that in an earlier testimony given by the district deputy coroner, he had stated that other than the usual bruises about the throat of the victim, the only other markings were a series of small scars at the base of the victim's spine. It was in my client's interest that I worked to discredit Mr. Lazarus's claim. If I could discredit this witness's testimony, then so could the prosecution. I offer now some enlargements of that scarred area—the base of her spine."

He projected the photographs onto the screen. We saw a design of crosses and warps in the skin. I had kissed those tiny scars a thousand times. I had once told Shara, "Scars become beautiful when you love the woman who bears them." In one picture her scars were darker, showing them in a slightly different depth.

Martin Lormer said, "There, your honor, is what I mean by a coincidence canceling out a coincidence."

The judge frowned at him. "Mr. Lormer, you are becoming increasingly unclear. I fail to see your point, or purpose."

The District Attorney stood up and shook his head as though puzzled. "Your honor, I appeal to the court not only to end this charade, but also to strike all of this from the record."

Martin Lormer stepped to the photographs and clapped his forehead as though startled by his own idiocy. He looked to the judge and grinned. "Your honor, I am truly sorry. I did not realize that I had been so vague in presenting these photographs. The enlargement of the scars you see before you are not only the scars on Shara Medford's body. These are two separate photographs. One belongs to Shara Medford and the other to Belinda Lazarus. Not only do they look alike, but they have the exact same scars on their bodies—and that, your honor, I submit is more than coincidence."

I had to grip the arms of my chair to stop from leaping up and shouting, "That is absolutely crazy! They can't be one and the same!" but the District Attorney jumped from his chair, almost upsetting the table. "That is just plain crazy, your honor. Shara Medford can't be Belinda Lazarus—it's impossible!" The jurors all leaned forward to look at the photographs of the scars. Some put on their glasses. Behind me, people talked and guessed and someone yelled, "Lormer has gone bananas!" The judge stood up, her breasts heaving under her robe as she slammed the gavel onto the wooden disc, demanding, "I will have order in this court!" She pointed the gavel at a bailiff, loudly telling him, "You will remove anyone who is not quiet. Remove them immediately." I felt myself grinning. Martin Lormer was as crazy as I thought I once was.

When the courtroom was silent, the judge, still standing, held her gavel toward Martin Lormer and spoke menacingly. "You will explain the meaning of those scars on the photographs, or I will cite you, not only for contempt, but for chicanery, and for at least seven other counts which I will name as I cite them." Martin Lormer rubbed his hand across his eyes and breathed deeply. I could sense he was excited, but not intimidated.

"Your honor, the only explanation that I had come up with at the time was that Shara Medford was Belinda Lazarus, but with a complete face and body lift that my client was unaware of."

I did not believe him. Shara's skin was smooth, it was tasty. There was no odor of age from her—not a blemish to disrupt the evenness of skin tone. Her motions were fluid. She could dance about the living room for hours and not show fatigue. I had never heard an arthritic grunt, a rheumatic moan. She was not an elderly woman prettied into youth by surgery. The judge sat down and shook her head.

"You said, 'The only explanation I had come up with at the time'—implying that your explanation at the time eventually proved unsatisfactory."

"Yes, your honor. Shara Medford had never undergone cosmetic surgery. The explanation was unsatisfactory."

"What, then, was the explanation you finally arrived at?"

"Your honor will recall in my opening statement to this court that I claimed there were many baffling aspects to this case. I have presented this one fact of the scars on both women as being the same—not as a device to startle or confuse. I have merely presented facts. If, as the court has stated, it cannot rule on the province of the supernatural, how then can I explain what cannot be explained, though it exists? The court asks too much of me. However, if this one odd fact is enough to influence the court in a negative manner, what then am I to do when other facts about Shara Medford are revealed?"

The District Attorney shoved closer to the judge's bench and shook his head as he spoke.

"Your honor, these facts, or whatever they are, referred to by defense counsel, still have no bearing on this case. Shara Medford's character or life is not on trial here. She was the victim, your honor, not the felon. It is Stephen Jerod who is being tried for her killing. It is not her character, but the defendant's act that is to be judged."

"Your honor, I disagree with the prosecution. Our defense is self-defense. A man does not defend himself against nothing. He is driven into that defense to save his life. How can the one who causes this defense of self be separated from the one who defends himself? The question is not only why did Stephen Jerod kill Shara

Medford, but what in Shara Medford caused him to kill her? And I must remind the court that we are not only dealing with the murder of a woman, we are also dealing with the motivation of reincarnation. Are we to be expected to employ conventional procedures in order to understand the unconventional?"

"Your honor, the defense of a crime does not establish the crime as existing in the manner it is being defended. It has not been established that Stephen Jerod killed Shara Medford in self-defense. *That is still to be determined.* I object to this line of defense on the grounds that it is irrelevant, on the grounds that it is without foundation, on the grounds that . . ."

"Yes, yes, counsel, you have made your objection obvious. The court, however, finds validity to defense's statements. Objection overruled."

The witness suddenly stood up and cried, "Stop! Stop this terrible thing!" He struck his clenched hands against his chest and moaned to the ceiling, "Now my Belinda's dead, she's dead, you hear? It's over for me—all over!" A bailiff rushed toward him as he huddled over and wept. People looked down, ashamed. The judge covered her eyes. When the bailiff reached the witness he shook the hand away and pointed his fist at me. "Why did you have to kill her, you bastard. I didn't kill her. No matter how she tried, I didn't kill her. Why did you—why didn't you just send her home to me!" I wanted to cry with him. I wanted to hold him and tell him I knew how he loved her, but it was not Shara he loved. No other man, in this lifetime, loved Shara as I loved her.

The bailiff spoke to him, softly, and gently took his arm, leading him from the witness stand. The judge said, "Let him rest in my chambers. Stay with him." Before he left he cried, "How I loved her, oh God, how I loved her."

I sat with my head bowed, knowing the people were looking at me, hating me. Slowly, because the jurors were staring at me, I raised my face to them, and smiled. I widened my mouth into a leer, showing my teeth and the tip of my tongue. Three women gasped at my viciousness. I winked at the men. The male jurors sneered at me, silently damning me.

The judge, as though hurrying the proceedings, told Martin Lormer, "Call your next witness." She knew that turning the people's interest back to the proceedings would quiet them. Martin Lormer announced, "I call to the stand Professor Carlo Guidobaldo, of Florence, Italy."

A small man strolled jauntily up the aisle, carrying a large leather portfolio. A newspaper artist began sketching his roundish face. He was a short man wearing a dark blue pin-striped suit. His hair was dawn gray and groomed to a celebrity fluff at the sides. His beard was neatly trimmed. He was sworn in and Martin Lormer waited for him to arrange himself comfortably.

"You are Professor Carlo Guidobaldo, curator for the *Museo nazionale*—The National Museum, in Florence, Italy?"

"I am. It has been my position for thirty-one years. Before me, it was my father who was *curatore*."

"Would you tell the court why you traveled from Italy to testify at this trial?"

"*Certo.* It was my interest in your defendant, Signor Jerod. He has caused a great find to my country—to my *specialità*—my own interest. When information of this *omicidio* reached Florence, a *telegramma* was sent to his representatives to place our people at his disposal. I am here, presented before you, to provide information to his *causa*."

All this man would do was prove that I had led his people to finding a treasure vault that had been hidden for centuries. His testimony would establish a probable relationship between my knowing of the treasure and the existence of Cesare Borgia. Martin Lormer would press the point that the discovery was unique because I had never been to Europe—thus making the relationship supernatural. He would jockey the witness to prove I was not living in a fantasy and that I was not insane. I listened to the man's voice. It was a lilt of sounds that were appealingly continental. But my interest was in understanding the meaning of the scars on Belinda Lazarus's back being identical with Shara's scars.

"How many factual histories have you written on the medieval centuries—the fifteenth and early sixteenth centuries in particular?"

"*Undici*—eleven."

"How many have been translated into English and published in America?"

"Nove—nine. They are, from translation, *Cesare Borgia: Statesman; Lucrezia Borgia: Mistress of the Nation; The Classical Renaissance; The Borgia Wars; Madman-Genius, Borgia; The Prince of Infamy; The . . .*"

The District Attorney stood up. "Your honor, the prosecution is willing to concede that Professor Guid—, that the professor is an expert on Renaissance civilization."

Martin Lormer stepped closer to the bench and shook his head. "While I appreciate the prosecution's acceptance of Professor Guidobaldo's credentials as an expert, that is not quite enough." He returned to the witness and pointed at him.

"This witness has come to America at great expense. My intention is not only in having him accepted as an expert on medieval Italian history—he must also be accredited as an expert on the life and times of the Borgia family—and those families and notables living in that particular era as well."

"Your honor, the prosecution has been apprised of this witness's credentials. For the sake of time and convenience, the prosecution agrees to accredit the professor as an expert on the life and times of the Borgia families and other families and notables of that time."

Martin Lormer looked to the court reporter whose fingers were skimming over the keys of his machine. He held his palms together and patted his fingertips.

"Professor Guidobaldo, when the secret vault of Cesare Borgia was finally located, what part did you play in the discovery?"

"It was my honor to enter the *volta* first. I cannot tell you of how thrilling I was made."

"Was the vault intact—untouched by anyone for, say, for centuries?"

"Only *polvere*—only dust. Then the treasure. A find of such magnitude, one cannot reveal the . . ."

I sat and thought about the strange scars on Shara's body and then I felt a mood of shuddering disgust being imposed on my thoughts. It was not my mood. My body began to feel dry, as though the fluids were being baked from me. And then my thoughts were not my usual thoughts—nor was my reasoning familiar to me. I was thinking about the scars on Shara's body and I was fixed into an aching hatred. Damn it, I cursed in myself. My stomach felt ulcerated and twisted and I knew that satan had transposed my mind and sensations to make me believe that Shara had lied about her age.

She had abandoned this man Arnold Lazarus because of sexual discontent. She was a bitch in heat—continually. She had then degraded herself through years of gross sexual experiences. Until the ruts and wrinkles of age had impeded her lewdness. Her last desire was to settle with a good and devout man. Then she read about my discovery of the Italian art treasures and decided upon me. Priests were scandalously ignorant about women. She engaged the services of a brilliant cosmetic surgeon who had stretched away her wrinkles and cleansed her skin of age blemishes. Except for the small scars on her back. That is why that poor fool killed her. He discovered that she was an old woman.

I squirmed in the seat and breathed deeply to cleanse the feeling of foulness from my body. I would not believe what satan was filling into my mind. It was only a complex coincidence that the scars on Shara's back were the same as Belinda's scars. I would not let myself believe another possibility. The witness clapped his hands together in a gesture of amazement.

Martin Lormer had shifted to where the jury was seated and he leaned against the rail as the curator spoke.

"To have read Signor Jerod's *diario*—he's journal, was my honor. The accuracy astounds. There is also information to bring huge bafflements into the light of—of understanding. Shall I explain?"

"Please do, Professor Guidobaldo."

"In a *baule*—a trunk there is to be found the *veste*—the garment for a *bambino*. From Lucrezia's rooms. Was this to be for her marriage to the Este's line? For preparation of children to come? No. It was *avanzata*—left over. From Signor Jerod's journal it is learned of her pregnancy which, from the Duke's order, the *dottore* Barthelamo Vecchio caused, how to say—ah yes, aborted. So—a fragment is brought to light on Lucrezia."

"That does not seem exceptionally precise, Professor. Is that the only means for determining that events, not yet recorded, or come to light, did actually happen?"

"*Un momento*—there is—how to say—cross-references. Letters, communications to verify findings. *Esempio*—example. Lucrezia Borgia did not ever remove her *calze*—stockings, hose. Why is that? There was *difformità*—a crookedness to her toes. All toes. It was her shame. It was believed she was one time tortured for secrets—it was believed to be by birth. So, which? From the find Signor Jerod led us to discover there was a letter from her father, written from Spain, to her brother Cesare. He is commanded to never permit her toes to be seen. It was like—how to say—ah yes, *stigma*. Shame. So you see, another enlightenment. It is interesting, no? Are not the people of history our children, our darlings?"

The District Attorney objected.

The judge patted her fingertips on a paper and pursed her mouth. She stared ahead, into the full courtroom, but there was no object in her sight. She sighed. "Objection overruled."

Martin Lormer glanced to me, then continued asking the curator questions about Lucrezia Borgia. I thought how nonsensical this was. The people in the courtroom could not know that what this man was telling them was a distortion. He was making of that historical time in the castle a glamorous and splendid existence when, in truth, people lived with illness and depravity and physical filth.

Their beards and hair and crevices in their skins were havens for lice of every known species. The tone and contour of their flesh was hidden below the rashes and boils and discoloring infections caused by constant scratching. Few men or women had more than half their teeth. Their gums bled, their necks swelled, they were bent with arthritis, rheumatism, and shuffled about with the pain of gout. They were tubercular, syphilitic, and all partially blind from uncorrected astigmatisms.

They believed that bodily dirt was the divine endowment and insulation nature had provided for their daily protection against ague and crippling maladies, even the plague. Often, when Barthelamo had to probe their torsos to find the source of pain or complaint, he would have to scrape away the hardened grime rubbed into their skins by the coarse underclothes they wore beneath their finery. They were addicted to promiscuous use of perfumes to disguise the rank odors of their parts. They sprinkled or saturated their clothes with all manner of costly aromatics and lotions. In time, even the perfumes turned rancid. No one was ever without a perfume soaked cloth ball attached to his wrists and which was held to his face when he spoke with someone—to avoid the smell of that person.

Their toilet habits seemed to have been learned at the pigherder's sty. It was not uncommon for a baron or earl or church prelate when urged with a need for stomach release, to find a shadowy niche in a vestibule where he would lower his garments and squat until he was emptied. It was common to see two or three nobles standing side by side near a storage room or a vault for armaments, each holding himself and dousing the wall while he talked of church revenues or affairs of war.

". . . what the court would like to know, Professor Guidobaldo, is the mental disposition of the people at that time. Would you say that it was rational? Tranquil?"

"It was a time of—how to say—ah, *diabolico*, and *scandaloso*. It was with incest. Mothers stayed with children. Fathers made mistresses of daughters. Lucrezia was lover to Cesare, her brother—and before him, to the father, Pope Alessandro. Morality was for to rule the poor. The power was for the church. Still, there was learned people. *Artisti, drammatici, filosofi.* There were diaries, ledgers, letters, to substantiate the journal of Signor Jerod. I have here with me a ledger from another Physician, Marius Vitto, who says on this B. V. whom Signor Jerod writes from."

He tapped the portfolio. Martin Lormer put his hand out and the curator opened the binding and drew out a photographed portion of an ancient diary. He brought it to the judge, requesting that it be entered into evidence. It was then given to the District Attorney, who studied it, commenting aloud, "It's in Italian." Martin Lormer smirked. "Did you expect it to be in hieroglyphics?" The material was entered into evidence and returned to the witness. Martin Lormer instructed him, "Would you bring this into English for the benefit of the court?" The curator drew a pair of gold-frame glasses from his pocket and studied the page.

I stared at one of the jurors, a dowdy woman with wide brown eyes. She did not seem immensely intelligent. She looked at me and I grinned and put thoughts into her mind. He's a psychic medium and doesn't even know it. His spirit guide comes from the Dark Ages. Whatever unnatural that he's done, his spirit guide made him do it. Aunt Wilma Mae's spirit guide was a gypsy in Rumania and it made her strangle cats.

I kept staring at the woman juror who was studying me. Her mouth was a taut bright curve of lipstick above an elongated chin. Her eyes were narrowed. He can get in touch with the dead and reap a marvelous fortune. Does he know his own? She began patting her hair as she glanced away and made herself listen to the Italian curator's testimony.

Martin Lormer pointed to the portfolio page the Italian witness held. "Would you be good enough to read this aloud, Professor Guidobaldo?" The witness touched his glasses and flattened the page onto the portfolio binder.

"Yes. I will begin with explaining this was not unusual, in that time. A prince composed letters of state, and messages of intrigue. He did not deign to write common communications. It was given to a *scriba*—a scribe. Here, I will read. '*Questa sera di gennaio. Nell'anno millecinquecento del nostro benedetto Signore, lo metto . . .*'"

The Italian words sounded lilting and poetic, though no one in the courtroom understood what he was reading. ". . . . *acquistarono dalla cittadella di Caterina Sforza. Ella era una opponente valorosa, ed una cagna.*"

He lowered the paper and peeked at Martin Lormer over the rims of his glasses. "Is interesting, no? Cesare Borgia, so fine a political genius can also love art—Uccello is, how to say—ah, *magnifico*." He glanced about the courtroom, concerned about the silence. He sighed. "I understand. I will translate for this court."

Martin Lormer held up his hand. "One moment, Professor Guidobaldo." He removed a packet from his briefcase and placed one before the District Attorney and handed up the other to the judge. He gave the remainder to the court clerk, saying, "Please distribute this to the jury," and turned to the judge.

"Your honor, before the Professor translates for us, I have issued a copy—an exact copy—of a portion of the defendant's journal, already read into the record and marked as evidence E."

He turned to the witness and nodded. "You may begin, Professor."

The man nodded. "Yes. I shall bring this into the English." People leaned forward to listen. The jurors all stared at their pages.

On this eve of January in the year of fifteen hundred, of our merciful Lord, I place within my vault three masterpieces by the artist, Paolo Uccello. Acquired . . .

Though the people frowned, trying to comprehend Martin Lormer's purpose, I was amused at how much foresight satan had. He could use an event which occurred four centuries ago to bring his purposes into this time. The note the curator was reading was exactly the same as the note I had written in my journal. I was not troubled by the devil's devices—I was troubled only about being duped by them.

When the curator was finished reading, the judge looked to the District Attorney, waiting for his objection. He sat, studying the paper. He did not want to object and cause the jury to be told about the exact sameness of the notes. Martin Lormer shrugged.

"Professor Guidobaldo, that receipt, so to speak, was written in the year fifteen hundred, almost 478 years ago. Have you ever read that note before coming to testify?"

"Yes. In Signor Jerod's journal. They are in different languages, but they are the same when translated."

"Is the note signed? The ancient note, I mean."

"It is. By the Duke, Cesare Borgia. It is *genuino*—genuine. There is also on the paper the initials B. V."

"The initials B. V., of course, represent Barthelamo Vecchio."

The District Attorney stood up and shook his head. "Your honor, objection. There is no way that it can be ascertained that the initials B. V. represent Barthelamo Vecchio."

The judge nodded. "Objection sustained."

Martin Lormer smiled at the witness. "Would you be good enough to read, and translate, from the other authenticated documents you brought—the additional references you have concerning the Italian Physician-Surgeon, whose initials are B. V.?"

"Objection, your honor. It has not been established that the initials B. V. belong to a Physician-Surgeon."

"Objection sustained. Counsel for the defense is reminded to be more discreet in the questions he asks."

"Sorry, your honor. Now, Professor, would you read the other references you have to the initials B. V.?"

"*Certo*. I have here, from the other *dottore*, Marius Vitto. It is dated for *settembre* in the year of 1499. 'I am made old by Messr. Vecchio. He is a Surgeon extraordinary. Our Duke would be dead had another drawn the arrow from his chest. Were Barthelamo Vecchio not a crookback, he would be elevated from his common lineage!' "

"Thank you, Professor Guidobaldo. Now, another reference, if you will."

"*Certo*. Here is from Gian Antonio Porcello dei Pandoni—he was a scholar. Once commissioned under Alfonso to report the Milano-Venetian warfare in 1451. He writes—I shall translate—'I am taken with dreadful chills. The blessed Virgin has brought me the hump-shouldered physician, Barthelamo, from Borgia's court.' There is more. It is, how to say—ah, yes, a *metter da parte*—an aside. It was found in . . ."

I was mildly startled to know that Barthelamo Vecchio had actually lived.

People were looking at me. They were seeing me as credible. I was not a former priest turned lunatic by a hyper sex drive. What had been drawing me away from reality had been real. The District Attorney, too, was becoming agitated with the realization that Martin Lormer was demonstrating to the public that I was an unusual human being, but not a madman. Ludicrous and mad as this trial was, Martin Lormer's skill might overcome public reason.

"Professor Guidobaldo, in the other references you have found concerning Barthelamo Vecchio, what kind of a man was he?"

"*Superbo*. Most compassionate. He was not loved, he was not hated. His practice was brilliant. For some, *sfacciataggine*—how to say, ah, outrageous in method. Most inventive. Effective, much more than other . . ."

"Objection, your honor. None of this is particularly relevant to the issues. Barthelamo Vecchio is not so unusual a name that it should be assumed that he is the one referred to in the defendant's journal."

"I'm going to overrule that objection, counselor. The witness has read several references to this doctor, Barthelamo Vecchio, who was also referred to as *crookback* and *hump shoulder*. It is unlikely that there were two such men at the same place, in the same time, conducting their practice at the Borgia residence. The defense may continue."

"Thank you, your honor. I have no more questions of this witness."

People looked to the District Attorney as Martin Lormer walked to our table. He was frowning. The District Attorney looked to the jury as he went to the witness.

"Professor, I will not question the validity of your records and documents. Are they within the public domain of your country? In libraries, in the museums, and so on?"

"Oh, yes. We are not ashamed. The heritage of Italy is for inspection. We have learned our lesson of concealment under Il Duce. Our national character is given beauty by our past."

"Then these records and documents are available for anyone who is interested in viewing them—even photographing them and bringing them to America?"

"Oh, yes. Many of them have been removed from our archives and brought to other countries. Our Renaissance is the grandest of all histories."

"Well, then, if anyone can view them, and copy them—there is no reason why someone can't use them for source materials for academic studies, for works of fiction—*even for use in personal journals*."

"That is so."

"Thus, the fact that B. V. was a real person, and deformed, indicates that he did live during the time of Cesare Borgia. But when he died, he died and his life was over."

"Yes, yes, he died, and it is over—*fini!*"

Martin Lormer said, "Objection, your honor. While it is advisable to believe that Barthelamo Vecchio died, there is no evidence to support the belief that his life was over. It is . . ."

The judge shook her head and smirked. "Objection overruled. Furthermore, counselor, this court does not appreciate your verbal manipulations." He licked his upper lip and I sensed he had become worried.

He muttered to me, "I opened a little door for him. I hope he overlooks it, but I don't think he will." He looked to me. I thought he was going to say, "Stephen, you must testify in your own behalf. Too much depends upon your testimony." But he remained silent. I was saddened for him. All his brilliance was becoming waste.

God would not allow him to win this trial.

I shifted around and sat with my eyes closed, not wanting to see his face and think about his defeat. I was suddenly overcome with a sense of sorrow for Barthelamo. The people in the courtroom could only hear about some of his life. They could not know what he was feeling during those long, endless days and nights when Cesare Borgia was searching for the murderer of Count Finiguerra.

Barthelamo was in a torment of alternatives—to offend God by destroying a human who was not an assassin, or to return happiness to his life. And because his love for Letitia was so achingly present in his every moment, he chose to deprive himself of his heavenly privileges, rather than lose his love with Letitia.

Each day away from Letitia was an unending pain. Each night without her asleep beside him was a lonely, agonizing plunge through darkness. Now that she was Lucrezia Borgia's body-servant—a position of esteem and opportunity—he had to rescue her from her ambitions and the wanton influences of the Duke's sister.

He suspected that Letitia's loyalty to him, and her love, was wavering: she had begun stealing from him.

One morning, when he had finished lancing several boils from the rump and neck of the Doge of Tintoretto, he encountered Lucrezia hastening along a corridor in her long silk nightdress. Her exposed skin was mottled from the cold. The rouge on her breasts had been caressed away. Letitia was hurrying behind her, carrying a heavy container of cosmetics. He had bowed and looked at Letitia, who subtly shook her head, silently saying, "This is not the time for loving greetings."

Lucrezia stopped and scowled at him. "Besides a demon Physician, have you also become a spying Physician?" The windblown flames of the wall torches sputtered in their brackets. He drew off the black cape he wore on cold mornings and held it to her. "Adored sister of my great Prince, accept this poor garment to protect you from a chill."

She pulled the cloak from his hand and flung it about her fragile figure. "Take heed, Physician Vecchio," she hissed in tones of hatred. "The number of years remaining for you are not as great as you anticipate." She stepped to the side and stared at his back. His deformity suddenly ached. He became ashamed of his physique. She snickered. "I have reduced those years to mere days."

She strode past him. Letitia pressed her small hand to her mouth and shook her head, warning him not to speak with her now. A large ruby ring adorned her center finger. He drew back and listened to their walk through the corridor. He was pained by his loneliness, angered by Lucrezia's threat—but he was fearful at the sight of Letitia's ring. She had taken it from a small casement filled with jewelry he intended giving her when they were together again.

Other valuables and objects were missing from his rooms. Probes and scalpels, a gold medallion the old physician Marius Vitto had given him. A jeweled caduceus he intended presenting to Borgia when the conquest of Forli was accomplished. A cauterizing iron, vials of oil and medicines. He had become so infuriated at Letitia's random stealing that he had waited outside of Lucrezia's apartment to accost her.

"Why are you stealing from me?"

"Master Vecchio, you accuse me falsely."

"Letitia, beloved, do not trifle with me. Why are you stealing from me when I would give you all I have—all!"

"Master Vecchio, I raise my hand to God that I am not stealing from you. In the eyes of my beloved Mary I swear that . . ."

She stopped when the door opened and Lucrezia stepped out. Barthelamo hurried away.

He had been forced—by Lucrezia Borgia's hatred of him, and his suspicions that she was contriving his downfall—to select Captain Vincenzo Valori as the assassin.

He had chosen Vincenzo Valori as the assassin because the captain, bedded with the mistress of Cardinal Riga on the night of the murder, had once tried to kill the Count. He was the adored cousin of Contessa Jeronima Finiguerra and he loathed the Count's continual abuse of his wife. One afternoon they had fought with knives. Vincenzo would have butchered the Count but was stopped by the Contessa, who feared his execution. When he could, the captain spoke damnations and slanders against the Count.

While preparing a powder and an anise-scented incense to alleviate a sharp ache in Cesare Borgia's side, Barthelamo feigned a puzzled expression. The Duke, alert to sense changes in disposition, inquired, "Do you diagnose this pain as more than pain?"

Barthelamo smiled patiently. "No, no, Excellence. It is another matter that troubles me."

Borgia roused himself from brooding to become scornful. "Has the Physician who can command both black and white spirits forgotten how to cast a spell? Come forth with an incantation and dispel its odious aura from your presence."

"My Sublimity honors me with his humor. I have no such dark powers or interests. I am not troubled for myself. It is for another. My affection for him has made me negligent in my loyalty to you."

Borgia brought the tray of incense closer to his nostrils and inhaled deeply. He fondled a great pearl pendant dangling about his neck. "Speak, Physician. Amuse me with your trifling catastrophes. It shall distract me from mine own."

Barthelamo stirred the powder in a jeweled cup of wine and spoke of how superb a character was the noble Captain Vincenzo Valori—but it seemed unlikely that the Contessa's cousin had been fornicating with Louisa del Sarto on the night of the murder. "She has been *incapacitata*, with a grave malady."

Borgia sat forward, seriously interested. "Why haven't you brought this to my attention before?"

"Excellence, I gravely doubted that anyone would indulge with the fair Louisa while in that dreadful condition—my reason told me this. Yet my heart now instructs me that true love disregards offensive maladies."

"Enough romance, Physician. What is her malady?"

"The curse of Venus—the dreaded infection of wantons."

Borgia shrugged. "Such information is *antico*—quite ancient." He sat back and sighed. A smile tilted his mouth. "The Cardinal himself told me of this. He claims to have escaped the infection. His humor is such that he encouraged the liaison between them."

"Rather than contradict my Lord, I would suffer the rack. Nevertheless, I doubt if the Cardinal has escaped the infection. You will notice the loss of his hair, the sallow complexion, the palsey of his touch, his lapses of memory. These are not the symptoms of a winter sniffle."

"Your conclusion then, Physician?"

"I do not conclude, my Lord. I merely assess. The love between Captain Valori and Louisa, which I once deemed as eternal, has passed into history. He now visits with another."

"Your assessment, then?"

"His presence in Louisa's bedchamber on the night of the foul deed seems questionable. If undying love can cease that quickly, then his ardor was never so exceptional that he would brave the contagion of her calamitous infection. And his hatred of the now deceased Count is known throughout the court."

Not more than an hour had passed when the dark-haired, tantalizingly bosomed Louisa del Sarto was escorted to the lower chambers of the castle, where she was cruelly interrogated. Barthelamo felt no guilt when he saw how they abused her. This was the risk of her profession. Her clothes were torn from her and she screamed her innocence as she was pushed into the *cartoccio di terribile*—an iron coffin raised above a brick forge. She continued screaming as the fire heated the metal. "*Misericordia!* I am innocent. *Disgrazia!* I was bedded with Vincenzo." Then her screams ceased and she fainted.

She was drawn from the heated coffin and Barthelamo swabbed her brutally burned and blistered skin. She was lowered into a vat of sewage water until she revived. Two men, hooded and completely covered with thick black leather protections, dragged her to the wasp chamber. When she saw the thousands of insects frantically crashing against the glass walls, she understood that she would be stung into either madness or death. She shrieked and fell to her knees and confessed that she had lied to save Vincenzo— that he had forced her to lie so he would not be suspected as the one who slew the Count.

Borgia began the torture of Vincenzo Valori by having him bound beneath a metal water spout and a *bostezo* was pushed into his mouth. The pronged device was slowly opened so his mouth was forced into a full yawn. A coarse tube of fabric was slowly edged into his throat. Water was dripped onto the cloth, causing him to swallow or else die of strangulation. As he swallowed, the cloth worked deeper into his throat. The black-hooded *tormentatore* then yanked the fabric from the depths of his body. Vincenzo could not even declare his innocence through the pain. The cloth, bloodied and scaled with gray tissue, was dangled before him until he could speak. "I am not the assassin. I confess only my innocence." This was done until the lacerations in his throat maimed his ability so speak. Barthelamo eased the captain's agony, though he felt no pity for him.

They dragged Vincenzo to another room. The floor was carpeted with sand and ember-ash to absorb the blood. He was stripped and flung upon a tilted chair. His wrists and ankles were chained and his head forced back until his mouth was fully opened. Borgia folded his arms across his massive chest and tapped his foot impatiently. "Come, come, Vincenzo, let us hear your confession now—while the words can sound clearly through your teeth."

The captain moaned, "I am innocent." Borgia chuckled and pointed to the exposed groin. "I see no putrid seepage from your glorious endowment, Vincenzo. Are you so favored by fortune that once having dipped your member into Louisa del Sarto's honeypot, you do not bear the stain of her malady?"

Barthelamo listened to the captain's pleas and would not reveal that the disease was not an instantly appearing infection. Bor-

gia snapped his fingers and a hooded rackmaster fixed heated pincers into the captain's mouth and began extracting his rear molars.
When seven were removed, the captain confessed that he had
murdered the Count. He sat, his face hung on his bloody chest
while more blood poured from his mouth as he continued confessing.

Barthelamo thought, "We are saved, Letitia, we are saved."

Borgia told him, "Repair this assassin that he may live long
enough to confess to the Pope and then to properly die." While he
opened his medicine case Barthelamo began scheming to have
Borgia return Letitia to his service.

Martin Lormer told the judge, "I would like to recall Edward
Jorden." The District Attorney looked at him, frowning. He believed that having discredited the significance of the Italian curator's testimony, he had pushed Martin Lormer into another dimension of the trial. He was alert now, and cautious.

I wondered what part of my journal the handwriting expert
would be required to read into the court records to prove to the
jury that my living under the impetus of reincarnation was not a
delusion. Perhaps the part dealing with Bianco and Onadyh leaving the village moments before dawn—carrying their water and
food—both dressed for their struggle through an expanse of desert
land. Onadyh wearing thickly cultivated animal skins to keep her
warm in the early morning chill. Bianco, not daring to leave any
portion of his sensitive white skin exposed to the sun, garbed in a
covering of feathers and wide plumes and looking like a grotesque
mutation.

I sighed. I did not care what section of the journal would be
read. I had been secretive, even timid, about writing of my relationship with Shara. My caution about recording my suspicions
that she was trying to destroy me, as the other women destroyed
their men, would bring on my conviction.

I had concluded that she was plotting from two dimensions—
to bring about my physical death or to drive me insane.

I began testing her.

I established the habit of standing on our narrow terrace, looking to the street three stories below. I stood with my arms crossed

on my chest, my legs eight inches apart. A slight push against my back would topple me over the waist-high railing. I was not taking a foolhardy risk. I believed myself capable of hearing or sensing when she would be behind me, moving to shove me to my death.

I was tense during those days.

I could feel her behind me. I could see her with the sight of intuition, the awareness of instinct. She was watching me. Estimating. Waiting.

The slightest sound made me pivot around, hands fisted, ready to fight her off. But whenever I whirled around, ready to strike her, she was somewhere in the living room, smiling at me.

Often, I would stand and listen to my own breathing. Was the tempo inconsistent, the tone unvarying, the feel of breath in me pleasing? I could see the alterations of color in the sky. I tried to memorize the clouds to see if the same cluster appeared the next day. I counted the cars that drove along the street. I studied the trees dotted along the sidewalks. People in the buildings across the terrace began to notice me but I ignored them.

Come on, Shara, do it, please. Don't keep me waiting until I feel crazy with agitation. Learn the difference between me and Barthelamo and Bianco. They loved unto death. I love unto life.

I knew the faces and activities of the people in the apartment buildings across the street. Many people slid their curtains across their windows if I stared for too long. One woman who lived directly across from our apartment was a vile peeper. She was a wrinkled crone who always wore black. She sat by the picture window dipping a cube of sugar into a glass of dark tea. She sucked on the sugar while she peered at all the windows. We would look at each other, then look away.

Days passed, then weeks.

The weather gradually became warm. Soon, it was going to happen, soon. On tippy toe and with a silent, villainous giggle, Shara would sneak up behind me, hands outstretched, fingers flared—prepared to push. Hurry, Shara, please hurry. This waiting bores me. It estranges us. Try to destroy me so I can love you more deeply.

I would stand on the terrace barefooted and without a shirt. I was not flamboyantly muscled but my physique was trim, and hard. I enjoyed flexing myself. Pretending, sometimes, to be a Greek statue come to life. I might crouch, like a wrestler alerted for combat. I would raise my arms and shift to my toes as a ballet dancer—wrists curved upward and hands cupped like inspired flowers. My favorite was a Hitler stance. Feet together, legs stiff, my right arm extended rigidly in a triumphant salute. The old woman across the way watched me and slowly shook her head. I knew she hated the Hitler pose.

I was not afraid.

If Shara pushed me, I would topple over the railing but while plunging down I would right myself into perfect balance and with cat-like grace, land on my feet without feeling pain or disarranging my hair. I would then hurry back into the apartment and embrace Shara, and console her, murmuring, "There, there, love, it's all over. You tried. The devil used you. But I defeated him. Now our love can grow in peace."

Sometimes Shara would join me on the terrace. Standing away from me, at my side, she would chat about her working day, about automobile repair services, the inconvenience of inflation, the planned unionization of her office staff, and then she noticed the old woman behind the wide window. I said, "She's a Peeping Tom, or is it a Peeping Tillie?"

Gently, she touched my arm. "No, Stephen, don't laugh at her. She's a blessed woman." Her hand was cool on my skin. Would this be the time? Was she cunningly preparing me?

"Why do you call her blessed?" I asked. "Only Mary, the mother of Jesus, is really blessed—above all women."

"Please, Stephen, you've become so literal. Can't we leave the Catholic Church out of our conversation? All I meant is that she seems to be growing old quite gracefully."

"You sound almost envious."

"Yes, I suppose I do. All that's left for her is some minor inconvenience like illness or physical discomfort, and then she's gone from the world. How lovely. I'm so tired of being young."

"I wish I were younger. I wish I were eleven years old again."

"Why eleven, in particular?"

"Then I would know what was going to happen to me at the age of twelve. And I could change it or avoid it. What age would you like to be?"

"That woman's age."

I shrugged, not understanding her. She continued staring at the woman until tears filled her eyes. She left the terrace and I was disappointed. I stood and counted the windows in the other buildings until the number became a lazy slur in my mind. It was obvious that I could not tempt her into acting before her plan. And I was fatigued with waiting.

It might mean five years of standing on the terrace like an idle idiot while she was devising some diabolic method for causing me anxieties that would numb my sensations. So I decided to provoke her.

I began stepping onto the terrace wearing only undershorts.

The old woman who sat sipping her tea did not leave her place at the window. Shara remained in the living room, watching me. I did not enjoy exhibiting myself and anyone who was observing me could not know I was in a terrible struggle. The woman I loved wanted to destroy me and I had to stop her so we could continue loving.

My groin was free of bandages and medicinal packing and I realized I was continually touching myself. I would pull out the elastic waistband and stare down at the black hair, the limp length of flesh. I became fascinated by the scar. It was like a ragged red ribbon bound around the pink flesh. I would raise it and stretch it to the fullest reach, plop it in my palm and whisper to it, "Get hard, you damn fool, I need you. Get hard without pain." Nerves had been severed when I cut myself and I could only feel the bottom of it. Sometimes I stared at it or plopped it for so long I would forget why I was standing on the terrace.

One day I was almost arrested.

It was early evening, just before the light faded. Our doorbell rang. I dropped myself into my undershorts and stood to the side, not wanting to be seen by any of Shara's friends. She opened the door and two wrinkle-suited men showed their wallets and stepped into the apartment.

Shara was silent while she listened to the detectives explain that some complaints of indecent exposure had been called in. I walked into the bedroom and began dressing. The other officer stood in the doorway, watching me. He glanced at the bookshelves and art prints framed on the walls. "You got a nice place here," he said. I nodded and did not want to speak. I knew Shara wanted me taken to the police station. She believed I would do something crazy when they questioned me.

While I dressed I felt stupid. My testing of Shara had been obvious and she had adroitly shifted her tactics. She did not have to corrupt her soul by pushing me from the terrace. She knew that people would complain of my near nudity.

The officer drew a notebook from his pocket and asked what kind of employment I was engaged in. I answered, "I'm an instructor at Calvin Coolidge University. My courses are in theology. Religious and ethnic mores of the Renaissance period." He wrote something, muttering, "Sounds heavy."

I did not look at Shara. The detectives stepped together and began speaking in whispers. Shara stared at the floor. Clever bitch, I thought. During our time together I had acquired a reputation for being unstable. An eccentric. If I became indignant or angry while being questioned the police would remand me to some psychiatric institution. If I was not a lunatic upon entering an institution, I would become one by remaining. Ergo—Shara would then know she had destroyed me.

I almost grinned and laughed aloud.

She was clever and diabolic, but she was only human. She could not alter the supernatural will. Or hurry it.

There were procedures and rituals that Barthelamo had endured with Letitia, that Bianco had endured with Onadyh. Their destruction has been arranged by Destiny, and the women had been only its human agents. They could not change their fate because they were ignorant of it.

In tormenting me with knowledge and sequences and details

of past lifetimes, the devil had given me the gift of *foresight*. Knowing allowed me to enforce change.

The detectives stepped apart and put their notebooks away. Shara looked to them. The chunky-faced man nodded. "This looks like some kind of misunderstanding to us."

The other detective said, "A man stands outside in his underwear and some old maids panic." The door was opened, and a detective said, "Once is a misunderstanding, twice can be a charge," and they left. I stood staring at the rug, suddenly wanting to cry. I could save myself only by leaving Shara.

I could not leave her. She would always be there, waiting for me, in one form or another.

She moved to me and touched my arm, whispering, "You need some rest, darling. It's been a long day." I let her lead me into the bedroom. She patted the pillow and spoke like a mother shushing an infirm child. "Why don't we have a good old American dinner tonight—hamburgers and french fries."

I lay down and closed my eyes, muttering, "Serve it with some pickled relish too, would you?" and because I felt childish, added "That would be yummy." I was feeling sad for her. We could not separate from each other. We would have to be ripped apart.

I could sense that the District Attorney did not like the handwriting expert. Tricky questions would not distress him. He held up the paper Martin Lormer had given him. "This photostat of an ancient document was brought to my office to ascertain its authenticity." Martin Lormer edged toward the District Attorney, who was studying his copy of the receipt written by Barthelamo Vecchio.

"Authenticate it? In what way?"

"To establish if it was written in the sixteenth century, as indicated on the date of the document. And to determine if the . . ."

The District Attorney interrupted him with, "One moment, please," and stood up. "Objection, your honor. The witness was examining a photograph of a document, not the original document."

The judge nodded. "Objection sustained." She leaned to Martin Lormer. "The document has already been verified and accepted as evidence. More expert testimony will not render it more authentic."

Martin Lormer turned to her and rubbed his cheek. It was one of his few nervous gestures. "Your honor, I appeal to your patience. I am seeking to establish another function of its authenticity."

Martin Lormer pointed to the paper the witness held. "Were you able to authenticate the approximate date of the document and, if so, would you explain, briefly, how you arrived at its authentication."

"Yes. We have a rich heritage of handwriting samples representing various ages and centuries. The cave drawings are, in fact, handwriting samples. We have been able to establish periods of migration from the cave drawings—or writings—the primitives left. The same artists—though they did not particularly consider themselves artists—left their picture writings on the walls of the various caves they traveled to and lived in, thus leaving a record of their movements."

"Counselor, will you advise your witness that the court, while appreciating this edification, would enjoy his getting to the point?"

"Yes, your honor. Mr. Jorden, could you be a bit more succinct in your testimony?"

"Yes, of course. Both samples of writing were meticulously scrutinized, under magnification and other tests. Handwriting can be distorted, deliberately altered, and so on, but it cannot be so disguised that under examination the similarity or dissimilarity cannot be determined. This Physician, referred to as Barthelamo Vecchio, was unusual in that he was both literate and precise in his writing. There are other records of doctors through the ages, and few of them were literate or precise."

"After you authenticated the date of the document, what were you then asked to search for?"

"To learn if there was any similarity between the document written by Barthelamo Vecchio and that of the defendant, Stephen Jerod."

The District Attorney stood up again and wagged a pencil at Martin Lormer as he spoke to the judge. "Your honor, this point has already been accepted by this court."

The judge clasped her hands together and placed them onto a sheaf of papers before her. Martin Lormer leaned against the witness-stand railing, waiting.

The judge unclasped her hands and nodded. "Objection sustained. The similarity between the documents has already been established."

Martin Lormer stepped closer to the bench. "Exception, your honor. My purpose is not to reaffirm what has already been established. It is to bring to light new facts."

"Then do it in another manner. Your present method is both time-consuming and repetitious."

"Yes, your honor."

He stood before the witness, his palms pressed together in a contemplative pose.

"Was there anything unique in your findings when making the comparison between documents?"

"Yes. If I may, I would like to clear away a misunderstanding. I was not comparing the documents for a similarity of *content*. I do not speak or read Italian."

"What, then, was the purpose of your comparison?"

"To learn if they were written by the same hand."

Martin Lormer paused before asking his next question. The District Attorney tilted his head and frowned. I put my hand to my face and grinned behind my fingers. The gross stupidity of the implication amused me. I could not feel that I was the defendant, the Stephen Jerod they were talking about. I wanted to scan the courtroom to find this fascinating defendant. Martin Lormer looked at the jury as he asked the question.

"In your *expert* opinion, what conclusion did you reach?"

"After many days of examination, and through consultation with other experts in the field, I concluded that though one document was in Italian and written in a medieval manner, over four hundred years ago—and the other document was written in contemporary English—*both documents were written by the same person.*"

I leaped up and had to clamp my hand on my mouth to stop from screaming, "You idiot, that's impossible!" The shock of what he claimed was a jolt of pain to me. I hunched over and wavered, feeling my legs and arms become limp, and voices stretched into long, haunting sounds, hollow and trembling as I gaped at the witness who twirled in my vision while others, as though floating to me, reached to grab my body, but I slowly slumped into a crumbling faint and they fizzled from my sight and senses and slowly, all was darkness.

Chapter 11

I was there, inside Barthelamo's life, and he was inside my life. I felt the hunch of his body, the weight of his deformity on his shoulder and back. I felt him wheeze when he breathed, saw that his vision was clouded when he stared at a distant object—because I was his body now.

I was in his rooms, preparing a vial of medicine, and I was startled when four of Cesare Borgia's *bravos* burst into my room to apprehend me. I shouted, "God's blood, have you taken leave of your senses?" They were surly and brutish and one reached to grasp my shoulder. I struck the thick arm down. The others jumped to me, grappling me toward the door, their armaments clattering. "Come peacefully to the Duke, or be dragged."

The mutation roosting on my body became a savage pain clawing for a strong hold. I demanded, "Release me. I will attend his presence without coercion."

We marched through corridors and vestibules. Wind struck the perspiration on my face, chilling my mind. The torches they carried lashed in the dark air. I did not know why this was happening and I would not permit myself to be afraid. Residents of the *palazzo* stared. Nobles stood in the midst of their affairs and intrigues and waved pomade balls—mocking me. Their derision was a blade across my senses. When the favored fall, they become odious to the ambitious.

The carved bronze door of the Duke's chambers was opened. Rudely, they pushed me to him. I struggled to aright myself. His anger caused him to tower. He loomed behind a table upon which were objects I quickly recognized as once belonging to me. Many of them Letitia had stolen. Behind him, seated grandly and with a cunning smile, was Lucrezia Borgia. Letitia stood beside the divan, her eyes fixed upon the tiled floor.

Borgia glared at me, yet I sensed him to be amused.

"Physician," he said, and his voice sounded enraged. "In all my court was there anyone I esteemed more highly, or trusted more?"

Not knowing the accusation, I did not speak. I looked at Letitia. Borgia leaned to the table and waved his arm, encompassing the objects.

"My affections have reduced me to a doddering sop. Were it not for my beloved sister's wisdom and obsession with my safety, your sorceries might have destroyed me."

"Adored Excellence, you speak beyond my reason. Name the accusation that I may deny it—that I may redeem myself in your heart."

"Here, upon this table, Physician, is your accusation. Immutable evidence of your betrayal. My armaments lie rotting in the fields. Here is the mandrake root you placed at the north juncture of my bedroom door to cause this catastrophe. Daily, in trickles and rushes, my army deserts me. Here is the *mantilla* of a widow, with the corners hardened by the blood of her dead husband—used to cast a corruption on the loyal among my troops."

I gazed at the black lace head covering. I was confused. His intention was to convict me for a crime. Why?

He picked a slender gold snuff box from the table and held it to me. "*Peste!* My army is famished. My lines are attacked, the supplies taken. Here is the cause." He pinched open the snuff box. "Three dried drops of adder venom, the tooth of a child dead from a black disease . . . and *usnea*, moss scraped from the skull of a murderer hanged in chains."

He raised a tubular vial and pointed to its contents.

"Am I a fool that you believed I would not know the mixture of your curses? The ash of a volcano and buried therein a toad's tongue and the hair of a wolf. Where, therefore, are my crossbowmen, my pikemen, my men-at-arms, and archers? Where then is my conquest of Faenza? It is taken from me by your sorceries, Physician, by your manipulation of the devil."

He did not believe any of these accusations. He did not need my devil. He had his own. I shook my head and bowed. "My Duke of glory, my Greatness. Not all these charms, these toys of a witch, are mine." He roared "Diavolo!" at me. I did not shudder though I was in fear. I held my hands to him in a humble gesture.

"Excellency—Duke of Destiny—I have no power to curse, nor to bless. I am a Physician, and a Surgeon. My power is to heal."

I heard frail and musical laughter. Lucrezia patted her hands. "Your Physician is a snake, beloved brother. His poison infects your reason." I glanced to Letitia. She stood with her eyes closed.

Borgia suddenly swept his massive arm across the table, flinging pincers and globes across the room. "I will not befoul this chamber with the accoutrements of your evil," he shouted, but I did not sense a fury in his anger. Be sly, be deft, I thought. This is Lucrezia's doing. He struck the table with a clenched hand, causing it to shudder. The *bravi* standing behind me snickered. This was all a charade Borgia was performing and I did not yet know why.

"You give me the assassin Vincenzo Valori, whilst the real assassin is concealed."

I forced my eyes to remain fixed upon his eyes as I lied. "I did not give you an assassin, my Lord. I proposed a possibility."

"Agreed. You did not accuse Captain Valori as the assassin. Yet you preyed upon my despondency. He did not murder the Count. Your mistaken proposal has betrayed my trust in you."

"Mistake, my Lord—yes. But distrust? Never. If you desire my life in your behalf, take it. Freely. You need no judicial pretense to claim it."

"I will not take your life while you pretend innocence. Circumstance will convict you and I will have your life at my discretion, and thus I will be cleansed of corruption."

"Captain Valori has been executed. What need is there for this mockery?"

"A man of nobility, of innocence, has been executed wrongly. Am I to spend my eternity toasting in the pits of hell because of it? For your heinous crime, my soul stands in stain."

I could not reply. I did not yet comprehend his depth. He did not believe in the menace of hell. Nor did I.

Lucrezia stood up and went to her brother. Her bosom

swelled in the lace cups as she leaned and whispered to Borgia. He drew an emerald ring from his thumb, huffed on the octagonal stone and polished it on his velvet lime doublet. He smirked at me.

"Do you begin to fear, Physician?"

"If my adored Prince desires that I fear, then I stand before you in unbearable terror."

"You do not yet know the depths of fear approaching you, Physician. You have gained too much power. Your influence has become too widespread. I am merely assuring myself that it will never transcend my own."

I smiled, though now I shuddered inwardly, with fear. My time with Borgia was closing. If he dismissed me from his court, Letitia would remain. I would need time with her. To persuade her to be exiled with me. I bowed to him, murmuring humbly, "A reminder coming from my beloved Prince is a jewel I will forever treasure." He chuckled softly and clapped his hands.

Contessa Ugolini entered the room. Her squat, ungainly figure moved to him as though carrying a burden of sand. Her complexion, below the thick covering of cosmetics, was an array of pits and pocks from a disease of birth. Had her father, a wealthy *Doge* in Urbano, not been blinded in the battle of Mantalio, before her birth, she would have been sold into service or secretly drowned to hide her ugliness.

"Contessa Ugolini, tell us of your complaint."

"The shame of it is beyond expression."

"Be not ashamed. Our reverence of you will cleanse our minds of any gross corruption."

"Excellency, whilst I was dazed with illness, this beastly Physician consorted with me. I did not consent. He has caused me a malady of horrifying disgust."

"A malady?"

"Yes, my Lord. In my privacy, I am plagued with vermin. I cannot sleep, so voracious are they in devouring me."

Borgia struck his hand to his heart and gasped in feigned horror, "*Dio mio!* I am astounded." She bowed her head in grave shame. Lucrezia sat in calm amusement. She reached up to Letitia and they held hands. Borgia pointed to me.

"Physician, reply to this accusation."

"The lie is too bold to countenance. I cannot refute her romantic dreams."

He laughed. His laughter shook my soul. The Contessa waddled to me. She smashed her hand onto my face, screeching, "Crookback devil! You used me foully—you implanted me with your demons."

I staggered backward but the hurt she caused me was nothing to the pain of not being able to choke her. Borgia commanded, "Leave us." She hurried from the room weeping. The silk cloth she held to her eyes was dry. I stroked my cheek and waited. If his purpose was to exile me from his court, why was he being so elaborate? He drew a gold-hilted dagger from his waistband and tapped it upon the table.

"What wench is there, in all my court, that I would not have offered for your carnal use—had you but asked."

"If I would not ask for position, nor for power, why would'st I request such lesser pleasures, my Lord? And which of my pleasures distresses you? My inclination for lonely hags?"

"Your preference could turn to roosters, for all I care. It is your use of privilege and power which offends me."

He cracked the dagger hilt against the table top. The narrow side door opened again to admit a bravo I recognized—Mario, the chief of Borgia's castle guard. I was chilled, knowing what he would say. He had viewed me in an isolated corridor, using a pretense of spells and curses to defend myself against death.

He stood before the Duke, the width of his shoulders tight against his purple jerkin. Borgia riffled his fingers at the soldier. "Speak." Mario did not turn to me.

"It was on the night you were near death from an assassin's crossbow. When this Surgeon saved your royal presence from death, you commanded that we hasten to protect him. He was beset by four of Count Beccadello's brutes. I believed we were too late to save him. Yet he held them off, to save himself."

"What weapons did he use? Describe the combat."

"None, my Lord. He held them at bay with the demons under his command. With incantations and spells. His assailants were powerless to move. He called up the demons of the dark. I cannot remember their names—I would not foul my mind with them. Smoke issued from his body. Strange lights shrouded his form. He was a specter."

The *bravo* crossed himself and muttered a quick prayer to God to protect him. The soldiers behind me edged back. Borgia slowly shook his head. I could feel his pretended sadness. "Physician, Physician," he said. "Shall I have you burnt to a stake, hanged in chains, led naked through the streets so the populace can stone you? You have put me into such a dismay."

"What I did was a hoax to protect myself from dangerous fools. They believed the hoax, thus I was saved. Would not my Lord have done the same—for his very life?"

Mario snickered. "The demons sprung from him like lice, my Lord. With my own eyes I saw them claw the throats of the Count's men."

Borgia waved his hand at Mario. He bowed and left. I looked at Letitia. Her hands rested upon the back of the gold-brocade divan. There were three rings upon her fingers. Lucrezia touched a perfumed kerchief to her lips and sighed. "Beloved brother, I weary of this trial. You have been duped and betrayed. Be done with what must be done."

He scowled at her. "Be silent, I will not be deprived of my satisfactions."

Lucrezia dangled lavender lace gloves above her breasts and laughed. "He hides the demons in his hump. By all the saints, I know he hides the demons there."

Borgia thunked the dagger hilt onto the table again and an old woman came in wearing a shabby, castaway velvet cape with a hood covering her gray hair. I did not know this stooped crone, who was a castle *cameriera*. What could a lowly scrub provide for Borgia, I wondered. A thick wooden *croce* hung from a rosary chain about her neck. He commanded her, "Speak." She quivered. Her voice was a dying moan.

"*Eminenza*, I was in my labors the night our blessed Count was slain. I stopped to rest the torment from my bones. The wind was breathing from hell and . . ."

"*Idiota*, stop blathering!"

"I saw the crookback Physician leaving his rooms. There was much blood on his cloak."

"Why did you not bring this to our attention that very night?"

"When is the Physician without blood on his garments, beloved Excellency? I believed it was from his work. I do not trifle with . . ."

"Enough. Leave us."

She brought the wooden cross to her lips and kissed it as she shuffled to the side door. Borgia stared at me and smiled. "You do not appear troubled at the consequence of such evidence."

I shook my hands in a trifling gesture. "Evidence, my Lord? What is evidence? Merely the manufacture of skillful minds. If your intention is to destroy me, why trouble yourself with evidence?"

Borgia looked to his sister. She brought her fingertips together and dabbed them. Borgia drew the beret from his head and stroked the long graceful plume. "Shall I bring you to the dungeons and wrest the evil from your soul?" He caressed the feather across his cheek and sighed as though in a lamentation—then suddenly flung the beret onto the table and bellowed in rage.

"It is not for any of the previous crimes that I desire your punishment. It is for what you did to my beloved Lucrezia."

I frowned, distressed at my own confusion. Had he joined the league of men made mad by unimpeded power? He pointed at me. "You have committed the vilest, the gravest blasphemy. Before you are judged by God, you must be judged by me."

"My Lord, forgive my complaint, but I fear your condemnation of me is unjust."

"Unjust! God's blood, unjust, you say? My adored sister, who is revered by all, was unable to contain her torment and has finally confessed the shame you have imposed upon her."

"Excellency, I am in a gross dilemma. My esteem for your beloved sister reaches beyond infinity."

"*Mentitore!* You lie. You abused her, shamed her, defiled her. I commanded that you heal her digestive ailment and you dealt with her as being *incinta*. Pregnant! *Dio mio!* God cannot forgive such sacrilege. The virtue of my beloved sister is intrinsic to the Borgia reknown. The offense is twofold when . . ."

"Excellence, my Excellency, this is madness. You told . . ."

"*Silenzio!* Had God allowed so unfortunate a condition to occur, the grief would be profound, but endurable. But to abort her. To destroy life God has caused in a woman! The blasphemy is unforgivable."

"Beloved Excellency, if she was not *incinta*—how then could I abort her?"

He struck his huge fist onto the table and roared, "You meant to abort her. *I damn you by your intentions!*"

The table shook. Objects clattered to the floor. Letitia gasped. Lucrezia yawned. I would not speak and remind him of his demand that I rid his whore sister of her burden. He was a vile fox. I was reduced and doomed. Yet in the knowledge of my doom, I was muddled. My belief that Letitia would cause my destruction had been misguided. It was to be Lucrezia. I moaned within me. I could have loved Letitia without fear.

I was afraid, yet I felt joy. She had not betrayed me. I wanted to reach to Letitia and touch her fingers. I might be bound between two fierce stallions and torn apart, and still I wanted only to have our flesh pressed together.

I heard Lucrezia laugh in girlish delight. Borgia scowled at her. "*Silenzio.* A man is dying before you. It is not a time for gaiety." He deepened his scowl at me.

"For these offenses alone I could have you torn to shreds. You are a sorcerer, a fiend of greater evil than the depraved witches my father burns at the stake. You feed upon the dying. You bewitch my armies and curse my campaign. You pervert the innocent and disease the lonely. You have rendered your Prince a fool by his affections for you. It is my beloved sister who has given me knowledge of your destructive intentions. Were it not for my beloved Lucrezia you might have usurped my rule. Your very presence befouls my sight."

I was stunned to know that he believed this about me. His love for Lucrezia, stirred by his lust for her, had dumbed his reason.

"Excellency," I said, holding my hands toward him. "I am not this vile creature being portrayed by these falsifiers. I have not, nor ever . . ." He struck his fist onto the table, shouting, "*Sucidume*—filth!" He stepped to me, enormous above my stooped physique. "I am Cesare Borgia, the Duke de Valentino—the Prince!" His voice lessened into a bitter sneer. "Are these people who speak of you fools? They know my sentence upon liars. Would they risk their lives to slander a common Physician? What is their gain? No, no, Physician. I have given you regard—yes—even now I give you esteem for having withheld your despicable nature from me. Yet your denial in the face of such testimony is an insult."

He put his hands on my natural shoulder and his fingers were hot pincers digging into my flesh. I moaned. He laughed bitterly. "We are not done, glorious Physician. Your life is not yet taken." He returned to the table and clapped his hands. A captain of his private Spanish guard entered carrying an ornately carved jewel box the size of a mature goose. He placed it onto the table and left. Borgia tapped the glistening silver lid.

"A nation that is ruled by the monarch's heart quickly becomes ripe for conquest. Rule is established by the use of a people's ignorance. Rule is maintained by the encouragement of fear. You have been ruined by love, Physician, and I cannot despise you. There was a time when I loved. One whose beauty was so perfect that God could not again create so wondrous a woman. Her passions were various and endless. She loved me with a love that could not be altered—or so I believed. But I was a bastard, spawn of corrupt affections. Thus it was believed I would not inherit or be granted a domain. Her everlasting love for me quickly died. Thus I was a fool. Now you, Physician, are the fool. You relied upon love as your measure of safety."

I could not follow his meaning for I was suddenly plunged into the living pain of the man I had once been. He was cloaked in strange feathers and peculiar skins of animals, slowly trudging a burning land. The woman was behind him.

Whilst I was still myself, standing before Borgia, who fondled the carvings on his treasure chest, I knew Letitia and I were the others trying desperately to live. I did not care if the windows of hell had opened to reveal this past of ourselves—this captive woman loved this alabaster creature my soul had once inhabited. And though I faced Cesare Borgia and his lethal intentions, I was joyous in knowing that Letitia loved me as she once loved Bianco, when she was the captive woman.

She walked behind him, in his shadow. She loved me then, as I knew Letitia loved me now. When the rigors of motion parted his garments she was quick to press the materials closed to keep the sun from his flesh. His desire for food often overcame his reason. When he sought food from plants growing in the waterless earth, she always stayed his hand from those that were poisonous or had ferocious barbs.

The blaze of afternoon had turned their bodies into heated shells. Though his eyes were covered with a mesh to protect him from blindness, the pigmentation of his pupils would become fiery. Soon, she was walking at his side, no longer frightened that his people were hunting them. He stopped, only to nourish her with drops of water from his animal pouch. She cupped her hands below her face to capture every drop. When he withdrew the bag she licked her mouth and fingers. He let her see him drink, to show he was not having more than his share. The land ahead was a vast stretch of long, dry hills.

The sun is dying and they seek a place to sleep. She points to the space beyond and he cannot see a pile of boulders. Lovingly, she walks at his side, guiding him from stumbling into craggy hollows. They drop to the grizzled earth and gasp into rest. He picks food from another pouch and they eat. They undress to blanket themselves in their clothes and gradually they couple in love and there is dry laughter in their embrace.

The darkness is speckled with lights from the sky. He sleeps. She opens her mouth to the fulfilled moon, then stiffens and grasps her stomach. The pain buckles her, makes her convulse. He does not see her tears nor hear her vicious cursing as she whimpers and gasps at the blood slowly streaming down her inner thighs.

She raises her face to the unblinking moon and sobs. In the distance she hears an animal howl. She curves her hand and fills her palm with blood and smears it across his ivory chest. He does not stir. She knows there is now no living child in her. The animal howls again. She sits and rocks, holding herself to stop the blood that oozes through her fingers. She listens to the animal's cry. She wants to steal his knife but cannot remove her hands from the blood.

Suddenly, they were gone from me. Borgia laughed and drew a slender silver key from a fold in his doublet. He looked at Lucrezia as he opened the treasure box. The jewels it contained were heaped in a mound—the spoils and loot garnered from his campaigns. Letitia edged closer to see. Lucrezia stared at me. She was relishing her hatred. Borgia placed his hand on the jewels and smiled.

"I will show you how dreadful is the risk of love. You have bedded with the wench you swore was malformed and . . ."

"Excellency, I have . . ."

"*Silenzio!* Else I shall have your tongue torn from your throat!" He pointed to Letitia. "Come forward, wench. You have been chosen by a stroke of fortune." Letitia hesitated. Lucrezia patted her hand. "Do not fear my beloved brother, child." She moved to him. She would not show me her eyes. She could see only the jewels.

Borgia spanned his fingers across her breasts and sighed to me. "So lush, so sweet. There are no fruits more succulent."

I gripped my curses in my throat. He placed his hand into her bosom and caressed her. She stood still, terrified, yet I sensed she did not feel revulsion. He drew his hand from her dear flesh and kissed his fingers. "*Meraviglioso, stupendo,*" he taunted me.

"This wench loves you, Physician. She has confessed it to Lucrezia. She has claimed that her love for you is her life. Such sentiment stirs my loins. Yet you have betrayed me with a lie. You claimed her to be malformed. When I gave her to the Count Beccadello to use, believing she would cripple him, you murdered him for using her. The Count was less to me than donkey droppings. Yet you have betrayed the trust of your Prince—for *love.* That was the choice of a fool. I will now prove this foolishness to you. Before your eyes, without intimidation, I will prove the infidelity of true love."

He held Letitia's wrist and drew her closer to the table. He riffled his hand through the jewels, allowing some diamond rings to drop through his fingers.

"Letitia, as of this moment you are elevated to lady-in-waiting to my beloved sister, Lucrezia. Does that please you?"

"Excellence, oh my Excellence, I am overcome."

"Still your heart, daughter of Fortune. I know you have bedded with the Physician. Lucrezia had set her spies to observe you. She learned of your dalliance days before the Count was murdered. Thus, my proposal is this. Deny this affair with the Physician, in such a way that I am persuaded to disbelieve my beloved sister, and I allow you both to leave my shelter to find residence and livelihood elsewhere. But admit, openly, that you have bedded with the Physician—that he has been your lover and that you are without a malformation—and I will grant you treasures beyond your most glorious imaginings."

We are free, I thought. Destiny has been thwarted by the caprice of the Prince of Conceit.

He drew a tiara glittering with diamonds set in a gold arc that might have been created by Donatello. He chuckled. "Here, a bedazzler once owned by Princess Filippo." He placed it upon the table. "There is a moderate estate in Urbano to which I hold title. It is yours. Now, tell me, wench. Have you a malformation—have you bedded with the Physician?"

How old was our love, I wondered. Could she withstand such temptations of immediate wealth and power? Lucrezia hissed to her, "Tell him. I will bring nobles to your bed. Handsome, straight-backed stalwarts to captivate your senses." Though my life was wavering in the balance of Borgia's guile and Letitia's greed, I sorrowed for her. All her small life she had been chattel—a mere groveler. Her look was now cunning, her desire enhanced with the promise of dreams.

She did not answer him. He cupped his hand into the jewels again and drew up a thrice-stranded necklace of pearls. He dangled it and she watched it sway, a pendulum of perfect snowdrops fashioned in Heaven.

"What is a Physician, wench? A dispenser of herbs, a dauber of poultices, a grub sack of tonics. Can he give you such baubles? Feel this. It will remain. Your passion for him will fade from your memory."

He grasped her hand and placed the necklace across her palm.

The precious orbs clicked. Her eyelids fluttered with anxiety. Borgia clenched his mouth. She placed the pearls on the table.

"Excellency, I was a child when the convent gave me into your service."

"You are a woman now. You are accountable for your choices. I have other gifts for the secret you hold. This estate you have just acquired will not serve as it stands. You now have furnishings and stables."

"My Lord, your generosity makes me faint."

"Yes, yes—now tell me of the first night you bedded with the Physician and I will be satisfied."

He scooped more jewels from the cask and held them to her. A coronet embedded with diamonds designed into stars. Her eyes squinted at the luster and flow as though being offered a portion of the sky. She was imagining herself to be a lady. No longer bringing bedpots and examining the excrement for the ingredients of disease. No longer exiled from the dance, excluded from flirtations.

Borgia juggled the jewels in his palm, two ruby rings the hue of pigeon's blood, a gold collar encrusted with sapphires. Letitia's bosom heaved. Letitia, Letitia, I have loved you in the Everlasting. The grandest diamond will crumble to dust before our love is diminished. She brought her hands together in a prayerful gesture. Borgia is toying with you, my thoughts screamed at her. Whatever he gives can be taken away.

I remained silent, waiting. I would not solicit her love with plea or prayer. Letitia slowly looked to me. Her eyes were opened and steady. My face and figure were being balanced in her soul.

Now I understood why the captive woman had taken blood from her womb to smear onto Bianco's chest. She desired the child she carried—caused by the son of the Great Burning Eye. Their struggle along the savage desert, their privation, had injured her body. And when they had loved at night, the violence of his desire had destroyed the infant. The child's death was now on his life. She had stained him with the blood of that death. She would now seek to destroy him. Revenge is deeper than love.

What had I done to Letitia that was suffocating her love whilst stirring in her a desire for vengeance?

"Speak, wench, I grow weary of this haggling!"

"My Lord, to be in your service, your court, became my greatest desire. To be the mistress of the Duke de Valentino, for only one hour, is a lifetime of remembered glory. When I was deprived of your love by reason of an unrealized malformation, I pleaded with Master Vecchio to correct me. It was in the correcting of my malformation that I was changed."

"Changed, you say? I'll have none of your evasions. Speak bluntly to your Prince, lest he become displeased."

"Master Vecchio's claim that I was malformed was untrue. I have bedded with him."

Borgia smiled. He wrinkled his mouth in mock pity and scowled at me. "How deplorable becomes the soul of one who trifles with the black spirits."

I was void of wit and reason and could not declare my virtue. I shook my head, moaning, "Excellency, it is all Lucrezia's doing— she has the heart of a witch, the mind . . ."

He suddenly smashed my face with his open palm, staggering me across the room. "*Diavolo!* You dare speak of my beloved sister!" The *bravi* leaped to me and held me upright. The pain within my skull was blinding. Blood spilled from a gash caused by his heavy ring. He strode to me, his thumb pointing at my eyes.

"You do not defile my beloved sister's name by bringing it to your foul lips. You have lied to me, betrayed my trust. The devil take your spells and incantations, your murdering of the Count. I care not a whit for these. It is the deception that I despise. For that dishonor to my name, my house, my cause, you will be bound between my stallions and your limbs will be torn from you. You will be dispersed, Physician. Fittingly dispersed. Your parts will be interred in separate and secret places. Not even satan will bring your parts into order again."

Letitia had turned to me. I sensed her shame to be a bloodless wound she could barely endure. "Letitia, beloved!" I pleaded. "I have jewels to give you," I shouted. "Come away with me. I will give you a manor and servants."

Borgia's laugh was a charge of hooves trampling my senses. "There are two possessions you cannot give her—*title* and *power*." His laughter was a roar of oceans. I struggled to reach her, to let her see and hear my love—to press my bloody face to her mouth.

The *bravi* pulled me back. I fought them. Borgia grasped my front and dragged me to him. "Love ruins not only nations, but men. You are doomed, Physician—your love has doomed you."

I quickly drew his ring from my finger and held it to him. There was a mad laughter in my voice. "Your pledge, my Lord. Your sacred oath to guard my life as your own."

He studied the great gold ring. His honor would demand that he release me. I would be exiled from the castle—perhaps from Italy. No matter. I would use my moderate wealth and legendary skills to return and rescue Letitia from his influence.

Letitia gazed at the ring. Her breath was rapid, her hope quickened. Borgia's eyes glinted with rage. His honor had trapped him. Lucrezia clutched her heart in feigned astonishment. "Oh, the depths of the Physician's evil."

She snatched the ring from my fingers. Her hand covered her forehead in a dramatic gesture of horror. "The Physician not only stains the name of Borgia with his devilry, he also steals my brother's ring."

Borgia wheezed a chuckle and the rage faded from his eyes. He shook his head in sham pity. "Your corruption is beyond language. I lay on my deathbed and whilst you draw an arrow from my royal chest, you rob me of a family ring. How ungodly, how depraved."

He returned the ring to his finger and spoke to the *bravi* as though to his tailor. "Bring the Physician to the dungeons. Have his garments torn from him. He will remain in that state until the afternoon he is fixed between my stallions. He will be torn as a weed." They began to drag me from his presence. Letitia shouted, "Wait!" Borgia and Lucrezia were startled. She bowed to him and spoke in a humble whisper.

"My Lord, Master Vecchio has been my lover. We cannot be parted in such a way—with so great a disaster between us. A fond kiss, my Lord. Allow me to kiss him before you bring . . ."

"Yes, yes, wench, you may kiss the crookback devil. Your loyalty to him does you honor. Be quick."

She hastened to me. I could not look upon her face. I stood before Letitia, my eyes closed, waiting for her mouth to burn upon my cheek. Her bosom brushed my shoulder as she reached up to cleanse some blood from my face. Her breath was a scented taste filling me. She whispered, "I will rescue you, Barthelamo. The stallions will not cause you a horrible death." Then she was gone. The *bravi* pulled me to the door. Her love for me was cunning. She would save me. Her betrayal of me was part of her plan to prove her loyalty. I would be rescued. My love would rescue me.

I awoke from my faint in the county prison infirmary. Four police guards were stationed in the long, dowdy white room. I lay staring up at the grimy ceiling, trying to remember why I had fainted. My lungs stung, the air was filled with a rancid, acrid smell. A chubby-faced doctor who chewed gum said, "He's coming out of it." He wore a white jacket. I shook my head to avoid the painful light. Martin Lormer leaned over me. "Stephen, are you all right?" I almost answered, "What happened?" He understood my unspoken question. "You fainted in the courtroom—after the handwriting expert's testimony." Then I remembered. The expert had proved that I was reincarnated.

It's a lie! I wanted to shout now. A trick of the devil! The evil spirit of Lucrezia Borgia is running the trial.

A hand touched my shoulder. "You can sit up when you feel like it."

I looked at Martin Lormer and hoped that he would explain why the handwriting expert had testified that the note written by Barthelamo and the writing in my journal were written by the same person. Martin Lormer could explain everything.

He held my forearm and helped me into a sitting position. He was smoking a cigarette. I watched a line of smoke drift up to his eyes. He smiled. "I warned you, Stephen. I told you that this might happen." His grip on my arm tightened, but his smile widened. "If you're going to faint every time you hear some shocking information, then we'd better bring a bed into the courtroom." I stared at his cigarette and did not think he was amusing.

I glanced about the infirmary, searching for someone. He whispered, "Shara is dead. Have you forgotten?" I tensed. He was beginning to understand my mind too clearly. The guard at the door asked, "Is he okay? What'll I tell the judge?"

Martin Lormer tapped ashes onto the floor. "Tell her he's fine. We'll be back in about ten minutes." The guard hurried out. I yawned. Martin Lormer shook his head at me.

"Fainting like that was the worst thing you could do—at that time. It suggests to the jury that your story of self-defense by reincarnation is a fraud."

I yawned again, then shrugged. He stared at me. He dropped the cigarette to the floor and stepped on it. He was suddenly angry and I did not know why. He turned to the three guards. "I want five minutes alone with my client. You can wait outside." I watched them leave the room. One guard posted himself at the door and carefully observed us through the narrow window. Martin Lormer pointed his finger at me. "I've had it with you, Stephen. I've had it with you, in spades." He stepped closer to me, his face pushing at mine.

"I'm Martin Lormer, do you hear me? Not some asshole shyster waiting for an ambulance to pass. *Martin Lormer.* I take only the important, the astonishing cases that become part of legal history. And every case I take puts my career on the line. Lose one— just one—and my career nose-dives. I'm not about to let that happen because some ex-priest has a rupture inside his brain and believes that he must die in order to save the world from the evils of reincarnation. That sucks, *Mister* Jerod. In my book you're just a soft, self-pitying loser who's making a Viennese operetta out of his last remains of life. Well, you can futz and fiddle with your life, but not with my career. After you, there will be a hundred other precedent-setting cases coming into my office. You'll not handicap my future, Mister *ex-priest.* Not in any way."

I could not look at the hating in his eyes. I could only see Barthelamo Vecchio being shoved into a dark and putrid dungeon and held immobile while the *bravi* tore the clothes from his body and dragged him to the grimy stone wall where a jailer forced his wrists and ankles into thick iron fetters. They laughed at his nakedness, how the winter air mottled his skin and made him shiver. One *bravo* clutched Barthelamo's black hair and forced him forward, suspending him on the chains while the other used the flat of his sword to strike the wrinkled hump on his shoulder and back—and while they laughed, all Barthelamo could think was that Letitia would soon rescue him, that her love for him was more powerful than Borgia's pronouncement of death.

I wanted to tell Martin Lormer that his anger did not upset me. His career, like my life, was some minor number in the vast statistic of people whose lives would be destroyed if our legal system sanctioned reincarnation as a fact, a daily reality. Martin Lormer's eyes were like charged sockets steadied on my face. But my mind suddenly became fixed on the vision of Bianco and Onadyh struggling through the desert land—could not soften the hating face she held when she walked behind him, staring at the feathered hood he wore. She was waving her arms and working her fingers at the sky in a silent incantation that pleaded with the Great Burning Eye, the father of her dead child, to lead her to her people.

Even as Martin Lormer reached out and clenched my arm to make me look at him, I could only feel the hatred Onadyh was feeling for the man who had saved her from being brutally sacrificed—who had kept her from being stoned by the village people. "He did not cause you to lose your child!" I screamed within me to the vision of them staggering across the oven of earth, their mouths cracked, their bodies parched—falling and then helping each other up only to stumble again.

Martin Lormer squeezed my arm until my flesh ached and I was forced to look at him. His voice was a vicious, cutting oath.

"I will win this trial, Stephen. In some way, and with resources I have never used before. Your silence won't defeat me, your courtroom cutups won't defeat me, the devil himself won't defeat me. I'll scare the piss out of people about reincarnation— but I'll do it through victory. I'll prove to the world that anyone who seriously believes in reincarnation and searches for his former life in some satanic depth of Time is believing in a doctrine of the supernatural that must lead to eventual insanity!"

While he stared at me, I could feel his ambition. It was a rage. A fanatic dedication. Suddenly, I hated him. He might win the trial. Dear God, he might win.

Sitting in the courtroom, being stared at by the spectators and the jury, I played a game with myself. I would listen to all that was said but I would not hear it. It would not penetrate my mind. Only through this mental insulation was I safe from fainting, from rage. All that I would let myself realize was what the Preacher, the son of David, wrote in Ecclesiastes: *"Is there any thing whereof it may be said, See, this new? it hath been already of old time, which was before us."*

There would be no more surprises for me. All that anyone would say from this time on, I already knew.

I felt Shara's presence in my senses. Her disposition was a caress. *It will be over soon, darling,* she was murmuring to me. I put my hand to my mouth and smiled. She had said that the night I choked her.

The courtroom was quiet while the handwriting expert sat in the witness box, waiting for the District Attorney's opening question. His gray pinstriped suit was neatly fitted to his lean figure. His eyeglasses reflected the rectangular neon ceiling lights. The District Attorney stood before him, his arms crossed on his chest. His stance and voice was belligerent.

"Mr. Jorden, you have testified that both the ancient Italian document—which is 477 years old—and the handwriting specimens you examined in the defendant's journal, were written by the same person. I find that testimony to be fantastic and I would like you to explain it."

"I cannot explain it. My responsibility was to make a comparison and reach a conclusion. The fact that I can't explain it does not disqualify it as a fact."

"Mr. Jorden, do you realize what your statement will do to your career?"

Martin Lormer raised his arm. "Objection, your honor. Prosecution is harassing the witness."

The judge shook her head. "I cannot accept that as a valid objection in these circumstances. The witness will answer the question."

The handwriting expert shrugged. "I am aware that some of my testimony will be detrimental to my reputation—but I am also aware of my obligation as a professional and that I am under oath. I can only repeat that they were written by the same hand."

"What you are saying, then, is that the defendant is over 477 years old."

"No. I am saying that both documents were written by the same hand. I cannot explain how that can be. I admit that I was shaken by my own conclusion. It seemed impossible. Thus, to ascertain that I was not mistaken, or incompetent, I sought other qualified opinions. I brought the documents to my colleagues. I have their names available."

"What did they tell you?"

"I included among the documents six other examples of writing from the period known as the Renaissance, and the handwriting of six other males made in 1978. I asked them to determine if there was any similarity between any of the documents. Three days later they informed me of their findings. They concurred with mine. The Barthelamo Vecchio document and the portions of the Stephen Jerod journal that were examined were written by the same hand."

"I find that impossible to believe. However, let me ask you this. Have you ever known anyone who believed or claimed he was a reincarnation of someone else in the distant past?"

"I have. But I do not believe in reincarnation."

"Did any of them ever show you a sample of their handwriting when they were someone else?"

"Happily, no. The people who believed they were reincarnated, that I have known, were either fools, emotionally disturbed, or phonies looking for attention."

The District Attorney paused. He paced before the jury, shaking his head. Martin Lormer shifted his chair closer to me. He whispered, "I've been reading the jury. They've passed their threshold of fascination. Now they want some heavy facts." He was talking to himself, really. The court stenographer scratched his nose. Martin Lormer muttered, "I've made one serious mistake, Stephen." He knew I would not answer him. "I'm going to assume that he's caught that mistake. I'll be able to tell by his next question." The District Attorney hunched his shoulders and sighed.

"There is something wrong here, something emphatically wrong. There's a time warp factor in here, or a sequence of circumstances that are so out of whack they have meshed into a meaning other than what they were intended for. There must be another . . ."

Martin Lormer stood up. "Your honor, I object to prosecution's musings and meditations. I request that he get on with the questioning." The District Attorney glared at him. The judge said, "Objection sustained."

"If the defendant, Stephen Jerod, seated before us, is not over 400 years old, then how could he have written both documents?"

"I can only state my conclusions. I can't always explain them."

"Isn't it possible that a man of the defendant's intelligence and cleverness could have fooled you and your colleagues?"

"That is possible, but not likely."

"Why? Are you people so infallible? The Italian document has been on display before the public since it was discovered. Couldn't the defendant have seen it and then forged or imitated the writing in his journal? Isn't it possible—since the defendant has a history of involvement in demonology—that he put himself into some weird trance and through the medium of automatic writing, duplicated, in remarkable exactness, a counterfeit of the Italian document?"

"That, too, is possible, but most unlikely. However, there is another fact that I will bring to the court's attention, to verify the accuracy of my and my colleagues' conclusion. The samples of writing we examined, written by the defendant in his journal— *were written at least seven years before the Italian document was discovered.*"

The District Attorney turned his back to the witness and glared at me. I winked at him. He crooked his mouth with disgust. He was confused. He wanted to hit someone. I glanced to Martin Lormer. He sat in a tired slump, impassively staring at his hands. What was the devil doing with Martin Lormer's mind? Was he becoming afraid and imagining himself to have been reduced to the asshole shyster he despised?

The District Attorney asked the witness, "Then it is your contention, in your expert opinion, that the defendant, Stephen

Jerod, who was once Barthelamo Vecchio, and before that Bianco—wrote that Italian document 477 years ago?"

Martin Lormer stiffened, about to object. He changed his mind. The front row of jurors leaned forward. The newspaper and television reporters squinted and frowned. The witness shrugged.

"All I'm qualified to state is that both documents were written by the same person."

"Then what you are stating as a fact is that the defendant, Stephen Jerod, is at least 477 years old."

The witness shifted nervously. The District Attorney looked to the judge. "I have no more questions of this witness." The handwriting expert left the stand. He walked to his seat, knowing that the entire courtroom was staring at him. I clasped my hands, feeling the texture of my skin. It was smooth and alive. I did not feel rheumy or calcified with age. Martin Lormer stood up. He skimmed his fingers through his hair.

"Your honor, I believe the time has come to rest this case."

People began to whisper. The jurors glanced to each other. The District Attorney leaned to his assistant. I felt hollow with sadness for my lawyer. The devil had frightened him. Martin, Martin, I wanted to plead to him. Give yourself to Jesus Christ and you don't have to fear the devil. He'll protect you. He defeated the devil at Calvary. Martin Lormer stiffened his shoulders.

"Your honor, although I have many more witnesses, I believe that beyond a reasonable doubt, innocence by reason of self-defense, because of reincarnation, has been proven here—even though the burden is on the prosecution to prove *guilt* beyond a reasonable doubt. Therefore, we have no further witnesses at this time."

"So you rest your case, is that correct?"

"Yes, your honor. The defense rests."

She stared at him with unusual steadiness. The two rows of jurors seemed startled. Someone called out, "Come on, Lormer, don't quit now—you're on top of it!" A tall bailiff moved from leaning against the wall to stand alerted. A jowly woman cackled, "You can't quit on the priest now. He needs you," and a man behind her snickered, "Hey, Marty, you got somewhere to go this weekend that you're hurrying?"

The bailiffs turned to the judge, who had not moved. Only I knew what was happening.

A gaunt-faced newspaper reporter hurried to our table. "Father Jerod, how do you feel about Lormer resting your case at this crucial time?" I ignored him. Martin Lormer grasped his arm and pulled him back. "Stay the hell away from us, vulture." The bailiffs strode to the courtroom aisles, waiting for their instructions. The judge stared, her eyes glazed, her mouth slack.

Satan had entranced her. She was paralyzed. Unable to act. I had an intimate view of her mind. She wanted to smash the gavel onto the bench top and demand that the courtroom be cleared. Her body was a constant pain as she strained to move. Behind her glazed eyes, tears were trying to burst free. Below her pain she was numb, like a toothache that had not yet reached the nerve. She knew what was happening while she wondered what was happening. Poor woman, I thought. To know you are helpless and not know why you are helpless.

Two men at opposite sides of the courtroom stood up and shouted advice to her. The county clerk rushed to the evidence table and guarded the items. The District Attorney pleaded to the judge, "Your honor, I suggest that you . . ." but was interrupted when a woman flung a newspaper at his head, screeching, "Shut up, you vicious bastard!" Another television reporter shoved a hand-sized tape recorder near my face. "Tell the American people what you believe about our judicial system." I deliberately let my mouth fill with spittle and stared at his eyes as I carefully drooled onto his black machine. He yanked it back.

The judge still could not move. Satan might hold her that way for two years or release her this instant. The people were free of their restraints. The District Attorney looked to Martin Lormer, who shrugged. He suspected what was happening. He would not interfere. He did not want the satanic focus to swing to his life.

A young man with streaky blond hair spoke to a juror. "There are greater causes than life or death at stake here. You are dealing with supernatural and spiritual principles." I squinted at him. How

could he know that? A transistor radio was snapped on. The raspy
voice of a country and western singer trailed into the air. A stout
man in a shine-worn suit clapped his hands, yodeling, "Go get'm
Merle." I saw Althea Jackson stand up to leave. Bishop Carmondy
placed his hand on her arm. She sat down. The Italian museum
curator wagged his head, complaining, "This should not be—this
is *scandaloso!*" Then satan released the judge.

She smashed her gavel onto the top of the bench and shouted,
"Bailiffs, stop this disorder!" The noise quickly ceased. She struck
the gavel again. "If this court is not absolutely silent in five seconds, and everyone seated, I will clear the court—forcibly, if need
be." The people shoved and scurried to their seats. Martin Lormer
narrowed his eyes at me. "All this is just more demonic crap, isn't
it? Scare tactics—supernatural extortion." I did not answer him, of
course. He had been allowed to prove that reincarnation was possible. He did not know if he felt blessed or cursed.

The District Attorney stood up. The judge said, "The defense
has rested his case. Do you intend any rebuttal?" He nodded. "I do,
your honor." She looked at some papers before her and pinched
her lips while she studied them.

I felt annoyed with this waiting—and though I had no place to
be, I wanted to be someplace else. I was tired of being gawked at,
bored with looking at others, annoyed with legal procedures and
satanic shenanigans. The hell with it. Pronounce the felon as
guilty and sentence him to death.

The tall juror at the end wanted me dead. His judgment was
obvious. He fidgeted his eyeglasses, rubbed his knuckles, crossed
his legs and scratched his ankles. He wanted the trial over so he
could be home, to be given celebrity for having punished the
"Reincarnation Killer." But the woman seated beside him would
settle for my lifetime in prison, without a chance for parole. She
was a loving woman and desired that I live but also carry the
weight of memory of my crime until I was aged and broken. She
did not want to cause the death of anyone. But it was the little man
seated in front whom I feared. He had the rabbit eyes of the
reformer, the sallow complexion of the do-gooder, the wetly
pursed mouth of the professional forgiver. He would argue to set
me free.

I listened to the muted coughing, the clearing of throats, the scuff of feet shifting into different positions, the squeak of a bench when a heavy body slumped back, the sound of a car horn from the street, the slight humming of the neon lights in the ceiling.

The judge turned a page over onto its blank side and looked to the District Attorney. "You may proceed with your rebuttal." He put his hands on the back of his hips and stepped closer to the bench.

"The defense has proven, it would seem, that Stephen Jerod and Barthelamo Vecchio and the Albino are one and the same. I hold here photostatic copies of portions of the defendant's journal. It was written by the defendant about himself. When he was Barthelamo Vecchio, when he was the Albino. He is not only revealing their character, he is revealing his own. This journal has been admitted into evidence. He has, therefore, become a character witness for himself, *although he has not spoken one word during this trial.*"

Martin Lormer muttered, "That shrewd son of a bitch really catches on fast. Hold onto your wig, Father. Your hot, smelly past is about to blow you down."

The District Attorney shook the papers he held and smirked. "It is not my intention to maliciously slander the defendant. But I don't believe the jury is free to reach an impartial verdict after what they have heard. The *effects* of this trial have been more fascinating than the *facts* of this trial."

Martin Lormer again raised his hand as though brushing away an annoying fly. "Objection, your honor. The prosecution is presuming to judge the mind of the jury."

The judge tapped her gavel and looked at the District Attorney. "I am overruling the defense's objection. You may proceed with the rebuttal."

Martin Lormer reached across the table and gripped his hand on my wrist. "Stephen, all I ask you to do is keep yourself under control during this ordeal of hearing your past. Trust me. I have not abandoned you." We stared at each other and I thought of what Jesus once said, *"I will never leave or forsake you"* and I wondered if I could allow myself to feel the presence of Jesus Christ in this satanically ruled courtroom.

I tried to find a profound historical parallel between myself and Barthelamo Vecchio. He had been chained to a dungeon wall, unable to sit because his own weight caused his arms to strain at the shoulder sockets. He was able to move his feet far enough to kick away the rats skulking to nibble his toes. Vermin crept up his legs and swarmed on his sides and stomach. Stretches of leather covering the barred windows were torn and did not stop the winter wind from making him shiver. Barthelamo was being held in chains, unable to help himself—and I was held in a courtroom chair, unable to help myself. But it was not the same. He was scheming to live, waiting for Letitia to arrange his rescue so they could be together. I was scheming to be found guilty so I could die and thus never again meet Shara because I had killed her—smashing the cycle of reincarnations—and when I died, I would utterly die. Thank God.

A police officer was brought to testify that I had once been stopped from behaving like a female impersonator. "Stop this stupid corruption of the truth," I wanted to shout. I had merely bought Shara a blonde wig for a party we were going to attend and I wanted to wear it only for the length of time it took to fill the synthetic hairs with my aura, my loving vibrations.

While the people in the courtroom stared at me, all I could wonder was where the District Attorney found these people. Was their yearning for a pinch of fame so desperate that they would distort a harmless action into a corruption of sanity that would be judged dangerous? I stared at Martin Lormer and felt that I should pray for him. Pray that this procession of anonymous witnesses that were using man's life for their own vain purposes did not so disenchant and sour him that he left this trial hating humanity.

And as other witnesses were brought forward I gradually diminished my prayers for Martin Lormer and began thinking of Bianco and Onadyh and I no longer whined and pouted for myself as I saw their circumstances.

Bianco had stumbled over a loose stone and fallen into a narrow gully and lay stretched on the sere, gravelly earth, too exhausted to raise himself. The lower portion of his feathered cloak had torn open, exposing an area of his stomach. While he gasped in semiconsciousness he also moaned from the burn of sunlight searching along his flesh. It was all the power of the Great Burning Eye sworn to turn him into flames for having killed his beloved son.

Onadyh had staggered down the incline and when she was beside him, she pulled the protective animal skin from about her waist and placed it across his stomach. Gently, she raised his head and lifted the mask from his face. She cupped her hands near his mouth and poured trickles of water onto her palm. He drank quickly and sucked on her skin until all the dampness was used. She sat down, resting her back against the slant of the gully. She shaded her eyes with her hand and looked ahead of her to see if she recognized their direction.

He listened to his breathing mix with the sounds of the land. The ground prodded into his bones. His flesh was an oven baking his body. The dry wind was a beast's mouth above him. He strained to hear the distance. There was only a scraping noise near his face. When he was a god again he would make a spell. They would always be protected from thirst and harm.

He lay with his eyes closed, remembering the bones and skulls of others who had tried to cross the Body of the Great Burning Eye. Once—he did not know how long ago—he had stooped over a huddle of three who had died and scooped up the hand bones and rattled them for Onadyh, telling her that he would cast them and read the tellings. She shuffled away from the heap blown together by the night wind. He shook the bones and dropped them at her feet. He told her the signs were happy. They would not be as the others. Onadyh stood and shifted sand over her feet. He did not like the words in her look. He knew she did not believe his readings.

He heard Onadyh move closer to him. She was bringing him more water. He would not drink. It was for her and the carrying in her. He slitted his eyes to see her in the glare from the Above. She stood above him, holding a large stone. He suddenly wanted to cry out that she should not kill him. No. No. She should not kill him to steal the water. His father in the Dark Above would save them.

She screamed a hating noise and smashed the stone toward his face. He whimpered.

When he felt no pain he struggled up. She pointed to his side and laughed. He saw a large animal, thick with wattles and scales, and long jaws now crooked beneath the shattered skull. He rolled away as the animal still thrashed, its clubby tail beating the ground, throwing grit at their faces. She reached behind him and drew the knife from his clothes. She raised the stone again and again flung it onto the head. When the coarse body stopped writhing she flopped it onto its back. While she gutted the slick, pleated underbelly to give them food, he held up his arms, offering love to his father who was behind the Great Burning Eye—guarding them.

He waited for her to finish cutting the beast. The Great Burning Eye had sent the animal to kill him and his father had changed the vengeance into food that would give them strength. He reached out to touch her leg—to speak his love. She stepped back, kicking at his hand. She flung the waste guts into the sand and pointed to the long stretch of hills ahead of them. He understood. They were reaching her people.

He made himself stand. He watched her chop and slice the flesh and prepare it for carrying. When they came to the village of her people and he was again brought to his god-ness, he would never be afraid that she wanted to crush his head with a large stone.

While they walked toward her people, the heat that came from above would burn such a fear from his mind.

I knew his yearning to become a god again, his hidden fright that Onadyh might want to destroy him. His desire and fear had transpired through millenniums to affect Barthelamo and myself.

The District Attorney called the man who owned the Costume & Novelty Shop in San Francisco. I sat and felt ridiculous. When I had gone into the man's shop my intention was not belligerent. I wanted to use a Renaissance costume to test Shara. To know if she secretly believed she was a reincarnated woman.

I would wear the Cesare Borgia costume and hide in the closet. When Shara returned to the apartment I would leap from the closet and shout, "Aha, my Letitia, there you are!" Her spontaneous reaction would reveal the truth. But the shop owner claimed the only Borgia costume he had was already reserved. Jokingly, I had decided to bully him into renting it to me. I had grasped the lapels of his suit jacket and bawled, "*Sozzura*—filth—bring my doublet or I shall feed you to the castle dogs!"

The man suddenly shoved me back, screaming, "Help! Police!" I fell against a display counter, tumbling it over. I was infuriated at his stupidity, his hysteria. I yelled, "*Stupido!*" The people who were examining costumes looked at me. I grabbed a short leather whip used for controlling bulls and began lashing it at their faces, roaring, "*Bestia! Animale!* Begone from my presence!" I was still lashing the walls and costumes and masks when the owner returned.

The District Attorney asked the witness, "When the police arrived, what happened?"

"He calmed down. I told him, you pay up for the damage, or you get put in the cooler. That, plus the cops being there, scared him. He wrote me a check on the spot. Then you know what? He's got the gall to ask me to recommend him a place to rent a Renaissance costume in Oakland."

The District Attorney looked at the wall clock and said, "I have no more questions to ask this witness." Martin Lormer shrugged. "No questions, your honor." The District Attorney stepped toward the judge. "Your honor, it is only a few minutes before the lunch hour. Could we break before I bring my next witness?"

She stood up and I yawned, blocking her voice from my hearing.

Chapter 12

I was escorted to a holding cell behind the judge's chambers. I was not handcuffed. I stood against the wall, staring at the backs of the deputy sheriffs guarding me. I stood with my hands pressed against the stone wall and though I had never been Barthelamo Vecchio, I felt as he must have felt. Fixed into one place and alone. Awaiting the time of his death—or rescue.

I heard a metal door open and a deputy sheriff said, "Hi-ya, counselor. Come to confer with the priest?" He opened the cell door and I knew Martin Lormer was going to work at persuading me to break my vow of silence. He sat on the metal bench bolted to the concrete floor. He stared at his shoes.

"Stephen, let me confess something. I am out of my depth in this supernatural conflict that is happening in the courtroom. And you are right in your assessment of the situation. You are not on trial. Reincarnation, as a doctrine and a living condition, is on trial. Thus, I must win this trial. Not to free you, which will be a secondary issue—a by-product—but to reveal to the public what actually happens to a person who believes he is reincarnated and is forced to live by its dictates."

I looked away from him. I was allowing my life to be taken by the judicial system to eliminate the possibility of people believing that reincarnation was a glamorous reality—and he was trying to thwart me in this purpose. I disliked him for being obvious.

"Stephen, we haven't much time left. I don't expect this trial to go into another day. We have different methods, but we are struggling for the same goals. You want people to shun the doctrine of reincarnation by revealing that it has destroyed you—and I want people to become terrified at the possibility of being reincarnated. What reincarnation has done to you is only part of the example. What it will cause you to do after you are released is the other part I must show to the public."

I stood and listened for strange sounds in the cell. The crawling of roaches, the nibbling tick of mice, the music from a transistor radio—anything—to avoid listening to him. I would not fight his battle with the devil. I had not yet won my own.

His hand stretched toward me. I shifted back. His touch might be persuasive.

"Stephen, don't be angry with me for believing you are a lunatic. It isn't madness you fashioned for yourself. God is now using us to promote the truth that the devil is real, that he is an egomaniac, an extremist, and that he uses the doctrine of reincarnation as a weapon against us."

Oh, how clever, oh, how sly this lawyer is. Tell the addled defendant what he wants to hear and distract his commitment. Tell him that God has given him a mission he cannot shirk. No, damn it, no. I have been a fool for so long I know all the tricks that turn men into fools. Take your psalm-singing, prissy-piety into another cell and con another con with your theological palaver. His voice was an urgent plea.

"I have proved that you were once Barthelamo Vecchio and before that, Bianco. But I did not prove it on the truth. I *proved it on fact*. When I began this trial, I had accepted a challenge. Can I get this lunatic off by using a unique, unprecedented defense. What I told you about my ambitions, earlier, still holds true. But many terrible and splendid things have happened to me. Now I must win for the sake of other people, not only for my career. If I lose, then the act of murder will be absorbed. It will be overlooked, while the issue of reincarnation will be promoted into dangerous public acceptance. They will see only your reincarnation, not your homicide. And the *truth* is that you are not reincarnated."

I wanted to laugh at him. He had used the church's money to conduct research, to bring people into Alameda from all over the world to prove I was reincarnated. And he had proved it. There was no way to deny the sameness of handwriting between Barthelamo and myself.

"Stephen, you are thinking about the handwriting comparisons, aren't you? What you have written and what Barthelamo had written become the same handwritings *only when they are examined*. When no one is studying them, they are totally different. It is a supernatural, satanic device, a trick of illusion. The devil has lived longer than you and me and even before the time of Bianco. He is a master illusionist. He has all the time in the world to arrange these illusions—and delusions."

I was listening to him but I was not believing him. Though I did not want to be reincarnated, I could not deny my reincarnation, even while I denied it. I knew my thoughts did not make sense. Only the feelings within my thoughts felt sensible.

"If you let yourself be convicted, then every disturbed person with suicidal inclinations will leap into the act of self-destruction. Their satanic torment will tell them that the next life is better than this one. They will recognize only the fact that I have proved you to be reincarnated. But when I win the trial and you are freed, *then the truth will be revealed*. Because we both know what you will do after you are released."

I will wander, I thought. The world will know me. "Reincarnated Man Visits Herrington, Kansas" and "Reincarnated Jerod Travels to Tonga." I will be given universal celebrity but I will avoid it. I would find a monastic retreat where the latest communication from the world came in by a Spanish frigate and work out the remainder of my life cultivating grapes.

I heard Martin Lormer snicker. He stood up and leaned to me.

"I'm not a mind reader, Stephen, but I know your thoughts. You believe you will become a recluse until the world forgets you. And you are wrong. When this trial is over, and if you have allowed me to win, you will walk out a free man. *And in less than three days you will kill yourself.*"

I turned my back to him. I did not want him in my presence. He was a spokesman for the devil.

I moved toward the cell door to shake it and alert the guards. I would tell them I wanted to be alone until court convened again. He laughed softly.

"Do you think you're the only one who has been bumped by the devil? He has affected all our lives, in strange and bizarre ways. The devil is a liar and *God is truth*. I'll put my trust in God. Whom do you put your trust in?"

I was suddenly indignant and swung around and glared at him. How could this heathen, this corruption who manipulated our judicial system, slander a former priest? His relationship with God was in shifts and starts and when the crisis was over, God was forgotten.

My glaring did not cause him to look away, to stop his smirking. I will never kill myself, I silently told him. And I am not a lunatic. He rubbed his hands together, then pointed to me.

"Stephen, the only reason the doctrine of reincarnation has survived all these centuries is because it is an *abstraction*. All the occults and satanic communes and ridiculous religions keep growing because they exploit our *real* fear of death. They promise us the abstract continuation of life after life. And life after that. Only our bodies are meat for the worms and dust for the wind. Our souls go endlessly on, picking up new bodies along the way, in another time, in another place. Therefore, reincarnation continues to exist. *Because it has never been factually proven to exist.* People will not believe in anything that is provable. The abstract does not frighten them."

Don't let me believe him, Lord. His tongue is slippery silver. He is being controlled by the devil.

"I have committed myself to a dangerous action, Stephen. I have eliminated the abstract factor from reincarnation. Now you must let me extend that reality into a *truth* by winning this trial. If the abstract allows for a soothing escape from reality, the reality of continual incarnations must be made terrifying to people. You must become the example. What I'm asking of you is to destroy yourself for a cause, not for a heroic but illogical gesture."

Although I heard him, he knew I was not listening. The more my silence denied his purposes, the more ridiculous they would become to him. He had only brushed with the supernatural. I had come into agonizing contention with the demonic. Shara had known this fleetingly. Sometimes she was given quick insights into my mind.

"Darling, why are you looking at me that way, and for so long? I have the feeling you are examining me as though you were a doctor."

"What the hell are you talking about?"

"I have no idea of what I'm talking about. Something made me ask you that question."

"Well, the next time it happens, ignore it."

"Darling, have you ever thought of killing me?"

"Shara—are you crazy? Why in God's name would a thought like that ever touch my mind? I love you."

"I know you do, darling. But I have the feeling that you've been thinking about killing me. That doesn't displease me, or frighten me. If you have to think about killing me, then you should think about it."

"Will you stop that foolish talk? Why should I think about killing you when I've never thought about killing you?"

"Because only by thinking the thought through, completely, can you ever be free of it."

"That's silly. An idea is not a static thing. It has vitality and direction. If you don't stop it, or control it, it can become an obsession."

"I'll take the risk, darling. I'll rely on your doing the right thing, at the right time."

The memory of that conversation made me shudder. Martin Lormer lit a cigarette and blew the smoke toward the guards. I no longer hated him for telling me that if I was freed I would kill myself. I understood his reasoning. He was becoming biblical. An eye for an eye, a life for a life. But he was not truly biblical. "*Vengeance is mine, saith the Lord.*" If it was in God's preference, He would kill me. I watched him inhale deeply and allow the smoke to skim through his lips. He tapped ashes onto the cell floor.

"Let me ask you this question, Stephen. What will happen to you if you are found guilty, and are not given the death sentence? What if the sentence is life in prison, without hope of parole? How long will you survive in prison before your madness becomes so obvious that you are transferred to an insane asylum? Face it, Stephen, you are doomed. You are utterly and unequivocally doomed. You lived for the wrong reasons and now I want you to die for the right one." I felt his hand grasp my arm, and he shook me until I looked at him. Anger was tightening his face.

"This trial has been easy for you up till now. You have heard parts of your life that have totaled you up to a reincarnated man. But what have you heard about Shara?"

He laughed meanly. His eyes narrowed. He dropped the cigarette and stepped on it.

"Sweet, innocent, adoring, ever-loyal Shara. Except for some small oddities, she was the epitome of womanhood—the dream come true. But is that true? Will her character, her life, stand up under my examination when I go into surrebuttal? You think she was Letitia when you were Barthelamo, and before that Onadyh, when you were Bianco. Do you want to find out, or will you be content to die without knowing?"

God, let me scream at this man who hammers into the guts of my soul and will not relent.

"Yes, Stephen. When I begin my surrebuttal I will deal almost exclusively with Shara. Her life, her character, your relationship. And if you force me to win the trial by bringing in evidence that I have carefully held back, what I bring in might very well drive you into a state of ungovernable insanity. I will do something that is rarely done in the courtroom. *I will make the inconceivable believable.*"

I went to the metal sink and turned on the water faucets to stop from hearing his voice. He shouldered me aside and shut them off. "You can't avoid listening to me."

I leaned my hands against the wall while he told me what he intended doing to Shara's character and life. I squeezed my eyes closed and forced myself to concentrate on recreating Shara. I recalled the night she had told me she had been listening to my sleep-talk and wanted me to tell her about Barthelamo and Bianco. I denied that I knew such people, or those names.

"Then what about the journal you're keeping? Tell me about the journal."

"It's only a personal journal. The random thoughts of a man who believes his philosophy will one day be meaningful. It's nothing more than that."

"Stephen, darling, you are such a poor liar. What are you really putting into your journal?"

"I am writing my thoughts. That's all I'm going to say about it."

"All right, darling. You don't have to show it to me. But let me offer you a contribution in the form of a riddle."

"A riddle?"

"Yes. *When does life remain after it vanishes, and what prevents life from continuing while it continues?* Put that riddle into your journal and if you ever solve it, let me read your answer."

"Do you know the answer to it?"

"Why, of course, darling. A riddle without an answer is not a riddle. It is an unanswerable question."

Martin Lormer shook my shoulder.

"You must be freed, Stephen. It is absolutely crucial that I bring about your acquittal. The sacrifice you are making of your life depends on your freedom, not on your conviction."

I stood before him, staring at his eyes. I wanted him to see into my thoughts, to know that I was shutting my mind to his pleas. He shook his head, bewildered. He was trying to see into a shuttered window. He clenched his mouth, realizing that I was no longer present in his reality. He walked to the cell door.

"All right, Stephen, I'll do it all on my own."

He sighed. His body seemed to inflate. He became larger in my sight. Stronger. His mouth tilted into a cynical smile.

"The first thing I want you to do is find a mirror and look at yourself. See the physical changes that have happened to you. Then ask yourself some questions. Why did Shara stay with you so long? Why did she live with a man who humiliated her, who brutalized her, who violated and degraded her. A man who made himself impotent and sexless."

I did not hear him. All I saw was the motion of his lips, the aggressive jut of his chin, how his shoulders were hunched forward like a fighter ready to punch.

"You'll never answer those questions because you haven't the guts to face the answers. Where did Shara come from—and I mean *originally.* Why did she need you? How did she use you? That's what I'm going to answer when the trial resumes. I'm going to turn you into a martyr. And then you are going to die by your own hand. And when you are dead, you will be dead forever."

He tapped on the door. "Open up." The deputy sheriff unlocked the cell and handed him his briefcase. I did not release myself from the confinement of myself. I would return to the courtroom and sit there in the same condition. Insulated from the world and closeted in my own life. It was the only protection I had against being freed.

I stood with my back against the wall, my arms stretched up, my legs spread as though held apart by chains. I knew that I was imitating the way Barthelamo Vecchio stood in his cell, awaiting his rescue. What was he thinking while he was waiting? He was frightened. While he loved Letitia, he could not trust her. Her greed, her ambition, might overcome her promise to rescue him. Then he would be led from the cell to be marched naked through the streets to where Borgia's horses were waiting.

He had seen a man torn apart by horses. It was in Urbano. The execution had taken place in the cobblestoned square. Wooden stands had been erected for the nobility. The populace had gathered along the streets, waiting. Vendors hawked foods and novelties and protections against the desires of the devil. The murderer was dragged by the arms to a thick wooden post with wrist and ankle locks to hold him from escape—from collapsing in faint. He was naked. His flesh was discolored with lash welts. Ten yards from the post a border had been marked with purple coloring. People stood in line and placed wagers that they could strike his genitals with the rotted fruit they carried. Soon the murderer's head and body were covered with the slime of their accuracy. Great black stallions with leather harnesses fitted to their sleek, muscular torsos were led into the square.

The murderer began screaming and begging for mercy. Two aides of the executioner released his wrists and ankles and attached them to the grips on the harnesses. They forced him to remain standing. The executioner, a small man with thick legs and a rubyhilted ceremonial sword dangling against his thigh, carried a black leather whip with two golden bells tied to the tip. He raised the whip and gently jiggled the bells. The horses stiffened and edged apart, pulling the murderer's arms level with his shoulders, spread-eagling his legs. His screams became shrill, his flesh quavered, he wagged his head fiercely and began shrieking.

The executioner looked to the center of the stands. The Doge, a white-bearded, palsied elder surrounded by his lavishly dressed children, his wife, and recent mistress, raised his hands to his sunken chest. The executioner jiggled the bells again. The horses separated again, stretching the murderer's arms taut, his legs parting wider until his feet were off the ground.

Food and debris and excrement were flung at him. People broke from the crowd and struck him with slender branches. Nobles threw coins at the executioner. The murderer still shrieked. His eyes bulged with agony, sweat pooled on his skin and streamed across his elongated legs. People shouted and demanded, "The bells, the bells, the bells!"

The Doge patted his cheeks to cool the flush and raised his right hand, holding the thumb down. The executioner suddenly lashed the flanks of the horses. They bolted. The murderer's body stretched like soft taffy until his arms were ripped from his shoulders, his legs torn outward from his hips, severing his middle— blood burst from all of him as the horses charged forward, the bloody members clumping across the cobblestones, splattering some of the cheering people who rubbed it on their faces as a protection from the devil's evil eye.

Barthelamo cringed against the wall, horrified at the pain he would soon feel. He despised himself for being so infantile with terror. I have changed death, I have brought death, I am a Physician-Surgeon. He heard a key turn in the cell door and he clenched his mouth to stop an urge to laugh triumphantly. It was Letitia come to rescue him. She had given away the fortune Borgia had bestowed upon her. She was bringing clothes. They would skulk through the castle where horses awaited. The thick door wavered in the tears blocking his sight. The ragged, thick-bearded jailer slumped in and stood aside to let Cesare Borgia pass.

342

Date: 1500   Month: February   Time: Evening
"*Venite ad me omnes, qui laboratis, et onerati estis, et ego refi-
ciam vos.*"
(Come unto me, all ye that labour and are heavy laden, and I
will give you rest.)
Matt. 11:28

I did not curse the Duke with the hatred I felt. I now feared for
Letitia. He had discovered her plot to rescue me and had come to
gloat.

He stood before me while the jailer brought a wooden stool
with an embroidered cushion. He was warm in the wealth of his
attire. I shivered. He told the jailer, "Leave us." When the cell
door closed he arranged his sable-collared cape and sat upon the
stool, his long muscular legs struck out in a casual posture. "Physician, you will answer me in truth, lest you earn my displeasure."
There was no mockery in his tone.

"Why does the living choose to converse with the dead, my
Lord?"

"Until you embrace your death, there is still the hope of
life."

"Do I perceive the emergence of a promise from the mighty
Prince, or has this cold given me a feverish delusion?"

"Physician, I have given you a trust offered to no other man.
Speak with me. My soul is in mortal danger. There is a curse upon
my life. How may it be removed?"

"You are not cursed, my Lord. You are frightened."

His legs stiffened, anger marked his face. He shouted, "Borgia, afraid? You dare slander me whilst I hold your life in the balance of my mercy?" I smiled and spoke as though impatient with a
child. "My Lord, we have no cause to wear the mask now. I am
near death and you are afraid of life. Why indulge in vexation and
pride?" His large figure eased of tension and he touched the ring
he had once given me. I sensed he did not want my execution.

"What is the curse upon my life, and will you remove it?"

"You are not cursed. Destiny has blessed you with greatness
but the man in you shrinks from its demands."

"I am cursed, I say. My military campaigns are stilled by

forces beyond the realm of the military. My sleep is plagued with horrors unspeakable. My waking is a horde of visions that come from the depths of the damned. I have begun to plot against my father—to murder him—and I tremble at my own ambition. I am driven by a curse, I say."

I did not remind him of the irony in which we were held. He was a vile and selfish brute, yet I pitied him.

"Physician, I give you a choice. Remove this curse from me and I will consider your life. Allow the curse to remain and I will devise a torment that will follow you after death."

"You have rule over my life, Excellence, but you have no jurisdiction after my death. Your promise is vague and untrustworthy. Your oath is but a sweet treachery."

Our eyes held each other, and I believed him. The truth was in his eyes as certainly as I knew the world was outside my cell. My heart heaved with expectation. There was no curse upon him. His superstition was my rescue. I closed my eyes upon his gaze and prayed to God to let me use the devil for powers that God was too merciful to grant me.

"Excellency, I accept your promise. Do exactly as I say."

"For this time only, my life is in your power."

"Confess your lecherous desires for your own sister, Lucrezia."

He leaped from the stool, bellowing, "*Serpente*—filthy snake! You accuse me of such profanity? I'll have you quartered and fed to my animals!" He was before me, his hand on the hilt of his sword: intimidating, massive. I did not wince at his intentions.

"My Lord, can you frighten a dead man with death? Can a curse be removed if the accursed will not admit to its cause? Confess this incestuous desire or hasten to your doom."

"Will that free me?"

"It will begin your freedom."

"Then I confess to this. My sister has touched a devil in me. Although the desires are fleeting—merely fleeting."

"Confess that you desire to murder your father, the Pope."

"I confess. Yet only to prevent his murder of me."

"You lie. Cesare Borgia lies. The confession is destroyed."

His rage flexed his body into a giant muscle. His huge hands reached for my throat. I was not afraid. God had granted me my prayer. He had allowed satan to give me power. Were I to laugh, fire would flash through my lips and burn him. He gradually edged back. He knew my power. He was in a sweat of fear. I mocked him.

"To lie in this confession is to increase the curse. You desire to murder your father so that you, a mere Cardinal, can be elevated to Pope."

"*Dio Mio*, yes, I confess. But tell me, Physician, how can you know that?"

"I am transcended beyond my mind to become your mind. You do not want me destroyed—I know this. My betrayal about Letitia's malformation is minor to you. It is Lucrezia who wants my death. She has become your ruler and in the bowels of your love for her, there is fear, and hatred."

His breathing sobbed. I was saved now. Letitia need not sacrifice her gains. He would welcome me to his court. He would revile my scorners. Lucrezia would be encouraged to leave the castle to marry for political advantage. I was whimsical with my power. My words were given to me.

"Kneel before me, my Lord. Place your sword at my feet. Spit upon the blade three times, then cover it with your cape. You must cross yourself and feel the piety in your soul—to loosen the grip of your curse."

"Will I then be free of it?"

"The freedom comes from what you return to replace what you have taken."

"What have I taken?"

"Life."

"Then it is life I must return—and how is that possible?"

"It will be told to you. As the curse loses its power over you, the truth will become your guide."

While he performed the ritual concocted by impulse, I thought, how childlike are the great when they are afflicted with doubt. There he is, the great Cesare Borgia, kneeling at the feet of a filthied and feverish crookback. See him, oh masses of people, see him placing his sword, worth a manor, at the grimy feet of his prisoner. Hearken, Letitia, and observe. The one who rules the mighty is mightier. Like an addled child he spits thrice upon the magnificent weapon and now he places his cape upon an earthen floor mottled with vermin. Do you doubt my power now, Letitia? He has crossed himself and now he believes the curse is done.

"Physician, it is done."

"Yes, my Lord, it is done. Soon you will be free. Your armies will conquer. Your rule will increase. The influence of Cesare Borgia will rest in the glory of history."

"All that is left to do is replace what I have taken."

"Then it is done, and you are utterly free."

"Advise me, Physician. I am without resources for this satanic endeavor."

This was his trick. Were I to name myself he would sever my head from my neck for deceiving him—for using his fear as a ploy to save myself. He rose and returned his sword to the jeweled sheath.

"The answer is in your soul, my great Excellence. I can remove the curse but your choice provides you freedom."

"Why have you aided me, Physician? Tomorrow you die. The animals are being readied."

"Even in death, I will remain loyal to your cause."

"How is that possible?"

"When I am relegated to my place in hell, I will negotiate for a cool station to be reserved for your arrival."

He glared—then laughed. He strode to the door and kicked the base. "Turnkey!" he shouted. The jailer hurried to open the door. He turned to me and chuckled. "I have never known one like you. I have promised you nothing, yet this does not mean my heart lacks promise for you. Think on that, Physician."

The cell door slammed upon my laughter and I continued laughing to have him hear the challenge in my voice as he left. He believed that anyone who could remove a curse from his destiny could place another upon that same destiny. I was free. There would be many nobles he will want me to curse.

He would allow me to remain chained in the cell, to establish his sovereignty. My execution would be postponed. Several times.

Until he believed I had regained my fear of him. Then I would be released.

Letitia, Letitia, we will be one again. Letitia, my beloved, we have triumphed. Oh, Letitia, my love for you weeps with joy. Prance about with your jewels and gifts whilst you wait for my freedom, that we may love again as one.

Chapter 13

I sat in the courtroom, being stared at, and no one could know the horror I was feeling. Barthelamo had turned his soul to satan to gain dominance over Borgia. "*Stupido*," I silently cursed him. *Stupido!* The power the devil gives you is the same power he turns against you. Satan is viciously possessive. He never lets go.

The District Attorney began calling other witnesses who testified that my presence in their lives had been destructive. I did not listen. Then he realized the jury was tired of hearing about my bizarre behavior. Knowing that I was already branded as a sadomasochist, he then turned to the judge and stated, "Your honor, the prosecution rests," and Martin Lormer announced that he was now prepared to conduct his surrebuttal.

I could sense that the people were nervous and expectant. Two jurors in the back row were whispering while the county clerk fidgeted with the array of evidence at his table. He kept snicking his thumb on the binding of my journal. I was not troubled by that desecration.

I allowed myself to notice that Martin Lormer had brought some objects into the courtroom, probably to be used for evidence. A large portfolio with the name "Klaymore Montecello" was on an exhibit easel. A box with the label "Magnifying Glasses" was beside a thick manila envelope marked "Enlargements." He had placed an unidentified globe-shaped device at the end of the table. Its content was hidden beneath a gray quilted covering, like a teapot cozy.

Martin Lormer walked over to the bench and looked at the judge who smiled at him. He placed his hands behind his back and interlaced his fingers. He said, "Your honor, I ask for the court's tolerance at this time. What I am compelled to do and say will require patience and latitude. It is, in all probability, an unprecedented request, but vital to the proceedings." His voice was softly toned to sound respectful, but audible enough to reach the jury. The judge folded her hands before her, waiting. Martin Lormer separated his hands and held them at his side.

"If there is reasonable doubt in deciding the action of a crime, or the state of a person's mind, then we can presume there is also the possibility of *unreasonable doubt*. I do not want this to happen, your honor. If there is any doubt as to the innocence of the defendant, then it must be *reasonable* doubt. But his defense, as the court has begun to realize, cannot be based on what we understand as reasonable information. The reason the doctrine of reincarnation exists transcends our natural abilities to comprehend its meaning. I have provided conclusive proof that Stephen Jerod is a reincarnated man, but my reason cannot accept it.

"As the act of murder cannot be justified in this lifetime, it cannot be justified in previous lifetimes. The defendant's life and past behavior has been mercilessly bared to the bone of his existence. All we have heard about is Stephen Jerod. But justice cannot be humanely dispensed unless more is known about the victim, Shara Medford. I do not place her on trial. I do not desire to slander or demean her life or her reputation. My only concern is to bring out what she may have caused. It is in this area where unreasonable doubt may occur."

"Mr. Lormer, this court, and I'm sure the people as well, are not quite certain of what you mean. Either make your point so it is clear to all those present—or, as the prosecution has requested, get on with the business of the day."

"All right, your honor. Here is my point. I am going to produce information concerning this crime that will not be believed, although it is absolute fact. It will be unreasonable, startling, bizarre. I am most reluctant to proceed, and possibly afraid to proceed. I ask, therefore, that if there is a priest, or a minister in this courtroom, that he call upon God to place this courtroom under His Divine protection and to allow this trial to be conducted without added hazards, interruptions, or unnatural catastrophes."

The District Attorney rose to object, then slowly sat down, knowing he could not refuse the possible presence of God and keep the jury's favor. The judge stared at Martin Lormer and it was clear that she approved of his desire and admired his skill in gaining sympathy. Everyone uses God.

In the rear, to the left, Bishop Carmondy stood up. He drew a white breviary from his pocket and placed a gold crucifix onto the embossed leather. I wondered if he also had a collapsible aspergillum to use for sprinkling the court with holy water. Althea Jackson, seated beside him, edged away as though afraid his religion was contagious. He patted his clothes, fussed with his tie. He opened the breviary and slowly flicked through the pages. Three rows before him another man, tall and with a blotchy complexion, impatiently stood up. He said, "I am Pastor of the Open Bible Church. Will all present please bow their heads." Bishop Carmondy returned the book and crucifix to his pocket and scowled. Althea Jackson giggled. The other man's voice rumbled with reverence.

"Dear Lord, in the beloved name of your Son, Jesus, we call upon your mercy and your mighty powers to stop all satanic oppression coming against this trial, and this people. You are above all, You are the great I Am. Grant us peace and deliver us from this evil. You are the God of love and joy and You do all things well. Prevail over this assembly. Jesus Christ is ever victorious and we bless you, beloved Father, for your precious Son. Amen."

People raised their faces and glanced to each other, uncomfortable, but not ashamed. The judge said, "Thank you, Pastor." Martin Lormer stood beside the witness box. "I call, at this time, Klaymore Montecello to the stand."

A middle-aged man in a black suit pushed a wheelchair that held a scrawny and wrinkled man who looked a hundred years old. He was completely bald, the skull flecked with brown liver spots. His skin was deeply grooved. The thin flap of flesh below his narrow chin quivered. The color of his eyes was hidden under a rheumy yellow. He wore a pale blue cashmere sweater. His shoulder bones prodded up the soft material. His hands, though bony and littered with veins, seemed powerful. The black-suited attendant stopped the wheelchair at the witness stand and slowly turned it around. Martin Lormer stepped to the judge.

"Your honor, Mr. Montecello is ninety-seven years old. Although his hearing and his sight have not been abnormally impaired by age, an operation for cancer of the throat has destroyed his voice. His manner of communication is by the sign language of the deaf. If it is acceptable to the court, Mr. Montecello's aide, Mr. Rodney Nemoy, will serve as his interpreter."

"Does the prosecution have any objections to that arrangement?"

"None, your honor."

I remembered once attending an exhibit of Klaymore Montecello's meticulous etchings. His eyes and hands were so exactly matched to the reality of what he was depicting that only by preinformation could the beholder tell they were etchings and not photographs. Many years later, when his works were again exhibited in San Francisco, I wanted Shara to see them. She had refused. Martin Lormer leaned over the wheelchair and touched the aged artist's hand.

"Mr. Montecello, in order to expedite this questioning, so as not to cause you undue fatigue, I will establish your background for the edification of the court. If I am incorrect in any of my statements, would you please inform us through your aide, Mr. Nemoy."

The aged man raised his right hand and manipulated his fingers. They were spry and surprisingly flexible. The aide interpreted. "I am in no hurry. I am enjoying the attention." The aide's voice was a nasal drone.

"You are Klaymore Montecello, an artist of worldwide repute. You were born ninety-seven years ago, in the small town of Council Grove, Kansas. In 1903, at the age of twenty-two, you were practically tarred and feathered and forced to leave town for displaying your portraits of nude women who were recognized as the wives of Council Grove's leading citizens. In 1909 you married Emily Barton. There were no children as a result of that marriage. Is that correct?"

The old man nodded. He raised his left hand, elbow resting on the wheelchair armrest, and spoke with his fingers. The aide said, "Your information is correct. It can be found in any brochure where my works are exhibited." If fingers had a tone of voice, his response would have sounded pleasantly sarcastic. Martin Lormer grinned. Some jurors leaned forward, becoming interested. The District Attorney fidgeted.

"Your last work, titled 'Nudebirth,' depicting a woman giving birth, sold to the Langely Museum, in Detroit, for $78,000. I cite this sale only to inform the court of the value placed upon your work. In 1954, when you announced your retirement, the Chicago Art Institute held a retrospective exhibit of your etchings. After the exhibit, an article was written by Jonathan Gilder, commenting that there were no works done between the years of 1911 and 1914. Would you tell the court why you did not work in those years?"

He raised both his arms and the aide studied his fingers and gestures. The finger motions were rapid and stark. The information was assertive.

"I was a resident of the Rogers Institution—a place where the mentally unbalanced were sent when they had what is known as a nervous breakdown. I was there for three years. I had become suicidal. The institution staff would not trust me to have the equipment I needed for my work."

"Could you tell us what you believe was the cause for your nervous breakdown?"

"It was during my marriage to Emily. She was a superb beauty. She was also strange and remarkable. Her demands were more than I could withstand. I have committed her to portraits many times, and was unable to capture the catastrophes in her soul."

"There are twelve portraits of her in existence. I have a portfolio of all twelve, in reproduction, of course. But these are not ordinary reproductions. They were done by the notable photographer Johann Krauss. I would like you to identify some of the portraits for the court."

Lormer walked to our table. He did not look at me. He picked up the box of magnifying glasses and the thick manila envelope. He motioned to a chubby bailiff to come to the table.

"Your honor, I have other reproductions of the portraits I will ask Mr. Montecello to identify. I have also provided magnifying glasses for a closer inspection to ascertain the meticulous, lifelike quality of the etchings. If it please the court, I will have them passed to yourself, the prosecution, and the jury."

The judge looked to the District Attorney. "Is there an objection from the prosecution?" He shrugged as he stood up. "No objections at this time," and fixed his tie while the bailiff distributed the materials.

Martin Lormer walked to the stand and stood beside the easel holding the portfolio. His manner was casual. The District Attorney was glaring at him, wishing he could move with such ease. He opened the cover of the portfolio and saw a portrait of someone who looked like Shara.

The jurors leaned forward, ignoring the copies they held on their laps. Martin Lormer picked the first etching from the group and held it up. It was a partial torso nude of a woman who had Shara's face and figure. Drawn with a hair-fine pen, the portrait was an intricate maze of lines brought into the exactness of human proportions. There was innocence in her eyes. Her nudity was a splendid repose—that of a tranquil child pleasantly delighted in being seen, but without vanity. A beautiful woman who accepted the truth of her beauty.

The jurors began studying their reproductions. I watched Martin Lormer point to the portrait on the easel and squint at the aged artist sitting in the wheelchair. He faced the portrait but his eyes were closed.

Martin Lormer tapped the portrait's surface. "Mr. Montecello, I know this is difficult for you—but would you tell this court something about your former wife Emily?" The District Attorney did not object because he wanted the deception to continue. He wanted the jury to first believe Martin Lormer—then when he pointed out the lie, the sleazy deception, the jury would hate Martin Lormer for tricking them. The old man edged his face from the direction of the portrait, then opened his eyes. He began moving his fingers and the aide slowly interpreted.

"She was the most beautiful and fascinating woman I had ever known. We met at a sculptor's studio in Chicago in 1909. Three days later we were married. For awhile I was the happiest man on earth."

"Why did this happiness take a turn for the worse?"

"It began with her refusal to have children. I wanted many children. I demanded that we have children. She said that she was incapable of having children. An accident, when she was young, she claimed. I insisted that she prove it by a medical examination. She agreed. The doctor—and at that time medicine was not as advanced as it is today—could not come up with a positive determination."

"Was that the only basis for your unhappiness?"

"No. She was involved in all manner of black magic, and the occult. She was looking for a secret. Whenever I asked her to reveal what secret she was searching for, all she would say is 'The secret of life and death.' I finally determined that she regretted marrying me. That she despised me."

I watched the District Attorney write something on his memo pad. He passed it to his narrow-shouldered assistant, who quickly read it and stood up. He walked toward the doors, his carefully tailored jacket covering the bulge of an unwieldy stomach. Some people watched him leave the courtroom. I did not care to know the information the District Attorney had assigned him to find.

"Tell me, Mr. Montecello, do you know if Emily ever learned the secret she was searching for—*the secret of life and death?*"

"During a spiritualist séance in Baltimore, I believe she learned the secret of life and . . ."

The District Attorney tapped his pencil onto the table, snapping the point. "Objection, your honor." The judge nodded. "Objection sustained." Martin Lormer looked at the old man and smiled. "Why are there only twelve portraits of Emily in existence? You said you did many of them?" The old man closed his eyes and lazily moved his fingers. The aide said, "Mr. Montecello would enjoy a moment's rest." Martin Lormer sighed. "Of course. The court will wait on him."

I looked at the old man, pitying him. He opened his eyes and looked to Martin Lormer, who smiled, asking, "You said you did many portraits of Emily. Why are there only twelve left?"

"I made over fifty portraits of Emily. It was after this séance we attended in Baltimore that she started tearing them up. If I hadn't hidden the twelve that remain, she would have destroyed them as well. This séance was conducted by a medium of great repute. I did not want to attend. But I believed it to be a fine opportunity to cure Emily's obsession with the occult. I invited a dear friend of mine, Harry Houdini."

"Is that *the* Harry Houdini—the famous escape artist and magician?"

"Yes. His mother had recently died and he was trying to contact her in the spirit world. As the world knows, he was also crusading to expose the corrupt spiritualists who were exploiting the public. Harry was offering a large reward to any spiritualist who could reveal the message he had locked into an uncrackable safe. He intended challenging the medium to reveal the message. The medium was very convincing. But Harry Houdini was busy during the séance. He was searching for devices, for hidden wires, for spiritualist contraptions."

The old man paused again. The judge was becoming impatient. She wanted the end of the story. The reporters held their ball-point pens above their pads. The courtroom doors opened and the District Attorney's assistant hurried to their table. He put down a white index card and shrugged. The District Attorney frowned as he studied the information written on the surface. Martin Lormer licked his lips. The old man blinked. Martin Lormer's voice was gentle.

"Did that great magician, that great crusader, Harry Houdini, find any devices or spiritualist tricks?"

"Not one. Then the medium began moving among the guests. He either answered their questions or told them private information. Some people offered him money. He turned them down. He explained that he was a millionaire in his own right. His purpose for conducting séances was to further the cause of spiritualism. He then went to Emily and told . . ."

He stopped speaking to gasp for breath. He wheezed and his rheumy eyes bulged. Martin Lormer edged closer to him. The aide began gently patting the old man's curved, spindly back. Someone said, "Get him a doctor." The aide turned to the judge. "This happens now and then. It will pass."

I silently prayed that God would keep him alive. I did not want my trial to cause anyone's death but my own. Slowly, the old man's breathing softened. The aide used a tissue to dab some spittle from the wrinkled lips. He nodded at Martin Lormer. He was ready to continue.

"It was at that séance that you believe Emily learned the secret of life and death. Why are you so certain of that?" The old man scowled as he moved his hands to let the aide interpret.

"It was not the secret of life and death concerning the universe. It was only as it applied to Emily. She was shocked—actually stunned—by what he told her. I began believing in the spiritualist when Harry Houdini could not discredit him. I was standing beside Houdini when the spiritualist handed him a paper and whispered something to him."

"Did you hear what he said?"

"Yes, I heard. He said 'I have given you a copy of the message you have locked in your safe. Give your reward to a cause more worthy than your own. You are a passing trend. Only spiritual life remains.' After he read the message Harry became furious. He had to be restrained. He must have known the medium had contacted Harry's mother in the spirit world and Harry was crazy with jealousy."

"Mr. Montecello, could it be possible that your former wife, Emily, was also Shara Medford?"

The District Attorney jumped up, furious. "Your honor, I object to this despicable display."

People began whispering to each other. The judge leaned closer to the bench and pointed her gavel at Martin Lormer.

"The defense has been duly warned that any breech of decorum or abuse of privileges will be dealt with in a severe manner. I warn you for the last time, Mr. Lormer. Do not continue trying the court's patience. You have about reached those limits."

Martin Lormer fingered his tie and moved closer to the old man. He cupped his hand on the bony shoulder. "Your honor, I submit that the court is being prejudicial in its attitude toward the defense."

"Your honor, what is the point of Mr. Montecello's testimony?"

"Counsel for the defense, I want that question answered. I want the purpose of Mr. Montecello's testimony revealed now!"

Martin Lormer suddenly flung up his arms and shouted, "All

right, your honor, all right!" startling the judge, making the District Attorney step back in worried caution. He stomped to our table, his face grimaced with agitation though I sensed that he was performing and in full control. He grabbed three reproductions he had set aside and brought them to the easel. Angrily, he slapped them, face down, onto the wooden stand, shaking it. "Here, your honor, right here is the purpose of this witness's testimony. I want the court, the prosecution, and the jury to use their magnifying glasses to study the lower portion of Emily Montecello's portrait." While the District Attorney hurried to his table, Martin Lormer quickly turned over the reproductions and shouted, "There you are!" He touched each one.

"These are three enlargements of the lower back area of Belinda Lazarus, Emily Montecello, and Shara Medford. Each one reveals three sets of scars set in the same pattern. All scars on each of the three women—in texture, size, shape, and pattern—are *all exactly the same!*"

The old man bowed his head and sobbed.

I was too stunned to react. There was no sense to this, no sanity.

I sat and waited for sensation to return to me. The jurors were studying their reproductions, the judge was crouched over, her face almost against the magnifying glass. The District Attorney's shoulder was pressed to the assistant's shoulder as they scrutinized the portrait. I sat, deliberately not feeling, probing my mind for an explanation. How could three different women, separated by generations, have the exact same scars?

A reporter left his section for the District Attorney's table. A bailiff snapped his fingers, warning him. The reporter cursed and returned to his seat. People in the courtroom were leaning forward attempting to see over the District Attorney's shoulder. The old man let his head fall to the side to rest. The aide bent over and took a metal flask from a compartment in the wheelchair. He poured a cup of milky liquid. The old man sipped from the rim.

There was no natural explanation for the scars except that it was a satanic trick. Martin Lormer knew this. He had said as much about my handwriting being exactly as Barthelamo Vecchio's handwriting. They became the same handwritings " . . . *only when they are examined.* It is a supernatural device, a trick of illusion." And now the devil was using the same deception by causing Shara's scars to appear on Emily Montecello's portrait, as he had done on Belinda Lazarus' photograph. Yes. Yes. I knew the devil was real, and Martin Lormer knew the devil was real. Yes. Yes. That was the only explanation. Shara had never undergone cosmetic surgery. She had died in her natural beauty, and in her youth.

Martin Lormer was using the powers of the devil to win this trial, as the devil was using him to gain my acquittal.

Now I wanted to speak. To stand up and tell the befuddled people what any priest is trained to know—that only God has greater power than satan—that Bishop Carmondy could authorize an exorcism this instant—and if the devil was cast out of this courtroom, and the ferocity and evil of his powers brought to heel, this would become an ordinary murder trial and, bless God, I would be convicted.

But I was afraid.

I sat, gripping the table edge, feeling fear as though it was an abcess in my soul. The people were already confused. I could not risk an explanation they would believe to be impossible and lunatic.

And if I betrayed my vow of silence, Martin Lormer would dupe me into further testimony. He would niggle and badger and taunt me into statements that would malign Shara. He would guide the sympathies of the jury to appreciate the horror I had lived with since I was twelve years old. He would maneuver my statements until the jury became overwhelmed, and doubted. Then I would be freed.

No. I would not leave my rigid silence. To hell with them. I could only suffer my own existence, until it was done. They were suffering within the miniature realm of this trial. I was suffering for society.

The District Attorney rose from the table. He stood in solemn heaviness and shook his head in despair. I now understood why he had not harassed Martin Lormer with a multitude of objections. He wanted this information presented to the jury so they would know the hoax that was being imposed on their natural logic. He

said, "Your honor, the prosecution is baffled by the court's willing-
ness to put up with such shabby courtroom tactics." He held up
the reproduction of Emily Montecello and angrily flung it onto the
table.

"The court has been exceptionally lenient with the defense. I
see no value to this witness's testimony. Had the defense apprised
us—through prosecutorial discovery—of what it was going to introduce, it would have been a trifling matter to come up with
many other women—starting from perhaps the turn of the century—who resemble both Emily Montecello and Belinda Lazarus. . . ."

"May I remind the prosecution that the defense has no obligation to provide your office with discovery. You have every right
to examine this evidence further, if you choose to. I will permit
you a brief period of time in which to do so."

"There is no need for that, your honor. It is quite obvious that
all the defense is doing is burying the facts of a viciously premeditated crime under astonishing coincidences. Therefore, I fervently
move to have this entire testimony, and the evidence of coincidence, stricken from the record. And that the court censure the
defense for his shoddy and unethical practices."

"Before I move on such a motion, I will first hear what the
defense has to say."

Martin Lormer left the old man's side. The collar of his white
shirt poked into his neck. He drew a folded handkerchief from his
pocket and dried his hands. There was no sympathy in my admiration for him. He had tried to convert the grave process of law
into a carnival, using my life, and Shara's, as the clowns.

"Your honor, I admit, openly, that I cannot explain what I
have just revealed. My responsibility is to bring facts into light
that are pertinent to my client's defense. I am to offer them in as
logical and convincing an order as I can arrange to persuade the
jury that Stephen Jerod's act does not warrant conviction. If I cannot completely explain the facts I present—because they are not
within the realm of the *natural*—I am still obliged to present them.
I admit, again openly, that much of what I know about my client's
defense cannot be explained by reason. Yet I cannot conceal those

facts, whether they be natural or supernatural. I cannot, before God, do that."

"Counselor—where the court can accept the similarity of scars on the bodies of Belinda Lazarus and Shara Medford, it cannot sustain its credulity by assuming another such coincidence between the scars of Emily Montecello and Shara Medford. In the first instance the similarity is represented through the objective and mechanical eye of a camera. In the latter instance it is produced by the subjective eye of the human being."

I heard the District Attorney snigger. Martin Lormer refolded his handkerchief and again wiped his palms. There was no sound in the courtroom.

"Your honor, the court demands too much of me. The noted pathologist, testifying for the people, indicates from his autopsy report that there was never any cosmetic surgery performed on Shara Medford. She was in her mid-twenties at the time of her death. Therefore the possibility of her being past ninety years of age is utterly impossible. I am no scientist, yet I know that scars upon a person's body are unique and individual, like fingerprints. I can accept a billion-to-one coincidence between Belinda Lazarus and Shara Medford—but two such coincidences? No, your honor, you ask too much of me."

"They why have you introduced an inconclusive coincidence into the record as specific evidence?"

"Because my client's state of mind at the time of the crime is of great significance. The greater part of my defense depends upon it. How better can I show what his state of mind must have been like but by revealing that there is more to this murder than the natural and understandable facts can define? If this court and its jury are troubled by what is visible and tangible, *but incomprehensible*, then imagine the state of mind of Stephen Jerod. I introduce such evidence, not to astonish or to shock—but to reveal that I believe Emily Montecello, Belinda Lazarus, and Shara Medford *could actually be the same woman*."

The judge struck her gavel and stood up. "But that is impossible!" Someone in the courtroom shouted, "Lormer's as nutty as the priest." People shushed the excited man. The jury began looking at each other. Some put notes onto their memo pads. Every person in the news media section was bent over, writing. The old man in the wheelchair was asleep. I imagined his scrawny, veiny body hugged against the succulence of Shara's body. I breathed deeply to stop from puking. The judge sat down, embarrassed by her loss of presence. Martin Lormer stepped closer to her.

"It is up to the prosecution to prove that Emily Montecello, Belinda Lazarus, and Shara Medford are not one and the same woman. Prove it, not by declaring it impossible, or contrary to natural law, or by denying the existence of God and the devil and reincarnation. Prove it with irrefutable fact!"

The judge pushed back a lock of hair from her damp forehead. I noticed dark hollows under her eyes. The District Attorney shrugged. "I would appreciate a ruling on my motion to strike this witness's testimony from the record." Martin Lormer walked to the wheelchair and spoke softly, as though afraid to awaken the aged artist.

"Before your honor rules, may I remind the court that the history of common law is created in the courtrooms throughout the country—not in the legislature. The insanity defense, the diminished capacity defense, were developed by lawyers who believed in their clients' defense. My defense of self-defense by reason of reincarnation has been accepted by the court. Having gone this far in allowing us to present evidence—startling though it may be—as to the reality of reincarnation—it would be a violation of our rights to tell us that further evidence is not acceptable. Therefore, I beg the court to allow me to continue."

The judge squeezed her fingers on the gavel. She was not certain if Martin Lormer had trapped her. She stood up. "I am calling a fifteen-minute recess while I speak with both the prosecution and the defense in my chambers. The defendant will be returned to holding during that interval." She left the bench and strode to her chambers.

Chapter 14

I shuffled to the holding cell and stood, slumped and drained, while the deputy sheriff opened the door and directed me in.

He closed the door and thunked a lock into place. I rested against the bars. Too much, too much, I kept silently repeating. I was once a priest who loved God in the simplicity of my soul. "Verily I say unto you, Whosoever shall not receive the Kingdom of God as a little child, he shall not enter therein." Tears warmed my eyes. How did all this happen? What sin, what impulse, what unremembered evil had allowed the devil entry into my soul?

Shara, Shara, who are you? Shara, Shara, was I always a lunatic, or did your love convert me?

I lay down on the narrow bed, believing that if I could sleep the world would be in another place when I awoke. Perhaps I would die in my sleep and awaken reincarnated again—into the twenty-third century. I might be a clerical worker, a mousy man, intimidated by an unruly breeze. How peaceful that would be.

I began to cry. There were no sounds in my sobs, yet they were deep. I was lonely.

Shara, Shara, Shara, Shara.

It was lush to cry now. My tears were company. They softened my confusion. How could Shara be Belinda Lazarus and Emily Montecello when she had also been two other women— Onadyh and Letitia? I licked a tear that had leaked onto my lips.

I closed my eyes and listened to the sink faucet drip. I could hear the faint incantations of some religious group outside the courthouse. They wanted me free. The muffled chanting of their voices was lulling. Tiny creaks, like the opening of a dried skin, told me that the building foundation was sinking.

There was information about Shara that I had not written in

my journal. I wanted her in an ideal image. I would not slander our love with facts.

She detested animals.

One afternoon I shopped for a canary. I was not happy when Shara was home alone. I brought the bright brass cage into the apartment and held it before her, laughing. "Look at it. Isn't it cute?" She had crinkled her face and hissed, "Get that creature out of my sight!" I shrugged and brought the cage to the terrace, placing it near the wall. The bird tweeted and chirped in the cool air. When I left for the university the next day, the canary was gone. I cursed myself for not having latched the small cage door. In the street below our apartment, I saw one of its tiny yellow wings crushed on the sidewalk. I was saddened for not having remembered that some people in the apartment building had cats.

I bought her an aquarium with four goldfish and a year's supply of flaky, tissue-thin food. "Here, Shara," I said. "They're so lovely and graceful, they remind me of you." She clenched her hands, damning me. "Will you stop bringing me such stupid, filthy presents!" I became annoyed and set the aquarium atop the television set. "Well, I like them, and I want them." In the morning, when I awoke to feed them, there were no fishes in the glass tank. I remembered being disturbed during my sleep by the flushing of the toilet bowl. I was not angered. Without concocting weird motives for her hatred of animals, I believed she shared that attitude with Onadyh when she was crossing a furnaced, infertile land, leading Bianco to her people.

There was always the menace of animals near them. Watching them, following them. While they staggered through burning hours, their bodies like ovens heating juiceless muscle and bone, the great black beasts that ate flesh were circling above them cawing, shrieking. He walked behind her, blindfolded. His eyes had become swollen and pulpy from the relentless sunlight. She led him by holding one end of the staff. When he fell and would not stand she would push him, poke her finger into the watery bruises on his skin, hurting him awake—until he cursed her abuse to his god-ness and rose again to plod behind her. He did not see the ground beasts she kept away from him. She left him only when she saw a lone cactus plant—the Ears That Stick—which she hacked with his sacrificial knife and then they chewed and sucked from its wetness until their swelled tongues and cracked mouths softened.

There was never sound or touch between us as I watched them live an interval of themselves through me. They could not know I was observing. They were alive in their own Time, and as authentically alive as I was while watching them. There was only sight as I followed them to an area of land that had once been almost fertile and was now a hardened mud flat littered with the blanched bones of animals. The surface was a maze of ruts and deep fissures. She tapped the staff onto the stony earth and listened. Insects crawled on the splits between her fingers. Livid welts and rashes encircled her neck. He stood, swaying with fatigue, waiting for her to lead. The leather wrappings on his feet were stiff with dried blood.

I knew many of his thoughts. When I tried to realize what she was thinking there was only flat, inarticulate space. Though he was shamed by her endurance, he wanted her to save him. When you kept a god from dying you became a god. He would do a ceremony before all her people, making her a god. Then her village would be folded into his father's protection and never know terrible hungers or the fear of being attacked and enslaved. Two gods, of the same father, brought all of the power from Above.

While he struggled the sound of the hot wind became laughing voices—the children of the Great Burning Eye mocking as they watched their father's enemy slowly die. He listened. Their laughter flung earth to his face, at the openings of his covering where his flesh was raw. He knew he would not die for their pleasure. His father, the Great Cold Eye, was greater.

They happened upon an abandoned village. She stopped. He stumbled and collapsed to the ground, moaning as his knees struck small stones. He edged up the blindfold and squinted against the pain of brightness. She was pointing to a line of low, twig-thatched abodes that had been deserted. His thought was to hate his father for taunting them. The beasts of the land would have eaten all the scraps of food the people left. Her arm moved to a mound of earth piled with thick rocks. He saw the dried well as a blurred shadow. He understood now why the people had left. She told him,

"Come," and dragged her legs to the mound. He raised to his hands and knees and moved to where she was lifting away the stones.

I am in my holding cell, cool and snug. Why do I ache and groan as I watch them? There is no suspense for me. I have seen, so many times, the way Onadyh strained her body, no longer lush and vibrant with the animality of woman, to lift the stones from the dried well—to drop them to the side—lifting and dropping until her hands became bloody. I've seen—so many times—how Bianco had roughly pushed her aside because only his arms had strength, while he blindly clawed and hefted the heavy stones. His thoughts were that there would be no water. He was lifting only to reveal that he was still with his god-ness. That he was allowing her to lead so she could be rewarded with god-ness. When all the stones were lifted out he fell back and lay gasping on the ground while she took the staff and began stabbing it into the dry depth.

I was watching them now because I was compelled to watch them. The powers that transcend the human will and concentration wanted me to take meaning from their life. I could not cup the hands of my compassion about the voice of my mind and shout to them, "Be careful!" I could not bawl out instructions to them as I scanned the landscape to tell them that a dense dust storm was blowing toward them—hurry, hurry, find shelter in one of the abodes before you are so blinded by the storm you are lost to each other.

She had not stabbed the staff into the well because of rage. She was digging into the loamy soil, stirring it, probing for hidden dampness—and then her cry of happiness, the sound of a choking animal—awakened him. He saw her bent over in the hole, scooping up handfuls of soggy ground and pressing it to her mouth. She sucked the wetness. He knew they were saved until his father could raise his Cold Eye and blacken the Burning Eye.

They heard the dust storm and felt the lacerating force of its beginning. She scraped a large mound of wet earth and carried it into the closest abode. He groped to the edge of the well and dug his portion and followed her sounds. They huddled against the abode wall and packed the earth to their faces and wounds while they squeezed gritty drops and licked them. There was a skeleton sprawled at the opposite wall. When she could speak she told him it was an Elder who could not travel when the people left the village.

My palms holding to the metal cot sides were cool. The water faucet, dripping in the enamel coated bowl, dripped from the cold water tap. I drifted from Bianco and Onadyh and gradually become one with Barthelamo.

The dark Italian night was windy with winter. I was in the dungeon cell, joyful in knowing that Borgia had altered his decision to kill me and must soon remove me from the cell so I would not be killed by the uncaring winter.

When the morning chapel bells rang, the gruff jailer and two *bravi* entered my cell and I was unchained from the wall. I was brought an embroidered blanket to cover my nakedness. It was used for the Duke's favorite steed. A silver tray bearing silver bowls and plates of succulent food was placed before me by a lowly page. I did not care that they beheld me, Physician-Surgeon Barthelamo Vecchio, gluttoning the foods. I was no longer engaged in dignity and ritual. When I was done shoving the food into me, they withdrew, leaving me only the blanket. It was the only food I was given for the day. Thus far there had been eleven such servings. At evening, when the chapel bells rang the canonical hour of nine, the jailer and two *bravi* returned and I was again chained to the wall. The blanket was taken from me.

Yet I did not fear.

Earlier this day the jailer had informed me that Borgia had taken the wealthy township of Barstella. He knew now that the curse he believed was strangling his Destiny had been removed. He would not have me torn apart by near-wild steeds. A man who could remove the curse of enemies was too valuable to him. His taunting me now was the royal manner of asserting majesty over my life, or my death.

Until the twelfth day, when I gravely wished that he had killed me.

I was pacing the cell, thinking of Letitia and of demonic powers. Did I possess them? Could anyone by the mere requesting of them be endowed with such terrifying power?

I wrapped the stable blanket tighter about me. The light had

faded from the day. The chapel bells rang. I waited for the jailer
and *bravi* to appear. Were I truly in possession of demonic powers I would have pointed my fingers at the cell door and commanded it to remain sealed. I did not want to sleep naked, hanging
from a damp wall, whilst the vicious Duke pondered when to
release me.

The jailer and *bravi* did not appear. I was afraid of the supernatural life within me. I did not want to possess demonic powers.
In time, I knew they would possess me. I shivered beneath the
blanket. Tears welled my eyes until the cell door trembled. "It is
opening," I cried aloud. It is opening. I am not cursed. I am not the
devil's pawn. Still I could not hear the sound of voices, the grate of
a turning key. I heard instead, laughter. In the courtyard outside
my barred window I heard laughter. I turned and saw the flicker of
torches and the laughter whirred and was drunken.

I stood upon my toes and grasped the bars, losing my blanket
as I raised myself to see into the courtyard. A line of red-wigged
pages held their torches high, surrounding an obese Doge I knew
as Pietro Rodozzi. He was floundering after Letitia. She laughed as
she escaped his reach. Her gown was of purple velvet fringed with
lavender laces, open at the bosom. "Letitia," I moaned, entreating
her to remain beyond the Doge's clumsy grasp. Her breathing was
heavy. I gasped when she stumbled on the train of her gown and
the Doge caught her. "Letitia!" I roared, my knees bursting with
pain as I tried to climb higher.

I lowered myself, nauseated with strain and horror. Letitia,
Letitia, I wept. Borgia is using you to torment me.

The laughter quickened. I leaped to the bars again and
strained upward. The Doge held her, his great stomach pressed to
her slender body, his huge jowls burrowed between her bared
breasts. "Letitia!" I screamed. "Letitia! Borgia is using you!" She
could not hear. The Doge's arms were clasped about her buttocks,
the thick fingers searching the delight of her crevices. "Letitia,
beloved," I shrieked with inhuman power. "I will live, Letitia, I
will save you!"

The Doge staggered at my voice and gripped her arm as he
searched to find me. His clothes were disarrayed. Food stained his
doublet and finery. Letitia swayed, her expression dazed. She

laughed in childlike innocence. Lucrezia Borgia stepped past the pages and pointed to my barred window. "Behold, the mighty Physician, Vecchio!" She curved her gloved hands to her mouth and called to me, *"Demonio!* No man shames Lucrezia and lives!"

I cursed, *"Prostituta!"* and spit at her pale blonde face as I tried to see beyond her. In the slashing of flames I could see Letitia's dull eyes, the slackness of her face. Lucrezia strolled to my window, amused at my agony. The Doge had torn open Letitia's bodice and was kissing her breasts. Lucrezia did not block my view. She wanted me to see. "Physician," she mocked whilst I sobbed. "Why does a dead man observe the lusts of the living, eh, Physician?"

I gripped the bars with my fury and again spit at her. *"Escremento!* You royal filth. God shall cut out your soul and feed it to the devil's swine!" Her laughter shrilled to me and Letitia leaned backward as the Doge pulled her hand and placed it upon his parts. I shook with strain and screamed in weeping, "I am not dead, my Beloved. I will be freed on the Duke's return!" The pages kept their circle as the Doge buffeted Letitia, trying to make her fall. He would take her before the castle servants. She was not herself, else she would have cut his throat.

Lucrezia stepped to my window, shielding her nostrils with a perfumed pomander. "She does not hear your cries, Physician. She delights too much in dalliance. The Doge will reward her handsomely for her ardor."

Again I frantically tried to climb upon the window ledge to rip the bars from the stone. My skin tore, my fingers felt broken. "Letitia," I begged, "beloved—resist. This Doge is a pig!" He heard my babbling and released Letitia. The circle of pages opened as he reeled to my window. I continued my pleas. "Resist that filth, Letitia. I will take you from this."

Lucrezia stepped aside, patting her brilliant hair. The Doge kicked the bars, smashing my fingers. I fell back, cracking my spine on the stone floor, splitting the flesh of my deformity. I hugged my fingers and writhed with pain and Lucrezia laughed. "If my beloved brother does not return, then you are mine, is it not so? You are my inheritance from him. For my amusement, marvelous Physician. You will never—not by order of king or God—deprive a woman of her love-child! Your death will free me of such loss." I sat and rocked and listened to her laughter and my tears soothed the pain in my fingers. I prayed for Borgia's return—the devil you use is less fearsome than the devil who wants to use you.

I was struck from Barthelamo's life in me when the deputy sheriff shook the cell door. "Court's in session again, Father." I sat up, waiting for the ugliness to leave my sensations. He calls me Father, I thought. What service have I ever done for God that I should still be known as a priest? He opened the cell door and the guard behind him said, "Get yourself ready for another hot session, Father."

I walked between them. I was not handcuffed or chained. Thank you. This minor courtroom recess had taught me that I must not let myself remember. I must not harass myself with memories of lives that were not my own.

I would have to pray to God to help me not remember. I could not continually forget through my own will.

Again I saw the people in the courtroom stare at me. I kept an indifferent glaze over my vision as I was escorted to the defense table. If I did not see sharply, I would not be seen clearly. I sat in a posture of numbness—as though posing for a mid-Victorian portrait. Martin Lormer and the District Attorney had left the judge's chambers and both seemed subdued. I wanted to grin. The judge had given them their comeuppance, I was sure. I sat and imagined what had happened in her chambers. She had probably slammed her hand onto the desk and, with controlled rage, had warned them:

"My court is becoming an arena of disrespect and controversy. I'm being harassed by the national, state, and local media for interviews. I do not approve of the court being used for news promotions and ridicule. I will not allow this fiasco to continue. If you two illustrious specimens of the legal profession force me to take drastic measures, I will take them."

She had probably opened the center drawer of her large desk and grabbed up a handful of memos and wagged the clutter at them. I imagined that anger turned the muted tone of her lipstick to dark red.

"Judge Jessica Rona Tries the Devil. Is God in Rona's Court? Will Judge Rona Pass Sentence on Satan or Christ? I warn you, gentlemen—and my word is my bond—if precedents are going to be established during this trial, I will establish precedents that will not only be historical but ruinous to both your careers, and I will be most ruthless!"

She had then pointed to Martin Lormer and studied him with disgust, and some hatred. He had probably cringed back in pretended fear—to assure her that she was the ultimate power.

"I warn you, Martin Lormer. If I find one tawdry gimmick, one sleazy deceit in how you conduct the remainder of your defense, I will not only hold you in contempt, but I will have you charged. I will, personally and with gusto, vanguard the disbarment proceedings."

I imagined that Martin Lormer had remained silent. He was not intimidated. I could see the District Attorney shifting nervously, licking his lips. He did not want her to remember his existence. I could almost hear her strangely contemplative voice.

"I have been a good Catholic all my life. I have enjoyed my relationship with God. But I want this trial ended, and ended quickly. I cannot allow myself to be divided in attention or responsibility—either to God, or the proceedings. We are engaged in more than a trial. I believe, in my heart, that we are engaged in an enterprise in which we are being used for greater meanings than the trial itself. I want this trial ended, and quickly!"

The courtroom was quiet. Martin Lormer ignored me. He studied some typed papers and the duplicate of a medical chart. Through the glaze over my eyes I was about to place the newspeople into a blur. I did not like them. They groped among the leaks and grubs of local scandal and magnified them into catastrophic world events. I wanted to be in another place, with Shara—barbecuing spareribs on our apartment terrace, or walking in the rain.

Martin Lormer stood up. "I recall Dr. Virgil Welch, the deputy coroner, to the stand." The District Attorney shifted to his assistant and they whispered. While the witness was being reminded that he was still under oath, I carefully closed myself off from listening to them. I did not want to hear them dissect Shara again. It would mean that she was dead with a finality not even imagination could revive. I began to attend the jury while the doctor was being questioned. Who were these twelve people—these twelve odd people? To them I was a crossword puzzle being filled in by the legal profession.

The lead juror had a deeply cleft chin. There was a pimple in the cavity. I suspected that he did not like me. He believed I was sinister, arcane. He probably had a daughter who believed in reincarnation. She delved into exotic religions. When she had left his home to live with a man who could levitate himself and solid objects, he had piled her masks and amulets and made-in-Japan jim-gigs into a cardboard box and brought them to the Alameda dump. I liked the man. He was God-fearing and moral. He would condemn me to the other jurors, emphatically. First degree murder. Hallelujah!

" . . . and were there any unusual circumstances surrounding the autopsy?"

"None that I can recall."

"Nothing odd, or unexpected?"

"None that I can recall."

"How were you able to identify the body as that of Shara Medford?"

"The usual means. In this instance, a friend, Althea Jackson, and, of course, the defendant, Stephen Jerod."

"That was the only way you could ascertain her true identity?"

"It was sufficient."

"When a check was run on her, as is the procedure, were you able to identify her through her fingerprints? For a previous criminal record, or whatever?"

The witness hesitated and glanced at the District Attorney. I was absorbed in the woman juror seated behind the juror with the cleft chin. The absence of eyebrows made her look goggle-eyed. A frog searching a swamp for a fly. She probably thought I was a homicidal pervert. That I had given up God and church for the worship of sex. Good. Good. Gas the dastardly bastard and spit into his face.

"Would you please answer the question? Did you also identify the deceased through her fingerprints?"

"No. She had no fingerprints."

Only the people in the courtroom were surprised by his answer. I had known Shara had no fingerprints. Long before I had injured myself and was not able to make love without pain, I had been playful with Shara. I began kissing her fingertips, reciting, "This little piggy went to market, this little piggy stayed home . . ." and then I noticed that the tips of each finger were enamel smooth. "You have no fingerprints," I said, amazed. She had shrugged. "An accident, when I was a child. A fire. The surgeons grafted some skin from my inner thigh and something odd happened." Then we became imaginative and thought of all the crimes she could commit and never be identified because she had no fingerprints.

"Why wasn't this fact brought out in your earlier testimony?"

"The deceased's lack of fingerprints was not at all contributory to the way she died. Also, an absence of fingerprints is not as rare as most people think."

"Really? How could that be?"

"Often, older file clerks have that happen to their fingertips. The prints actually wear off from the constant filing. It is not at all rare."

"How old would you estimate Shara Medford to have been?"

"In her early twenties."

"Then it isn't likely that her fingerprints wore off from constant filing—since she was never a file clerk and she was in her early twenties."

"I suppose not."

"Then how would you explain her fingertips, that had no fingerprints?"

"Frankly, I can't explain it. It never seemed important."

The District Attorney stood up and casually objected to the relevancy of the questions. The judge nodded. "Objection sustained." Martin Lormer pinched his lower lip and sighed. I flicked my vision to the other end of the jury section. The tongue-chewer was in the front row. His jaw muscles bulged from the exercise. He was a man who boasted he could not hurt one of God's teeniest creatures. Yet he would find me guilty and feel no moral discomfort. I had murdered a woman he had been having sexual fantasies about. As long as he didn't have to kill me personally, it was suitable that I die. He was a sanctimonious boob, whom I was pleased to have against me. They never changed their minds.

" . . . Would you, Dr. Welch, tell the court what your determination was when you learned that the deceased, Shara Medford, had no *handprints?*"

I concentrated on a woman juror in the rear. She had a sprawled, fleshy nose. She seemed like a romantic soul and I guessed she wanted me to be innocent. She believed my love for Shara had been so savage that Shara could not endure its intensity. The greatness of my love, so exceeding the dictates of common morality, transcended the restrictions others must obey. I had killed her upon learning she was a banal shadow unworthy of such love. I almost giggled. To avoid shouting at her, "Madam, you are a dip-silly bitch!" I placed my hand to my mouth and yawned.

"In California, it is the common procedure to run a test on the blood type of the victim, is it not?"

"It is not mandatory, but it is procedural."

"Would you tell the court what you learned about Shara Medford's blood type?"

The District Attorney drummed his fingers on the table and pleaded to the judge, "Your honor, I strongly object to the inconsequentiality of this information." The judge shifted forward. Martin Lormer frowned at her. "Your honor, this information is highly pertinent to the defense's case." She edged back and adjusted her eyeglasses. I could feel a quality of despair begin to alter the casual stance of Martin Lormer. He wanted to create the impact of a vital point and the legal structure of a trial would not allow it.

He waited. He brushed back his hair and walked to our table to stare at his notes while the judge decided. He glanced up at me, then held his gaze until I felt studied. There was shock and pity in his eyes. I moved my face until I could see the entire jury as a rectangular blur of faces. Ignore me, all of you—you too, Martin Lormer—why not judge Bianco and Onadyh. How would you now judge them? You read my journal.

They did not die in some abandoned, desolate abode, covered by the scrape and loose refuse of the earth. When they had rested, they left the abode and the beasts that tore flesh returned to again circle above them. The relief of sleep did not revive their strength. They moved as though in a feverish, sluggish convulsion, then for long spells dropped to their hands and knees and huddled over, panting like the starving animals they once flung food at. The heat became solid on their bodies. The wind blew with scalding steadiness. He begged her to stop—to find a deep shadow behind the large boulders where they could sleep and not have the Great Burning Eye touch them—when his father was in the Above they could move without such scorching death in them.

She spoke in coarse gasps, telling him she could not find the signs of her people because his father's eye was weak. She clenched her hand and held it near his face. The signs her people left were the size of her closed hand. He had begun to hate her. Not with killing. Only with punishment. After he drew the child from her body he would use his staff on her back. He moved with the joy of what his god-ness would allow him to do to her. Until, through the gauzy cloth bound over his eyes, he saw her village and she would not believe him, and he wanted to crush her head.

He had pointed ahead of him, trying to shout, "There!" She heard the squawk of noise and looked to where he pointed. She shook her head and tugged the staff to make him move. He cursed her. He could see her people in the distance waiting for them. He kept tugging at the staff, straining to pull her to him, to make her see the people.

She suddenly smashed her bleeding hand against his face. He screamed in pain and blisters burst and he fell. She kicked his thighs, then kicked earth at his body. Her voice was ropy and torn as she damned him as a "sick one" who chewed the god-plants and lay on their backs and howled and clawed and ran to bite their own tails. He crunched together at her attack, until she fell beside him, struggling to breathe. He opened himself and looked to where he had seen her people. The land was a long barren blanch of earth shimmering in the heat. He could hear the pain screeching into his eyes from staring at the fiery space. He would not hate her anymore.

He lay back, watching the beasts that ate flesh circle lower to them. While she wheezed and gasped the air and shuddered with exhaustion he shook the staff at the black shrieky beasts in the Above. They circled lazily. When he tired, he dropped the staff and gently caressed her back. She tensed her body and rolled away from him. She raised herself to her elbows and watched the two animals that were stalking them—starving jackals. She knew they would attack as hunger maddened them.

Slowly, she drew the sacrificial knife from her clothes and began sharpening the end of his staff. She pushed him, demanding that he stand. He remained resting. She prodded the staff into his side. "Stand!" Behind the blaze of his eyes there were cool tears he could not cry. He strained himself to standing. She warned him to not be afraid if he heard an animal charging at him. He was too enraged in his cursing her to understand. She began hollowing out the earth to fix herself into a crouch while appearing to be laying on the ground. He swayed as he stood. They waited.

I did not want to remember what would happen.

I watched the judge use a pink tissue to clean her eyeglasses lens. She shook her head slowly. "Unless the defense can justify the question concerning the deceased's blood type—through its contribution to the crime, the objection will be sustained." Martin Lormer stood with his back to me, leaning against the table.

"I am attempting to build a foundation for a point of character that will be enormously significant in a little while."

"That is not satisfactory. Objection sustained."

The witness intertwined his hands across his stomach, and waited. The despair altering Martin Lormer's posture became heavier. He moved to his left and turned to lean over and study his notes. I concentrated on directing my thoughts to the jury to make them see some thousands of years back—to observe Bianco standing while the desert air, like dry sauna fumes, encased his body. The wind forced gravel motes through the rents in his covering. He was afraid to remove the blindfold and have the sun burst his eyes. Onadyh, crouched below him, hissed to him to be silent. The small, spear-faced animal slinked closer, its nose flared, the black line of flesh taut over its bared teeth. The yellow, scruffed coat was bristled. He could smell it, hear its harsh breath, feel the madness driving it to attack them. The other animal remained in the distance, huddled, alert.

She could see the wet sores on the animal's eyes, the opened gouges of flesh on its scrawned neck. It lowered to the ground, its chest pumping, then suddenly lunged ahead, kicking ground into flurries, and leaped at Bianco. While it was in the air, Onadyh sprung up, straining to thrust the pointed staff into the soft, unguarded belly. The animal screamed as it slammed into Bianco's chest, tumbling him over. He lay sprawled, waiting for his throat to be ripped open. She rushed to the thrashing beast and shoved the staff deeper into its body, impaling it to the ground. Bianco whimpered, asking what she was doing. She sliced the knife across the animal's neck and waited until it was fully dead. While she dismembered it she told him they had food and were saved a while longer. She gutted open the belly and ripped out the entrails. Ahead of them, the other jackal waited. She flung the oozy green and bloody insides as far as she could. The animal raced to them as they fell, and began eating.

How would you judge them, I silently asked the jury. Are the men of this reincarnation cowards and felons because we are not fierce and do not know how to save our women?

Martin Lormer traced his finger along the yellow sheet of paper and tapped a heavily underlined stretch of words. He turned to the witness.

"On the day you were to do the autopsy on Shara Medford, you received a telephone call from Dr. Jonathan Houseman. It is a matter of record. Now, will you tell the court the content of that phone call?"

"Dr. Houseman told me that he had been retained by the firm of Doty, Rice, and Lormer. He requested that I allow him to observe the autopsy. I agreed. Dr. Houseman and I have been friends for many years."

"More than friends, wouldn't you say? At one time, Dr.

Houseman was the deputy coroner, your immediate superior. When he retired to return to private practice he recommended you for the position."

"Yes. We have been friends for many years."

"I imagine you were pleased to have him present during the autopsy."

"I am always pleased to be in the company of Dr. Houseman."

"Even though you disagreed about your findings during the autopsy?"

"Disagreed? I recall no disagreement. The cause of the deceased's death was a simple matter to ascertain. There was no disagreement."

"What about your differences concerning that peculiar substance, that foreign matter that was lodged in the uterus of Shara Medford?"

The witness frowned. He looked to where Dr. Jonathan Houseman was seated. People followed his eyes. They saw a husky, middle-aged man with dark brown hair and a down-curved mustache. He did not stir. The District Attorney crouched closer to the table edge, undecided about objecting. He chose to remain silent, sensing that Martin Lormer was about to commit a serious mistake. The witness pinched his lips.

"Yes, I recall the incident now. There was some foreign matter lodged in the uterus of the deceased. Since it was not contributory to her death I conducted a cursory analysis of it. I recall that now."

"What did your cursory analysis of that foreign matter come to?"

"I could not make an adequate determination. I discounted it as being unimportant in relationship to her death. Dr. Houseman, on the other hand, thought it was an interesting bit of tissue and wanted to conduct a further examination. Our disagreement came over its value, not in its contribution to Shara Medford's death."

"How did that foreign matter get into her uterus?"

The District Attorney raised his finger, muttering, "Objection, your honor. This line of questioning appears to be irrelevant." She sighed. "Objection sustained." Martin Lormer edged to the witness.

"Was it possible that this foreign matter lodged in the deceased's uterus—this strange tissue—could have been an inoperable and agonizingly painful cancer the deceased never revealed to anyone and . . ."

The District Attorney stood up to object. I quickly understood what Martin Lormer was doing. "Your honor, objection, objection. The defense is trying to intimidate the witness into an issue that has no bearing on this trial. I most strenuously object." The judge looked at Martin Lormer. She, too, understood that he was trying to introduce the idea that Shara had been deathly ill and, because she was a moral woman, had compelled me to an act of euthanasia. I almost snickered aloud. Martin Lormer was becoming desperate. I was feeling cheered. The judge admonished him.

"The defense's line of questioning seems to serve no purpose. Objection sustained."

Martin Lormer glanced down as if searching the floor for a coin. He mumbled, "No more questions," and slowly moved to our table. The District Attorney grinned and spoke with disdaining emphasis. "I have no need to ask this witness any questions." Martin Lormer sat in a discouraged slump. He seemed to study his list of names. The jury watched him. He idly placed his hand on the globular object on the table. He patted the quilted cover. I tried to guess what was concealed beneath the cloth. My mind was void of images or information. I watched his hand. The fingernails were evenly clipped. They spread full across the domed top, spanning the curve. The fingers moved together and gently stroked the object.

The way he stroked the globe made me think of how Onadyh had suddenly stopped walking to drop to the ground to grasp a white hand-sized oval stone—cuddling it to her breasts, caressing it, holding it to her cheek and rocking while Bianco, gasping and tense to keep himself from falling, asked what she had found. She reached up and placed the stone in his hand, telling him that if she finds another one nearby, and then others, they were reaching their people. The stone, stark white and carefully smoothed into the shape that the flying beasts slept upon until other little flying beasts were born, contained the soul of the Searching-god, Death. Her people always made many Death stones and encircled them a great walking distance from their village. The Death stones were used to show the Searching-god that his children belonged outside the village, that her people would not steal his children. Then the Searching-god would have no reason to bring his Death into their abodes.

She tugged his arm, telling him to sit. He brought himself into a tight huddle to hide his face and the exposed flesh from the sun. She rested beside him, waiting for strength to wet the insides of her legs. She asked her god of Finding to bring her other Death stones.

He did not speak. An animal with hooked claws was in his throat. He felt her leave. His father was greater than her Finding god. When the child she carried gave signs that he was ready to be taken from her, he would make a large mixing of his colored flesh. He would draw the child from her. He would cover the child with the mixing and her people would give god-ness to him. They would believe he was his own child. When the mixing faded from the child he would tell her people he had done a magic. Now the child had the god-ness of them and he would be their god.

He heard her call to him. He remained huddled over. She shouted, "More." He heard her coming to him, carrying more Death stones. He cursed her god of Finding—his father should have led them to her people.

Martin Lormer slid his hand from atop the quilt-covered globe and stood up. He called a Doctor Ralph Dewitt to the witness stand. I watched the man move along the aisle and recalled him as the doctor who had been on duty the night Shara and Althea and myself had been in the automobile accident. The doctor was a rangy man with long upper teeth. He wore a pastel gray denim jacket and a pants belt with an oval jade stone fitted into the buckle. His hands looked like bony skinned pigeons. One held a small black notebook.

"On the night of March 16th, approximately two months before Shara Medford was murdered, you were on duty at the Kennedy Memorial Hospital in Milpitis. Three people were in an automobile accident. Would you tell the court about that incident."

He opened the notebook and flicked through the pages. "I was driven to the scene of the accident. Three people were involved. A Stephen Jerod, a Shara Medford, and an Althea Jackson, a black woman. The male was mildly bruised. The woman Shara Medford suffered only a minor shake-up. Ms. Jackson was seriously injured."

"What was the nature of her injuries?"

"Heavy contusions in the chest. Apparently she was driving. A deep slash across her forehead above the left eye, which later on required fifteen stitches. Lacerations across her shoulders and neck, and a severed brachial artery in her left arm."

"Why was the patient, Althea Jackson, given blood in the ambulance?"

"The ambulance crew found that Ms. Jackson had a severed brachial artery which had been bleeding for at least fifteen minutes. She was already in shock. Waiting until she reached the hospital would have been fatal."

"What type of blood was Ms. Jackson given?"

"O-negative, which is universal donor type."

"Universal donor type blood can be transfused into anyone, is that correct?"

"Generally, yes. O-negative blood will not cause a transfusion reaction, so it can be given to a patient of any blood type. A, B, or O."

"But you stated that Althea Jackson, after receiving a blood transfusion of O-negative blood, suffered a reaction. What went wrong?"

The doctor studied a page in his notebook. I was not interested in what he would read. All Martin Lormer would do was reveal to the jury that Shara had behaved stupidly, cruelly, on the night of the accident. Martin Lormer was snipping away at her character.

I was feeling elated with the memory of how Onadyh and Bianco had been greeted by the people. They had reached the border of the village as the sun sifted behind a long hill. Three dogs barked at them. Some children, wearing leather and wool clothes, their long black hair held behind their necks with tines—ran from them. They screamed. Men rushed from low-roofed, mud brick abodes. Onadyh waved her arms, speaking as they spoke, and they remembered her. Elderly men in cloth coverings tapped small sticks on flat metal discs and the people stepped aside so they could examine Onadyh. Bianco drew off his blindfold and tried to see them. They edged back, afraid at the sight of his enlarged, reddened eyes.

Onadyh calmed them. Cautiously, women brought bowls of water. They placed them before Bianco, fearful of his feathered head covering, the torn and broken plumes attached to the cloth on his body.

Onadyh splashed herself, then flung water onto Bianco. When he could spit away the animal clawed inside his throat, he hoarsely began telling them of his god-ness. They did not understand his speaking. Onadyh went to him, saying, "Show them." She reached up and carefully drew off his head covering. The people cringed back and gasped at his flair of white hair, the swollen whiteness of skin covered with festering blisters and insect bites. She pulled away his body covering. When they saw his total whiteness they dropped to their knees, protectively grasping their children. The warriors extended their arms and began bowing to him. The blaze of the day they had just left was still in his eyes and he could not see them clearly. Only shadows moved below him. He heard their language chant to him. They were giving him his god-ness.

What Martin Lormer was asking the witness seemed so trivial. How lifeless was talk when compared to survival, to being made into a god.

"Come now, Doctor, surely you can recall why Althea Jackson went into shock after the blood transfusion. Or are you still surprised at what you learned? Tell the court what went wrong."

"Nothing went *wrong*. The ambulance crew acted in an acceptable medical fashion. When the patient arrived at the hospital I detected signs of a reaction—she experienced chills, her skin was clammy. She was rushed to the emergency room. Her temperature was low when she came in. But it suddenly elevated. Also the laboratory had typed her blood, which came out O on the forward type, but A on the backward type. This discrepancy indicated that the patient was not really type O. In fact, the only explanation for this is that the patient is an extremely rare blood type known as Bombay. This was confirmed in a subsequent test."

"Bombay blood type. Would you tell the court . . ."

The District Attorney tapped his pencil on the table and stood up. "Your honor, I object," he said, shaking his head. "I will give anyone in this court a ten-dollar gift certificate for Taco Bell burritos if they can tell me what all this talk of blood transfusions has to do with this case." The judge picked at a flake of varnish on the wooden handle of her gavel. Martin Lormer stepped away from the witness stand and faced her. There was no servility in his posture.

"Your honor, I have a specific purpose for this testimony. There are facts in this very testimony that are crucial to our defense—*and the understanding of Shara Medford's character.* It is also pertinent to another testimony and to many of the testimonies already heard. I entreat this court to allow me to continue."

She brushed the flake of varnish from the gavel and drew off her glasses. She said, "The court will allow the defense to carry on a bit longer. Objection overruled." Martin Lormer thanked her and turned to the witness.

"Is it true, Doctor Dewitt, that only about six people in our country—say in over two hundred million people—possess the type of blood known as Bombay?"

"Yes, that is correct. It is extremely rare."

"Did you have any Bombay blood in the hospital? Was there any in the local or state blood banks?"

"No."

"Then you had to get some quite quickly—or Althea Jackson would die. Is that correct?"

"Yes. There was no other way to save her."

"If there was no Bombay type blood in the hospital, no Bombay type blood in the state or local blood banks, then where did you get the extremely rare Bombay blood you used to save Althea Jackson's life?"

"From the other woman, Shara Medford."

I ignored the sense of surprise in the courtroom. One night, after trying to make love to Shara and failing, she substituted liquor for sex and got drunk. Her eyes rolled lazily in their sockets, her body was a slump moving about the apartment. Sometimes she laughed moronically, sometimes she stood near a wall and kicked the baseboard. She did not curse me for my sexual failure. She harangued, loudly and in slurs, about how God controlled us by implanting an irrevocable sexual drive in our souls no matter what age we were. She flung a vase of flowers against the wall, shattering it. She stumbled to the sharp pieces and began picking them up from the carpet. She held one pointed shard near her wrist and her face grimaced with rage and I was afraid she wanted to kill herself. "Leave them alone, darling," I urged her. "I'll pick them up. You might cut yourself." She stood and swayed, bringing the jagged glass to her lips—her eyes cunning with mysteries as she shushed me to secrecy. "You're right, my lover priest. You'll have to fly to Bombay—'cause I'm Bombay blood, with a *kicker* in it." Then she began laughing again.

Martin Lormer raised his arms, palms facing the witness, saying, "How did you ascertain that Shara Medford had the same rare Bombay type blood? Did she tell you?"

"After receiving the laboratory report and understanding its consequences, I went to the other people who were in the same accident. I wanted to contact Ms. Jackson's family. It was then that the male, Stephen Jerod, told me that the woman, Shara Medford, was also a Bombay blood type."

"And the woman, Shara Medford, readily agreed to the transfusion?"

"No, quite the contrary."

"What? She refused to give a blood transfusion that would save her friend's life? Well then, since Althea Jackson is still alive and obviously doing well, how did you manage to persuade her?"

"I had nothing to do with it. It was Stephen Jerod who managed it."

The doctor looked to his notebook, studying his notes. That night I had been stunned by Shara's refusal. I pleaded with her, "You can't refuse, Shara. I have no love for that black bitch, but even I would give her blood if I could." She had turned her back to me. "You don't know what you're asking me to do. I won't agree to the transfusion."

I grabbed her shoulders and forced her around. "What kind of a heartless bitch are you?"

She struck my hands away from her. "You don't understand. My blood has an unknown factor in it."

I squeezed her arm and my other hand clenched. "If you can live with that unknown factor in your blood, so can Althea." I angrily pushed her against the wall.

The doctor tried to step between us, complaining, "Come on, you two. You're in a hospital, not a barroom." I shoved him back and grabbed the side of her neck, forcing her face close to mine. "You're a vicious, hypocritical bitch," I hissed—then felt a vomiting disgust for her and stepped back. "Look at how Althea loves you, and this is how you return her friendship—by letting her die. I can't stand to look at you!"

Then she laughed and I wanted to smash her mouth. "All right," she said in her laughter. "All right," and kept laughing. "You might fail me again, Stephen, and then I'll need a friend, won't I? I'll have a life-long friend and I won't be lonely."

She stepped around me and smiled at the doctor. "I agree to the transfusion."

Martin Lormer and the court listened to the doctor tell what I had remembered. The doctor closed his notebook and placed it into the tabbed pocket of his jacket.

"Tell me, Doctor Dewitt, did any complications result from the transfusion—because of the unknown factor Shara Medford claimed to have in her Bombay blood type?"

"There were no complications, but her claim was correct. The factor is still unknown and still being investigated."

Martin Lormer nodded. "Thank you, Doctor. No more questions." The District Attorney left his table, carrying a yellow pad with him.

"Doctor Dewitt, about this unknown factor in the murdered woman's blood. Might it have caused the already dying woman to die more quickly—even more horribly?"

"It is still an unknown factor, so I can't really say. But it might have. Bombay blood does not have the precursor substance that is subsequently changed into A substance for A blood type, and B substance for B-type patients. Moreover, Bombay blood has an antibody called anti-H, which causes the destruction of red cells in all blood types—A, B, and even O. Hence the transfusion reaction."

"That's all very interesting, Doctor Dewitt, but could you answer in such a way that the average person knows exactly what you are talking about?"

"Yes, I'll try. Bombay type people all have anti-H, making it almost impossible to give them blood because they will *destroy any blood given them*, except their exact own."

"Then what you're saying is that with an unknown factor present in Shara Medford's Bombay blood, giving a blood transfusion to someone, though they have a *similar* rare blood type, could have been dangerous—even fatal?"

"Yes. There is always that possibility."

"And Shara Medford, knowing that her Bombay blood contained the unknown factor, might have been refusing to provide a blood transfusion because Althea Jackson's death might have been hastened—Shara Medford was not being cruel, but loyal and loving to her friend."

"I did not know her background in medicine, if she had any, but from the human standpoint, I would agree to that possibility."

The District Attorney grinned. "No more questions." As the witness left the stand, someone to the left of the jury said, "Excuse me." The voice was toneless, timid. The doctor walked to the witness area and sat down. The voice became louder, slightly annoyed. "Excuse me, please." The judge and jurors looked to the dark-suited attendant of Klaymore Montecello. He had his arm raised as though in a classroom. "Excuse me, please—it's just that—well, just that I believe my employer, Mr. Montecello is— well, he's dead."

The judge leaned forward, touching her ear. "What was that?" she said, while she squinted at the aged man slumped in the wheelchair. The attendant edged the wheelchair forward. People raised themselves and stared. I saw three women cross themselves. The District Attorney crimped his mouth and glanced at his wristwatch. Bishop Carmondy lifted himself to a dignified stance and fussed with his clothes, ready to officiate. The dead man's arms dangled over the sides of the chair. Some newspeople left their places and went to the attendant, ignoring the artist's body and the judge's warning to return to their places, as they asked quick questions. "How long have you been in his employ?" and "Are there any immediate heirs?" and "Do you believe the pressure of this trial caused his death?"

Two bailiffs hurried over and escorted them back to their section. Martin Lormer sat and shook his head, muttering, "It doesn't feel right. It's got to be something else. I feel it." The judge breathed deeply and flattened her hands before her. She looked to where the witnesses were seated. "Would Doctor Dewitt please attend to Mr. Montecello and confirm this gentleman's claim."

The doctor patted his western-type jacket and cleared his throat. "Yes, of course, I will, your honor."

Martin Lormer studied me. I glanced away, examining the flag of California decorating the wall behind the judge. I did not kill the old artist, I thought, for Lormer's benefit. I liked the peppery old codger. Martin Lormer's eyes did not move from my face. I shifted my sight to watch the doctor who had opened the old man's clothes and placed a stethoscope to his chest. He stood stooped over, listening. All the people in the news media section were standing, waiting. The doctor drew the stethoscope prongs from his ears and sighed. "I would say this man is dead." The judge's mouth trembled.

A young woman, a familiar television newscaster, spoke to the judge. "Your honor, I believe it only fair that the court be recessed for at least an hour so this information can be transmitted to the country."

The judge touched her gavel, annoyed at having to decide. Martin Lormer stood up. "No, your honor. Klaymore Montecello is not dead. I'm sure of it."

The judge glared at him. "Mr. Lormer, you are out of order." He walked from behind the table and stood before her.

"I beg of you, your honor, listen to me. I have a premonition about this. There is more to life than some doctor's examination and premature pronouncement."

She raised her gavel as if to fling it at his face. He turned from her and pointed to the pastor who had prayed for the safety of the court. "You—Pastor—of the Open Bible church—isn't there something in the Bible, in Acts, about Chapter 20, that can deal with this kind of situation?"

The tall man rose from his seat, pinching the red splotches on his chin. His pale green checkered suit was wrinkled at the shoulders. He blinked, startled with a remembrance. "Why, yes, there is—when the Apostle Paul was preaching in Troas."

The District Attorney began smacking his hand on the table, shouting, "Your honor, this is utter madness. There is a dead man in the court and we stand around chattering about the Bible." The pastor left his area and walked toward the wheelchair. A bailiff moved to stop him. The judge ordered, "Let him perform his calling—or the last rites." The doctor stepped before the sagged body, protectively. "This man is dead."

The pastor sidestepped him and placed both hands on the ashen bald head. "Jesus, Jesus, Jesus," he began intoning, then spoke in a flurry of sounds and tones that were not words. I have heard this glossolalia articulated before. The priests, during Communion, were careful to find anyone praying in "other tongues" so they could be chased from the church. True spirituality disturbed priests. The pastor's voice swayed and trembled in the silence. Some people lowered their heads and gripped their hands in prayer. Bishop Carmondy sat with his mouth clenched. I did not breathe as I listened. This was the language of the Holy Spirit and I didn't want to offend Him with my corrupt breath. The District Attorney said, "Oh, my God," and I looked at the old man. His right hand shuddered. Four jurors leaned over the railing. The doctor strode back to the wheelchair, softly cursing as he refitted his stethoscope.

Martin Lormer returned to the table and smiled at me. I looked past his left shoulder and watched the doctor again examine Klaymore Montecello. The pastor continued praying though the artist's bony hands were slowly opening and closing. The pastor's voice was lyrical, the sounds an eerie swirl of strange phrases expressing his thanks and praise to God. The doctor told the attendant, "Let's get him to emergency," then swiveled to face the judge. "I do not understand what has happened. I would have sworn, *on the Bible*, that he was dead."

The judge called to the bailiff at the wide double doors. "Let them pass through. The doctor is excused from this court until the necessary measures are taken—at which time he will be required to return." The pastor became silent. Sweat oozed on his forehead. When the attendant had wheeled the old man from the courtroom the judge pursed her mouth and looked at Martin Lormer.

"Mr. Lormer, I would like to know what prompted you to believe that the man was not dead."

"I can't answer that, your honor. I merely believed that the man was not dead. I doubt if anyone can explain one-tenth of what this murder and this trial is really all about. I can't, in all honesty, answer your question, your honor."

The pastor moved to the aisle. People whispered to him, "Thank you," and "God bless you," and "That was a true miracle." Others reached out to touch his arm and mutter, "Pray for me, pastor." He spoke softly to them. "I did nothing. It is all the power of Jesus Christ!" The judge struck the gavel hard, ordering, "The court will remain in session while I retire to my chambers for fifteen minutes." She left the courtroom.

God, God, I thought. We had just been in the presence of God. We had all witnessed His mercy. I felt chilled. I wanted to stand with my arms raised and shout, "Praise the Lord! *For His mercy endureth forever*." God was alive—dear God. His touch was now in the heartbeat of an aged man. God—dear Jesus, Lord of my life—while you are still here, forgive me.

We waited. The people felt no need to talk. A man had died in their presence and the same man had been revived. They were quiet in wonderment and awe.

I slowly moved my eyes until I was looking at Althea Jackson. I knew she was beautiful but I did not feel her beauty. She was just some black bitch who was monumental in sex and minimal in mind. She was chatting softly with Bishop Carmondy. Her dark skin, almost prune black, made his complexion seem like a badly peeled grapefruit. I could not hear their conversation, but I imagined what they were saying.

"Why are you still here, Bishop Carmondy? Your part of the trial is over."

"Wild horses couldn't tear me away. I will stay to the very end."

"Then we share the same attitude. I want to see that honky killer get his ass nailed to the gas-chamber chair."

"You put it rather harshly, young lady. However—well . . ."

"I know, Bishop, vengeance is the Lord's, not yours. Well, in this instance, the Lord can use a little coaxing."

"I don't believe that God is ever undecided. He's a rather independent spirit, you know. Perhaps we could discuss it at another time."

"Why, Bishop Carmondy, are you making a pass at me? Shara told me you had the charisma of virility about you. I wonder who would experience the novelty more? Could you handle a . . ."

"My reasons are purely theological, not social, I assure you."

"I'll tell you what, Bishop. After that son of a bitch Jerod is found guilty, I'll discuss any damn thing you like—from faith to fornication—after he's sentenced to die."

I saw the Bishop shift away, his face suddenly flushed. I wondered if I had actually guessed their conversation. I had to admire him. He was past sixty years old and still hustling for new sexual experiences.

The District Attorney kept glancing at the judge's chambers. Martin Lormer reached to the globular object on the table and dabbed his fingertips on the cloth. The pastor who had prayed for Klaymore Montecello returned to the courtroom and went to his seat. A newspaper woman called to him, "How is the old man?" People waited for his answer. He grinned, then put his finger to his lips. I thought about Barthelamo because he was accredited with being able to revive the dead through his medicine, with his devilish skill in removing curses, and through his mixtures of potions. I closed my eyes, trying to remember how I began the last part of

Barthelamo in my journal. It was the most painful, saddening section I had written.

Date: 1500   Month: February   Time: Evening
"Sed et serpens erat callidior cunctis animantibus terrae."
(Now the serpent was more subtle than any beast of the field.)
Genesis 3:1

I waited patiently, enduring the cold of my dungeon cell, enduring the maddening knowledge that other men might be consorting with Letitia. I instituted attempts to place a curse upon Lucrezia Borgia. I used all my knowledge of the prevailing superstitions and witchcraft. I kept myself warm by conjuring up dreadful images of how Lucrezia was destroyed through fire, by monstrous diseases that caused her fevers. I ignored my indignity through the excitement of scenes of what my life would be like when I was released and reunited with Letitia.

Gently as though drifting through a murmur of time, I allowed myself to leave the presence of the courtroom to remember Barthelamo in his cell. I could feel the chill wrapped about his nakedness, see the scrawny rats slinking along the walls, waiting for him to sleep. I am you, Barthelamo, we are one.

While I dozed, dawn drifted into the cold dungeon. The thick door groaned open before I could fully awaken. I saw Letitia gliding toward me as the jailer fitted a torch into the wall. I sighed, "Beloved," as she stood before me. The fullness of her beauty changed the dungeon into a place of decoration. A woman, yet still a child, just stepped from a tapestry. The delicacy of her face was a cameo perfection. Only a crease of despair at seeing me chained marred her glow. She closed her eyes, lamenting, "Oh, Barthelamo," and her sorrow was a caress. She removed her fur-lined cape to cover my icy skin.

"No, beloved, there is no need to warm me. I have become inured to the cold. Without your wrap you will gain a chill."

"How monstrously he has treated you. His abuse is inhuman."

"He is Cesare Borgia. No more need be said. I thank God his heart has become softened to me."

"You are feverish, Barthelamo, you know not what you speak. Borgia is a monster. His soul cannot be altered."

"No, beloved, his cruelty will soon be over. He visited me and we spoke. Though I be bound in such a manner, still he sought my services. I removed a dreadful curse from his destiny. Thus, he will not destroy me. I have become his necessity."

Her eyes gleamed with tears. I laughed, softly. At such times, when she cried, I remembered she was still a child, merely seventeen. She dabbed a silken cloth to her tears and whispered, "I have come to rescue you the only way your rescue is possible." How good of her to love me so, I thought. I pursed my mouth to her in a silent kiss.

"I bless you for your love, Letitia, but I am already saved. When Borgia's whim no longer amuses him, I will be freed."

"No, Barthelamo, your goodness and trust has ruined you. You are a fool to believe in Borgia. He has not relented. Preparations for your execution are being made. The Pope will attend your death and his presence is for adventure, not blessing."

"Letitia, hear me, beloved. Borgia is allowing them to continue preparations to avoid aspersions upon his honor. He has a plan in which all the court will know it is expedient that I live."

"Plan? There is no plan. It is the fever in your mind."

She closed her eyes and I could not know her thoughts. Why are we speaking in the heat of dissension. I am to be freed. We should speak of love. The ice in my body will soon be thawed by wine. I will gorge myself from the succulents of Borgia's kitchen and we will then steal to our bed chamber and become one again.

I shifted to rattle the chains to make her look upon me. She was a child and often possessed by a great stupidity. The flesh beneath her neck throbbed.

"Go from me now, beloved. There may be danger in your presence here. Seek the warmth of our rooms until I return to you."

She placed her fingers to her mouth and shook her head. Now

there was no youth in her eyes. Sorrow had turned her absolutely woman.

"There is no rescue for you, Barthelamo. Lucrezia has already blessed her brother for redeeming her honor by your death. He would rather cherish the devil's curse in his life than lose her blessing, or cause her displeasure. Other princes, and dukes, and royalty from far places have already arrived. He cannot save you."

I heard low, mocking laughter, and glanced about the prison to see if another one was present. We were alone. The flame in the wall torch danced anxiously. The laughter was in my mind. Suddenly, I believed that she was not lying. "Letitia," I whispered, inspired by a strange hope. "Accomplish my rescue now, and come away with me. I will be welcomed in Rome—nay, in France I will be greatly esteemed. Our life will be exorbitant with love."

She stepped back and I saw her draw a stiletto from behind her gown. The long, pointed blade reflected the dim morning light. She held it toward me. "I cannot endure to witness you torn apart by the Duke's stallions. This is my rescue, Barthelamo." She was a child again. How could so thin a blade sever the thickness of chain? She held the blade to me and then I understood and I was transfixed with horror. Circumstance had changed my executioner.

"Letitia," I hissed. "You cannot do such a thing. You will damn your soul."

Her eyes were dulled, unseeing with regret. I flared in anger. She was being duped. All of it was an arrangement of Lucrezia Borgia's. The slow dullness in her eyes was a spell placed into her mind. "Letitia," I barked at her. "If you are doing this in Lucrezia's cause, you are doomed to become her assassin. There will be others she will want destroyed." The blade quivered in her small hand.

"No, Barthelamo, I swear. The day will come when I will stand by Lucrezia's grave and mourn her, or laugh. The Prince, too, will be gone before I am taken from life. I do this for you—for how you have loved me."

"I love you still."

"Yes, dear Barthelamo, and so I am bidden to make haste in

rescuing you from Borgia's demonic amusements. While there is yet time."

How could I deny her? To hear her speak of love I would have laid bare my heart for her to puncture. But she was not herself. She was under a spell and not alert in ways political. There was a Captain Gargiolo who once betrayed Borgia by announcing the Prince's penchant for cheating in games. The Captain was imprisoned and tortured. Borgia promised him a cunning death. The morning of his execution he was released. The Captain's military skills were necessary for Borgia's campaigns. My life too was vital to him. I could shroud him with virtuous protections against other curses. She must believe this. I spoke softly, in pretended calm.

"Letitia, my beloved, you have become bewitched by Lucrezia's powers. Let me pray against the spell she has clothed you in."

"I am not bewitched. I am only honoring the love you have given me."

She edged closer to me, the slender blade pointed at my heart. I closed my eyes. This would not happen. I listened to the fullness of laughter in my mind. Laughter coming from so distant a time it seemed to be a shadow's echo. Who was laughing in my mind? Was it the white creature whose existence had been with me all my life—or was it his savage woman's laughter? For she had destroyed the white creature—Bianco. How did he die? Please, adored Lord, cause me to remember Bianco's death. He died within a scream to the savage woman, to not destroy him. Was I now to be grateful to Letitia for killing me in such a way that I need not scream?

"Letitia," I spoke with closed eyes. "Pause a moment, I beg you. Are there recollections within you of another time, when we were lovers? A time so long ago there was no way to measure time?"

"I will not speak of such things. It is unholy."

"There is no unholiness in love. Do you remember another time between us? We spoke other languages and I was another man. Not deformed as I am now. Think. How did you destroy me then—I have forgotten."

"Barthelamo, I must hurry. Lucrezia will note my absence and search for me."

"Letitia, my beloved, grant me the choice of death. Rather than have my death cause the corruption of your soul, I will risk my life on Borgia's whim."

"Close your eyes, dear Barthelamo. I cannot do this whilst you look into my heart."

I did not close my eyes. The laughter, coming from the darkness of Time, would not leave me. I strained to remember Bianco's death, to see it happen, so I could know my own. There were no tears in Letitia's eyes.

"Letitia, if you plunge the blade into my heart, only my body will perish, not my love."

"Pray that I am forgiven for what I do, Barthelamo."

"But you have done this before. Were you forgiven then?"

"I ask for forgiveness for now."

"Kiss me, then—send me wherever I go with your taste upon me."

"I fear—you are too cunning for me."

"Letitia, Letitia, how can I harm you? I am chained. Kiss me, beloved, I require that you do."

She placed the blade behind her and moved to me. The sense of her nearness was sky and space. I whispered, "Beloved," as she placed her mouth to mine. She spoke into me, "You must forgive me," and I suddenly bit her mouth and desperately held her flesh between my teeth. She cursed, *"Diavolo!"* and struggled whilst I held to her to cause her pain to break Lucrezia's spell. She smashed my face and neck, kicking at me. Then I gasped in shock as she drove the knife into my chest. She leaped back and I stared at the golden hilt jutting from my body. The pain flamed in me, yet I was not in agony. The laughter in my mind was shrilling whilst I watched my body shudder with the horror I was feeling. I could not see her clearly. Only the blood issuing from her mouth. She had missed my heart but organs of great need had been stabbed. I was dying while yet alive.

"Letitia," my waning voice mourned from a closing throat. "Draw the knife from me." I could not speak. The laughter began to soar in my mind.

I love you, my beloved. I am love for you, Letitia, my glorious Letitia, you did not destroy me, I compelled you, I saved you from sacrilege, Bianco did not forgive you, he cursed you, I remember. Her image wavered and streamed into a glittering flow and the sparkle of her burst terror into me. "I love you, my loved beloved," I spoke, though the sounds we heard was the gurgle of my blood. We are not done, this death has not ended us, and I will not be humped of back again, I will be whole for you—and then I was without pain and my form was still and I heard only my inner confession of love and another man's laughter.

Through my tears I saw Martin Lormer studying me. Though his expression was blurred I knew he was afraid I had reached the endurance of my sanity. He could not know that Barthelamo was finally dead in me—again. That I was sitting in a state of funeral and mourning.

Barthelamo had died in me so many times that my grief was habit. I cried now because he would never again live in me. When I was executed, Barthelamo's death would be irrevocable, for I would not become reincarnated to become the burden of another man's consciousness in another Time. In killing Shara I had broken the flow of incarnations. We would all be finally dead.

And there were pulsations of laughter in my sorrow. None of this could be true. All of this must be an arcane, evil lie. Reincarnation was a demonic delusion.

Martin Lormer began calling an assembly line of inconsequential witnesses to characterize Shara as a bitchy, viciously ambitious young woman who provoked people to despise her. The legal ploy did not seem impressive. The District Attorney offered the required objections to reveal that he was alert. He fulfilled the methodical procedure of discrediting the people who maligned Shara. He was not accepting the list of witnesses as a threat to his pending victory. He knew the jury was bored.

He was not a subtle, sensitive man.

I wanted to warn him. Martin Lormer was not boring the jury, he was deliberately wearing them down, lulling them into wearily accepting the credibility of statements. To eventually shock them—to suddenly awaken them with an astonishment. And by the habit of accepting, they would accept.

Barthelamo was dead and my memory of how he died had emptied me of feeling. I was lonely to relive him again. I enjoyed his life. But there was such happiness now in Bianco's life, that I was pleased to leave the dismal courtroom to be with him.

Onadyh recovered quickly. In the passage of days, treated by the women who bathed her skin in salving preparations, her welts and swellings diminished—the sores and rents in her flesh began to heal. They had brought Bianco into a long rectangular abode built of carefully fashioned stones bonded with a gray putty that became one with the stone. A scented smearing, like whitewash, covered the inside walls. The roof was a stretch of sturdy trees stripped bare and bound together with a cross netting of thick ropes. The warriors lay him in the center of the abode, softening the tamped-solid earth with blankets.

Women were allowed to enter only to bathe him. His body, distorted by the swellings, leaked pus—large scabs, like spatters of caked mud, were cracked on his flesh. The women did not look at his eyes as they cleansed his face. They were small in stature and deeply bronzed. The warriors who guarded him stood in attendance, holding heavy shanked spears. They were brawny men, squat in figure, with broad faces and almost flattened noses.

He did not allow them to know his pain. When his festered skin was touched he lay in taut silence. They must not know his god-ness was not yet returned to him by his father in the Above.

When he was cleaned, the women bound him in gauzy strips of cloth saturated with scented ointments. He was told to remain unmoving. Though he did not know their speech he understood their instructions.

He lay in stillness while his eyes cooled. He heard singing and the thump of dancing outside the abode. He knew that large fires had been lighted by the flows of heat that entered the abode's openings. He began carefully recalling himself as he had once been, so that when he was healed he would not be changed. He saw the stark whiteness of his hair flared from the sides to sweep back into a spill across his shoulders, the near glow of whiteness of his skin that stunned all people to believe he had bathed in the full

Cold Eye of his father. The rims of flesh around his eyes and the tips of his fingers felt like the tongues of the beasts that barked about the village.

I sat in the courtroom, hearing the hum and jabber of voices of people asking questions and offering testimony, but I was squirming within my body, for I was not separate from Bianco. He was the origin of our suffering. I did not know how many of us had been born from him between the time of Bianco and then the time of myself. I squirmed with his pain, feeling pity for him.

When it was time to remove the ointment-saturated wrappings, four Elders arrived with the women. They chanted and jiggled their legs as they uncoiled the gauzes. Though the Elders held their torches away from him, he could feel the heat. He felt lengths of his hair being worked from his head. The Elders leaned over him and spoke. He believed they meant for him to stand. They shifted away from him until he was steadily balanced.

He spoke through the opening framed on his mouth. He asked them to bring Onadyh. He wanted her to see their fear when his eyes could touch their eyes. They did not know his sounds. He did not anger. He could see beyond the snug covering over his eyes, past the abode walls. Onadyh was at the Temple commanding many warriors to place his god-ness throne where all could see it. He tried to see her face clearly but the Burning Eye inside his mind blocked his vision.

Onadyh had already been given her god-ness. Women brought their children to her. She touched their faces, caressed their chests. She picked chewy food from a pouch she wore and fed them. She was being given his god-ness by his enemy. He angered at his father in the Above. His father was not giving him strength to leave the abode so he could beat her before her people. She had the enemy's carrying in her that would become a child. He had a carrying of the enemy in his mind—a Burning Eye. Silently, while the Elders looked upon his flesh, he wept to his father to wet the Burning Eye in him—to put out its fire.

The Elders tapped metal tipped sticks onto flat, circular discs. They wailed and hummed and swayed. The women's voices became like small beasts that flew and sang. He could feel that his flesh was no longer swollen. There remained only a smattering of cuts that were like long clumps of hair on his skin. The women were told to uncover his face. He could smell their nearness—hear their motions as their wearings tinkled. He felt lulled. Slowly, he did not fear the enemy who had placed an inflamed carrying in his mind. Others had gone to cross the enemy's great land and had fallen and were picked as food for the flying beasts that tore flesh. He and Onadyh had not fallen. The Burning Eye in his mind was a gift. It was drying and smalling the Cold Eye of his father. It gave him powers.

He opened his mouth to let them hear his sounds. He raised his arms and waved his hands, clawing and jabbing his fingers, suddenly wailing and singing his voice. There would be no sickness in their village. Their children would become great warriors and hunters. The ground would fill heavy with food. Their wells would never dry.

The Elders and women had stepped back while he shook and incanted and flung his arms and shuddered his shoulders. They bowed before him. When he became silent, the women reached up and gently unwound the gauze from his eyes. He opened his eyes, then quickly clenched them closed. The whiteness of the abode walls reflecting the flare of torches burst the Burning Eye deeper into his mind. He grasped at his eyes, squeezing them. He hooked his fingers to tear them from his face. The Elders rushed to him, pulling his hands away and gently lowered him to the blankets while he kicked and pounded with pain. They dripped a sweet liquid into his mouth and soon he slept.

The pain passed but the inflaming in him remained. When his father was in the Above and flesh shivered, his mind throbbed with warmth. He could see, but there was a hurting below his sight. He waited for his father to douse the fire-gift his enemy had put into him. He watched the days enter the abode, and then leave. There were waist-high apertures cut into the stone walls. When his father was ruling the Above and there was no light, the people built mound-fires about the abode and the glare sliced through the narrow openings. He ate the food they brought and did not return the bones. He used them for castings. The throwings told him that he must wait until he was without a scratch or marking, and then he would be granted his god-ness. He must appear before the people without blemish.

He knew they were watching him while he slept. Their faces pressed against the abode openings. The women, always led by the Elders, carefully rubbed salves on his skin and smeared thick golden oils onto his sores. They wore necklaces of green stones that clicked as they moved about him. The Elders always dressed with long lines of green stones held in gold strings over their torsos. They sang and muttered as they healed the flaws and cracks. When he was alone he screamed at the enemy god. The inside of his mind was embers and sizzling stones.

He studied the village through the wall spaces. The abode was encircled with the small oval stones. Within the border were small arrangements of bones, honoring him. He saw the temple he would rule. Balanced on the long rise of steps was a great man-sized oval stone. He stood at the abode opening, watching the builders patiently fashioning the throne he would sit upon when his god-ness was returned.

Onadyh sat upon a tall gold-decorated wooden seat, directing other males where to erect a large, three-sided abode into which his throne would be placed. Her skin was oiled, her hair was a blackness spread across her back, hiding the heavy necklaces and amulets the Elders had given her. Women brought her flowers to touch. She did not look to where he was sheltered. She knew that soon he would beat her. Then his god-ness would be known to be greater than hers.

The sides of the abode that would guard his throne were fashioned of evenly separated thin trees bound with thick ropes. The space between each pole would allow only a hand to push through. Each one was adorned with thin windings of golden cloth. Further away he could see other builders setting the narrow trees into another wall.

He began calling to the people through the apertures. There were some children who were swollen in a sickness, he told them. "It is from the well," he shouted. He could heal them. The women hurried to bring more mounds of bones, but hid their children.

He stood at the walls, straining to use the Burning Eye in his mind to flame a passage through the stones. He brought the thickest bones and clubbed the walls until the bones splintered. He cast the splinterings. He huddled back, afraid. They would not give him god-ness until he did a spell, until they saw his power. What spell could he do? He lay on the blankets and rolled. He struck his hands onto the faces and stories woven into the blankets. He pulled the cloth from his front and stroked himself. The women screamed. The Elders fell to the ground and crawled from the abode. He cast the bones and listened to the speaking of the Great Burning Eye. It would tell him the spell to do.

I felt a hand grip my arm and I opened my eyes and saw Martin Lormer staring at me, asking, "Are you all right?" I realized that I had been shuddering and squirming. The courtroom of people was one enormous face focused upon me. I drew my arm from his grip and sighed. He turned to the judge. "My client is fine, your honor. If I may, I would like to continue." She nodded. "So be it." A woman with a petite face and thinly plucked eyebrows was on the witness stand. I ignored her. If there had been some madness in Barthelamo Vecchio, and there was some madness in me now, Bianco was the origin. You could not walk over a hundred miles across a desert and remain the same as when you began. I sat with my eyes closed, trying to listen.

Then I was startled when Martin Lormer asked the woman, "When did the deceased, Shara Medford, tell you about the journal she was reading?" The woman spoke with an affected lisp that did not distort her words. "It was at least a month before she was murdered. Frankly, when she told me what the journal was about, I didn't believe her." Martin Lormer placed his palms together and touched his fingertips to his chin.

"What did she tell you about the journal? Try to recall her exact words, if you can."

"I can't recall her exact words. Only what it was about, in the main. About this man who was alive in other times—reincarnated. He was killed in those other times, and he blamed some woman for doing it. Shara said the man she was living with, Stephen Jerod, believed he was that man."

"Did she say that he was the man writing the journal, or the man the journal was being written about?"

"Both. I thought she was making up a television soap opera. Everybody thinks they can write those silly soap operas. But she wasn't making it up."

"How can you be sure of that?"

"Because she brought the journal to the office."

I almost shouted, "You're a lying, simpering and crazy bitch!" Shara had never read the journal until the night I killed her.

Martin Lormer went to the evidence table and brought the journal to her. "Is this the journal she showed you?" The woman opened the binder and stared at the pages. She nodded. "Yes."

She had lied. The journal had been hidden at the bottom of our clothes closet. In a metal box with an unusually complicated lock. I kept the key taped underneath the kitchen sink where there was never a reason to clean. Shara had not found the journal.

I sat, gradually hating Martin Lormer. His struggle to create Shara as a devious, backbiting and malicious bitch was beginning to impress itself on the minds of the jurors. But it would not alter the verdict. It would only make me appear less sadistic, not quite as mad. Merely a man who did not know how to cope with a troublesome woman. My epitaph would be, "He was pussy-whipped!"

I sat and concentrated on returning to Barthelamo's life again. I wanted to become again that crook-backed Renaissance Physician-Surgeon illegally dissecting a corpse in the back room of a filthy tavern—unaware that soon he would be summoned by Cesare Borgia. But only flickers reached me. They were forced memories.

I strained to fix myself into Barthelamo. I sat with my right shoulder hunched, imitating the grotesque mutation on his body. I sucked in my cheeks to narrow my face. I touched my nose, pressing and squeezing to remodel it into a sardonic thinness.

But there was no Barthelamo in me now, and I knew why. I would have to complete the life cycle of Bianco before I could return again to Barthelamo so that former lifetime could begin in me and then I could also become Bianco again, from his origins, when he first saw Onadyh being brought into his village as a captive woman. Damn, damn. I was disgusted with the control other powers had over my mind. I combed my fingers through my hair. It felt scruffy and unkempt. Time bulges with mysteries while we live in the skinny reality of Now.

I pressed my hands onto the table edge and pushed myself to standing. All voices stopped, all motion stiffened. I wanted to moan with sorrow. This was the time of my death and I was scheming to avoid it.

I reached up my arms and stretched. The bailiffs near the door hunkered forward expectantly. I wanted the aches and agony of Bianco out of my sensations. Martin Lormer strode to me, asking in snickered whispers, "Have you changed your mind, or do you intend to sing something from 'La Traviata?' "

I continued stretching, opening and closing my fingers. I looked up to the ceiling, thanking God there was still some God in me. The newspaper people stared at me, all wanting to urge me to speak. Martin Lormer smirked. "Would you like me to bring your ex-priest robes and let you conduct a service? Why don't you sit down." There were thick lines under his eyes that I had not seen before. By the tilt of his mouth and mocking tones he was telling me that he was reaching the conclusion of the trial and any outburst I performed would not contribute to his case. I rubbed the knuckles of my hands into my eyes and yawned, then sat down.

The judge struck her gavel, telling Martin Lormer, "The defense will please instruct the defendant to stop distressing this court with his unusual behavior." Martin Lormer muttered, "Yes, your honor." He remained at our table, studying some notes and idly stroking the globular object covered with gray quilting.

I was martyring myself for a cause no one today would understand. But later in time, I would become the enduring symbol testifying that the doctrine of reincarnation was a delusion that destroyed sanity. I was not like unto Jesus. Had He been crucified for His own crimes, who would have known of Him? Had He been resurrected from the dead merely to demonstrate some gimmicky miracle, He would have been remembered only as the patsy of a demented magician. He had died to redeem the lives of all men, and was raised to offer them salvation—and I'll die to deny the joys of reincarnation and, in time, the world would resurrect me.

Go, go, man—wheee—and hallelujah—glow-ree bee tuh Gawd!

I was feeling giddy with justifications. This trial, this publicity, this promotion was worth it.

Martin Lormer sensed my change of mood. He turned over his notebook and leaned to me, whispering, "You know, Stephen, it really isn't easier to walk a tightrope one foot from the ground, than it is to walk a tight rope a hundred feet from the ground above a pit of starving alligators." He tapped the back of my hand. "It's the height you might fall from and the beasts below that hunger for you that makes it harder."

I did not frown at him to show I did not understand. He left the table and stood near the judge's bench. "I now call Dr. Jonathan Houseman." The middle-aged man who had once been deputy coroner left the witness area and walked to the stand. I closed my eyes and listened to the tone of his voice, knowing that Martin Lormer would compel him to reveal something important about Shara.

"Dr. Houseman, would you tell the court what transpired on the day you were retained to be present during the autopsy of Shara Medford?"

Martin Lormer's tone of voice was pleasant. I could sense a mutual respect between them. I felt envious. I had never been respected by other men, as a man. I had drifted from childhood to priesthood and then to a university instructor. What was the virile, strong male world like?

"I was called in immediately after the death of Shara Medford. I was told that from various data, and a journal, there were peculiarities about the woman and the event that were enigmatic—puzzling. I had been retained by Mr. Lormer's firm on seven other occasions. All of them proved most interesting."

"While the autopsy was being conducted, did you discover anything distressing or unconventional?"

"Only when Dr. Welch discovered that the victim had no fingerprints, or hand prints. That was most unusual in someone so young."

"Were you ever able to come to a determination about that unusual discovery?"

"No. We discussed it at length but could come to no conclusive determination based on what we know. It was a medical first, for both of us."

"In the length of time that has passed have you been able to come to a determination?"

"No. I have sent my findings to other pathologists and several dermatologists and have not yet received data to direct my interests. While it is a rarity it is no more unusual than children born with their hearts exposed, with eleven toes on one foot while the other is a stub—or other biological mutations. Many of which occur because of a chromosomic combination going out of whack. Some can definitely be traced to the influence of drugs—prescribed or otherwise."

"Are you then suggesting that Shara Medford might have been a user of, let us say, exotic drugs?"

I shifted to the side and concentrated on not listening. The pathologist said, "No. There was no evidence that she was a drug user."

I was disgusted, almost nauseated from imagining how they had autopsied Shara. Burrowing into her body with scalpels to snip out her slippery liver. Whittling off scraps of tissue and dropping them into plastic bags.

The courtroom felt sweaty. Tension gave the air an acrid aura. My bones felt like narrow rods encased in hardening cement. Even the roots of my hair ached. I wanted a thick blanket to suddenly descend from the ceiling to fall over me so I could be concealed from the people staring at me.

Therein was a comparison between Bianco and myself that proved us different. He wanted the people of Onadyh's village to stare at him. He could not be worshipped if he were not seen.

His skin was now clear of flaws and wounds. Onadyh's people would now give him god-ness.

Outside the abode he could hear their ceremony.

They struck heavy sticks onto long hollow logs. The sound was a charge of great beasts. The women of the Elders stood at the temple steps and tapped stones together and pulled taut strings they had cured from animals. His throne was finished. Though the light was fading, its goldness glowed. It was positioned inside the abode they had made of slender trees. The abode had been placed beside the great white stone they worshipped until Onadyh had led him to her people. After he had beaten her before them—to make them know his god-ness was greater—they would bring her smaller throne and fix it behind his.

He could not look through the apertures for too long. The Burning Eye in his mind had not left him. It had become a voice with a speaking that told him to curse his father in the Above. He wanted to stand at the wall and strike his head upon the stone to loosen the inflaming, to silence the speaking. He sat on the blankets and did castings while he listened to the noise of their ceremony.

At the top of the temple steps, above the people who were crowded about the Elders, Onadyh walked around the walls of his god-ness abode. She held a golden staff forked at the end. She touched each pole. She was brought a long, tubular tray with white powder. She stepped into the abode and sprinkled the large throne. Three warriors pushed heavy stone steps to the wall. She walked up the steps and touched each pole that was bound together to make a roof. She sprayed the powder through the openings. Young males formed a line at the temple steps, holding unlighted torches.

The Burning Eye in his mind suddenly inflamed. He stood and writhed and grasped his head. He pressed his body against the wall, then quickly jumped away. He did not want to cause a marking on his skin. The voice within the inflaming demanded that he hear the words. If he let them give him the god-ness then the Elders could remove it. His god-ness had never left him. When he had killed the son of the Great Burning Eye, he became the son, alive, and with powers.

He squeezed his head and moaned. He pulled his hair and wanted to beat his eyes. Faces appeared at the apertures and gaped at him. He must do a spell. He fell to the blanket and rolled and shuddered across the stories woven into the cloth. The thunking of wood upon wood became faster. The air flared with light as torches were held near the abode. He heard the breathing of the people.

He made himself stand and walk to the entrance. The two

warriors stepped before him. He told them to move apart and let him pass or he would cause them to die. Their blunt faces frowned at him. They did not understand his sounds. He raised his arms and chanted. His voice spilled and flowed into a wailing shrill. The noises of the ceremony stopped. The inflaming in his mind crackled, he could feel smoke from the burning in him. He incanted sounds and words given to him. Slowly, the warriors swayed and one slumped to the ground. Women began to cry. They pushed their children behind them. He flared the Burning Eye higher until he wanted to scream with agony. Then the other warrior fell. Crowds of villagers watching cowered back. He strode from the entrance of the abode.

Onadyh left the temple steps and walked to him. She carried the golden staff upright. He felt his god-ness. He stood and waited. She was the same as when he first saw her being dragged into his village. Below the leather cloth around his waist he felt bulged for her. This god-ness would not be the same as with his people. Her carrying was now his. The Great Burning Eye would change the child's flesh.

Onadyh lowered the staff and bowed before him. He held his arms toward her. She wore a slender metal circle encased with the green stones. He suddenly struck her face. She stumbled back. The people gasped. Four warriors rushed to her. She waved them away. She smiled at him. He walked to the Temple and stood before the Elders.

Torches were lighted and the Elder began cutting off his hair. The white clumps were dropped into the bowl. The people formed a long line and each one took some hairs and placed them into a small pouch dangling from their necks. Onadyh, standing behind the Elder, made her eyes steady at his eyes. Her face was swollen where he had struck her. She held his crown. It was a gold circle with glittering white stones.

He laughed. His voice was a crumbling of bark. The air was cool on his shorn head. They would all carry his god-ness with them. When the whiteness upon his head grew long again they would give the cuttings to the children. His god-ness would protect them. He looked to the dark Above and did not see his father watching him. His father was hiding. In the glow of his mind there was the Burning Eye of his enemy. There was laughter in his mind as there was laughter coming from his mouth.

Bianco did not wait to be given his god-ness. He had used the power offered him by his former enemy, the Great Burning Eye, and had boldly, aggressively, asserted his god-ness.

The ceremonies continued. He remained at the Temple steps, reveling in the honor of this worship. The darkened air was cool on his flesh and skimmed along his shorn head. Elders brought him adornments. His torso was draped with slender gold chains holding small white oval stones. He stretched his arms outward and slowly turned so the people could see his splendor. The Elders touched their metal-tipped sticks onto the circular gold platters and walked up the long stretch of stone steps. When they reached the top they stood beside the man-sized white oval stone. Bianco held out his hands to Onadyh, beckoning her to stand near his god-ness. Four warriors carrying sturdy poles placed them at the base of the great oval stone. As Onadyh moved upward, eight warriors holding white-haired, aged people in their brawny arms, formed her train. They placed the bony, toothless men and women into his throne-abode. He was to do spells and bring them to health and youngness again.

He raised his arms and shook his fists at the darkened Above. The Cold Eye of his father now looked at him. He shifted his feet and began singing as he danced before the people and he knew they would soon understand the sounds. He told them that he would be the god with love and bring them curings and cause their fields to spread with plenty. They would be protected from the raiding people of other villages. He swayed and skipped to Onadyh and clapped his hands. She raised the crown and slowly placed it upon his head. The flaming in his mind became many bursts of pain. He swung from her, knowing what he must do. He curved his arms as though scooping the air and again shook his fists at the Above.

The people below the steps separated into columns. The warriors with the thick poles jammed them at the base of the great oval stone. It tipped forward, then rocked back. They strained until their strength bulged against the gold collars on their arms. The huge stone tipped forward and fell over. It crashed downward, shattering the steps as it tumbled and joggled. His laughter swirled above the noise. While the great stone was still falling he walked to the abode sheltering his throne.

I wanted my memory to stop at his expectation.

In the time left to me, I knew I would never achieve the sweep of his festivity, his joy, as he sat upon his throne. But I felt suddenly heady, almost swooned with a strange scent.

I looked about me to see if anyone else was being affected by the peculiar, tantalizing aroma. The jury was quiet and attentive, listening to the testimony of the pathologist. Only the District Attorney fidgeted, anxious to begin a series of loud objections.

"Tell me, Dr. Houseman, what was your reaction to the three strange scars on Shara Medford's back, at the base of her spine?"

"There was nothing *strange* about the scars. They were merely three small scars which might have been acquired through a burn, or possibly a coarse puncture when the victim was a child."

"You know, of course, that the exact same scars, located exactly in the same place, also existed on two other women."

The District Attorney patted his hand on the table. "Objection, your honor." He stood up and sighed. "Unless the defense can prove the scars in question have some bearing on the death of Shara Medford, this line of questioning is irrelevant."

The judge spoke to Martin Lormer. "Objection sustained."

"Dr. Houseman, you and your former assistant, Dr. Virgil Welch had a serious disagreement over some strange matter discovered in the uterus of Shara Medford."

"The word *strange* is not particularly suitable. I would prefer to use *foreign* instead."

"Would you tell the court about this *foreign* matter?"

"In acts of violence, it is common practice to examine for the presence of male sperm, to determine the possibility of rape. Dr. Welch discovered what appeared to be a fibroid—an ordinary uterine tumor. I believed it might be malignant."

"On what premise, Dr. Houseman, did you decide that the foreign matter in the deceased's uterus warranted further investigation?"

"Curiosity, mainly, and some intuition. It had no relationship to any substances that were recognizable in my references. I had the time, the equipment, and the interest to indulge my curiosity. I gained permission, through a court order, to conduct a further analysis of the foreign matter."

"What did your investigation reveal?"

"It was a shriveled sac containing a greatly macerated embryo. In other words, the deceased, at one time, had been pregnant and had experienced a miscarriage."

The jury looked at me as though they were one face. I sat and wanted to moan with despair—God, how awful—if I had only realized. We could have had a child. A son. Why didn't she tell me, damn it, why didn't she tell me?

The District Attorney was grinning. Martin Lormer had just lost his trial. A man could kill a woman for a thousand perverse reasons and be acquitted of the murder—but if she's pregnant at the time, he's a degenerate beast. The judge did not look at me. She did not want the courtroom of people to observe her prejudice. Shara, Shara, why didn't you tell me? I would not have killed you. I would have risked your destroying me, to have a son. His birth would have changed our lives.

But whose child was he? We hadn't made love in over five months. Martin Lormer rubbed his temples as though confused.

"Did you report your findings to Dr. Welch?"

"I certainly did."

"But there is no mention of Shara Medford having had a miscarriage in Dr. Welch's report. Can you offer an explanation for that?"

"At that time, he believed that the only things he was responsible for reporting were scientifically verifiable facts in regard to the homicide. His report was to indicate the cause of death, which was strangulation—and not to speculate about other factors not contributory to that death."

"Why didn't Dr. Welch, or yourself, immediately identify the foreign matter in Shara Medford's uterus as a fetus?"

"After fetal death, if the embryo is not spontaneously expelled, but is retained for months, or years, it takes on the characteristic of old tissue and blood, and dense calcification. I can state,

with certainty, that it was not the result of the relationship between the defendant and the deceased."

The District Attorney jumped up, shouting, "I object—I object!"

I could tell the judge was now deeply interested. She wanted
to know—and she had the legal power to find out. Martin Lormer
walked to the bench. "I will guarantee your honor that the court's
time will not be wasted." He placed his hands in his back pockets
and stood with his side to the pathologist, facing the jury.

"When you claim that you can, with certainty, state that the
fetus found in the uterus of Shara Medford was not the result of
her relationship with Stephen Jerod, how can you verify that?"

"After the fetus attains considerable proportions, and is not
aborted, it becomes depressed because the amniotic fluid is absorbed. It becomes desiccated and shapes into a *fetus compressus*. It
begins to degenerate. It becomes milky in appearance, and in time,
it dries to the point of becoming mummified. The fetus in Shara
Medford's uterus was quite old."

Martin Lormer came to our table and placed his hand on the
globular object. He drummed his fingers on the quilted covering
and turned to the witness.

"Were there any other peculiarities about the fetus?"

"Yes. It did not belong in her uterus. There was no way her
body could have produced so old a fetus—and I knew of no scientific method that could determine how that fetus was present in
her uterus."

The District Attorney stood up to object but remained silent,
not able to form a sensible objection. People began murmuring.

Martin Lormer lifted the globular object from the table and
brought it to the witness and drew off the covering. It was a
bleached walnut floating in clear liquid. "Is this the fetus you
extracted from the uterus of Shara Medford?"

The pathologist studied the fetus and nodded. "It is. "

The District Attorney walked to the container and leaned
over to study it. Martin Lormer said, "I offer this into evidence
as . . ." But the District Attorney cited his objections, and I did
not listen. My stomach was pounding with nausea, my head felt
expanded with a heat of pain as bright as the Burning Eye fixed

into Bianco's brain. I hunched over and clamped my hands over my ears.

Shara, talk to me. Explain our life. I'll hear you. I have gifts and powers now. Had something gone wrong in your reincarnations?

I opened my fingers and heard the judge say, "Let it be marked into evidence as exhibit M." I slit my eyes and peeked at the fetus swaying in the liquid as Martin Lormer placed it amongst the other evidence. He pointed at the pathologist.

"When you realized the fetus's great age, what did you do?"

"When I determined it to be petrified, I began testing for its true age. I used the Carbon 14 test to ascertain its age as closely as possible. Upon learning the results I was astounded. To be certain I was not mistaken in my findings, I brought the fetus to the University Hospital, to the Chief of Pathology, and asked him to analyze it. He came to the same conclusion that I did."

"Was he able to explain how the fetus became lodged in Shara Medford's uterus?"

"No, he could not."

"Did he confirm, exactly, your findings as to the age of the fetus?"

"Yes, he did. There was no discrepancy in our findings."

"What is the age of the fetus found in Shara Medford's uterus?"

"It is approximately two thousand five hundred years old."

I wanted to laugh then. Shara had not lied to me and I had not loved the wrong woman. The courtroom appeared paralyzed—a motion picture suddenly stopped on a courtroom-scene frame. I heard voices whispering, asking, "Did he say twenty-five hundred years?" and "It couldn't be that much, do you think so?" and "I heard two thousand five hundred—what did you hear?" Martin Lormer stood next to the exhibit and stroked the top of the glass. The fetus floated to the side. He shook it again. The District Attorney scratched his head and chuckled to his assistant. "When I read his report I thought he meant two, point five years, and didn't bother to correct it." The assistant frowned. "That Lormer's no schmuck. Watch him." A newspaper man raised his arm, asking, "Your honor, did he say two thousand five hundred years?"

and she scowled at him. "You are out of order." She looked to the court reporter and asked him to read the witness's last statement.

"It is approximately two thousand five hundred years old."

She spoke to the pathologist. "Are you sure you quoted the right figure?" He was not troubled. "That is the correct figure." The silence continued until Martin Lormer said, "I have no further questions of this witness." The District Attorney shouted, "Well, I most certainly have some questions to ask him."

The pathologist had found the child that had been miscarried by Onadyh. The dead fetus had not been dropped in the desert. She had retained it. And when she passed away, when she dropped her body, when her essence had shifted into the cosmic orbit, the dead fetus had remained within the ebb and flow of Time, hovering about from generation to generation, like a weightless prune suspended by supernatural forces—until Shara was born. When Shara herself was a fetus in her mother's womb, the fetus was then implanted into her uterus. There was no other explanation.

"Tell me, Dr. Houseman, do you believe—truthfully—that the fetus is two thousand five hundred years old?"

"What I believe is of little consequence. The fact is, through examination, analysis, and corroboration, the fetus has proved to be two thousand five hundred years old."

"And you have no way of explaining how it got into the deceased's uterus?"

"None."

"Then how do you explain its age?"

"The only explanation I can come up with—and this is only speculation, nothing more—is that the fetus contained a rare disorder known as Cockayne's Syndrome. It is believed to be caused by some metabolic or endocrine imbalance."

"What is Cockayne's Syndrome?"

"It is an acceleration of the growing, or aging process. Every year the child grows it ages about twenty years—so by the time it is five years old, the child actually takes on the appearance of being a hundred years old—experiencing the same symptoms of advanced aging. Deafness, arthritis, cataracts, high blood pressure, mottled skin, senility, and so on."

The District Attorney waved disgustedly. "I have no more

questions to ask this man," and someone laughed. Martin Lormer said, "I have no more questions. Thank you, Dr. Houseman."

The pathologist shrugged and left the stand. Martin Lormer motioned to the judge. "Your honor, before I call my final witness, may I have a moment to confer with my client?"

She tapped her gavel. "If the prosecution has no objections."

The District Attorney looked at the jury as he answered, "If he needs time to dream up something as wild as what we just heard, we have no objections."

Martin Lormer ignored him and sat beside me and spoke in whispers. "I have only one more witness to call, Stephen, and then your ordeal is over. I want to ask you this one important question. You don't have to speak to answer. Just nod, or shake your head. Were you ever involved in any black magic, any occult rituals, at any time in your relationship with Shara?"

I would not nod or shake my head. I let him see my eyes. If God was truly directing this man's conduct then he would know. He studied my eyes, but I did not see his. I was remembering the afternoon I sat in our kitchen dealing out Shara's deck of tarot cards, then reading the astrological horoscopes she had collected— trying to determine the day, the very hour, when she would attempt to destroy me. While I used her demonic paraphernalia I felt crawly and stupid. But the premonition I had that the day and hour of my destruction was near was just as crawly but not stupid.

Martin Lormer sighed and reached out to grip my wrist. His voice was gentle, almost loving. "If you're found guilty, your torment will take a long time before it is ended. If you are acquitted it won't be longer than three days before you will end it yourself. I am truly sorry for you, Stephen. Win or lose, you lose."

He stood up and spoke to the judge. "I am now ready to continue."

She pushed her glasses closer to her eyes and looked at the paper before her. "Will you be presenting any other exhibits?"

"None, your honor."

"Well, then, I notice in my notes that six of your exhibits, D, F, G, L, N, and P, have not been moved into evidence. I believe this would be an appropriate time to deal with such matters. Do you wish to move them into evidence at this time?"

"Yes, I do, your honor."

"Does the prosecution have any objections to the introduction of these exhibits into evidence?"

"Yes, your honor, I have."

He placed his fingertip onto a list. Martin Lormer looked down at the list before him. The District Attorney tapped a notation.

"Yes, your honor. Exhibit F, the photographs taken at the archaeological digs of the ancient city credited to the defendant's information. I reiterate my original objections that this is mere coincidence rather than affirmative proof of his . . ."

Drone, drone, drone, will they never stop bickering, badgering, and chattering? I was feeling the need to speak, to explain every exhibit that would be brought into evidence against me, and for me. All of it was fact and only some of it was true. Those pictures are authentic. They show the village of Onadyh's people. There are the steps Bianco walked up, the pedestal upon which the massive oval stone once stood. Those are jade necklaces and golden amulets that were like the adornments Onadyh once wore—and that crown—the one with the oval alabaster stones set into the sturdy golden frame, that was Bianco's crown. You have the photographs but you can't see the pagan pageantry as I have seen it. There was splendor, the rituals were lavish. All the people were there to witness Bianco's god-ness and his enthronement.

The people were divided into orderly columns. Torch bearers strode in long lines upon the plateau expanse of the Temple. Golden bells were attached to their anklets and they made music as they walked. Bianco stood near his god-ness abode. He was taller than the many warriors positioned about him. An absolutely white statue, his hair scruff cut to the skin, the crown slightly atilt on his head as he shouted in sounds they did not understand.

At the base of the elongated rise of steps the people held up the pouches containing his hair. He waved his arms and blessed them, wailing and howling his voice in a spell that would bring curings to their diseases. He was delirious in the swells of his power. Women without coverings on their breasts moved about him carrying aromatic smoke pots, shrouding him in the perfumes of holiness. Artisans with gnarled hands and broken fingernails adorned his chest and thighs with long slender gold chains holding the white stones. Crone-like women, toothless and crooked in body, entered his throne-abode and removed the wearings of the aged people lying on the floor. An elder knelt before him and carefully drew off the covering about Bianco's waist and he stood naked before the people. Onadyh, now arrayed in a golden garment with symbols designed into the cloth, stood by the abode and called his name. She held her hand to him.

Bianco, Bianco, I remember now.

I had to hold the sides of the chair to keep from standing in the courtroom. I wanted to rush to the judge's microphone and speak into it and tell the people the glory of the rites of god-ness. Then they would mock this puny ticktacktoe legal procedure, scoff at the petty lawyers bickering over exhibits and evidences. They would see Bianco's time and his fulfillment.

It was all returned to me now.

He stepped into the royal abode. The old people crawled to the sides. He turned from the people and knelt before his throne. He spoke in a loud singing prayer to the Great Burning Eye, accepting his new father, and his greater god-ness. Onadyh raised her arms to the warriors holding the fourth barred wall. They carried the heavy structure and fitted it into place. Some of the aged began to cry. He stood up and laughed to the Above where his father was hiding.

Onadyh clapped her hands. The artisans rushed to the abode and quickly bound the final wall with thick chains that interlocked and clamped together. Suddenly, the people became shrilly jubilant and danced about. He smiled at their joy and held the bars and tried to push the wall away. It did not move.

Onadyh raised her arms again. The people quieted. She stood before the abode and spoke to him in the sounds she had learned from his people. "You are the Searching-god, Death. You cannot leave to take my people." She pointed to the huge white oval stone that had been toppled from its altar. He pressed himself hard against the bars. She told him the people had placed that stone before their temple and had prayed for the true Searching-god to visit their village. To see the honor they gave him. The fear. He began shaking the bars. The aged people huddled to each other and covered their eyes.

She jabbed the forked staff she held and laughed. "I have brought you here. I am given the god-ness." She swung the staff, striking the bars at his face. He jumped back, falling against the throne. She laughed her telling. Now he could not come from the dark Above and touch their children and warriors and women in birth. He can only have the old ones who cannot work, who cannot hunt, who cannot do battle.

"You will live here. For all the people to see." She pointed the staff at him. "You are Death." She turned to the people and lifted her arms and shouted, "We have captured Death!" Their voices roared happiness, they clasped each other and danced, they rushed to the rear of the Temple where there were three hills of sand and grabbed handfuls.

He clenched his hands on the bars and shook them, calling her to have him released. He was not Death. His god-ness was life. He hit the bars with his fists and screamed, "I am not Death!" The aged people cowered and moaned at his feet. He began pleading with Onadyh, promising that if he was released and given his god-ness he would give god-ness to her carrying. She hefted the staff as though a club and began beating the bars, screaming in his sounds that she had no carrying, that he had killed the carrying. His touch, his mating with her, his Death-ness, had killed the child of the son whose father's god-ness was the living. She stopped beating the bars and stood gasping to breathe. "I speak no more to you." She turned to the people waiting below the altar. She waved her arms and clawed her fingers and prayed to the Above that was beginning to turn light.

The people suddenly rushed up the steps and began flinging their sand at his face and body. He folded himself into a crouch and covered his face. The coarse sand stung and he felt his skin begin to ooze films of blood. When everyone had flung their shaming at him they stood at the base of the Temple and silently waited. He slowly raised himself and he was smeared with blood. He saw the lightness in the Above and he became afraid.

The people began swaying and humming in a chanting drone. He leaned against the bars and softly pleaded to Onadyh to release him. The Great Burning Eye was beginning to see him. She stood before the people, her golden robe glistening with reflections. He could feel the heat crust the blood dried on his white flesh. He shook the bars, trying to topple the abode down the steps to smash it so he could free himself. He slipped in the sand at his feet and fell against an aged woman. He became enraged and tore the chain adornments from his chest and flailed the old people until they bled and some lay still in death.

The Great Burning Eye was now above them. He begged her to bring him water. The Burning Eye in his mind began to swell. He had to gasp to breathe. The humming chant of the people became shrill to him and his hands and eyes became embers. He lay on the floor, trying to cover himself with the sand. He crawled to the aged people and began hitting them, then choking them until they were motionless. He pushed their bodies into a mound of limp flesh and tried to creep beneath them to hide from the Great Burning Eye. The bodies slipped from him and he began burning. He grasped the bars and used them to pull himself to a standing position. He called to Onadyh. She turned to the strange steadiness of his voice.

He knew the Great Burning Eye would soon turn him into a flame. He brought his hands together and began a spell. "I curse you," he told her. "When I return to kill you," he moaned, "you will die." His spell was giving him strength. Behind the Great Burning Eye his father was watching. "You will know me," he hissed. He tensed his body to feel rage, to enfury the power of the spell, to cast it into the Great Burning Eye to be remembered. He opened his mouth and wailed to his father and stood while the burning in him slowly spread and broiled while he repeated the spell.

Bianco, Bianco, Bianco—I wept in the guts of my life. She left you to die peeled of all protection. How could you do that, Shara? He loved you. Your loathing was small compared to the worship in his love.

He remained in the cage, slowly basted by the sun. He knew she was watching him die. The sun squeezed down on his bared head. There was no sound in his screams but his voice was fire. He moaned his spell again and again, until there was no sound in his spell. He breathed the spell into the flame of the Burning Eye in his mind. He died like an ashy log with his spell, as smoke, streaming into the Above.

Chapter 15

There is no grief after centuries have passed. There is only regret and anger.

I wished that Shara was alive again so I could beat her. To avenge Bianco. She had destroyed me for the esteem of god-ness, though she had none. I had possessed these powers—the divinations, the curings, the spells, the curses—I possessed even the capacity for recalling my lifetimes. Onadyh had no powers, Letitia was devoid of the prophetic, Shara contained no knowledge of the concealed.

I saw her image in my mind and raged at her, "You covetous, greedy bitch!" and hated her for deceiving a gentle and loving Bianco. I gripped the table for restraint until my hands became numb. I must be calm—serenity is my only salvation during this trial. Shara could not destroy me again. Shara was dead beyond resurrection. It was done between us. Erased from the surface of Time. What I was doing now was my last payment for the cost of Time.

Martin Lormer said, "I would like to recall Althea Jackson to the witness stand."

I blinked, feeling surprise. I allowed myself to watch her from the rim of my peripheral vision. She moved like a cobra, wearing a lavender pants suit. The trial had not wearied her. The males watched her—violating her in a variety of sexual fantasies. Were the women in the courtroom also using her? She sat on the hardwood chair, almost demure, while the judge reminded her that she was still under oath. She crossed one leg over the other, waiting for the questions she would quickly turn into responses designed for my destruction.

Martin Lormer seemed troubled. His wide brow was split with deep creases. He held the long white medical record and studied it. I sensed his reluctance to question her. She was clever. He was in a predicament of risk, and worried. She stared at him, her broad lower lip slightly pouted.

"Ms. Jackson, I would like to return to the night of your automobile accident. You were driving, weren't you?"

"I was. Shara was seated beside me. He—the defendant, Stephen Jerod—was in the back. He was harassing me."

"Harassing you—in what way?"

I knew she would now begin a sequence of facts cunningly ordered to prove I was vicious. But she was being truthful. I had been using her to leak out my anger and fear. I knew, that night, when Shara would try to destroy me and I did not know how to stop her. When we died in this century—of old age and creeping infirmities—I wanted us to remain dead.

That afternoon had begun in an ugly disposition. I had returned from my classes and lay on our bed to rest. I was agitated. I wanted to determine what method Shara would use to bring our lifetime together to its conclusion. Would she thrust a knife through my heart as Letitia did to Barthelamo? Would she set me on fire to burn as Bianco had? I left the bed to begin searching her dresser for her tarot cards. I would deal out my fortune and perhaps learn how she would kill me.

It was then I discovered that most of her clothes were missing.

Shara was intending to leave me. The black bitch had spellbound her, as Lucrezia Borgia once had done to Letitia. In the car, I had told Shara that she was involving herself in a disgusting, perverse relationship—then cursed Althea as a degenerate bitch who lived off the lifeblood of young victims, and I branded her a vampire. Shara said, "Stephen, you're being ridiculous." She did not turn when she spoke to me. I gripped the back of the cushioned seat and snarled, "Are you denying that you have gone to bed with this bitch?" She still would not turn to face me.

Althea had laughed. "If she ever did go to bed with me, you would never see her again."

I knew then that Shara was going to use Althea to destroy me. She had removed her important clothes from the closet. The drawers in her bureau were empty of scarves and lingerie. She would leave me. In this lifetime, my destruction would not be physical. I was to be driven insane with loss and jealousy—to become a catatonic lump huddled in the messy corner of a state institution, until I wasted with the decay of death. Of course. How ingenious.

The car gyrated over a rough stretch of freeway. Althea lit a cigarette and blew the smoke back at me. I did not want to go on this farcical dinner of reconciliation. A huge truck with high headlights began tailgating us. Althea cursed the driver as a "honcho flake" but would not veer into a slower lane. I blurted to Shara, "Where are your clothes?" wanting to trap her. "What sort of a question is that, Stephen? They're at the cleaners."

Althea laughed again. "I wish one person would send his priestly mind to the cleaners." I dug my fingers into the seat cushion.

"I want you to shut up, Althea. I'm trying my best to forgive you."

"Forgive me! Listen, you honky-turd, don't lay that saint trip on me. Stick your forgiveness into your uptight priestly ass."

"Althea, I warn you. Stay out of our lives. You're a sick lesbian bitch who is punishing all men because you're incompetent with them. You're a diesel dike who can't . . ."

"Incompetent with men! I blew the brains out of your skull the night we partied. You couldn't get it stiff if we wrapped it in splints. And what about now, *Father* Jerod? A premature baby has a more functional dick than the one you . . ."

In rage, I struck my clenched hand against her neck, cursing, "Filthy bitch!" She moaned and slumped against the door, her hands dropping from the steering wheel. The car careened across the white dividing lines. Shara did not move. "The wheel," I shouted. "Take the wheel, Shara!" as I lurched over, reaching for the steering wheel. Just as Althea recovered enough to grasp the rim we were all blinded by the brutal smash into the concrete pillar.

"When the defendant, Stephen Jerod, struck you, what did Shara do?"

"I have no idea. I blacked out."

"But the result of the defendant's violence against you was your near-fatal smashup, is that correct?"

"Yes."

"What was your attitude toward the deceased, Shara Medford, after learning that she had refused to volunteer a blood transfusion?"

The District Attorney cleared his throat. "Objection, your honor. Defense is leading and trying to influence the witness's response." The judge nodded. "Objection sustained."

Martin Lormer turned his back to Althea and spoke toward the news media people. "Did you know that you had such an incredibly rare blood type as Bombay blood?"

"I did. Ever since I was a child I have avoided any physical activity that might cause me an injury where a transfusion would be necessary. I've always worn an identification tag indicating my blood type. During the smashup the tag was probably torn from around my neck."

"Then Shara knew your blood type."

"Yes. I told her about it."

"Did you know that her blood type was also this rare Bombay blood?"

"Yes. It was a binding element between us. We believed we were slated—predestined to love each other."

"Did you know that her Bombay blood had an unknown factor in it?"

"I did not know that her blood had an unknown factor in it."

"Do you believe her refusal to volunteer a blood transfusion when you needed it was due to her knowledge of this unknown factor?"

"Absolutely. Her love for me was so strong that she did not care if she appeared cruel or disloyal to other people. She did not want to risk what little life there was left in me."

"Yet she did, eventually, offer you her blood."

"It was an understandable, and forgivable, risk. She didn't know if her Bombay blood would save me or kill me. She opted for the risk. I'm forever grateful to her."

"I can appreciate your sentiments, Ms. Jackson. Yet, in that unfortunate accident you experienced a severed brachial artery in your left arm. Is that correct?"

"Yes. Among other injuries. All caused by the irrationality and hysteria of Stephen Jerod."

"Ms. Jackson, I have no interest in causing you embarrassment but, for the sake of confirmation, would you open your blouse and reveal the area where your brachial artery was severed?"

The District Attorney stood up, noisily scraping his chair on the floor. "This is ridiculous, and extreme. Objection, your honor."

The judge stared hard at Martin Lormer. Her mouth was grim with annoyance. "Counselor, I have been enormously liberal, but this line of questioning has gotten out of hand." Martin Lormer stepped away from the witness stand.

"Your honor, I am building a foundation for a series of circumstances, and *facts*, even more incredible than the circumstances and facts already revealed during this trial. I request your continued patience in our behalf—in the behalf of truth. Otherwise some exceptional—no—extraordinary truths will be lost."

"Either justify this line of questioning, or the prosecution's objection will be sustained."

"This is a trial in which the element of the miraculous must be considered. A miracle not only defies the laws of nature, it *denies* the laws of nature. This must be taken into account. All I require is two more questions of this witness."

"I will allow for those questions, Mr. Lormer. But I warn you—if they do not prove to be of enormous contribution, you will not be pleased with the ruling that will follow. However, the witness will not be required to expose any part of her person."

There was no one in the courtroom who was not frowning with curiosity as they stared at Althea. She sat, untroubled, with a gentle smile. An antique carving of enigmatic beauty. I sensed Althea's glory. The courtroom was gripped in her life by wonderment. Within her depths she mocked them. I am savage—I am life. There was a power in her beauty that touched me with the same want I had for Shara. I did not want to love this woman.

Martin Lormer waited. I pitied him. He could not whittle her into nervousness to make her seem the hostile fool. He was straining to avoid her eyes as he gradually edged to the side, facing the jury as he asked his question.

"Since the court is so adamantly opposed to your showing where your brachial artery was severed, would you kindly point to the area of your forehead where you were given fifteen stitches."

Althea tilted her mouth contemptuously as she reached up and touched her forehead above her left eye. Martin Lormer slowly turned to her. He placed his right foot on the step and leaned his face close to her forehead. She did not shift back. They could taste each other's breath. He said, loudly, "You are the most superb healer I have ever seen. It is a miracle." He moved back and shook his head as though confused.

"I cannot believe a woman of such impeccable character would perjure herself."

I felt people begin to stir. I heard whispers. The District Attorney stood up again and bawled his objections. "Your honor, I protest this callous and calculated demeaning of this witness's dignity and veracity and . . ."

Martin Lormer stopped him by pointing at Althea and shouting, "You show me where the hell her scar is, from those fifteen stitches, and I'll apologize immediately!" He strode to the District Attorney's table and struck his fist onto the wood, yelling, "Where are the scars? Fifteen stitches must leave a terrible scar—where, in God's good name, is her scar?"

People stood up in their seats and stretched their bodies for a clearer view of Althea. The judge pounded her gavel and spoke sharply to Martin Lormer. "Counselor, you are out of order. The court will not tolerate such behavior." But her voice dimmed as she was drawn to staring at Althea, who kept touching her forehead as if trying to find the scar herself. The District Attorney began wagging his head, whining, "Your honor, this is highly irregular and I . . ." but stopped when he could not articulate his objection. Martin Lormer waved his hand, challenging the District Attorney.

"If the prosecution does not believe my claim, perhaps he would like to inspect the witness's forehead for evidence of scar tissue or cosmetic surgery."

Althea crouched back. Her cheeks twitched. She kept looking
to the jury, then to the judge. Althea's voice trembled and she said,
"I don't understand," and Martin Lormer quickly replied in a
strong, shoving sound.

"You have no scars because the blood of Shara Medford is
running through your veins—the blood of a woman who was never
sick, never menstruated, never experienced any fear of injury because her blood was strange, magic. I could slash your body with a
butcher knife and when you recovered your body would bear no
scars. There is no other blood in the world like the blood of Shara
Medford."

He quickly turned to the judge and raised his arms as though
pleading to the heavens to hear him. "Your honor, the defense
rests!"

I stood up, my hands flattened on the table. The courtroom
became silent. I would tell them that to save my life Martin Lormer was turning Shara into an outer-space creature. There were
other reasons why Althea did not scar. There had to be. He was
distracting them from my act of homicide by declaring that Shara
was a freak with witch blood.

I swayed on my feet. People poked each other and asked what
I was going to say. Althea slumped in the witness chair as though
drifting into a coma. "Don't believe him, Althea," I prepared myself to say. I breathed deeply to feel the substance of my voice.
Don't destroy your love for Shara by believing she was unhuman.
But there was no voice in my throat. I had forgotten how to
speak.

Martin Lormer walked to me as the judge instructed him,
"Counselor, you will advise your client to please remain seated so
the prosecution can question this witness."

Martin Lormer smiled at me and touched my shoulder. "Here
we go, Stephen, here we go." His voice was soothing. "It will all be
over soon."

The District Attorney went to Althea and quickly asked her,
"Have you ever been seriously injured before?"

She answered from a dazed depth. "No, never."

He leaned to her, his voice persistent. "Has your flesh ever
been so deeply cut that it destroyed irreplaceable tissue?"

She shook her head, beginning to recover her presence—able to understand what his questions were leading her to believe.

"Then you have no way of knowing how your flesh responds to a serious cut, have you?"

She blinked and made herself smile. "No, no way."

He turned to the jury and shrugged. "Then you don't know if it is natural for you to heal without leaving scar tissue."

She sat straighter, her shoulders stiffening. "This is the first time I have ever been cut deeply. It must be that my own body heals in that way. Not Shara's blood."

The District Attorney nodded and grinned. "Of course. There is no other explanation. No more questions, Ms. Jackson."

I did not watch her leave the witness stand. I felt sluggish, exhausted. Not because of what I had heard, but from all the death that was in me. The judge summoned both lawyers to the bench. Before he left the table, Martin Lormer touched my hand, reassuring me. "We're at the closing arguments now. The D.A. will crucify you a little, then I'll wipe away some of the blood, then he'll come back to *really* crucify you. It will all be over soon."

He was a good man, I thought. Kindly, sympathetic. He moved closer to me, whispering, "While you're in the holding cell, I'll have them bring you the finest meal you've ever eaten—undrugged." He went to the judge and I thought about food. I would request a hamburger. A fat, back-yard sized hamburger. The judge told the District Attorney, "The prosecution may now proceed with his closing argument."

He wiped his palms on a folded white handkerchief. I suddenly remembered his name. Charles R. Solenzi. He walked in casual steps to the jury section. His black hair was smoothly combed forward to conceal his baldness. He stood, trying to straighten his rounded shoulders.

"Ladies and gentlemen of the jury," he began. He held black-rimmed glasses in his hand. "This has not been a trial as much as it has been a theater of strange events and shrewdly devised riddles concocted by the defense." He tapped the eyeglass frames on his fleshy chin and sighed.

"First let me apologize, on behalf of myself and my staff, for subjecting you to the humiliating hoax perpetrated by the defense. I doubt if anyone here has ever heard such outrageous fabrications. A sadistic and masochistic man has killed a lovely and trusting woman, and what defense does his attorney use for trying to get him off? Self-defense by reason of reincarnation. I would say that is a remarkable hoax to try and put over on an intelligent and objective panel of his peers. But this attorney, this *superstar* of our legal system, goes even further. He comes up with coincidences like two other women looking like the deceased, with a fetus in her womb that not only doesn't belong there, but which is two thousand and five hundred years old. The discovery of hidden Italian treasures, Cesare Borgia, Pope Alexander, Lucrezia Borgia, pre-Mayan rituals and albino witch doctors—it taxes the imagination to keep up with all the flimflam and razzle-dazzle the defense has used to try and get this vicious murderer set free."

He walked to our table and pointed at Martin Lormer. "This man is trying to pass off the most fantastic lie in the annals of legal history." Martin Lormer rubbed his nostrils and smiled as though patronizing an addled child. The District Attorney clapped his hands and laughed. "But we must esteem our superstar. He is no penny-ante phony. He has imagination, daring, and an extraordinary capacity for risking another man's life." He suddenly strode to the jury box and struck his fist onto the rail, startling the jurors. "But he will not get away with it!" He wagged his fist at them.

"No, no, no. We are not fools. In a cold and calculated state of mind, Stephen Jerod premeditatedly murdered Shara Medford. His record for cruelty, brutality, and deviance is as long as his record for self-mutilation, self-abuse, and self-destruction. He strangled a lovely woman to death. It was a planned murder, right down to the very costumes they wore that night. He humiliated her, debased her, violated her—but that was not enough. He killed her because she wouldn't obey him, because she finally understood that he was an incurable sadomasochist and that she must leave him. Friends warned her, friends told her that she would die if she remained with him. Her loyalty was stronger than her common sense. Until she realized that even she could not help him. Then he strangled her to death, maliciously and with premeditation. And he must pay for his crime."

He swung around and pointed at me, his voice mocking. "There he is, today's reincarnated man." He snickered. "No matter how clever his attorney is, his attorney is not as brilliant as Stephen Jerod.

"The defense has labored to establish the credibility of Stephen Jerod's reincarnation. When he was Bianco, he was killed by Onadyh. When he was Barthelamo, he was killed by Letitia. Now, as Stephen Jerod, he kills Shara before she can kill him. And the alleged justification of his killing her because of reincarnation becomes absolutely invalid because *Shara Medford was not reincarnated.* Proving that Stephen Jerod was reincarnated is not enough. *The defense must prove that Shara Medford was also reincarnated.* And because the defense has not proved it, Stephen Jerod's alleged reincarnation is only a clever trick, an interesting gimmick."

He clapped his palm to his forehead and moaned as though in deep despair. He went to the evidence table and gestured his arm in a sweeping motion and laughed in contempt.

"All of this is garbage. Photographs of ancient sites, a mummified fetus, nude pictures of women who resemble each other. Garbage! Stephen Jerod killed maliciously. He murdered, with premeditation. And unless you bring in the verdict of guilty, for the crime of first-degree murder, you not only release a monster into society—you open the door for other monsters who will justify their crimes by the deceptive excuse of self-defense by reason of reincarnation. Shara Medford died because she loved the wrong man. Stephen Jerod killed because he is a killer."

I did not trouble myself to question what he said. He was unerringly correct. I was like satan. I believed myself to be wiser than God. I had taken upon myself the labor of altering my own destiny. I should have waited on God to do it, for it is written, *"And let us not be weary in well doing, for in due season we shall reap, if we faint not."*

Martin Lormer left the table and slowly walked to the jury. People shifted forward. The judge nervously licked her lips. He stood before the jury, his head slightly bowed as though in prayer. He was a solemn, heavily contemplative figure. I was certain the entire courtroom knew he was acting.

"Ladies and gentlemen of the jury, Stephen Jerod is not on

trial for his life. He is on trial for having *returned* to this lifetime. That is ironic. Here is another irony. I have been struggling to save the life of a man who is deliberately trying to die. He wants the state to kill him. Why? Because it is unforgivable for a priest, or an ex-priest, to commit suicide. Suicide is a guaranteed one-way ticket to hell. If the state kills him, his soul is saved. Why does Stephen Jerod want to die? Because his intention was to shatter the cycles of reincarnation he has been living through so he could be with the only woman he ever loved. Until old age and natural death did them part. His intention was to save his soul, and Shara Medford's soul."

Martin Lormer stepped further away from the jury and faced them.

"I'm not going to plead for Stephen Jerod's life. I am going to solve a complex riddle. The solution to that riddle will prove that Stephen Jerod is innocent of murder and justified in believing he had cause to defend his life. I have already proved, unquestionably—by history and fact—that Stephen Jerod is a reincarnated man. His reincarnation is not a fantasy, not a clever deception. And if the facts prove that he is reincarnated, then he cannot be faulted, condemned because he believes he is reincarnated. His *state of mind*, ladies and gentlemen, his state of mind at the time of the homicide—that is what he must be judged on. His state of mind."

He walked to our table and put his hand on my shoulder. I did not shrug it away. The odds he was trying to overcome were awesome. He was doing his best. I was not relenting in my desire to thwart him. I wanted him to know I did not hate him.

"I am going to take apart the riddle, piece by piece, as I know it, and reveal its astounding meaning. It will shock you. All I ask is that you consider the defense's evidence and, no matter how wild, unnatural, or fantastic it is, think on how it also proves the troubled, the confused, the frightened state of mind of Stephen Jerod. Let me show you what I mean."

He picked the stack of stiff, colored photographs from the evidence table and began passing them to the jury. "These are the photographs taken at the archaeological digs that Stephen Jerod was responsible for locating." He pointed to the weapons and decorative blankets, the abodes and temple, the amulets and pottery.

"These photographs deny the prosecution's argument that Stephen Jerod is fabricating about his reincarnation. He once died there, many centuries ago."

He held up one photograph and tapped its surface. "This is the cage—the throne-abode—that Stephen Jerod writes about in his journal." He brought it to a woman juror and placed it near her face.

"Study the many skulls and bones scattered on the floor. Can you see poor Bianco in that golden cage, being burned to death by the sun? Rotting away while the village looked on, and Onadyh laughed."

He swung around and pointed to me. "Shara Medford murdered that man when he was known as Bianco." He shook his hand at me and shouted.

"Stephen Jerod is the only man alive today who can review the skull and bones of his own remains!"

People stared at me. I did not look at the photographs. I did not want to see what I had once been. It was disgusting—frightening. Martin Lormer returned the photographs to the evidence table.

"In the first part of his closing argument the prosecution asked one outstanding, one shocking question. How can a man who is reincarnated kill a woman for having destroyed him in two previous lifetimes, *when it has not been proven that Shara Medford was ever reincarnated?* The prosecution asks a most puzzling question. I have not attempted to prove that Shara Medford was reincarnated. It is actually critical to our defense that I prove Shara Medford *was not reincarnated.* And Shara Medford was not a reincarnated woman. And here is one part of the complex riddle I must unravel. Though Shara Medford was not reincarnated, Stephen Jerod still defended himself against the right woman."

I would not listen to the damned misguided fool. Before she died Shara knew she was reincarnated. I had let her read my journal.

When the premonition that she would destroy me was returned to my awareness, I also received the method for altering our destinies. The supernatural can direct us only when we do not exercise our free wills. Shara could not exercise her free will because she was ignorant of her reincarnations. When she read my journal she would be shocked into that recognition *and remembrance.* Her role in our reincarnations was to destroy me. Together, with the concentration of our wills, we would dominate that ancient supernatural edict.

I rented our Renaissance costumes and gave her the replica of Letitia's dress. "Shara," I told her. "It's time for you to read my journal." She was pleased that I was no longer secretive. I cupped my hand on her cheek and smiled. "I have a special dress for you to wear. Indulge me, just this time, by putting it on for tonight. After you read my journal, you'll know why." She laughed gently. "I'll do it because I know it's important to you." Reading about Letitia and wearing what Letitia wore would shock open the mind in her soul and she would reach deeply into herself, even back to being Onadyh.

It would be a festive evening.

Later, when I returned from my university classes, I could hear her in the bathroom. I called, "Shara." She laughed. "Don't come in now. I'm still dressing." I went to the closet and touched the black velvet doublet I would wear. On the shelf was the plastic case holding the gold embroidered scabbard and ivory-handled stiletto. The metal safety box that contained my journal was open. Had she read all of it? Did she believe any of it? I went into the bedroom and undressed.

I put on a close-fitting *jack* with small *bombarde* sleeves. The hood draped behind me and formed a collar about my neck. The gold piping and fluting sewn into the velvet was royal in appearance. I stood still, trying to hear the sounds of Shara dressing. I began to feel like Barthelamo. My right shoulder ached as though I bore a deformity. When I took the plastic case from the shelf, the stiletto was not in the scabbard. I smiled. Shara had no cause for being afraid. On this night we would blend all the loves we had shared in other times, and we would be complete. I hummed softly, happily.

I set the pearl-strung cap on my head at a rakish angle, then a small leather coin pouch with golden tassels. I stepped into a pair of thin leather *poulaines* to keep the chill from my feet. I draped a black cape—a *soccus*, with slits at the sides—over my back. The collar was imitation ermine but Shara would not know that. I walked to the full-length mirror in the living room and gazed at myself. I wore the clothes with casual familiarity.

I went into the kitchen and took the bottle of white wine from the refrigerator. It would be the Sicilian wine Letitia favored. I brought two fragile goblets and placed them on our coffee table.

I was giggly with joy.

Tonight we would force the supernatural powers to obey our wills. Then I would be able to burn my journal. Perhaps I would also learn a way to destroy our memories.

The bathroom door opened and Shara said, "Barthelamo." I spun around and did not breathe. She was Letitia and I instantly adored her. She posed before me. Standing as though a pedestal sculpture. "Letitia," I whispered, "beloved Letitia." Her face was delicately hued with powder, her mouth faintly red as perfect petals. Her hair was held in a tiny seed-pearl *fillet*. Her neck was slender and enhanced with an amulet bearing the Borgia crest. I was momentarily confused. The amulet was not part of my rental. Slowly she turned, modeling herself.

Her gown was a glory of scarlet with billowing sleeves and fur-trimmed cuffs. The triangular cut of her bodice was laced tight with golden strings revealing the cleft between her breasts. Beneath the rich cloth I knew she was wearing the clinging undergarments Letitia once wore. It was then I noticed she was holding a black leather Bible. I chose to ignore it.

"Beloved," I said. "How *amabile* you look," and bowed low. She curtsied with graceful ease. "Master Vecchio, how delightful it is to see you again." I touched the perfume ball on my sleeve and brought it to my nostrils. The aroma was of ailing moths. "*Favorita*, you carry the Bible. Do you have cause for God?"

She sighed, "*Caro*, it soothes my troubled soul. I greatly fear Borgia suspects us." We saw each other's eyes. It was happening. I felt now, as I felt when I was Barthelamo, plotting to deceive Borgia. She was becoming Letitia.

I stepped to her and softly we kissed. Then harder. Our

mouths ached with our love. She drew back to gasp. I laughed. "Wine, *carina?* Some *fior d'arancio*, from the Prince's private cellar?" She patted her hands in delight. *"Splendido!"* I poured the wine and we drank.

Fondly, I crooned the lyric of a madrigal. "There is a lady, sweet and kind. T'was ne'er a maid so pleased my mind . . ." and hummed the remainder. She held her arms to me and I encircled her waist and gracefully we danced. We were airy with song, lilting with affections. She danced with her head back, her eyes to the ceiling. They were dulled with reverie. "I have known you so many times, my Barthelamo. Always you possessed a deformity," she said—her voice wistful, remote. I kept humming. She was being changed. Returned. I hummed in hushes.

"You were once a zealot in the service of Gaiseric the Vandal. Your deformity then was obesity. Your were repugnant with piety and cruel dispositions." Our dancing slowed. I asked, "How did you destroy me, then?" She sighed and spoke of my former death as chatting. "To appease Attila, I led you to be crucified like unto St. Peter, head down. I cannot now recall the reason." We stopped dancing and I stood in an unreality of Time. How could she know all this whilst my consciousness was void? "Letitia," I whispered, shaking her. "Is this truly so?" The distance, the dimness of her eyes, did not change.

"Yes, Barthelamo, it is so."

"Then I have had lifetimes other than the three I know?"

"Yes. Five times before, I found you. Your journal is incomplete. And always you failed my need of you. Another time I found you in . . ."

"Enough! I will hear no more."

She brought herself to me, her mouth brushed upon my mouth. "You are blessed with forgetfulness for all the other times. Yet what of me? Is your torment more than mine?" I clasped my mouth to hers. Her taste was a decaying pressure. I suddenly pitied her. I grieved at my savage stupidity. I had returned recognitions to her that she loathed containing. She was unlike me. When her remembrance of former lifetimes had filtered into her awareness, she strained to hide from them—to drape an amnesia over that dimension in her mind. Now I was imposing on her the madness she had once suffered. Yet I could not cease. Together, we could defeat its demonic will.

"Shara, beloved," I whimpered, ashamed of the ridiculous costuming. "It is in this lifetime we must cure our disease of reincarnations." She stepped back and swayed with inner melody and began unlacing her bodice. I flung aside my cape. I was stirred with expectation.

But I could not recall what happened as she was undressing before me—a voice was burrowing into my remembrances and I sharpened my vision to see Martin Lormer's hand pointing at me while he told the jury, "The prosecution claims that this man is lying, that his intention was to kill, with malice and premeditation. That he concocted this defense I am presenting." He lowered his hand and walked to our table. He touched my shoulder.

"The prosecution believes itself to be clever by posing questions impossible to answer. I can pose more seemingly unanswerable questions. Onadyh was dark-skinned and had black hair. Letitia was fair-skinned and was blonde. Shara Medford was Caucasian and had brown hair. How can one male, who is also three other males at different times, recognize the same woman who does not look the same in any of the lifetimes he recognizes her in? Is that question unanswerable? No!"

He held up his right hand. He began touching his fingertips as he talked—counting off the reasons.

"Is it possible that in the process of reincarnation the body is changed but the vision within the soul remains the same? Though Shara Medford did not even resemble the women he loved when he was two other men, in *this* lifetime he loved the same woman from the vision in his soul, and it did not matter that she was different, in appearance, from the other women."

He paused and frowned as though analyzing what he had just said. He shrugged and sighed. "I'm not quite sure I understand that myself." He touched another finger and pinched the tip. "Although I have not yet answered the riddle of Shara Medford—why was there a twenty-five-hundred-year-old fetus in her body, her Bombay blood, and so on—I assure you, ladies and gentlemen, there is an explanation for Shara Medford, and it will be offered before this trial is over."

He came to our table and studied some notes. The pulse in his neck throbbed. A faint film of sweat was on his hands. He turned his note pad face-down and turned to speak, leaning against our table.

"This is the first time in the history of American law that a defense of this nature has been brought forth. I could have defended Stephen Jerod in other ways less fantastic. But unless a defense is based on truth, it will fail. I have proved, without a shadow of a doubt, that Stephen Jerod is reincarnated, and not only that—but that he had just cause to rely on the information within those other lifetimes. To defend himself *against Shara Medford's premeditated plan to murder him.*"

He nodded. "That's right, ladies and gentlemen of the jury, Shara Medford clearly intended to kill the defendant, Stephen Jerod."

Speak louder, Martin. Your voice is too theatrically studied. Let it boom throughout the court. Let it reverberate in my mind and stimulate the voices of memory.

Shara had paused in her disrobing to ask for more wine. "More, Master Vecchio, more. To have found each other again deserves celebration." I did not know if she was pretending. She had succumbed so quickly. But I did not sense play-acting. I, myself, was Barthelamo. Whilst I poured the wine into our goblets she twirled about and laughed. "When you slew Count Finiguerra, I was not drugged. Nor he." I could not be Barthelamo now. I could only listen as Stephen. I could not let myself be constricted with jealousy.

"The Count suspected the wine contained a potion. His greeting to me in the bed chamber was 'adorabile damigella!'—adorable damsel. How quaint. *Dio mio!* His stomach was . . .'"

"Enough, Letitia. I will hear no more."

"Forgive me, Master Vecchio. I did not know you would be distressed. *Amante*—lover of the ages, why are we so burdensomely clothed?"

She drank the wine in gulps and flung the glass to the divan. I did not reveal the sorrow I felt, and asked, "When we loved, then, Letitia, was our love true?" Her mouth tensed, her voice became hoarse. "When I knew you would not serve my needs, I hastened your death. Oh the years, the lonely years I awaited your return." I gripped the goblet stem. Her laughter was crafty, cutting. "You believed me so innocent. I was the vessel of the priests—the sweetmeat of the holy sisters, before the Prince chose me for his pleasures."

God, stop me from hearing this, I prayed.

Her laughter became girlish.

"When you claimed that I was malformed, to deceive the Duke, I was delighted. How droll, was my thought. In his return to this new life my ancient lover—my continual lover—has become bewitchingly droll."

I would stop her ugly chatter. Her laughter became a thrashing snake in my soul. "You loved me too deeply, Barthelamo. Had you loved me less we would have ended in that time." I reached to her bared shoulders and shook her. "It is enough, Shara. That time is gone. We have our lives again. Let us use them with love."

She placed her small hands on my wrists and caressed me. "*Favorito*, it is not done yet. We needs must complete this night for it to be done. This time you love enough, though not too much."

She drew away from me and twirled about again, and laughed. Her gown billowed and curled about her. An enchanted *danzante* moving in the rhythms of a strange universe. I whispered to her, "I forgive you, Letitia—beloved, I forgive you." She did not hear. She danced and I beseeched God to fill my heart with forgiveness for her. I would not carry dead hatreds into this new life. The recognition is the resolution. The craven devil could take the bygone times. We would never again be reincarnations.

But I could not stop myself from wondering about another time.

I grasped her arm and held her still. "You led me to the village of your people, knowing they would believe me to be the Searching-god, Death. Knowing they would kill me. Why?" Her breath was gaspy, her eyes flashed with her excitement.

"I wanted the god-ness they would give me for imprisoning

Death, more than I wanted your love. Had I known, had I believed you possessed powers, I would have led you elsewhere. We began then. We end here."

I believed her. We would end here. Her recovery of the past now gave us mastery of our wills. "*Beniamino,*" she hushed to me. "Why are we so clothed?"

Slowly we undressed and our clothes formed shimmering pools at our feet. I was without fear now, cleansed with my forgiveness, aroused by my release from deaths. I was transposed from pain and I bulged with sensuality. "*Superbo!*" she cooed. I was a staff swelled with the blood of centuries of lust. She clapped her hands—"*Enorme!*"—at the rigidity of my power. I stepped to her. I would have her now. The savage consummation would shock her from the past. Then her laughter honeyed with sentiment, her eyes clouded.

"I stood at Lucrezia's bedside when the Lord took her. I loved Lucrezia, though she hated you."

I did not want to know of death. I would be normal. I would be now.

"It is a grim irony," she murmured, her tone fragile with sorrow. "Lucrezia died shortly after childbirth. A daughter Isabella Maria. A dear, dear child. Had you been the Physician Lucrezia would have lived."

The force of my manhood softened into indifference. I stared at her flesh to harden myself. The nipples were blooded holes. I closed my eyes, suddenly afraid. I felt now the same wonder when she had come into the dungeon cell, concealing a dagger. She sighed and said, "Lucrezia wore a hair shirt all her life for letting you destroy the soul she carried. I could not ever speak your name. She spit upon your memory."

I felt sweat seeping over me. She touched my hand. A coolness separated our skin. "Shortly after I rescued you, Borgia was slain." She clenched her hand and shook it at the ceiling. "How I loathed that vile *bastardo!*" And then I recalled that as Letitia she had told me she would live to see Borgia dead, and his sister.

The past was clinging to me, drawing me back. Softly, I asked her, "When you slew me, beloved, what did Borgia do? Did your saving me from his monstrous intentions cause your death?"

She patted her hands and tittered as a child. "No, oh no, he could not cause my death. He accused Cardinal Foiano of influencing you to become a *suicidia*. Oh, the scandal it caused." I brought her hand to my mouth and touched her fingertips, whispering, "Where was I buried, beloved? Was my grave marked?"

She drew her hand from my lips and covered her eyes. "You were not given a grave." She shuddered. "The Duke's rage was monumental. He would look the fool. The preparations, the festivity—the Pope was in the castle. Yet his cunning was *fantastico*. He viewed your death. He drew the blade from his royal person and fitted it into the wound I caused you. He commanded his *bravi* to bring you to his balcony where your death could be seen by the great assemblage. His oration was *magnifico*. 'You will not be deprived of your games. This spawn of the devil, this birth of darkness will not cheat us. He will be rent asunder that his soul may not have no other habitation but whence it arrived from—the bowels of hell!' The people cheered. He raised you above his head and flung you from the balcony. You struck the ground and your head was shattered. You were bound to Borgia's stallions and they were whipped and you were torn as though a doll. Your members were later gathered and you were dropped into a sack to be deposited on the dunghill north of the castle. Only I went. Only I grieved."

I stood in a trance of horror.

She stroked my chest and brought her cheek to my shoulder. "Barthelamo, Barthelamo," she moaned. "He is long dead. All that is left of him I have in a memento." She stepped from me. "I will bring it. I have kept it all these years."

She hurried from me. I stood and silently wept. I was utterly dead from the time of Borgia. I was no longer anyone but myself. Yet Shara was no longer Shara. She was Letitia now, searching in our bedroom for an ancient memento that did not exist in this time. I had destroyed her present. I must return her to this time or I would be alone. Unloved.

I stood naked in the living room, awaiting Shara's return. I was cold now, as I was cold that bleak night when I was in the dungeon, waiting for Letitia to rescue me. I was also hating her for having pierced me with a knife.

Yet in the dark recesses of my soul I knew all this was a lie.

I had never been Barthelamo or Bianco. I had never before died. I was fully myself now. It was the sickness of reincarnation that had changed me. All the years of my torment of living other lives had been imposed upon my consciousness by the devil. He had used my sins, my corruptions, to influence me. But tonight all this evil would be expended. I would reach out to God, bringing Shara with me—and we would become actual and forgiven.

I did not know Shara had returned until she was before me.

"Barthelamo," she whispered. I forced my sight from staring inward and looked to her and gasped at what she held. It was the brass canary cage I had once bought her. It was polished to appear golden. Inside was a black velvet pillow with a stiletto resting on its surface. The handle bore the Borgia crest. I wanted to snatch it from her hand and fling it out the window.

She smirked. "Here, beloved—symbols of your former deaths."

I struck the cage aside, knocking it to the floor. I clenched my hand at her face. "What have you arranged for me this time?"

She stooped down and took my cape from among the clothes and covered her back. There was no dream in her eyes. "Your journal is quite stupid, Stephen," she said. I felt taut at the flat cruelty in her tone. "You were the one who always loved. I allowed you to love me." She went to the bird cage and set it aright, placing the dagger on the pillow.

"Stephen, I'm going to tell you a strange tale of life. All humans live in two worlds simultaneously. The real world, the tangible world where we are now—and the supernatural realm in which we are constantly being reincarnated. The supernatural world is a mirror of this visible world. Only the time values are different. You might live a hundred lifetimes in the span of years it takes to live one lifetime here. Or only three, or three thousand. For most people the real and the supernatural worlds never touch. For some they touch briefly, then separate. That is the cause of déjà vu or partially recalled lifetimes. But your worlds collided and mixed, and portions remained together. We have no . . ."

"Shara, stop. We are not mystics, we are people. I've been damned for . . ."

"And I've been cursed. Something unbelievably horrible happened to me when I was very young. Only you can relieve that horror. But you have always failed me. Bianco and Barthelamo were weaklings. They loved to the intensity of worship. They let themselves be destroyed, not by a woman, but by an idol."

I was standing naked before her and I was becoming afraid. She was not any of the women I had once loved. Her eyes were brittle, her nakedness plastic. Someone inside her was using Shara's life to harm me. I almost laughed then. I would not let anyone else but Shara kill me. I placed my palms on my bare thighs to feel that I was real.

"I have never loved you, not even as Stephen Jerod. I have tried, believe me, to keep you from being weak. But there is something unwholesome about you in this life. I never understood what it was until I read your journal. You are insane, you see. Quite insane."

"Shara, please. Listen to me. The journal is a lie. I no longer believe it. What I wrote never happened. I know that now. My mind was being controlled. Pushed here and there and into that and into this. Tonight we can regain control over our lives. That's why I let you read my journal, to . . ."

"To awaken in me the memory of those lifetimes I have lived through. Your plan was stupid. I have always known about them. You have been afraid to find me because I would confirm your reincarnations. I have always been *searching for you* so you could set me free. But you won't, because you're insane."

"Stop calling me insane. It isn't true. The only reason I haven't gone insane is because of God's strength that is still in me."

"God! In every damned lifetime we have met, there has always been God hovering about like some smelly cloud. Do you think this was the first time you were committed to God? You haven't been given the recall of when you were a monastic—a devotee of that flagellant monk Anthony. I found you then—back in the fourth century—and you gave up chastity, poverty, fasting, because you loved me. But God would not allow you to . . ."

"You're lying, Shara. I will not let you burden me with another madness."

She pinched open the door of the canary cage and withdrew the dagger. I knew she was right. I had an insanity in me. The devil is an insane spirit constantly maddened from his rejection by God. He was harassing me to get back at God. I was standing naked before Shara while she fingered the dagger and within me I was beginning to see a scrawny man, covered with a ragged, dark wool cloth, sitting in a cave and warming his hands. Behind him was a straw pallet. Scratched onto the coarse cave wall was a crude cross. I had to shake my head to flick the image from my mind. The devil was still using me.

I watched Shara balance the knife on her palm. Her flesh was as white as the hilt. The blade flashed hot darts at me. She smiled. "This dagger is familiar, isn't it?" I would not agree that I had seen it before, in another lifetime. I was done with the insanity of reincarnations.

"When Borgia found it in the dungeon, he kicked it aside in his rage. I retrieved it and have kept it with me always."

"Shara, darling, put the knife down. Let us fall upon our knees before God and pray to Him for release from this supernatural insanity. Only God can help us. And He will. He has always loved us."

"I spit on the name of God. Do you know how many gods I have believed in? Hundreds. Long before Jesus and long after He was killed, I was searching for a god. No, Stephen, I will end your agony and later on, in another century, we'll meet again, and perhaps you will be different. Stronger. A man who loves his life more than his love for a woman. I'll find you again."

I wanted to begin dressing. I was ashamed of my nakedness—the deep scar I had stupidly cut into my manhood. This night had become a solemn disaster. I wanted to be done with it. I spoke in tones controlled by not breathing.

"Shara, you're talking foolishness. You have no desire to hurt me. This isn't Borgia's time where murder was as common as farmland. There are laws in this time. Serious laws."

"Laws? What have laws to do with me? There will be no fingerprints on the knife. Except your own, if you try to draw it from your heart. The law will consider it suicide. You have done enough insane things, on record, to justify that conclusion. Come, Stephen, it is time. Let me place this blade into your heart. You're weary of this incarnation. Let me end it."

Her absolute calm peeved me. She would push that dagger into me and I still did not know why. I edged back and she shifted to me. I suddenly pleaded, "You must help us, Shara. We must present ourselves to Jesus Christ, in truthful confession. He will intercede for us to the Father. Or we are doomed. Absolutely doomed."

She hissed, "What have I to do with Jesus Christ? I would confess to satan before I confessed to Him." She swiped the blade at my face, forcing me to jump back. She moved her mouth but her soul did not smile.

"You are a contemptible creature, Stephen. You and your Jesus Christ. You're a soggy, limp man with a spiritual deformity uglier than any physical affliction you could bear. You are crippled with love. I despise your love. Your love is ooze. Your love is putrid, it offends me. Your love is decay, it rots me. *Why can't you refresh me with hatred!*"

I raised my hand to smash her mouth and she laughed and lunged the dagger at my chest. I grasped her wrist and also her neck and held her, shaking her. "Stop it, Shara. This is wrong." She spit at me. She kept trying to slash me. I squeezed her wrist and her neck harder. She struggled her head. Tears blurred my sight. Love, love, I wept. Rescue me from hurting her. Dear God, help me. "Shara, please," I begged. "We have lived in hell long enough. We can leave it now."

Again she spit at me, her eyes bulged with hatred. Her hand became furious with strength, forcing the dagger up and close to me. Then I wanted to ease my hand on her throat, on her wrist, so she could plunge the knife into me. The hell I would go to might be better than the one I had already lived. Her hand weakened and I gripped her tighter. Her back arched and I tried to open my hand. The fingers were locked on her neck. The dagger dropped onto the cage and she fell back, pulling me with her. We stumbled to the floor. Her eyes gaped at me. I released her wrist to grasp my other hand and tear it from the crushing grip on her neck. I could not move it. Her mouth was twisted into a horrible smile and no breath came from her lips. "Shara," I shouted, shaking her, joggling her head. "Shara!" I screamed at her. "Shara! Shara! Shara!" I kept screaming until there was no voice in me, only aching air rasping in my throat—shaking her and mutely screaming as her head pounded on the floor, her face discoloring. I shook her, but the louder pounding was on the door while I cradled her neck in my locked hands and I crooned to her like an enchanted lover and told her we were finished, we were free—and my tears dripped onto her opened eyes and I believed I was washing our sins from our existence.

Chapter 16

I sat huddled over and did not care that the mass of people were staring at me. There was no sound in the courtroom, except for the murmur of the air conditioning, the steady hum of the wall clock. The hardwood table pressed against my forehead. I was drained of grief.

I heard the judge say, "Counselor, if the defendant is over-wrought, I will call for a fifteen-minute recess, until he can compose himself."

Martin Lormer answered, "The defendant is probably tired and hungry. I know he will be all right."

I was not hungry. The sides of my stomach were collapsed into a wrinkle.

The judge said, "Please continue, then." I flattened my hands on the table and forced myself to sit. I kept one eye open. I would see outside while I was looking inward.

Martin Lormer walked to the evidence table and carefully raised the laboratory container. He brought it to the jury and held it forward. The small, mummified clot swayed in the liquid. The jurors stared at it.

"Here is the oddest mystery of them all. One that violates all the laws of nature and biology as we know them. Yet if we deal with the supernatural laws within the jurisdictions of the supernatural realm, it is no mystery at all. You will recall, from Stephen Jerod's carefully notated journal, that the woman, Onadyh, was pregnant by the son of the Great Burning Eye. In the course of their flight, the woman, Onadyh, miscarried. *This*, ladies and gentlemen, is the fetus that Onadyh once carried, twenty-five hundred years ago."

With my opened eye I saw the District Attorney shift to his

assistant and grin. Several news media people shook their heads with disbelief.

Some jurors edged back from the exhibit he held, as though it might pop from the container and leap onto their eyes. Martin Lormer jiggled the container, making the fetus loop and roll. "How can I make such a statement?" he asked them. He patted the container. "I have already stated that I know, for a fact, that Shara Medford was never reincarnated. How do I know that? I know that by knowing that Onadyh never died. She has lived all this time. She, Shara Medford, once known as Onadyh, never died. *At the time she was killed, Shara Medford was two thousand five hundred years old!*"

The District Attorney applauded and laughed. "Your honor, a little madness is not too unpleasant. But isn't this a bit too much?"

She leaned to Martin Lormer, asking, "Do you realize what you have just claimed?"

Before he could reply, a newspaper reporter rushed up the aisle to leave the courtroom. An alert bailiff grabbed him around the waist. The judge pounded her gavel. "Bring that fool back to his seat, and keep him there." Martin Lormer held the container against his stomach. The fetus drifted down, then floated up.

Martin Lormer said, "I will repeat my statement. Shara Medford was approximately two thousand five hundred years old. She appeared in the world as Onadyh and lived all those centuries, probably with many other names, to be eventually known as Shara Medford. *She could not die until she was killed by Stephen Jerod, and she knew it.*"

The District Attorney became annoyed and stood up. "Your honor, I object."

She looked to Martin Lormer. Her voice was soft, almost pitying.

"Counselor, your claim is physiologically and humanely impossible. I offer you this opportunity to reconsider the claim and to withdraw it. The court is most appreciative of your zeal—however, it is also our responsibility to caution you."

Martin Lormer clutched the container closer to his chest. He slowly shook his head. A thin film of sweat was on his forehead.

"I cannot retract that claim, your honor. I believe it to be absolutely true. What is impossible in the world of the natural is not at all impossible in the realm of the supernatural. In the realm of natural laws and biological truths, the doctrine of reincarnation is impossible and actually stupid. But because the world, and the majority of people in this court, have accepted the credibility of reincarnation *long before this trial began*—then the possibility of everlasting life is also credible and must be open for acceptance. When witnesses are brought to the stand and placed under oath, they put their hand on the Bible. They clearly swear to not lie before God. They swear on the Bible, the work of God. Yet is there any book in existence that contains more supernatural events? Are we then to throw out the Bible, which is the Christian foundation of this nation, because what has happened in that record of former events appears impossible to us now? No, your honor, I will not retract my claim that Shara Medford was two thousand five hundred years old and, if allowed to, I will prove that claim!"

She touched the rim of her glasses. "Mr. Lormer, you are asking the court to believe that Shara Medford was alive for two thousand five hundred years. In all human reason and common sense, that is not reasonable."

"Your honor, if we destroyed our calendars and our clocks, would the seasons stop arriving? We can explain the cause of plagues and earthquakes—but can we stop them from happening? We are not in control of nature. We are controlled by nature. And there are mysteries of nature—natural and supernatural—that we cannot explain. No, your honor, I will not retract my claim. With unerring and tangible evidence, I will prove my claim."

The judge wrote some notes onto a pad. The people in the courtroom sat in patient, expectant silence. I felt myself tremble and there was no humor in me. I was cold now. Standing outside a cave on a tall hillside. I was rubbing my flesh to warm the surface. I wore a dark, ragged cowl and covering. Before me, several miles away, was a village with smoke drifting up stone stacks. I had been in those houses before. There were fires inside the flat-structured, dirt-floor homes. People in loose fitting wool garments were moving about the small rooms, some were sitting at bench tables, spooning hot broth from wooden bowls. I heard the sound of steps crackling on the dried leaves and twigs on the path. A woman was carefully moving up the rough hillside. I stepped backward into the hollow of a cave. I hurried past a straw pallet, kicking aside some bowls and the ashes of a former fire. I was frightened. She must not see me. Must not speak with me. I rushed further into the cave and crouched within a large, black cavity. I was bearded, my hands were thin bones. Tears, like coarse hair, scratched in my eyes. I knew she would come into the cave and find me. I knew that I would love her.

I shrugged and denied the vision of another lifetime Shara had assured me we had once lived. I would now allow it to begin in me. I shifted forward, concentrating on what Martin Lormer was doing at the evidence table. I watched him bring a group of photographs to the easels and place them onto the slanted frames.

"When Bianco, who was serving the village as a shaman, saw the warriors returning from a raiding party, among the captives he recognized a woman and felt an immediate, unexplainable love for her. He watched the warriors drag her and the others to the area of imprisonment. A warrior slashed his whip across her back. Bianco sees the wound that is inflicted on her. Three punctures in her skin, at the base of her spine. Over a thousand years later, as is noted in Stephen Jerod's journal—Barthelamo Vecchio, when examining Letitia, for the pleasures of Cesare Borgia, notices the same three scars."

He pointed to the photographs. The people in the jury box leaned forward.

"About five hundred years later, the great artist, Klaymore Montecello, draws meticulous portraits of his wife Emily. The same scars appear at the base of her spine. About fifty years later, Mr. Lazarus, a professional and expert photographer, does portraiture of his wife Belinda. Again, the same scars appear. As part of the autopsy procedure, Shara Medford is photographed in detail. Once more, the same scars are present, in exactly the same part of her body. Added to that, Emily Montecello, Belinda Lazarus, and Shara Medford look exactly alike. What can be considered incredible is the odds against five women, in different centuries and decades, over a period of two thousand five hundred years, having the same—the exact same scars in the exact same places on their bodies. What is not incredible is for *the same woman* to carry the same scars on her body for *as long as she lives.*"

He paused, letting them think about his statements. I knew that soon I would be reacting to what he was saying about Shara. I was being patient. Letting my anger slowly simmer in me. Only Shara's beauty was as old as Time. Her taste was a fresh, exotic cream. To touch her was caressing a newly budded flower. Soon, when my anger was fused, I would stand up and ask the judge if I could speak just one sentence—then I would denounce Martin Lormer as being a bona fide lunatic and a fraud.

"Onadyh miscarried and was rendered sterile. None of the other women she appeared as could have children. Not Emily Montecello, not Belinda Lazarus, not Shara Medford. If Shara Medford, born Onadyh twenty-five hundred years ago, was never sick and when she was injured, was never scarred because of the still unknown factor in her Bombay blood, how then could Onadyh, when she was whipped, bear those three scars? And when she had a miscarriage, why didn't she immediately heal and remain fertile? Well, ladies and gentlemen, the answer to that mystery is quite clear and logical. Her scars and her miscarriage and her sterility happened before Bianco cursed her—telling her, 'When I return to kill you—you will die!' And then . . ."

He was interrupted by Bishop Carmondy, who demanded, "This blasphemy must be stopped!" The people were startled as he waved his arm at Martin Lormer, shouting, "You, sir, are committing mortal sin by such profanity. You will be cast into everlasting hell for what you are saying!"

The District Attorney grinned and nudged his assistant, who chuckled. The judge raised her gavel, but stiffened her arm, realizing the Bishop's title and status. He pointed his finger at Martin Lormer. "You cannot trifle with the dear departed's soul. You are maligning God's handiwork. You will be condemned for your sacrilege!"

Martin Lormer pushed his hands into his pockets and stood slouched over as though in glum penitence. I enjoyed the Bishop's interruption. It had distracted the jury from the spellbinding fiction it had been listening to. The judge said, "Bishop Carmondy, while I appreciate your outrage, you must understand that this is a court of law. The church and state are separate entities. That is constitutional."

He brought his hand to his chest and fingered the sturdy silver cross. "If this is what is allowed to go on in our courts, then it is no wonder our nation is in a condition of collapse." He began moving toward the aisle, stepping on some people's toes. He unfastened the cross from its silver chain when he reached the doors. He held it to Martin Lormer as though trying to terrify a vampire. "You, sir, are an unscrupulous scoundrel. You are tampering with the laws of God and you will be damned for it!" I saw groups of people cross themselves and look to Martin Lormer to see if he had suddenly disappeared.

The Bishop spun around and scowled at the bailiff. "Get out of my way—you agent of the devil!" He raised his cross as if to club him. The bailiff quickly stepped aside. He shoved the doors open, sputtering, "Damn'd infidels!" Before the bailiff could close the doors a young woman with dark brown hair ducked under his arms and hurried into the courtroom. She moved to the last row of seats. She held a folded newspaper to her face as though intimidated by the fluorescent ceiling lights. Some people shifted closer together to create a sitting space. Outside there was shouting and complaining by the people who wanted to witness the conclusion of the trial. The judge looked to Martin Lormer and shrugged. "The court apologizes for the untimely interruption." He drew his hands from his pockets and flattened them on the beveled jury rail.

"Ladies and gentlemen, I ask you to believe that I have no intention of offending anyone's theological convictions. I am only trying to arrive at the truth that will save an innocent man's life. In Haiti there is voodoo. In America we have black witches and white witches, the satanists, the occultists—and daily they curse people and daily, people have unexplained accidents and deaths. In the Philippines there are spiritualist doctors who perform open-heart surgery without medical instruments. They run their hands along someone's chest and, as if by magic, it opens. They close the human chest the same way. No scars are left and these spiritualist doctors do not even wash their hands and there are no after-infections. That is not reasonable or believable, yet it happens. Therefore, why should we be astounded at the possibility of a woman being cursed into everlasting life?"

He wiped his palms on his jacket and raised his right arm and pointed at the jurors.

"Let me reconstruct the event that happened on the night of the homicide. Part of the mystery of Shara Medford can be learned by knowing what happened on that unfortunate night."

He brought his hands together and stretched his fingers. He paced four steps toward me, then turned back to the jury.

"Stephen Jerod believed that on that night he could not only interrupt the pattern of their reincarnations, but that he could stop them from ever happening again. He did not know that Shara Medford had never been reincarnated. Then Shara Medford brought out the bird cage and dagger that was found at the scene of the homicide. *To taunt him. Yes. To taunt, to enrage, to drive him insane with fear and fury.* The cage being the symbol of how she had killed Bianco. The dagger, the symbol of how she had murdered him once before. At that moment, ladies and gentlemen, Stephen Jerod was absolutely rational and eagerly anticipating living a normal life. And then she attacked him. Yes. He believed she wanted to kill him. But he was *wrong.* She did not want to kill him. She attacked him only because she knew that he was now strong enough in character and soul to value his own life over their love. Shara Medford planned her own death in the only way that she could die. *By forcing Stephen Jerod to kill her.*

"Shara Medford was desperate to die because she was bored with life. It had worn her sensations and her soul to a flat, uninteresting state. Just as it had worn down her fingerprints and handprints. Everyone she cared for had grown old before her eyes and died. The world changes but you remain the same. You drift from place to place, country to country—the eternal wanderer, a gypsy through Time. She became witness to the unalterable inhumanity and stupidity of mankind. You are unnatural and life is ugly. Because we are born to live in the world for a common span of time; if we live beyond that span which is common to our lives, then the monstrous character of the world makes us want to die. She

wanted the release of death. And she had told this, in effect, to
Stephen Jerod. But he did not understand. He loved her too
deeply."

He paused to walk to our table and drink some water. He
looked at me over the rim of the styrofoam cup. His eyes were
variegated green and steady.

He put the cup down and returned to the jury.

"What did Letitia tell Barthelamo Vecchio before she killed
him? *'The day will come when I will stand by Lucrezia's grave and
mourn her. The Prince, too, will be gone before I am taken from life.'*
One night Shara is roaring drunk and she curses God for *'implanting an irrevocable sexual drive in our souls no matter what age we
are.'* On another occasion she plants the idea that he should kill
her. *'If you have to think about killing me, then you should think
about it.'* When Shara Medford was using the name of Emily Montecello, she attends a séance and asks the psychic, *'What is the
secret of life and death?'* and the psychic's answer shocks and stuns
her. Why? Because he was a psychic and in touch with the supernatural world and he told her that *her* secret of death was in the
curse Bianco placed on her. *'When I return to kill you—you will
die!'* "

He clapped his hands and shouted, "But Shara Medford is
dead, isn't she? Yes. Shara is dead." He strode to the District
Attorney's table and pointed at the prosecutor's face.

"The prosecution will claim that I am contradicting myself. *If
Shara Medford could not die, then how can she now be dead?* The
answer is in the first part of the curse—'When I *return* to kill you.'
Shara Medford could only be killed by the man who cursed her and
that man died in a cage while she looked on. But Bianco did
return—*reincarnation* returned him. First as Barthelamo Vecchio,
then as Stephen Jerod. And Shara Medford's greatest agony was in
having to wait all those centuries for the essence, the supernatural
being of Bianco to return so she could finally find peace by having
him kill her."

His words were having an impact on the minds of the jury.
Yet I knew that not one man or woman believed him. They kept
looking from Martin Lormer to the three nude photographs posed

on the exhibit easels. There was no flaw, no wrinkle, no ancient aura about the women who resembled Shara.

"Shara Medford had to find him again. How many men did she live with and marry before she married Klaymore Montecello and Mr. Lazarus? We will never know. Both men ended up in mental institutions. Why? Because Shara Medford, in hopes that they were the reincarnations of Bianco, tried to drive them into killing her. They were not men who killed to save their own lives—they defended their lives by retreating into temporary insanity. When they returned from their mental institutions, she was gone. Gone, in search of another man who might be Bianco. And then, finally, she found Stephen Jerod. She found the only man alive in this time who could kill her."

He picked the nude photographs from the easel and quickly replaced them with similar sized photographs of Cesare Borgia's private treasure room and an aerial overview of the village in which Bianco died.

"How did Shara Medford know Stephen Jerod was the right man, the Bianco. Quite simply. *He advertised that he was.* When he sponsored the location of Cesare Borgia's storeroom of fabulous treasures, the find was communicated throughout the civilized world. It was brought to Shara Medford's attention. She quickly went after Stephen Jerod. Upon discovering that he was a priest, she was quite discouraged. Possibly uncertain. Then, when Stephen Jerod was responsible for locating the pre-Mayan village in which she was born—as Onadyh—then she knew. Bianco, who had been reincarnated to become Barthelamo Vecchio, was now reincarnated as Stephen Jerod. She had finally found the right man again, but he was a priest. His commitment to God would not allow him to become involved with a woman. But Shara was now over twenty-five hundred years old. That length of time was certainly sufficient enough to teach her about men. Century after century she had become involved with men in her search for the man who had once cursed her. Getting Stephen Jerod to give up the priesthood to begin living with her was not extraordinarily difficult. He was a man who knew little about women—she was a woman who knew everything about men."

I placed my hand over my eyes as if shielding them from glare. I was beginning to believe him and I hated him for his cruel stupidity. If I had cursed Shara into life everlasting—until I could return to kill her—then I had cursed myself into the inhuman, supernatural flow of reincarnations. Dear God, dear God, how could that be true? You had cursed me. It had to be you who cursed me.

"Little by little, Shara Medford began working on his sanity. Fueling his confusion about reincarnation. And he began cracking up. Having a mental and spiritual breakdown. Yes. He fought over her. Became paranoid with jealousy. Schizophrenic with doubt. Manic-depressive with helplessness. An exhibitionist, a flagellant, a near self-emasculator—because of Shara Medford. But still there was a core of strength within his psychology, within his character, and he was about to avoid insanity. But Shara Medford kept driving at him. Then, when he struck Althea Jackson, ignoring his own safety for the sake of releasing his violence, Shara knew it was time for her centuries-old plan to be placed into action. She set Stephen Jerod up—primed him—and now she was ready to detonate him into killing her."

He went to the evidence table and picked up the dagger and scabbard. He stroked the hilt. He drew out the blade and balanced it on his palm as Shara once had. His voice was gentle, almost respectful.

"I do not mean to make a monster of Shara Medford. She was living through the power of a terrible curse. Yet she was not totally vicious. Once, she almost sacrificed her own plan, her death, to save another woman from sharing her terrible way of life. When Althea Jackson needed a blood transfusion of Bombay blood, Shara Medford refused to give it. What did she tell Stephen Jerod? '*You don't know what you are asking me to do.*' She knew what her unknown factor was. But he threatened to leave her. So she relented. Because—and this is what she told him—'*You might fail me again, Stephen, and then I'll need a friend, won't I? I'll have a lifelong friend and I won't be lonely.*' She allowed her blood to be poured into Althea Jackson. And here is the vileness of Shara Medford's centuries-old character. Not only will Althea Jackson never be sick, never be scarred, never be fatally afflicted—*Althea Jackson will never die!"*

There was a scream, horrible and without end, until Althea Jackson clamped her hands over her own mouth and stood gape-eyed and shivering. The judge became confused. Althea Jackson opened her hands and screamed again, and clutched her throat and wailed, "She told me and I didn't understand. She said we could be together forever—friends and lovers for ever and ever!"

She grasped her hair and began pulling, twisting her hands and moaning, and suddenly shrieked, "That filthy white bitch!" and rushed from the aisle and ran to me and I huddled over while she struck my head and neck, screaming, "Why didn't you kill her sooner!" The frantic power of her fists were hammers striking my head and I wanted to faint, I wanted to die from her violence, but I would not let myself faint or die. She was pulled away from me by two bailiffs who dragged her out still screaming, "Why didn't you kill her sooner!"

Before the courtroom could recover, Martin Lormer suddenly raised both arms above his head and shouted, "I did not want this to be revealed." The people turned to him and he swayed and waved his arms, still shouting, "I want only to save an innocent man's life, not destroy a good woman's hope!" I saw tears brighten his eyes. He sobbed. My head felt bruised, my neck ached from Althea's pounding. Martin Lormer hurried to me and gripped his hands onto my shoulders and spoke without shame for his tears.

"We cannot decide whose life has meaning and whose life is trivial. Only God can judge. But what is to become of Althea Jackson? Althea Jackson, who now has Shara Medford's blood—the blood that protects its possessor from ever dying. It is the blood of ages. Supernatural—devilish. Our grandchildren and all the generations of children that come from them will one day know of Althea Jackson, who will be wandering throughout the world, desperately searching for someone to end the tedium of everlasting life *by killing her."*

He released my shoulders and strode to the jury section and smacked the rail. The sound was the snapping of an animal bone.

"Will Althea Jackson find someone to kill her as Shara Medford found Stephen Jerod and made him kill her? Will she devise a plan for attacking, for assaulting, for threatening the life of that man as Shara Medford did to Stephen Jerod? Forcing him to defend himself. That is why Stephen Jerod is absolutely innocent. The facts and history in his reincarnations proved to him—*in his state of mind*—that Shara Medford would one day try to kill him. He did not know of her plan, her desperate motives. He knew only that Shara Medford was coming at him with a knife, and so he defended himself. The motive of premeditated murder, in attempt, belongs to Shara Medford. All Stephen Jerod was doing was defending himself. There is no reason to acquit him even on reasonable doubt. There is only justified cause to find him innocent for reasons of self-defense."

He turned his back to the jury and muttered, "Thank you," and walked to our table. The silence in the courtroom was like a tight shroud allowing only the hush of breathing to leak through. I did not believe what Martin Lormer had claimed about Shara's blood. I pitied Althea Jackson for being persuaded that she now had everlasting life. In a little while, when the first wrinkle etched on her cheek, she would know the truth. But I felt tinged with nervous doubts. I recalled a statement of Galileo's: *"There is no greater hatred in the world than ignorance for knowledge."* I would not believe that Shara was two thousand five hundred years old. It was impossible. Dear God, it had to be impossible.

Gradually, people began to look toward the District Attorney—waiting for him to begin the conclusion of his closing argument.

He stood up and cupped his hands over his ears and wagged his head and moaned with theatrical loudness, *"Mamma mia!* Where has human reason fled to?" He kept shaking his head until he reached the jury. He clapped his hand on his forehead, wailing, "Is there no end to the human imagination!" He swung his arm toward me as though trying to fling his fist at my face. "That man is a murderer. If he is allowed to leave this courtroom a free man, then reincarnation, which is now an entertaining pastime, will be turned into a weapon of public destruction more lethal than the machine gun!"

I counted the heavy breathing of Martin Lormer sitting beside me. He smelled of fatigue. The District Attorney lowered his arm and spoke in tones of appeal.

"I am not the exciting performer our legal superstar, Martin Lormer is. I am a simple man. When a woman is mercilessly strangled to death in cold-blooded, premediated murder, I believe the murderer should be punished. *That is the law.* It has been in existence since the time that primitive people congregated into communities. It is a law that has protected them, as it protects us. People cannot go around planning the death of other people. It is unlawful. Stephen Jerod has committed murder."

He walked toward our table and poked a finger at Martin Lormer. "Magic blood, everlasting life, supernatural curses. Dear Lord, that takes guts and gall to use in the defense of a murderer. But when logic fails, when reason is insufficient, when truth is meaningless, it is always expedient and wise to use *the great lie.* Yes. I envy this man's daring, but I do not envy the cuts and scars on his immortal soul for abusing the tenets of his profession and the sacred laws of God—merely to win a trial."

The District Attorney suddenly whacked his palm onto the table, shaking the styrofoam cups. He shouted, "The defense will not get away with it." He jabbed his thumb at my face. "This man is a cunning and devilishy cold-blooded murderer and he must pay for his crime." He rushed back to the jury.

"Let us, for the moment, consider the supernatural—how dare the defense subject reasonable men and women to such superstitious drivel? It is a strategy designed to confuse. A woman has been murdered, and a man killed her. That is realistic fact. The supernatural should be kept where it belongs. In the peejinker and knickknack shops."

Some jurors grinned. I wanted to listen because he was interesting. But visions of a gaunt, fourth-century monk who had withdrawn from the world began to intrude on my awareness. I squinted into my mind and his image gradually assumed clarity. He was shuffling along the stone corridor of a monastery. His cloak was soil-brown and coarse. It scraped at his bare ankles. Waiting for him in an arched doorway was another monk. His superior. He was a short man, and stout. His cloak was smooth and dawn gray. A long strand of wooden beads ending at a cross was about his neck. His chubby face was grimaced into a scowl.

The image began to fade. It soon returned, but it was not the same. I was watching a silent film unreel in my mind. The stout monk was hitting the man Shara said I was in that fourth century. I could not hear their minds but I knew from the cowed way I stood, by the smears of tears staining my face, that I was being punished and threatened. The monk-superior stamped his sandaled foot onto the floor and again started smacking the side of my head. I huddled over and did not complain. I was being censured for having broken my vow of poverty, or chastity, or silence. Let me hear your minds, I silently pleaded to them. Let me hear your minds as I heard the minds of the other men I once contained.

I saw the gaunt and scraggly haired monk standing outside the monastery, his body pressed against an ivy matted wall. He was hitting his fists against the stones. Behind him, in the distance, was the figure of a young woman I could not see clearly.

It was not Shara, but it had to be her.

It is not true, I assured myself. I am highly suggestible. Mention that I had lived another lifetime, as Shara claimed I did, and I quickly become that lifetime. I am not a man, I am an imagination. Yet I am done with having lifetimes. I have overcome them. I have killed to overcome them.

Yet I was not pleasured by this knowledge. I felt now, as I felt when I was twelve years old. Frightened, and fascinated by my fear, and pleading to God to show me more.

The sight of the District Attorney waving his hand at me grabbed my attention. "I have branded that man as a sadomasochistic murderer. I am not a psychiatrist, but I know a sadomasochist when I meet one." He stepped to the evidence table and held up the knotted rope I had once given Shara. He dangled it before the lead juror's face. There were still some bloodstains in the fibers. The man edged back. "Any male who makes a woman beat him with this weapon of perversion is a masochist." He put the rope down and picked up a blue razor blade. "Any man who attempts to cut off his—to emasculate himself, is a masochist, getting worse." He brought Althea Jackson's medical report to the jury and waved it. "Any man who becomes violent against a woman while she is driving a car and endangers the lives of the passengers and himself has become an uncontrollable *sadist*." He flung the chart down and shook his fist at me.

"In law, the *scoff argument*, the mocking argument that one attorney imposes on the other, is not a valid or reasonable argument. Therefore, I will not scoff at what the defense attorney has said. I will flatly and forthrightly deny it. Not with a counter-argument. But with all the evidence and facts present in the testimony of witnesses. The truth will scoff the lie of the defense."

The District Attorney began a methodic, calm presentation of his evidence and supported it by reading portions of what the state's witnesses had said about me. Martin Lormer shifted closer to me. He whispered, "There are only two points we have to worry about. If he brings them up, we could lose." How marvelous, I quickly thought. I did not believe that he ever considered losing. He looked to me and spoke in hushed sounds. "I predict that in two months Althea Jackson will become a madwoman. From now on you have to be careful. She will try to kill you." I sighed and listened to the District Attorney's voice and tried to distinguish the words. I had the sudden feeling that God wanted to speak with me.

". . . and there is a point that a jealous man reaches where he cannot reasonably deal with his problems. Thus, he resorts to the elimination of those problems. Shara was going to leave him. She was afraid that he would kill her. And time and circumstance proved that she had cause for this fear. He did exactly that—kill her."

I watched the portraits of the three nude women being placed on the easels. The District Attorney touched them with a schoolroom pointer. The black tip thumped Shara's faces.

"The defense uses these pictures of three different women who resemble each other as his proof that they are the same woman. And what is the basis of his proof? They appear to have the exact same scars located in the exact same place. Upon this fractional, this enormously speculative theory, he tries to convince us that this now murdered and dead woman had everlasting life. I tell you it is only a remarkable coincidence. And hear this. *The frequency or the uniqueness of the coincidence does not change it from remaining only a coincidence.* Photographs and hand-drawn portraits are not people. The pose, the lighting, the shading and the equipment used to create these artificial images of a person, all influence the appearance of the subject. The coincidence is not in the three women looking alike, *but in the three photographs looking alike.*"

He faced the jurors, tapping the pointer on his thigh while he allowed the impact of his statement to affect their judgments.

"If any of you, for one moment, seriously consider the defense's plea, self-defense by reasons of reincarnation, let me explain what a shabby and fraudulent defense you are seriously considering. *We can all claim to be reincarnated.* The validity of reincarnation depends solely on how convincingly you can prove that you once existed in a previous lifetime—without ever having to bring forth physical evidence to substantiate your claim. The proof of reincarnation is not in declaring that you lived in a previous lifetime, but in how convincingly you get a group of egg-headed dabblers in the occult or psychic sciences to believe you once lived before. *The proof of your claim depends upon their ability to disprove your claim.* If their tests are inadequate and your preparation is thorough, they will happily give you the reincarnative credential. *They want you to be reincarnated.* Their employment, their funding, depends upon how many subjects they can find to justify their expenditures on a frivolous theory."

He took the photographs of Shara from the easels and returned them to the evidence table. He was happy now. My conviction of first-degree murder would be his political launching. He would write articles about the sanctity of the law, the need for dedication to justice. Then he would begin promoting himself in a campaign to become the mayor. Use me, use me, I thought.

"Since the defense has offered such fantastic coincidences as the substance of his case—let me throw in a few more. Stephen Jerod located the ancient village and the Borgia treasure trove through his interest in history and by a fluke of circumstances. Nothing more. Not because he lived there at one time, in other lifetimes. He found them through plain old luck. And the defense has used this lucky find to persuade us that it is all part of the motive for murder. No. Stephen Jerod is a murderer who . . ."

I could not listen because I was saddened with thoughts of Althea Jackson. I no longer hated her. What was she doing now, I wondered? Praying to God? No. She would be testing the blood in her veins to know if it was cursed blood—satanic blood. She would be in her bathroom, sitting on the bowl, preparing to slash her left wrist. Not to kill herself. Only to learn if she could bleed in a normal manner and if the flesh would heal without leaving a scar.

The District Attorney paused in his argument and began pacing before the jury—and then the monk returned to me again. He was in a field, using a thick-handled hoe to till the ground. His cloak was rolled up to his calves. There were sores and scratches on his legs. Then he was in another place. A tavern of sorts. Hunkered over a slat wood table, spooning a brownish gruel into his mouth. There was a woman standing behind him, patting his right shoulder and speaking to him. I could not see her face. She wore a full-length, dark green robe that concealed her figure. While I watched him eat I could hear the District Attorney's voice, and I could feel the touch of the woman's hand on my shoulder.

I was afraid.

A voice outside me was telling people that they ". . . must not be moved by the fascinating tales of a master spellbinder. You must let the *facts* lead you into your judgment. . . ." Inside my mind I was straining to turn the woman around so I could see her face.

Then the image flicked away and was replaced with the same man carrying a rough bundle of his possessions strapped across his back, walking along a cracked and neglected road that did not seem ancient. It might have been tar or macadam. The landscape about him was not clarified. It was either barren or being slowly renourished by the seasons. The grass was finger-long stubble. The erratically scattered trees were slender and without leaves. In the far distance there was the vague appearance of structures I could not define. They were either spires or skyscrapers. He was haggard in his coarse cloak bound against his waist by a bowed rope. There was a dark wooden cross tucked into the crude belt. He walked in a mood of despair. I did not know his mind or hear the language of his thoughts, yet I did not feel this monk to be of a fourth-century mind as was the monk Shara had described to me. Yet the man I observed within me seemed an authentic eremitical monk who had given himself to the service of God at the sacrifice of natural avarice, and lechery, and idolatry. While I did not feel this gaunt-looking monk to be me, he was not a repugnant, threatening stranger in my consciousness.

I don't understand. I just damn, damn don't understand. What Time is he in, and in what country is he living?

I sat at the courtroom table, aware of Martin Lormer beside me and the District Attorney's voice talking to the jury. I was conscious of the people who were intermittently watching me and then shifting their attention to the judge. I was remembering what Shara had told me on the night I had killed her. "You haven't been given the recall of when you were a monastic—a devotee of that flagellant monk, Anthony. I found you then—as far back as the fourth century—and you gave up chastity, poverty, fasting, because you loved me."

I had begun to believe her, but warily. The vision of this monk beginning to happen in me gave me the sensation that Shara was lying. He was beyond her Time—further into the time of centuries.

I could feel him, but I did not know him, as I knew the others—myself. Was I observing another lifetime I had once lived, or was I being given a projection of the lifetime being prepared for me?

Would Shara be there—or Althea Jackson?

God, help me. All I have left is you. Am I filling with a remembrance or am I grasping toward a prophecy?

The District Attorney stood before the jury, waving his hands as though erasing chalk scrawls from a blackboard.

"All right, ladies and gentlemen, let me be generous with the defense. Let us overlook the trumped-up fable the defense has offered and presume that Shara Medford chose Stephen Jerod to kill her. *Does that absolve the act from being a crime?*"

His voice became harsh with contempt.

"Isn't our superstar attorney familiar with the law of the land? There are no provisions for *aiding and abetting anyone in a desire for suicide.* There are laws which specifically prevent the aiding and abetting of another human in the act of suicide. Because when someone desires to commit suicide, they are not in their right state of mind. No matter what your state of mind may be, if you help someone to kill herself, you are a murderer."

He went to the evidence table and poked his finger onto the glass container. The ancient fetus joggled in the liquid. He raised it toward the ceiling and stared at the wrinkled clot. He shook his head. "Let us now deal with this matter of a woman who is doomed to everlasting life." He placed the container onto the table and walked to the jury.

"How dare the defense openly and without conscience tell us that there is a provision in the law which entitles us *to kill every twenty-five-hundred-year-old woman we meet!*"

He suddenly pivoted around and hurried to our table and shook his fist at Martin Lormer and shouted, "How corrupt, how evil!" He shook his fist at me. "What a wretched, dreadful person that man is." He lowered his arm and strode back to the jury.

He was interrupted by the sound of crying, and I was annoyed. We looked to the area where a woman was hunched over, holding a newspaper to her face. I remembered her hurrying into the courtroom when Bishop Carmondy left. A stout man beside her patted her shoulder, comforting her. The judge cleared her throat and called to the nearest bailiff, "Will you please see what's troubling her?" Martin Lormer muttered, "We just got a break. The D.A. was murdering us."

The young woman moved the newspaper from her face to dab a hankie at her eyes. A round-shouldered woman said, "Look, hey, look at her!" People shifted and stretched in their seats to stare at her. The bailiff reached her row and looked at her. He stepped back, startled. Martin Lormer gasped, "I don't believe it." I stared at the young woman and I was staring at Shara.

I stood up, wanting to scream to her, "Shara!" and charge ahead to embrace her, but my throat was still void of sound. I shoved the chair back to go to her but Martin Lormer swung his arm to my chest, forcing me still. "It's not Shara, you fool. It's another look-alike."

I didn't believe him. I kept trying to move to her but I was weak and exhausted and could not shove past his arm. I had not killed her. The trial was now canceled and we were alive. Shara rose from the seat and looked toward the judge. It was Shara. Her mouth, the arch of her brows, the way her fingers held the white hankie. Martin Lormer was right. She was everlasting. Shara. Shara. The judge began striking her gavel, silencing the chattering people. The District Attorney suddenly shouted, "It's a setup, a filthy, disgusting trick!"

Martin Lormer shoved me onto the chair and struck his hand onto the table, protesting, "I know nothing about this, your honor. On my sacred oath, I do not know that woman." The judge stood up and patted her black robe. Her glance flicked about the court-room. The District Attorney rushed to the jury and swung his arms at them, yelling belligerently, "Now you see the tricks and the gimmicks I have had to put up with during this entire trial!"

Again I reached to her. Martin Lormer jammed my hands down. "Stop it, you damn fool. You killed her and it's not possible for her to reincarnate so quickly." He turned to the young woman and called, "Who are you? Please identify yourself."

She shifted into the aisle. People inched away as though afraid she would fizzle before them. "My name is Christine Cheney. I'm from Montreal, in Canada." Her voice was Shara's. Her look, her presence, were Shara's.

And I felt overcome with sudden anger. Why aren't you dead? Cremated and powdered into a sealed jar. Please, Shara, be dead. Stop tormenting me. I have been made lunatic enough.

The judge asked her, "Why have you come here?"

She held out the newspaper. "I was going to San Francicso to visit my aunt. She's dying of cancer." She touched her cheek and sobbed. I wanted to taste her mouth, caress her. I would not kill her again.

She controlled her sobs. "But something made me leave the bus and come to Alameda. I don't know what it was." She opened the newspaper and pointed to the front-page photograph. "When some people stopped to talk to me and tell me I was supposed to be dead—I bought this newspaper. I had to come here."

Martin Lormer turned his back to me and asked her, "Was Shara Medford your sister?" The judge slammed the gavel onto the bench, demanding, "The defense will please shut up!" then softened her voice to ask the young woman, "Are you in any way related to Shara Medford?" She began to sob again. I knew what she would answer—that she was not related to Shara, that she had no memory past a few days, that she saw my picture in the newspaper and felt an unexplainable love for me.

And when she said that I would rush to her and we would escape from this awful place.

Everyone waited for her sobs to stop. Touch her, somebody. Comfort her. She is newly reborn.

Martin Lormer held his hand near me. He knew my intentions. Her breath heaved and she bit her lips. She pressed the hankie to her eyes. "No," she wept. "I'm an only child."

The District Attorney curved his hands around his mouth, shouting, "How old are you?" A scuffle suddenly broke out in the news media section. Two men were holding another reporter who was trying to break away and leave. A bailiff jogged to them and pulled them apart. They straightened their clothes and shrugged. I felt strangely sexual, excited.

The young woman said, "I'm twenty-one years old," then raised her hand like a shy schoolgirl. "Please, your honor, I didn't mean for this to happen. I have to go to my aunt's."

The judge smiled. "Yes, of course, you may be excused." She pointed to the bailiff. "Escort her from the courtroom and to her transportation." She hit the gavel on the block of wood, adding, "And do not allow—I repeat—do not allow anyone else in!"

Martin Lormer pressed his hands onto my shoulders, holding me down before I could rush to her. "Stay put, damnit! That wasn't Shara. Shara was killed in the only way she could stay dead." His fingers were rivets fastening me to the chair.

Before the courtroom doors were closed, the District Attorney swung around to the jury, wagging his hands at them, demanding their attention.

"You have just seen living proof of what I have been telling you. That woman—that Christine Cheney—is nothing more than a remarkable resemblance to Shara Medford. Perfect likenesses, commonly known as *Dopplegängers*, are merely likenesses, nothing more. And we all have such likenesses. Yes. Somewhere in the world there is one, or several, people who look like me, who look

like each of you. We have just not yet met our *Doppelgänger*.
Shara Medford is dead. Strangled. Deliberately murdered by
Stephen Jerod. With malice aforethought and long-standing premeditation, he murdered Shara Medford. There is no cursed Shara
Medford, no Shara Medford with everlasting life. There is no longer a Shara Medford. She is dead, killed by the hands of this vicious
and brilliant sadomasochist murderer, Stephen Jerod. He is
guilty, guilty, guilty of murder in the first degree and that must
be your judgment—no other judgment can satisfy justice or the
law."

His hand pressed onto his heart when he stopped speaking.
He walked to his table, face raised—the resolute hero who had just
bested the reputedly invincible dragon.

I was too overcome to even be unreasonable.

Now I knew the full cunning evil of the devil. He had
arranged for another woman to begin tormenting me. There remained only a few months to my life and he would not allow me to
live them peacefully. "She is a vicious lie!" I shouted within myself. She is not Shara. She is a demonic deception! But even as I
understood the truth, I would not believe it. God, could it be Shara
again?

My eyes were open and I could see clearly but I did not know
what people were doing. I heard voices but could not understand
what they were saying. I was drawn into the vision of seeing the
gaunt monk sitting silently in another monastery while another
gray-robed superior spoke to him—a man I may have been or still
might become. I knew the superior's words were not approving.
He was shaking his head and stabbing his thumb onto his desk top.
It was a cold and large office. Bare of furnishings. The walls were
dark and of smoothly fitted stone. My cowl was on my shoulders
and I saw my hair was black with faint strands of gray. I could not
hear what was said, but I sensed that I was being refused admission
into that order. I looked past their figures to the arched stained-
glassed windows. Sunlight shone on Jesus Christ being crucified.
The blood coming from His side was cracked. I stared through the
clear panes to see the outlying land. There was only sky. The
monk-superior began beating the gaunt monk's skull, but when I
looked at them, he was still sitting in his silent, obeisant posture,

and I knew it was me pounding on our courtroom table, enraged and helpless because I did not know what Time I was in or where I was in that Time.

My hands hurt as I struck the wood and Martin Lormer grabbed my arms and forced them still. "Stop it, Stephen. It's just about over!" I looked up at him and let him see my tears, my anguish. He patted my shoulder. "I'll see if I can get you out of here." He looked to the judge. "Your honor, may I approach the bench? I would like to make a motion in the interests of my client."

She became alert, her shoulders stiffening. "All right. However, *both* council will approach the bench."

I had stopped pounding the table and sat sprawling across some pads and notebooks, sobbing. I sobbed in rhythm of the young woman's name, Christine Cheney, Christine Cheney, knowing I must not forget her name. Forcing her name into my memory even as I heard the others speak of me.

"Your honor, I would like to request that my client be excused from the courtroom during the reading of the jury instructions. As you can see, he is quite overwrought and wants permission to leave at this time."

"I am very reluctant to grant such a request, council. Does Mr. Jerod understand his constitutional right to be present?"

"Yes, your honor, he does."

"Mr. Prosecutor, what is your attitude in this matter? Have you any objections?"

"We have no objections, your honor."

She nodded. "So be it" and turned to the court reporter. "Let the record indicate that Mr. Jerod, through his attorney, is waiving his right to be present during my instructions to the jury." She looked to the bailiff, who had moved to me, alerted for any confusion or uproar I might cause. "You may take him to the holding cell."

My legs trembled as I stood. Martin Lormer said, "I'll come visit you while the jury is out." He held my elbow to be sure I didn't fall. The courtroom was a bright steady eye watching me. I tried to remember why I was letting myself be convicted. My shoes were shuffles on the brown linoleum tile floor. There was

another Shara in the world, I thought. If I had killed the right
Shara, the exact Shara, why was I beginning to have visions of
another lifetime?

A bailiff said, "Hold'm, Father, if you please," and I slowly
raised my hands. Martin Lormer told him, "You don't have to cuff
him. Look at him. He's too tired to even walk." The bailiff
shrugged. "Sorry, counselor, it's the rules." The steel was cold
about my wrists. He did not clamp them tightly. I had been told
that Shara's body had been cremated. What had brought the ashes
together again? I saw a door open and then I was in a corridor and I
no longer cared. I wanted only to sleep. The bailiff saw me moving
my lips and he looked away from me, believing I was in a phase of
insanity, but I was silently praying to God to relieve my mind of
dreams. Allow me to awake in someone else's dream. Let me be
cheerful to whomever would dream me.

Chapter 17

When I awoke I did not know if it was day or night. I was still more alseep than awake, and from time to time Jesus Christ would visit with me, and then drift into a shadow of the cell. I would soon see Martin Lormer sitting at the end of my bed and know that he was urging me to eat because I was chewing warm substances and sipping cool liquids while he told me I needed the strength for one more court appearance. Although the trial was over and my vow of silence had been fulfilled, I remained silent to save the first sound of my voice for someone who was not in the cell.

I could determine the passage of hours by the changes in deputy sheriffs patrolling and guarding my cell, by the shifts of radio disc jockeys playing the country and western music that blasted into the corridor when a steel-plated door was slid open, by the times Martin Lormer came into the cell to chat with me, by my intervals of sleep in which there was no substance of living or subterranean self, or dream—only a void of being.

I am someone, I know that I am. I am my own keeper, and my jailer. I am inside the explosion of a suicide and I cannot get out. Save me, oh God, save something of me.

But these hysterias were fleeting intervals. I was usually idle and indifferent to knowing.

The only meaning of the time I waited for the jury's verdict was in those moments when Jesus Christ appeared in my cell. He was no illusion, no projection of desire. He was there. As specific as the occasional presence of Martin Lormer, as specific as the permanent presence of the walls—but not as substantial. At first I demanded that He prove Himself to be Jesus. I would not accept His holding out His hands to show me the nail holes gotten on His bloody cross. I believed Him to be Jesus Christ only when He told

467

me I had the God-given choice to disbelieve, and then He would remove Himself.

Gently, He brought my mind into the language of sensation. We did not use our voices, yet we spoke, as when I asked Him— why are you here, in this humiliating cell—He told me that the humiliation was in me, not in the cell. And then I asked Him how He could still love me after all I have done that was against His preferences, and He reached out and touched my forehead— When was there a time that I did not love you?—and I became serene. Then the cell door was opened and Martin Lormer stepped in and told me, "It looks like it's going to be a long haul before the jury makes up its mind. Do you mind if I stay with you awhile? The newspaper and television people are driving me crazy."

He sat on the bed and smoked a cigarette and smiled at me and told me about how unpredictable juries were, but I could hear in a deeper dimension of sensation Jesus telling me that I did not have to burden myself with guilt and shame and the knowledge of sin—I am the Intercessor. I will bring your burden to the Father, if you ask me to—and that told me that the jury would find me guilty because Jesus was here to administer the Last Rites—and He knew that I might just do that—ask Him to get me forgiveness. But a little later, perhaps. He was patient with my indecision.

The caged ceiling light was always on but I created my own darkness in lengths of sleep in which I experienced fever and then chills and often I awoke tightly clutching my groin in fear that a fiendish power was trying to amputate my parts. When I was lonely and desired a sense of love, a soft torrent of love, I always looked to Jesus, but when He reached to touch me, I avoided His touch.

And then I would see Martin Lormer, leaning against the cell door, looking at his wristwatch to know how much time had passed. He did not know that Jesus Christ was with us. And because I did not know why Jesus was in my cell I began feeling hostile. With the sweep of His single thought He would brush all delusion and distress from my mind. Merely by tapping my soul with one of His bloody fingers He could heal the infections caused me by reincarnations. Yet He sat there, smiling at me. Being God. What did He want?

I lay on the bed, counting time in my own meter, and remembering that there was a full and busy world beyond this holding cell. Slowly, I began to imagine what people were doing while I was confined to this small space. I saw Marsha Jenner remove some travel folders from a white bureau drawer and neatly place them on her pink-flowered bedspread. She wore a transparent sleeping gown. Her flesh was lumpy and not interesting. She knelt at the bed and reached under the tassled spread and withdrew a gray metal box. She opened it on the bed and began counting a thick stack of twenty-dollar bills. The money Shara had given her to hold. The money she had not returned to the District Attorney's office. One travel folder advertised, "Cannes: The Home of the Great Film Festivals."

I smiled and looked at Jesus. He knew the contempt I had for so low and shrewd a thief as Marsha Jenner. Jesus shrugged and He informed me, *"Every plant, which my heavenly father hath not planted, shall be rooted up."* I wondered when the root of God that had once been planted in me had begun to decay.

I must be wise now, and sincere. God was present in my cell.

Martin Lormer leaned against the wall, smoking another cigarette. When he saw I was alert, he winked at me. "The jury is still out. I don't feel like going home." He wanted me to talk with him but slowly he drifted from my vision and I was seeing the aged artist, Klaymore Montecello. He was seated in his study, staring at an etching he had never allowed the public to view. Shara was nude, decorously open to receive his lusting. But because he believed her to be his wife, Emily, I felt no outrage or jealousy, no loneliness for *that* Shara. How sad it was to be in love and still be alive without the woman that you love.

"Stephen," Martin Lormer said to me. "I'll tell you something I won't tell anyone else." He drew deeply on the cigarette and glanced to his left to see if a deputy sheriff could overhear. "I've broken with the woman I've been having an affair with for two years." He expected me to answer. I stared past him to know if Jesus had heard him. We were alone in the cell, but I could smell God's presence. It was a cooled sunbeam, aromatic, warm.

"It's been this trial, Stephen. I've been changed. We've *all* been changed."

I would not speak with him because I was saving my voice for the moment when I found Shara again. I would tell her, "I will never kill you again, Christine."

He tapped cigarette ashes onto the concrete floor. "I won't tell my wife," he sighed. "She wouldn't know how to handle it. But when the sex gets better, and more frequent, she might suspect." I wanted to tell him to stop talking about sex in the presence of Jesus.

And then Jesus touched my forehead and whispered what He had once spoken to Peter ". . . *what is that to thee? follow thou me,*" and I shook my head to move His touch from me, for I was afraid. He was God, but He was not Shara, now named Christine.

Martin Lormer said, "You know something, Stephen? I believed everything I said in my closing argument. Even to Shara's age." He inhaled deeply on the cigarette and blew the smoke at the bars. "But that seems so long ago, I wonder if I believe it now. And that worries me. Because that's how the jury probably feels too."

He was only talking to calm me though I was more peaceful than a summer pond.

There were times when I knew I was asleep because I did not feel or think or remember. Sleep is not darkness, inert and fallow. Sleep is only the absence of awareness and response.

If my food was drugged it was a clever chemical for I had no sense of change in me. There was only stillness in my sensations, while outside of me Time fulfilled its chore of moving. I enjoyed Martin's visits, I was pleased that Jesus favored me with His divine concern.

While I was being condemned by twelve people, I was feeling blessed.

I imagined Althea Jackson to be walking along Market Street in San Francisco. She leaned forward, aggressively pushing past people who moved slowly. She reached the corner and turned left onto Fifth Street. There were bedraggled, smelly drunks lumped in doorways. Some stood near radio shops and second-hand clothing stores passing brown bagged liquor bottles to each other. She stopped before a pawn shop with a thick metal grill on the windows. She stared at the merchandise. Two saxophones, an arrange-

ment of tape recorders, three pistols, some cameras—trays of rings
and pendants and watches. A pink Jaguar veered from the traffic
and slowed at the curb. A black man with a white ermine-collared
jacket and mirror-lensed sunglasses leaned to the window and
called to her. She pivoted around and raised her hand to him, her
center finger rigidly pointed up. She strode into the pawn shop.
There was a stark white bandage fastened about her left wrist.

It was only when I saw the gaunt monk that I might have once
been that I became tense and unsettled.

He was behind a masonry pillar that was thick and smooth
and reached upward to a jagged end. He was crouched in fear,
hiding within an area of ruins I could not identify. Strong winds
swept about him, making him hug the pillar as he shivered. He was
not wearing his monk's garb. His garments were dark and creased
and so carelessly fitted about him I could not distinguish their cut.
The swirl and flight of wind brought him voices—excited, angry
sounds that made him want to run.

He edged his face to the side and peeked at the distance. In
the dusk of evening light he saw crowds of people carrying heavy
clubs and crude weapons searching the terrain. Some carried
lights—I could not discern if they were torches or searchlights.
Ahead of the crowd he saw the woman who always appeared in the
times of these visions. The gaunt monk knew her but I could not
see her face. She was screaming at the people, waving her arms and
pointing to the ruins in which he was hiding. I could not fit my
mind into his thoughts but I could see that she was leading this
outraged mob to find him—to cause him to be killed—and he was
hating her but there was love in his hatred.

No, I shook my head, no. This was not acceptable. I would not
see a death I might have had unless I first knew why I had to die.
No. This was not acceptable, not at all.

Then Martin Lormer, as though prompted by Jesus, told me,
"It's all a lie, Stephen, your reincarnation, that is. Just a big frig-
ged-out lie." He sat on the bed and gently poked his thumb onto
my ankle. "All your life you've been victimized by a doctrine that
comes from the delusions of a supernatural narcotic. Not even the
devil can make you live over and over again. All he can do is come
into your one-and-only life and make you believe you have lived

many times before and will go on living many times after. It is all a
lot of supernatural, all-American faddist bullshit!"

But I was not really listening to him. I was carefully construct-
ing a scene with Bishop Carmondy. He was in the home of the
woman he had lived with for twenty years, seated before an expen-
sive, remote-controlled color television set, eating a leg of juice-
dripping chicken while he listened to a bland-faced newscaster tell,
"The Stephen Jerod jury is now in its second day, trying to decide
the fate of the ex-priest who strangled his mistress for reasons of
reincarnation. At the last report the jury was still sending out for
coffee and sandwiches and requesting that points of law be explained to them."

The newscaster was snapped away and only his voice could be
heard as a film of the business outside the courtroom was shown.
"Martin Lormer, prominent and colorful attorney, who has come
up with this unprecedented defense of self-defense by reason of
reincarnation, has been noncommittal about what he believes the
verdict will be, or his claim that the victim, Shara Medford, was a
two-thousand-and-five-hundred-year-old woman." My photograph
was flashed onto the television. "Stephen Jerod, the man who
claims to have lived in two other lifetimes, still has not spoken one
word." Bishop Carmondy pulled some chicken skin from his
mouth and flung it at the television screen, cursing, "You misera-
ble, pussy-whipped son of a bitch. If you're reincarnated, then I'm
the left tit of a syphilitic orangutan!" The chicken skin stuck to the
television glass like a mouse pelt flattened on the surface of a bulb.
A woman's voice nagged from another room, "Please, your Excellence, your language is a scandal!" He sat, snicking his thumbnail
on the large silver cross nestled at his groin.

When I become agitated, Jesus would sit beside me and touch
my hands. If I knew why He had come into my cell I would be able
to understand a mote of God's mind. Jesus did not have a beard.
His face was a blunt workman's face. He seemed to have just come
from a shop and had cleaned Himself and was now ready to social-
ize. His hair was dark and with a pronounced Hebraic wave. His
hands were broad and the knuckles thick. I was pleased that He
was not the fragile, dandelion-like pantywaist that the artists portrayed him to be. If He had a halo He must have left it at home.

I did not slide my hand from under His. He was listening to my thoughts—why are you here?—and though I did not hear sound in His answer, He told me—When have I not been with you?—and I wanted to yell at Him, that's a lie! but it is written, *God is not a man that he should lie.*" So I knew that I had not always acknowledged His presence in me. Why are you here now?—I asked Him, and I felt my hand raised to be held by both His hands—Before you leave this place, you will understand.

And I remembered an aphorism I had once heard—that Faith sees the invisible, believes the incredible, and receives the impossible.

Show me, Jesus—come on, show me.

Then Martin Lormer was shaking my shoulder, urging me to look at him. "The court has been notified that the jury has reached its verdict." I pushed his hand from my shoulder. I knew now why Jesus had come into the cell. He was offering Himself to me again. I sat up. What was Heaven to me? A myth, an unreality. I would rather have the doom I fancied than the salvation that could be an even grimmer delusion.

"It'll take a while yet, Stephen. I want you to relax."

I looked to Jesus, who was standing at the barred door. Behind Him was the solid, uniformed body of a deputy sheriff cleaning some clogged dirt from his wristwatch. Then I saw the long and narrow sanctuary of a church in which there were people kneeling in prayer while a black-suited pastor held his hands on the shoulders of a fourteen-year-old girl in a chrome-framed wheelchair. Her legs were soda straws encased in metal. He was praying, "Jesus, Jesus, Jesus, Father of mercy, Father of love, heal this child, let the healing virtue go out of you and let her faith make her whole."

Behind him was a smoothly planed redwood cross. The pastor began to tremble and pray in the glossolalia I was taught to hate, and the girl's thin hands gripped the wheelchair arms as she strained to leave the chair. The people kneeling before the altar moaned and clutched their hands and trembled and sobbed. The girl suddenly collapsed back and slumped over and began wetting herself, and the pastor stroked her hair and he cried while he promised her, "Another time, Laurie, another time it will be healed."

I looked at Jesus' face and His eyes were wet with tears and I remembered God saying that He had raised pharaoh to great power and strength only so He could be used as an example of the greater power of God when pharaoh was destroyed, and now Jesus was showing me that He did not have to heal. He wept because He was not healing the crippled girl so I could know all power was His. He wanted me to pray to Him to heal her. He wanted me to love the crippled girl more than I loved my own reincarnations. He wanted me to disbelieve that Self was a doomed Self, and gain my new Self, born again through Him.

He also wept because He knew my choice.

A deputy sheriff tapped on the cell door. "Jury's out and seated. The court's waitin' on you, Father." Martin Lormer held the suit jacket for me and I thought that I should be afraid. But I suddenly remembered why I had not contributed to my defense— so I could die and prove that reincarnation was a demonic evil that would turn you lunatic or suicidal or murderous. Jesus had moved away from the cell door and was now standing at the bed. I wanted Him to know why I had chosen to die, but He knew. *"The earth is the Lord's, and the fullness thereof."* The sensation of His mind was stern. The whole world is not your concern, Stephen, unless you love me. You cannot save a bird from falling or color a blade of grass. Your dying will be lonely and hardly mourned. Only if you love me can you have life. The faith you let me give you is your power.

I buttoned my jacket and flattened the collar tips of my shirt and let the deputy sheriff fit the steel cuffs about my wrists. We walked through corridors and Martin Lormer suddenly gripped my elbow and squeezed until the pain made me turn to him. "Stephen, listen to me." His voice was insistent. "You've gone through serious changes. Mentally *and physically*. Don't let them frighten you. Just accept them as natural—not *supernatural*." But I did not attend his warnings—I kept looking behind me and Jesus was still there. I passed other cells with men holding the bars, their faces pressed at the bars—some were silent and others called out that I would be found not guilty and to send them some cigarettes when I was outside.

The gaunt monk began pushing at my consciousness, trying

to reach me. I strained to ignore him and turned to look at Jesus and told him, just let me follow this new lifetime through, and then I'll give myself to you completely.

The tears were still wet on His face.

There's a woman in the world named Christine Cheney, who might be Shara—and Jesus told me that the Father who is in Heaven is eternally perfect and all He does is perfect and He does not need to create you again and over again—one lifetime is sufficient in His perfect reasoning.

But I saw the gaunt monk and the woman and they were on a high cliff and they were struggling and one would fall or be pushed from the cliff and be shattered to death on the rocks a long distance below—and then a thick steel door slammed behind me, shaking the vision, and I looked to see if Jesus was compassionate to my dilemma, but He was gone and the deputy sheriff was undoing the handcuffs and Martin Lormer told me, "Just have faith, Stephen. I've been praying for you." The bright courtroom lights made me blink and I began feeling hazed and musty with fog and I prayed that Jesus would be in the courtroom too.

I was not drawn from the haze within me. A fine spray of powder was over my sight. Dust had settled on my sensations. Procedures of law were going on about me and I did not perceive their meaning. The judge entered and we all stood and then we sat down and she spoke to Martin Lormer and the District Attorney and then to the jury foreman. The clock on the wall was a porcelain eye waiting to gain an expression. Someone walked to the jury foreman and picked a sealed envelope from his hand and it was presented to the judge. There was no breath of life in the courtroom because the flags on each side of her were still. While she slit open the envelope, I realized it contained my existence, and I was confused.

If I lived and wanted to become reclusive and die of old age, would Shara, now named Christine Cheney, find me? Then who would kill whom? The devil is playing his fiery fiddle—let us dance the gavotte of reincarnation.

And if I was guilty and duly executed, would the demonic music revive me into another lifetime and would I again be mated to my partner in death? If I lived or died I was neither dead nor alive—I merely always become and Shara always is.

Diddle-dee-diddle-dee-dee, the devil is playing his fiddle for Shara and me.

But Shara was dead. That was truth. Strangled for a purpose and sliced and severed for the information of autopsy and put together to be slid into a special oven and burned into some weightless flakes. She was not alive, not even as Christine Cheney. But I saw her, dear God, *I saw her.*

Shall we dance, beloved? The devil is warming up for another round. Doodle-dee-diddle-dee-day, we can kill each other while he plays.

There was murmuring and whispering while the judge studied the verdict.

Help me, Jesus, I prayed. But not right now. One more cycle, one more pursuit, one more lifetime of the strange anguish crying in my blood. I am immune to joy.

I swear, if You let me find her I will not kill her and we will let our everlasting love overcome the curse of reincarnation and we will present ourselves to You—that is my solemn oath.

The judge said, "Will the defendant please rise?" and Martin Lormer shook my elbow and I stood and allowed myself to pretend that I was in church and the priest was now going to baptize me into another name, and existence. It was a sobering occasion. I saw Martin Lormer cross his fingers.

It did not matter that the priest, who was really a judge, was female. She was not a pretty woman. Her eyes were flat brown behind her glasses. Her face seemed to slope toward her chin.

And I stiffened, because I no longer saw her. I was watching the gaunt monk and the woman who was always after him. She was bathing me. I sat in a wooden tub and she poured hot water over the deep creases of dirt in my flesh. She scooped up gobs of gray grease that was soap and slowly washed me. I shivered, I purred, her touch thrilled me. She cupped her hand and stroked and lingered over my parts, making me giggle with joy and crouch over with shame of how I bulged. She began hushing her voice to my ear, telling me of the ecstasies and fleshly festivities I had once whipped and lacerated myself to stop imagining. Her breasts caressed my face as she stooped over to cleanse my crevices and I tried to see my infirmity—where was the grim infirmity I carried throughout my lifetimes?—and then she began poking and jiggling her finger in tender places and I laughed and told her she must stop and she poked and jiggled harder and I bent over and laughed and laughed. . . .

. . . and when the jury foreman read the verdict, "We the jury find the defendant Stephen Jerod not guilty!" I was hunched over and laughing though no sound spilled from my throat—and the courtroom was silent, suspended in its astonishment while the judge spoke some instructions and said that I was to be released. I huddled over and whacked my thigh and laughed at how the woman was tickling me—what a glorious way to destroy a man—tickle him into such gasping fits that his heart burst him to death. Then there was an uproar so that I believed the entire courtroom was detonated into laughter. . . .

. . . but it was Martin Lormer jumping around me and lustily patting my shoulders and side, shouting, "We won, Stephen, we won!" and six deputy sheriffs were quickly surrounding me and though I wanted to think, wanted to know why I was innocent in public and guilty in soul, I was encircled by the officers and Martin Lormer laughed. "You're free, do you hear me, you're free!" and the people clamored at me, news media hands wagged pads at me, voices asked me how I felt about the verdict, and a woman screamed, "You lousy murderer," and spat at me—and Martin Lormer helped me walk in the circle of deupties who threatened the people to get them out of our way. . . .

. . . and Martin Lormer said, "I have a car waiting for us. I ordered it to be there, just in case," but I could not hear him clearly and I stood still, looking at the faces talking and calling to me, but none of the women were Shara, now named Christine Cheney. I was pulled to the doors and outside the courtroom the noise was greater and camera flashes blinded me and I cursed them for taking away my sight. Long camera lenses zoomed at me, microphones were pushed toward my face and batted aside by the deputies and Martin Lormer kept yelling, "No comment at this time, no comment at this time!" I heard sirens and Martin Lormer pressed his face near my left ear and told me, "You have about three days left,

Stephen. Be good to yourself in that time," and I stopped again to look at him, remembering that he had predicted that I would "wander about the cities, unquestionably mad. You'll be searching for the dead and not even an irrational person would want to become what a belief in reincarnation has done to you," and I wanted to smash his face but the roar of voices and the press of bodies made me feel dispersed.

I felt drained of strength and dizzy. I wanted to breathe silence, I wanted to drink aloneness. "What will you do now, Father Jerod?" a television commentator called to me, but he was elbowed aside by an angry woman who screeched, "Who are you gonna murder next?" I wanted to lower myself to sitting so I could gasp in air, and I held onto Martin Lormer's arm and he said something to the deputies and they formed an arc before us and he grabbed my arm and pulled me into a foyer and we were running past glass doors and the only one following us was an elderly man with white hair and a slight hunch. "Here!" Martin Lormer said, and pointed to wide brown doors. He shoved them open and we rushed into another corridor and the old man did not follow us and then we were outside and the daylight made my eyes tear and blink.

He pointed to a squat black car at the front of the courthouse steps. "There, Stephen, that's ours." There were jams of people on the steps, crowding and pushing each other, trying to get in and see. Standing at the rim of the crowd was the gaunt monk and his clothes were torn and blood was dripping from his fingertips. I was only seeing him, he wasn't there—he couldn't be. Was it his own blood on his hands or the blood of a woman?

Martin Lormer grasped my wrist tightly. "Come on, get ahold of yourself. We can sneak by them." I yanked my hand from him and tried to hurry to where the gaunt monk was sitting. I passed a wide and thick window and saw the old man with the white hair inside the building, following me. I cursed him, leave me alone, damn you, leave me alone. But he stood still and just shook his fist at me and he was damning me, and I became enraged—the gaunt monk would still be there—and clenched my hands and stepped to the old man to batter his face, and he stepped to me, prepared to fight—and I drew back because he was old and had a hunched body, and he stepped back, and I became suspicious and I made myself smile and he smiled, imitating me. I pointed at him accusingly, and his finger was poked at my face and I suddenly covered my eyes to blacken him from my sight, to stop seeing what I had become. Then someone yelled, "There he is, there's Jerod!"

They rushed to me and I looked at the albino-haired man with Barthelamo's humped body and suddenly the glass was shattered, crashing about me, and people began screaming and running, and I heard a pistol shot and Martin Lormer bawled, "Stephen, watch out, she'll kill you!" I turned and another shot burst in the air like the snapping of wood. "There!" someone hiding behind a concrete pillar yelled. "There. It's some crazy woman!" and I looked ahead and standing across the street, her arms outstretched to hold her gun steady, Althea Jackson was taking aim at me. I stretched my arms out as she fired again.

People shrieked at me to fall down, to run, but I slowly walked down the steps, letting her aim again. She deserved to kill me and if she did I would die, blessing her in my soul.

I saw two deputy sheriffs moving along the sides of the steps, their guns drawn. She shot at me again, and then again, and I could see her dark face through the smoke and a hard insect snicked my cheek before flying away. I touched my face and felt blood and I grinned and stood still to applaud her: come on, Althea, kill me, then you can have Shara for all your eternities—kill me, Jesus is waiting for me. I opened my dark suit jacket and exposed the whiteness of my shirt to help her. Blood leaked down my face, soaking my neck. She fired again and then the gun clicked and I was closer to her and I saw her left wrist was bandaged. A deputy sheriff bawled to her, "You drop that gun, lady!" but she kept clicking the trigger and when I was near her another deputy shouted to me, "Get the hell outta the way, Father!" She cursed me, and then her voice became a shrill cackle. "I have all the time in the world to find and kill you!" and she flung the gun at me. It struck at my shoes and skidded along the concrete. She ran. The deputies chased her.

Martin Lormer called to me, "Stephen, are you all right?" I shifted to the right where the streets were narrow, and began running. I kept looking behind me for Althea whilst in front of me I stared at faces to find Shara, now named Christine Cheney.